D0529832

Tamsin Keily studied psychology before completing a post-graduate degree in primary education. She now lives in Berkshire with her husband and cats, where she juggles writing with her job as a primary school teacher. She is the author of one other novel, *Daisy Cooper's Rules for Living*.

THE
Surprising Days OF
Isla Pembroke

TAMSIN KEILY

ORION

An Orion paperback

First published in Great Britain in 2021 by Orion Fiction
an imprint of The Orion Publishing Group Ltd
Carmelite House, 50 Victoria Embankment
London EC4Y 0DZ

An Hachette UK Company

1 3 5 7 9 10 8 6 4 2

A CIP catalogue record for this book is
available from the British Library.

ISBN (Mass Market Paperback) 978 1 4091 9108 7
ISBN (eBook) 978 1 4091 9109 4

Typeset at The Spartan Press Ltd,
Lymington, Hants

Printed and bound in Great Britain by Clays Ltd,
Elcograf S.p.A.

www.orionbooks.co.uk

To Alice, for there is nobody
quite like a little sister.

Prologue

Her mother told the story like this:

Once there was a gentle spirit of the ocean. She soothed the waves when they were filled with irrational rage. She whispered soft words to calm the storms so that the sailboats could be coaxed safely into shore. And when lightning sparked across her waters, she would wrap her arms around the panicking ships to keep them safe.

The spirit of the ocean had a sister. A fierce, whirling wind of a sister who scurried through coves with gleeful delight, who whooped with laughter when the boats were sent wildly bobbing across the water.

The spirit of the ocean loved her. It was a love not quite like anything she had ever experienced. A feeling in the deep caverns of her heart that she would rip the world in two to keep her safe. That she would sink a thousand ships if they threatened her happiness. A soaring sense of love that made the water sparkle and the fish leap joyfully into the air.

But the spirit of lightning was jealous of the young breeze and the way she danced effortlessly through life. The way she could bring life to a child's kite, the way she could lift the seeds from the air and spread them across the world. He was jealous of how she was loved by her sister whilst he remained alone, barricaded by his own sparks and heat. Nobody had ever loved him like that.

Jealousy wormed into his thoughts until one day he could hold back no more. The spirit of lightning sent his deadly sparks after the wind and struck her down.

When the spirit of the ocean saw that her beloved sister had been taken from her, she let sorrow fill her, let it send her waves into a frenzy. A storm howled across the coast with waves the size of mountains, crashing mercilessly into cliffs and harbour walls. People huddled around their fireplaces in search of warmth and light and hope, waiting for the night to pass and for the sea to calm.

And it did, eventually. A heartbroken wail can only last so long, fury eventually turns to empty grief. The waters became gentle once more.

However, her rage had carved new shapes into the coastline. On one beach, one cliff was swept away entirely, except for one mighty, towering slab of rock. The locals could not understand how it did not just topple down. But the ocean spirit knew that her grief had carved that monument, and it would not fall until her grief was gone. She knew it would stand forever.

And then, in her dreadful sorrow, she soaked the rock in her tears, filling each teardrop with a desperate yearning to see her sister once more, until time itself was forced to bend to her will. The ocean spirit found a way to the past she had been forced to leave behind.

Of course, nothing is ever that easy. For the doorway to the past required power. Power that only came from the very lightning that had stolen her precious companion away. She begged and pleaded, cried until the waters rose and spilled down the coastal village streets.

But the lightning would not listen. He would not help her, so blinded by white-hot jealousy. The ocean spirit, broken and distraught, disappeared. The waves were left to rage and roar to their hearts' content, the fish swam lost and unguided.

Time passed. Guilt grew slowly within the lightning spirit's heart, a constant and sickening whirlpool. Desperate for some forgiveness, he tried to make the ocean spirit's wish come true.

So lightning regularly strikes the beach where the ocean spirit's rock monument stands, desperately trying to hit the stone and fix his dreadful mistake. But the lightning always misses, blinded by his own remorse.

That's how her mother's story goes anyway. Read carefully from the old pages of her own childhood fairy-tale book. A story to explain the almost crippling weight of a family love, to explain the unusual column of stone that stands on the beach and weathers the storms. And to explain why the village has its name: 'Karrekoth' – 'old stone'.

A story, yes. But lightning does often come to Karrekoth. Still the stone stands, untouched, unmoved by the lightning that desperately strikes around it.

And the past remains closed.

One

Isla Pembroke sometimes wonders what it's like not to smell of fish. She can remember it, almost. That perfume she used to wear on nights out with her school friends; the sweet-smelling laundry detergent she always found oddly comforting. A distant memory now, replaced with the ever-present, ever-pervasive whiff of fish.

On the bright side, she's probably not the only one. You can't work at an aquarium and not smell of fish. She wasn't sure she'd ever look at *Finding Nemo* in quite the same way, not after battling for three hours to clear out the coral reef tank with a load of gawping tourists watching from the other side of the glass.

Still, she has a job. She has to remind herself of that when the fiftieth visitor of the day asks her where the sharks are, despite the prominent maps stuck everywhere. She reminds herself that while it may not be the marine biology career she was quite imagining, it does at least give her means to survive.

And it could be worse. She could be serving the dead version of her aquarium companions at the local chippy.

Isla stands outside, squinting up at the building she has spent the last seven years practically living in, trying to find some sense of prestige about the place. It's a struggle, as it has been since she first cast eyes on it. The 'quirky' fish sign is still wonky, the turquoise paint is still peeling. Nothing changes. Someone joked on her first day that once people worked here, they never left. Isla laughed back then, disbelieving. Why would anyone spend more than a few months here? She remembers how confidently she dismissed that idea. She wasn't going to be sticking around. It was just a temporary job, just until her dad got back on his feet after … everything.

But here she is. Seven years later. Stuck. Employee photo starting to peel a little off the staffroom wall. Name tag practically implanted into her chest.

'You off then, Isla?'

Dennis Baker, Isla's boss and proud owner of the peeling aquarium she has been squinting at, is heading out of the staff entrance and heading directly towards her. Isla watches as he steps carelessly over a discarded lolly wrapper and she feels her lips purse instinctively. They have a whole bloody exhibition on ocean pollution, for Christ's sake.

'Yes, I'm off. The front's all locked up,' Isla replies, and does her best surreptitious dance around her boss until she can scoop up the discarded wrapper and deposit it in the bin.

'Ah, you're a saint.' Dennis doesn't bat an eyelid at Isla's litter picking, already hoisting his keys from the depths of his pockets. 'I tried to get Mitch to lock up on the weekend; total disaster. Thank God he's temporary, Isla; not sure I'd have the patience otherwise …'

Isla feels herself holding back a wince. A grand total of three months; that's how long Mitch will have worked here by the time he leaves. Wouldn't that be nice.

'Isla?'

Apparently expecting some sort of response for his rambling, Dennis is now staring at her with a frown. 'Sorry,' she says hastily, though she's not quite sure what she's apologising for. 'Long day. Uh ... I should get home. Dad'll be waiting.'

Dennis gives Isla that sympathetic look that always makes her stomach flip. 'Sure, sure. On your way.' She's halfway turned towards her car when he speaks again. 'Oh, Isla – I meant to say ...'

When Isla glances back, Dennis almost looks uncomfortable. That's a new one. She frowns, feels that instinctive sense of foreboding that always seems to lurk nearby. 'What is it?'

'Look, I know you've got a lot on and everything ... but there was an email I got this morning. Some local ... ocean scientist—'

'Marine biologist?'

'That's the one.' Isla's exasperation with his complete lack of knowledge is apparently not obvious on her face because Dennis goes on, unabashed. 'This marine biologist, she's doing a talk in London about ...' He snaps his fingers, searching for the words for a moment. Isla feels her teeth grit as she resists the urge to tell him that it's most likely a lost cause. 'I think it's something to do with the ocean.'

'Probably a fairly good chance.' Isla's sarcasm seems to waft right over Dennis's head before disappearing out towards the nearby ocean.

'You're right. Anyway, it's in London. Two-day thing; they provide a hotel and that. It costs a fair bit but I'm happy to subsidise it, what with you being such a reliable employee and all that.'

Isla feels a swooping sensation in her chest which she eventually identifies as hope. But she swiftly buries it before it can get too comfortable. 'Oh. Wow. That does sound great.' For a second, quick as a blink, she considers what would happen if she took up his offer. She tries to imagine herself standing in London, attending a conference with other people who actually cared about the ocean and not just how many stuffed whales sold in the gift shop. But then she shakes her head and chases the idea away. 'But I can't. It's just... not a good time.'

Isla can sense Dennis's unspoken words hovering around her ears. *There hasn't been a good time for nine years, Isla.* But, to give him credit, he doesn't say anything of the sort. Instead he nods slowly. 'I get it, I do. Just give it some thought, though, eh? I'm putting up a sign-up sheet in the staffroom tomorrow. Plenty of time to think on it.'

Plenty of time, right. Just like she's had plenty of time to move away from this tiny corner of the world. Just like she's had plenty of time to fix the cracks wriggling through her life.

Plenty of time has a funny way of slipping past in the blink of an eye.

Isla watches Dennis stride off towards his car with the air of someone who is quite content with his lot in life. Must be great, she decides, to be settled with your life decisions. Even if they're somewhat misguided.

Then she feels the breeze from the sea kick up the ends of her curls, smiles a little to herself as she allows it to soothe that tightening of her chest that she always feels when she's leaving for home. She calls it instinct.

Her own car waits for her in its usual space. She knows she could be an hour late to work and nobody would park their car in that space instead, because that's 'her' space. It makes her feel a little sick to think about it.

Time to get home; the lesser of two evils. She thinks. Isla wrestles with the stiff lock, then the creaking door, then the sticky ignition. The silent car park is filled with the sputtering of an engine past its best, then Isla sets off for home.

It's a perfect early autumn evening, with the sunshine just

dipping behind the far-off horizon and casting a hazy glow over the ocean. As Isla drives along the coast, she feels the usual temptation to just turn and stare at the glittering water. To get lost in its wonderful unpredictability.

But she can't. There are hairpin turns to navigate every five seconds, as the road stubbornly tries to match the wild edges of the coastline. Her hometown, Karrekoth, gets its name from the unusual stone standing on its beach, but Isla has always wondered if perhaps it should be named after the heart-stopping route you have to take to get to it. 'Car-Off-The-Bloody-Cliff' feels more accurate but, then again, Cornwall is full of villages and towns that have heart-stopping routes to get to them.

As she feels the sunshine on her skin, feels the wind racing through the open window and agitating her curls, Isla lets the potential of Dennis's offer weigh on her shoulders, just for a moment. Here in the car, away from his sympathetic gaze and still a few miles away from her home, she's safe to consider it.

She doesn't hate her job, not really. The days pass at a steady rate and the wages are enough to keep them afloat, which is the most important thing. But it's hardly rescuing sea turtles or tracking blue whales. When she stood proudly in front of her class, aged seven, and told them that she wanted to be a marine biologist, this was not quite what she had in mind.

You're only twenty-eight. That's what her head keeps saying. There's still time. But it has been nine years since she put every-thing on hold, left university to come home, and told herself that she'd get the future back on track one day. And that dream job still feels far, far beyond the horizon.

Isla hears the clanking of boat masts and the shouting of fishermen and it pulls her back to reality. The road has wound its way up one side of a cliff and then down the other, bringing Isla and her dusty car to the harbour of Karrekoth. It's time to focus. She'll be home in four minutes, unless she gets stuck behind Bobby Mercer's bloody boat trailer, in which case it will be eight minutes. Bobby Mercer, who is far too paranoid to leave his prized boat in the harbour at night and so painstakingly and extremely cautiously drives it home at the end of every day.

Her phone rings just as she's accelerating a little past the harbour ramp to beat said bloody trailer. The sound makes her jump, the buzzing coming angrily from the cupholder by her elbow. A quick glance and she can see it's her father so she pulls into the bus stop, ignoring the dirty looks she gets from those waiting. Chances are that he wants something from the shops and Isla really doesn't want to have to come back out to the village again once she's home. And if it's not that then it's something worse and she *really* can't miss it.

She snatches up the phone and balances it against her ear, keeping one eye on her wing mirror in case the bus changes the habit of a lifetime and arrives on time. 'Dad?'

'Hey, bud. Where are you?'

Isla lets a small sigh of relief rattle down the speakers at her father's steady tone, though it's paired with slight exasperation. It's not like her routine changes. Ever. 'About three minutes away. I've just pulled into the bus stop so obviously I'm Karrekoth's Most Wanted right now. So what's the matter?'

Jasper Pembroke has become a man of few words but even by his standards he seems hesitant to speak. Isla can almost hear the gears in his brain grinding to a halt. 'Dad?' Isla prompts again, trying her best not to sound irritated. Practice should make perfect but it hasn't quite yet. 'I'm literally three minutes away... so unless it's something from town that you wanted, can it wait?'

'It's Morgan.'

The words spill down the speaker so rapidly that at first she doesn't understand them. Maybe Jasper senses this be repeats them a second later. 'It's Morgan, Isla.'

She can't remember when she heard that name last. Maybe that's why she finds the seconds ticking away in silence. Hearing her sister's name has doubled her heart rate instantly. Isla feels it smacking painfully against her ribs, as if it's trying to escape the pain that might be heading its way. And she's not sure if the icy feeling coursing through her veins is anger or fear.

'What about her?' Isla finally asks, feeling her suddenly dry lips sticking together as she tries to speak.

'She's back, Isla. Morgan's back.'

Two

The village of Karrekoth is located in a tiny inlet on the southern coast of Cornwall, far down enough to feel that you're one step away from tipping off the country entirely. It is known for two things: the towering and oddly-shaped rock on one of its beaches, and the thunderstorms. Isla never really understood the hows and whys of it all, just that Karrekoth has more thunderstorms per year than any other place in the country. She knows the folklore behind it of course, but she long ago dismissed that as credible evidence. Lightning has no personal relation with the sea, for goodness' sake.

But as Isla Pembroke completes the last part of her homeward journey, the sky looks calm. A few clouds loiter right off in the distance but they're white and fluffy, not dark and menacing. Nothing, except for a possible storm brewing between two sisters. Which some meteorologists might call more dangerous.

As she squeezes her car through the typically narrow streets of the village, Isla tries to remember the last time she heard from her sister. Two months ago, she decides. The same message as always: *Safe. M x*, as if receiving that on a vaguely bi-monthly schedule makes her abandoned family feel any less worried. It's been four years of those messages and they're yet to make Isla feel anything but a tightening sensation in her chest. She feels her hands stiffen against the wheel, forces herself to focus on not driving into a building. She just needs to get home. Probably best not to think about her sister until she's out of the moving vehicle. She just needs to get home.

She whizzes past the tiny line of shops that make up Karrekoth's commercial centre; the gift shop, the off-licence, the post office. Isla feels her eyes linger on the post office like always, almost catches the familiar scent of envelope glue and sherbet lemons. But then she's passed it, she's leaving the main streets of the village and the sea is back to meandering along beside her. The memory slips away, settles back into the dark. Isla lets out the smallest breath that she never realised she was holding.

The car gives a little creak of complaint as Isla brakes abruptly to avoid hitting Cora Myrtle and her ridiculously minuscule terrier as they make their way back from their evening walk on the main beach. Usually, Isla would leap at the chance to stall her trip home by talking to one of the few friends from school who still lived in Karrekoth, but Isla knows there isn't time. Still, Cora is waving at her in an impatient fashion and Isla knows she can't ignore her completely. She brings the car to a shaky stop, winding down the window with a series of squeaks.

'Hey, where's the fire?' Cora asks, once the barrier of glass is gone between them. 'You'll be all over the Karrekoth Watch Facebook page with driving like that.'

Isla suppresses a shudder at the thought. The sooner that particular Facebook page got banned the better. 'Karrekoth's Most Wanted, that's me.' Cora snorts at what both know to be a frankly ridiculous idea but gives Isla an expectant look. Apparently Isla is not giving off the casual attitude she's aiming for.

'Uh, Morgan's home,' Isla finally says, and is quietly proud at how she says each word without too much of a tremor.

'Fuck,' Cora's eyes widen. 'Are you serious?'

'Afraid so.'

'How long's that been?'

Isla pauses, tries to pretend as if she doesn't know the exact number of months and weeks. 'Um, four years, give or take a few weeks.'

Cora shakes her head. 'Shitting hell...' she whispers, never one for particularly eloquent statements. 'Well, you'd better get going then, girl! And give her hell from me, eh?'

Isla doesn't need to be told twice, though of course she knows it's not quite as simple as just giving Morgan 'hell', whatever that actually means. She shoots her friend a grateful smile, winds the window up, then starts off down the road again. In the rear-view mirror, Isla watches as Cora stands still for a moment, still apparently in shock. Well, at least Isla now knows she's not the only one.

The road sharply veers down a slope to the right, further away from the main village. The surface becomes a little more uneven beneath the car and Isla wrestles fiercely with the steering wheel to keep it straight. The car half bounces past the beach café, past the slightly decrepit-looking public toilets, then takes a left turn with a sudden burst of speed. Her homeward road is heading back up a hill and Isla knows that you need a run-up if you're going to make it.

The car lets out a groan of almost despair as it's forced into the steep ascent and Isla half expects to see smoke billowing out of the bonnet (again). But by some miracle they make it; up the hill, over the top, and through an open wooden gate, into the scrubby patch of grass that serves as a front drive for the Pembroke home.

Technically speaking, the whitewashed house in front of them should be called the Birch home, as it belonged to Isla's mother's family. Konan Birch, Isla's grandfather, stubbornly lived in it until the day before he died, and let it go slightly to ruin in the meantime. But then when Isla's mother, Marina, inherited it she began to turn it into something resembling a functioning home, with toilets that flushed, ovens that didn't pose a health risk, even internet access.

Isla remembers how she used to call it a castle. At the time, she'd never seen one in real life, and so her house, with its large windows, heavy doors, tight-cornered staircases, was close enough. Castles were always on hills, after all, and her house clung to the edge of the tallest one she knew back then. Castles had crumbling walls and her house definitely felt a little crumbly at times. Scruffy, that's what her mother called it. A pain in the neck, that's what her father calls it these days.

Isla finds something strangely comforting in the confident way her home presents itself directly to the elements of the sea, in the carefully arranged seashells cemented around the somewhat warped door frame. The grass that tickles around Isla's ankles is the grass she learnt to walk on, the sound of the ocean that crashes against the beach below is the sound that has lulled her to sleep since birth.

But all castles have dungeons. And sometimes she hears the echo of a locked door, feels the walls closing in around her.

It's with slight hesitation that Isla steps from the car and closes the door. The house looms over her and she can almost feel its incredulity at her stalling. She finds her shoulders stiffening at this imagined criticism. Why shouldn't she stall? It's perfectly reasonable, considering what's waiting for her on the other side of the peeling front door.

Suddenly, said door opens. Isla feels her feet take an instinctive step back towards the car. Four years and nothing has changed. She's still scared.

Except it's her father, not her sister, who steps from the house. Isla feels a distant sense of relief to see that he has at least got dressed today. His jeans need a wash and his shirt is incredibly crinkled but it's something. He may even have shaved.

Isla can tell from a few feet away that he's stressed, though. Usually his eyes are hollow, apathetic caves but now there's a frantic spark of panic instead. His shoulders seem more tense than usual and Isla feels her instinct to protect him rearing up inside her. Except there's nothing to protect him from. A father shouldn't need to be protected from his daughter. Especially not by his other daughter.

'Hey, Dad,' she says, keeping each word carefully level. 'What's going on then?'

By this time, she's reached his side. He touches her shoulder briefly, perhaps hoping to find some comfort from this contact. 'I just got back from fixing Paul's boat for him, you know, like we talked about. Bloody fool keeps using duct tape so it was a right mess—'

'Focus, Dad.' She says it kindly, holding back the fluttering impatience in her stomach.

'I came home and she was just there … in the kitchen. Didn't even think she still had a key…'

'Have you spoken to her?' A strange question, sure. But she never quite knows with her father.

'I tried to. A little. But she wouldn't say much.'

Isla takes these words with a heavy pinch of salt. Her father won't talk to her about the bills because he finds it 'uncomfortable'; she can't imagine him having much to say to the daughter who walked out on them four years ago.

'Right. Okay.' The heavy weight of responsibility sits on her shoulders. It should be familiar, almost comfortable by now. But it's not. It still makes her muscles ache. 'I'll go find out what's going on, okay? It's going to be fine.'

Jasper takes a step to the side and Isla feels the shift, like when aeroplane pilots switch control. Her aircraft now. As if it isn't always.

She pulls herself together then steps into the house. Leaving her bag by the door, she skirts around her father's toolbox, steps instinctively over the wobbly floorboard, straightens the constantly askew photo frame. Just like always. Little rituals that make it feel like a normal evening when Isla has the distinct sensation that it's not.

The kitchen is almost exactly how Isla left it this morning, right down to the abandoned bowl of cereal by the sink that she had to leave when she realised the clock on the wall had stopped and she was running late. The only difference now is that there's somebody sitting in a seat that has stayed empty for the last four years.

She looks younger. That's the first thing Isla notices about her sister. Morgan Pembroke has been gone for four years and yet somehow she looks younger than she did when she left. Though perhaps that memory has become muddied over the years. Isla can't actually remember exactly how she looked before she left; she didn't know it would be the last time for a while after all; she didn't take notes.

Morgan has the dark brown hair of her father, in contrast to Isla's – and their mother's – ginger curls. It used to be chin length but she's let it grow, judging by the size of the haphazard bun it's been scraped back into. Though the fringe has stayed the same, Isla notices. Still skimming just above her eyes, as if it offers her sister a strange sense of refuge. She's still hiding then. Isla feels that bitter thought lodge in her chest, burrowing down like a tick.

Morgan looks up from the table the moment she hears Isla enter. For a second, Isla is a little floored. Their father used to joke, long ago, that his daughters' green eyes could stop the ocean with a glare. Isla is used to seeing that fierce look in her own reflection; now she remembers how different it is to see it in real life, staring back at you.

Isla is also struck by the hope she can see there. What exactly is Morgan hoping for? Isla tries not to let this thought linger too long; she doesn't want to go into this interaction already irritated. She expertly fixes a smile in place, hesitates, then comes to sit across from her sister. 'Well, this is a surprise.'

Morgan blinks; Isla sees the hope disappear instantly. Clearly she didn't quite keep the irritation out of her voice, then. 'Hey, Isla,' she says, fingernails digging into the worn wood of the table. The scratching squeaks of the wood bring a wave of familiarity over Isla. Funny, the things she's forgotten her sister took with her, right down to the smallest sounds. 'Yeah. I came back.'

'You ... came back?' Isla echoes, trying not to sound as if she's picking apart her sister's words.

Of course, Morgan narrows her eyes in a way that suggests that's exactly what it sounds like. 'Yes,' she responds, voice stiff.

'Mogs ...' Her old nickname. Isla hasn't said that word in so long and it feels strange on her tongue, almost as though it doesn't fit any more. Yet it has arrived, without her really thinking about it. 'What's going on? We've been worried sick. You walked out on us, without a word. And all this time we've had no idea where you were, what you were doing.' Isla feels anger seeping into her words already and she grips her hands together tightly in a hopeless attempt to stall it.

'You knew I was safe. I told you I was safe,' Morgan says, but without much feeling.

Isla lets those words sit in silence for a moment, lets her sister feel how irrelevant they really are. Finally, she speaks again. 'Yes. You did. Every once in a while, we knew you were safe. That makes it all fine, I guess?'

Morgan sighs, rests her forehead against one hand. 'Isla, please.'

'You come home after four years of basically radio silence; you leave us in the middle of the night with not one word? A seventeen-year-old kid disappearing on us, after all we've been through? After all Dad's been through. And now you come back and ... what? You expect me to drop it? Do you even know me?' She tries to make it light-hearted, that she's almost telling a joke. But she knows she's failing. Of course she's failing. Some things cannot be said without bitterness at their core.

Morgan lets out a small sound, almost like a groan, of frustration. Or maybe it's fear. Those two feelings have always been entwined pretty closely within Isla's sister. 'I didn't ... I wasn't saying drop it ... Just ...' She trails off, each of those words seeming to have exhausted her beyond the point of continuing.

'Why now?' The question slams into the uneasy silence between the sisters and Isla almost considers whether she can still pull it back because she's not actually sure she's ready for the answer.

There's the creak of scratched wood again, as Morgan's fingernail digs deeper into the surface of the table. Isla watches how her eyes darken, how the green seems to become poisoned. Morgan shakes her head slowly, almost imperceptibly.

But Isla still spots it. 'We don't even get to know that?'

Something in those words, those seemingly innocent words, kick in that all-too-powerful Morgan instinct to run. She stands up, chair screeching loudly against the worn slate. Isla notices instantly that her sister straightens up with a certain delicateness, as if she's expecting to fall apart at the simplest of movements. Over her leggings, Morgan's wearing a man's sweater that seems to almost cocoon her. It makes Isla uneasy for a reason she can't quite find.

But then Morgan's gone, heading for the back door. Business as usual.

Isla lets her go, gives her five seconds of space, then follows her. A tried-and-tested technique. Sometimes it even works.

Behind the Pembroke house is a path that leads directly to the second, more remote beach of Karrekoth. It's narrow, steep and treacherous but the Pembroke girls could traverse it with their eyes closed. They know when to step around the exposed root, when to avoid the oddly slippery stone. They know which part will become a swamp after a storm, they know in May it will be swarming with mayflies and they know that it takes precisely three minutes to walk down when you're striding off in a huff.

The path winds down the hill then suddenly opens up onto the beach. The sea waits directly ahead, tall cliffs tower behind and Karrekoth itself sits off to the right, a mile or so away behind a lower set of cliffs. Sand can be seen ahead but, before it can be reached, a craggy and somewhat intimidating line of rocks need traversing.

The wind is calm but there's a chill in the air, causing Isla to tug her jacket a little tighter around her. Summer is most definitely on the way out. Morgan's not really dressed for beach scrambling but it doesn't seem to bother her, as she belligerently continues to ignore her sister's shouts. She expertly walks across the larger, dryer rocks that are at the back of the beach, her head down. Isla gives the sea a brief glance, makes a mental calculation about the tide. They've got a little time.

'Morgan! Will you just stop?' It's the third time she's said that, or something similar. But Morgan does not listen. She picks her way over stone, heading for the towering column of rock that stands proudly at their end of the beach, the rock which gave their town its name.

Now, as she sees Morgan making a beeline for it, Isla lets out a groan. Morgan found a perfect ledge halfway up the rock when she was seven and has considered this her bolthole ever since. It seems that apparent adulthood has not changed that.

But Isla is not particularly in the mood for climbing, not after a day of telling sticky children to stop tapping fish tanks. So she decides to use her last bit of energy to close the distance between them, until she can reach out, grab her sister's arm and tug her to a halt.

'I know we're all for dramatics, but can we not do the climbing thing? Just ... sulk at the damn bottom for me.'

Morgan pulls herself free. For a moment, Isla wonders if she's going to climb the rock anyway, just to spite her. It wouldn't surprise her. But one hand drifts to her side, pairing with a small frown. She takes a few more steps towards the large rock, then slowly lowers herself down onto one slightly protruding edge. Suddenly, she seems exhausted once again.

Isla peels off her plimsolls, leaves them by a cluster of barnacles, then sits beside her sister. There's not really room but somehow the two accommodate each other whilst also managing to avoid any direct contact. A temporary act of sisterly rebellion against the laws of physics.

Isla watches the way Morgan picks at the skin around her fingernails, the way she keeps her eyes fixed on the ground. She has a desire to snatch her sister's hand away before she can peel off a whole damn nail. But she resists that urge. This isn't her kid sister any more. She doesn't need Isla; she made that very clear when she left.

'We missed you.' It feels like an easy place to start. The truth.

'I missed you too.'

Isla can't help it. 'You could have come back. Nobody was stopping you.'

Morgan shoots her sister a weary look. 'You know what I mean. I forgot how pedantic you were.'

'And I forgot how dramatic you were.'

Morgan scowls. God, she could still be a child with that scowl, the same scowl she wore when she surveyed the subpar fifteenth-birthday tea Isla tried to make for her.

'I had to leave.'

It's a start. Isla presses her toes against the stone, feels the persisting stickiness of the leftover saltwater. Waits.

'I had to leave; I couldn't do it any more.'

Isla feels the memory sting, like saltwater, in her eyes. The open bedroom door, the neatly made bed, the ransacked chest of drawers. The flat dial tone on the other end of the phone. The blank expression her father wore when she tried to explain, in the gentlest possible way, that his seventeen-year-old daughter was nowhere to be found.

'We … thought you were dead. There was no sign of you, anywhere. We thought … until you sent that first text … we thought you must have fallen into the sea or something.'

Morgan sniffs, scuffing her feet against the edge of the towering rock they're sat on. 'As if I'd be stupid enough to go walking on the cliffs at night.'

Isla decides it's best not to say anything. She doesn't trust her own mouth right now. She feels Morgan staring at her, waiting desperately for some response. Maybe waiting for her to make it all better. But Isla's got nothing.

'Isla ...'

'Four years.' Isla winces immediately. Dammit. So much for keeping quiet. 'Did you not think about us for a second? Do you know how terrifying it is to not know whether someone you love is dead or not?'

Morgan is silent. Then slowly nods. 'I do know.'

Isla feels the heavy meaning in her words but she's not having it, not now. 'Yes, you do. So you should have known better.'

Morgan seems to withdraw within herself, sliding back against the rock and drawing her legs up to her chest. She does it slowly, carefully. Like she's expecting to fall apart at any moment. It's years away from the girl who once confidently scaled this rock as if she was on the school climbing frame. Isla can't tell if it's her words that have closed her up like this or something else. But she feels guilty anyway. Just in case.

She decides to move things on. For both their sakes. 'If you won't tell me why you're back, will you at least tell me where you've been?'

Morgan drums her fingers against the rock. 'Around and about. It's not important.'

Isla wants to believe that, she really does. But Morgan has never been that simple. 'I'd really rather you didn't hide things from me. Not now. Not after everything.'

'I'm not.'

'I know what you avoiding the question looks like, Morgan. You've been doing it to me long enough.'

Morgan sighs, resting her head against the stone. Eyes closed. She looks so exhausted. Beneath all her anger, Isla is just so damn worried. She knows Morgan's a grown-up, officially speaking. She's twenty-one; she can look after herself (apparently she's been looking after herself for four years after all). But she's still her little sister. Isla still remembers when she held Morgan in her arms days after her birth, how her tiny fist clutched at a lock of her hair and refused to let go.

'Did something ... happen?' Isla's voice is gentler now. Morgan sniffs and Isla sees one solitary tear travel down her cheek. But she brushes it away, shakes her head as if she's convincing herself against a course of action.

'I forgot how much you sound like her.'

'Like who?' As if she doesn't know.

'Mum.'

Isla is silent. She's not sure she remembers the last time she heard that word in relation to her own mother. She's heard it at the aquarium, of course. Over-excited children shrieking the word when the octopus finally comes out of hiding. Or screaming it when they're not allowed to buy a soft toy from the gift shop. But for her own mum? No, she's not heard that in a very long time. Jasper won't say it and Isla daren't, not when those memories still cause her father such trouble.

'Isla?'

Isla looks over to her sister as she speaks again and sees how she's looking right at her. There's desperation in her eyes. She's not sure what for.

This time, it's Isla who stands up first. 'The tide's coming in.'

Morgan glances out to sea and Isla knows that she's not buying her deflection for one second. But it seems as though she's willing to play along, for now. She stands up too.

'I'll have to make your bed up for you; we stripped it ... after you left.' Isla tries to find some solace in this normal sentence but finds very little. The words feel like they belong to someone else.

Morgan nods slowly. 'I just … I need time, Isla. I'll explain one day, I will. But I just need …' She trails off, a little helplessly.

'Yes, you said. Time.'

Isla knows that Morgan's heard the disappointment in her voice. She doesn't mean to sound disappointed; she's not even sure why it's there, not when she can usually hide her own feelings with such skill. Perhaps four years is too long to wait to hear the same sentence she's heard her father say, over and over, and not let that disappointment free.

Morgan hesitates, then slowly begins to pick her way back along the beach, towards their path home. With the aim of giving her sister a little space, Isla takes her time to stuff her feet back into her shoes, glancing out across the sea.

Out along the horizon, the sky is darkening; the clouds are thickening. And she knows what that means.

A storm is coming.

Three

But the storm doesn't come after all. Isla keeps expecting to hear the wind whistling through the gaps around the kitchen windows or to hear the rain pounding against the glass. But there's nothing.

Just a stony silence that settles over the house like a thick fog. Isla's not sure which is worse.

Morgan manages to wait downstairs long enough for Isla to find her some clean bedding and a towel, then disappears into her bedroom with nothing else to say except an awkward thank you. Isla makes dinner, and tries to tempt Morgan down with her favourite pasta dish. But when she comes downstairs, she sits in such unmoving silence that it might as well have been just Isla and Jasper as usual. Except now her father is even more withdrawn, barely answering Isla's borderline desperate questions about his day.

She feels as if she's taken a leap back in time and it scares the hell out of her. How hard has she worked to tug her father into some sort of normality? And one evening with her sister back in the house has sent everything tumbling back to square one.

Once Morgan makes her quietly murmured excuses and disappears upstairs, Isla finds it hard to stay up for much longer. She clears up the kitchen, reminds her father to take his medication before bed, then leaves him in front of the news. Then she goes upstairs, sits on her bed and stares at the opposite wall, which separates her room from Morgan's. Wills herself to somehow develop the ability to see through walls (and into sisters' brains). But it remains resolutely solid and all she can see is the whale painting her mother made for her fifth birthday.

At some point, she finds the energy to get ready for bed. Sleep comes patchily, for she keeps waking to what she assumes (or hopes) are imagined sounds from next door. Doors opening and closing, objects crashing, even hastily smothered crying.

When morning light begins to filter through her curtains, along with the persistent screeches of seagulls, Isla feels that she hasn't really slept at all. Bleariness drags at her eyes but she's determined to get somewhere with her sister today.

However, when she steps out of her bedroom, she finds Morgan's door open and the room empty. For a terrible moment, she thinks she's gone again. But then she sees her suitcase on the floor, open and spewing clothes out. She's not run away again, then. Yet.

It soon becomes apparent, though, that Morgan has not just left her room but has also left the house. In fact, the house is empty. All Isla has for company is a note from her father stuck to the fridge: *Gone to paint the beach loos, be back for dinner.*

Helpful. So all Isla can do is head to work and hope that she finds a solution there. For once.

South Cornwall Aquarium is unsurprisingly quiet when Isla finally gets to work. A few pensioners are sampling the questionable selection of fish-themed food in the cafe, a toddler is being wrestled back into his buggy to avoid him putting another toy starfish near his mouth and there's a lacklustre-looking Mitch sitting at the admissions desk.

'Shouldn't have bothered, Isla,' he comments with a grin as she comes barrelling in. Isla hoped there would be a sufficient aura of stress around her to ensure she would be left alone today but apparently that's not the case. 'Nobody here but the guppies...'

Mitch clearly thinks the fact that he's used an alternative word for 'fish' is worthy of applause, but Isla is certainly not the one to give it. She barely manages a smile, brushing past him. 'It *is* an aquarium, Mitch. The "guppies" are sort of the point!' she calls back, not quite able to help herself.

It's not until Isla is on her fourth round of feeding that she realises she's not concentrating at all. Her hand hesitates over the top of the octopus tank, as she suddenly becomes aware of the fact that she has no idea if she's actually putting the right food in.

A quick check and she confirms that, yes, it is a bucket of whelks and clams she's about to tip into the tank. The octopus is squirming irritably just under the surface and Isla hurriedly completes the job, before she's rewarded with an impatient slap of a tentacle (it's happened before).

The tank's lid is back on a moment later and the octopus is merrily crushing shells against a rock, a sadistic glee seeming to radiate from the creature. Isla knows she should move on, that she's got work to do, but she can't quite find the motivation required. All she can do is stand, staring at the octopus and wondering what it must be like to only need to worry about breaking clam shells.

'Does he always smash them like that?'

'It's a she,' Isla corrects instinctively, before actually registering the fact that someone has spoken to her, in a voice she barely recognises.

When she turns around, there's a man by the door. He's hovering a little uncertainly on the threshold, as if he doesn't quite want to intrude. Isla takes a second to examine his face and feels herself jolted, as if hit by lightning.

'Dylan?' she splutters. For a moment she wonders if she missed the damn memo about this being the officially designated week for long-lost people to return. She's sure she hasn't seen him since they both left school to pursue their similar marine biology dreams. And now here he is, mere hours after her sister reappeared, wearing the tan of someone who has not been in the depths of another disappointing British summer, and a slightly crinkled visitor sticker which he's somehow failed to stick properly to his polo shirt. Immediately, Isla resists the urge to fix it for him.

Dylan appears to notice Isla's bewilderment and steps forward, holding out a hand with a slightly lopsided grin. 'Dylan Burroughs. I'm with Professor Sawyer.'

It almost seems as if he's speaking another language and Isla has to really concentrate to make sure she's understood his sentence. The hand is still waiting in front of her, so she hurriedly puts down her now empty bucket, wipes her hand on her trousers, and shakes it, slowly. 'Yeah, I know. It's me – Isla. Isla Pembroke?' she manages to say.

'Oh, no way! Shit, I didn't recognise you at all.'

Isla feels her eyebrow raising. She's not entirely sure she believes that; they were in the same class for the entirety of secondary school after all and it's not like Isla's wild red curls have ever allowed her to blend into the background. No matter how much she's wanted to. Still, she decides to play along for the moment. 'Professor Sawyer? As in … jellyfish expert Professor Sawyer?'

Dylan nods rather proudly. 'Yes, that one … though I think she prefers just Professor Sawyer …'

'She's here?'

He nods slowly and Isla notices a sense of slight confusion in his expression. Well, at least she's not the only one. 'About the internship? The, uh, owner ... Dennis? He said you all knew about it.'

'Oh. Right.' Isla sniffs, turning back towards the octopus tank. 'Dennis doesn't really have a clue about anything, in particular running an aquarium. I would assume from now on that anything he says in regards to this place is nonsense.'

'I'll bear that in mind.' Dylan doesn't seem able to say anything without that crooked grin of his, which Isla is swiftly recalling from their time at school together. She seems to remember it distracting her back then as well, though perhaps she's currently more bothered by the way he confidently steps around her and approaches the tank. This is her domain after all; not Dylan bloody Burroughs's with his world-traveller tan and casual reference to a top marine biologist he's talking about as if she's his best friend. 'So ... is she a fan of smashing up her food?' he asks with a nod at the tank's solitary occupant.

Isla watches as the octopus curls one tentacle around a stone and hurls it at the final, apparently strongest shell. 'Uh, yes, she is. I mean, she never seems to do it another way. And sometimes she seems to do it even when she doesn't need to. Like it's entertainment, rather than a means to food.'

'Interesting. Have you tried feeding her without the shells?'

Isla feels as though she's being assessed. The thought makes her shoulders stiffen somewhat; this might be a tiny, seedy-looking aquarium but she's not a disinterested employee looking for an easy job. She knows what she's doing. 'Yes. She didn't eat it. She just sat waiting for me to do it properly.'

Dylan laughs at that, eyes fixed on the tank. Isla can see intense fascination in his gaze and she wonders if she looks this wired when watching sea creatures. Almost like he's trying to melt the glass away and be immersed in the water. 'What is she, then?'

Isla is almost tempted to just say 'octopus', just to make up for Dylan apparently not recognising his classmate of seven years. But there's that incessant desire to prove herself, still buzzing away in her ears. 'Giant Pacific,' she says. 'Though she's not that giant at the moment. She came from some idiot's basement a few months ago; we were amazed she made it.'

'A survivor. Nice.'

Isla thinks of her sister ignoring her questions, pushing her away, running off for four years. Being a survivor is all very well, unless your surviving only succeeds at the expense of everything else.

The thought makes Isla shiver. She doesn't know if Dylan notices it but she certainly doesn't want to hang around to find out.

'I, uh, should get on. I've still got a lot of feeding to do.'

'Of course, sorry for bothering you.'

'You weren't,' Isla lies immediately, as her instinctive need to please everyone kicks in. She grits her teeth with slight frustration. 'I mean … it's fine, it wasn't that much of a bother.'

Again, there's the crooked smile. As if everything she says is amusing. But perhaps he notices how it seems to rile her up because he turns a little more serious a second later, as he stands aside to let her leave. 'Dennis said you knew your stuff. Are you thinking of going for the internship?'

'I didn't realise it was anyone else's business.' The words are out before Isla can stop them. Clearly her own exhaustion and stress (and that stupid smile) has got the better of her. She feels her cheeks flushing because since when has she spoken to people like this? That's Morgan's remit, not hers.

For a moment, Isla is so shocked with her own words that

she finds it impossible to say anything else. Then, as Dylan's expression drops a little, she drags herself back. 'I'm sorry. I just meant ... it's complicated.'

Isla feels like even the octopus is staring at her now. Her cheeks are definitely flushing so she decides that the time has come to leave. Hastily picking up her bucket of slushy ice, Isla hurries from the room before he can say anything else.

It's the end of the day before Isla finds herself encountering Dylan again. She's successfully avoided most people by dealing with as many minor fish issues as she can. She cleans the filters in four tanks, checks the fin condition of as many tropical fish as she can manage and does a somewhat excessively careful stocktake of food supplies.

Isla knows she's hiding away and she knows that Morgan probably learnt her instinct of flight from her, but she can't stop herself. The world seems to be throbbing around her; people's voices seem to be on an entirely different, painful frequency. And her mind keeps drifting across the coastal winds back home to the bedroom that has suddenly found itself occupied once again. Back to the sister whose eyes are hollow with sadness and yet full of determination to not share one ounce of it.

Even with all that worry, Isla's not exactly rushing home. Hidden amongst the merrily bubbling tanks, she can almost pretend nothing has changed and there's something comforting about that. Something calming about knowing there's only fish to care for. They don't tend to come with quite the same complications.

But eventually, there's no more procrastinating she can get away with without feeling guilty. It's fifteen minutes past the official end of her shift and she knows her father will worry if she's too late, and that's something she can never feel settled with. After all, she knows what her father's worry can cause.

It's as she's stepping outside that she sees him. Dylan's standing to one side of the entrance doors, nursing a Thermos flask which is billowing steam into the rather sharp chill of the evening, and he's thoroughly immersed in his phone. Isla thinks she can perhaps get away with sneaking past him but no such luck; she's halfway down the path to the car park when she hears him call her name.

She turns slowly on her heel, finds him hurriedly snapping his Thermos shut so he can follow after her. 'Hey, I just wanted to say … about earlier—'

'It's fine, really,' she interrupts. He sounds as though he's going to apologise and Isla doesn't want him to, not really. 'You were just being politely curious, I'm sure. I really don't know what came over me.'

Dylan pauses, eyebrows quirked. 'Do you often skip through people's apologies?' he asks, grin back in place.

'Only if they're unnecessary.' Isla finds her retort snapping back immediately, which surprises her. Usually she's not one for quick retorts, unless it's her sister she's arguing with.

'And … do you often deem apologies unnecessary?'

Isla feels a small smile tickling at the corners of her own mouth now. The truth is the truth after all. 'Probably.' She shrugs, and tries not to think about how many pointless apologies she's sifted through over the years (*I'm sorry to hear the news about your mother; I'm sorry I can't go to Morgan's parents' evening; I'm sorry I stormed out of dinner last night*).

Dylan's surveying her with the same piercing, almost scientific gaze he had with the octopus. Isla's not sure she likes it particularly. It reminds her of Morgan's teacher when she had to go to that parents' evening in place of her father. The memory is cold against her back and Isla is keen to move on.

'Um, I should be going ... Unless there was something else?'

'Not particularly, I just wanted to catch you and check things were okay. And ...' Dylan pauses and Isla gets the distinct sense that Dylan is trying to say something quite important. 'I just wanted to say that I did recognise you, before. I don't know why I pretended not to. It was stupid ...'

A rumble of thunder rolls lazily across the sky above her. It makes Isla's somewhat frazzled brain struggle even more to focus. 'Oh. Right.' What else is there to say? She can't disagree; it *was* stupid. 'Don't worry about it,' she finally manages.

All around her the clouds are darkening, whirling around each other with increasing agitation. The wind picks up, causing Isla's curls to throw themselves into her face until she wrestles them behind her ears.

Just as lightning flashes out across the distant horizon, Isla feels her phone buzz in her hand. She glances down, sees the message from her dad: *Morgan's back again, what should I do?* The world blurs around her as reality sneaks back and demands her attention.

'Dylan,' she blurts out, not really sure if she's cut him off or not but finding it hard to be too concerned, 'I'm sorry. I've really got to go.'

Dylan looks a little nonplussed. She had cut him off, then. 'Oh, right. Sorry, look at me rambling on. Anyway, I'm here for the next few months or so. Professor Sawyer asked me to do some research from here while she's visiting different aquariums around the country ... so I'll see you around?'

'Sure,' Isla says, without really thinking. She's heard the inflection of speech that generally means a question and so has given what she hopes is the correct answer, but she's not really listening. Now her father needs her, she can't think of much else. Before Dylan can say anything else, she hurries off towards her car.

A moment later, as she drives out of the car park, she catches sight of Dylan shuffling back inside. Distantly, she can't help but wonder why he was standing outside in a gathering storm in the first place.

Four

By the time Isla gets home, Morgan has already retreated into her bedroom. She finds her father in the sitting room, staring resolutely into his cup as if he might find some sort of answer in there. She sees the way his fingers grip tightly enough to make his knuckles flare white. Then he looks up, sees her watching him. That's something, at least. There's been many times when she has sat opposite him and waited for him to acknowledge her, only for it to never happen.

'Oh, hey, bud.' He manages a smile, so small that it's almost just a twitch. 'She . . . she didn't want to talk to me. Said she was too tired.'

'Right,' Isla says, the word hard as rock against her tongue. 'I see.'

Jasper shifts in his chair. 'Isla . . .' It's a gentle warning tone, but he's not got much energy to put into it. So unsurprisingly it doesn't do much to quell the frustration that is building within Isla. She hasn't spent four years worrying about her sister for her to return and just not speak to them.

So, work bag gets dumped on the floor, shoulders get squared, and sister follows sister up the stairs. Isla wonders if Jasper will follow her but then she dismisses that idea immediately. Jasper hasn't intervened in a very long time.

Isla doesn't bother knocking. She rather forcibly smacks her sister's door open, finds her slumped over her phone on her desk. 'What is going on?'

Morgan stands up, drops her phone down. 'What is going on what?' she shoots back.

'You disappear for four years and tell us nothing, you come back and tell us nothing. You go out all day and tell us nothing. You come back at last and, surprise, surprise, tell us nothing? What part of that do you think is okay?'

Morgan shifts, one foot tucking behind the other. Isla remembers that classic Morgan stance of defence. 'I'm not a child any more, I don't need to tell you where I am.'

'You do if you're living under this roof. You're not on your bloody dreamy runaway adventure any more, Morgan.'

Isla sees her words sting against Morgan and she does feel a twinge of regret when she watches how her sister winces. But she's not going to apologise for it, not when frustration wraps around her like a hurricane.

'That's not ... That's not what it was like.' Her voice has become so soft that Isla can barely hear it over the rain smacking against Morgan's window. The eyes become hollow once more and Isla can feel her instinct screaming at her to offer comfort.

But four years is a long time for anger to grow and it won't just let go. 'Well, I've got nothing else to go on because you won't bloody tell me!'

The hollowness disappears in an instant. Isla can practically hear the crack in Morgan's knuckles as she clenches her hands into fists. 'Get out,' she snaps, teeth gritted.

'Tell me where you've been. Tell me *something*, Morgan!'

'Get out, Isla!'

Isla is struck by how familiar this conversation feels. How many times has Morgan yelled at her to get out of her bedroom because she didn't want to face the conversation heading her way? And how many times has Isla relented, when perhaps she should have stayed?

Maybe that's why she stays rooted. 'I won't get out until you tell me what the hell is going on with you. I'm trying to help, Morgan—' She's interrupted by a furious snort that sends her remaining scraps of calm scurrying out of reach. 'What?'

'Trying to help, right. That's what you're *always* doing …'

The sarcasm drips off her words, unforgivingly thick and heavy. For once, Isla is stumped. Brought to a halt by the almost hatred radiating from her sister. Oh yes, she'd forgotten how much that stung.

Isla waits, hoping for some sort of regret to flicker across her sister's face. But it never comes. Morgan looks at her, savagely unabashed.

'What do you mean by that?' Isla finally manages to ask the question that has been sitting uncomfortably on her tongue for the last few seconds.

Morgan stands up abruptly, eyes looking slightly wild. 'I mean that you're full of shit, Isla. You're not trying to help, you're just trying to feel better about the fact that you're still here despite all your talk about getting out. When are you going to stop bloody fooling yourself, Isla?'

Isla doesn't quite know how she ends up outside after that. She distantly remembers the slamming of Morgan's door behind her, the thud of her own feet as she half trips down the stairs.

She remembers that her sister doesn't come after her.

And suddenly she's all alone outside in the rain and Isla feels it dripping down her neck but she can't bring herself to go back. Stubborn Pembroke genes won't let her. It's not that bad out here, she tells herself. It would be convincing if she could hear her own thoughts over the growl of the wind.

But she storms on nonetheless, thoughts whirling around her and making it difficult to see. She almost trips over the exposed root, almost loses her balance on the algae-covered stone. The rain and her anger have transformed the familiar path into a treacherous jungle.

Somehow, the beach arrives. It's not the calm plain of sand, stone and sea that she saw yesterday. The wind has created furious, foaming waves that crash angrily against anything they can reach. The clouds sit heavy and low, crushing oppressively down on the world beneath. Isla knows this is no time to be on this beach. But desperate anger can work marvels at dulling rationality.

So with her better judgement scattered across the wind, Isla keeps moving. Tries to make sense of the words her sister has thrown at her feet. The anger's not new; she knows that. Morgan has been angry at her for a very long time and while Isla can't always understand it, she has learnt to get used to it. But there's something different now. A deep, bitter frustration that doesn't match up with the little sister she has spent a sizeable chunk of her life caring for. Does Morgan really see her like that? Does she really think she's cross with Morgan simply because she left while Isla didn't? No, she's cross because her sister has let her spend four years constantly worrying about her well-being.

A rumble of thunder pulls Isla from her despairing thoughts and drops her back into reality. The reality of being on a darkening beach in the middle of a thunderstorm that seems to be growing more furious by the second.

Isla pauses, briefly considers going back. But there's a flash of lightning a few seconds later, only a few hundred yards out to sea. She doesn't want to be out on this exposed beach for a second longer. She curses herself for allowing that impulsive streak of hers to fly free, then runs for cover.

There's a large cave set into the cliffs just a few metres away and Isla ducks inside it. Her curls weigh heavily against her shoulders, some flopping against her forehead until she pushes them back. She is becoming distinctly aware of how utterly soaked she is. Stupid. She's twenty-eight; she's a damn adult. And yet here she is, trapped on a beach in the middle of one of Karrekoth's infamous storms.

Stupid.

She sits down, winces as thunder booms again, echoing eerily through the cave. Waits, counts. Hopes for a pause before the lightning, for a sign that the storm is moving away. But no such luck. Almost instantly, the cave is bathed in hot white light as the sky flashes for a moment. No forked lightning yet; that's something.

Of course the moment she thinks that, it happens. The previous thunder has barely faded before there's another crash. And this time it's accompanied by a spindly line of lightning that wriggles right down to strike the sea. Isla feels herself wince; she should be used to this weather in this storm-battered village, but it's still a little unnerving for it to be so close.

The lightning seems to linger, or perhaps its bright light is just permanently seared against her eyeballs. Silence returns for a moment, even the rain seems to die down a little.

But then the whole ground seems to shake, as lightning cracks through the air once more. This time, though, it hits solid land, close enough for her to feel the heat from it. From her spot in the cave, Isla can see it clearly. She knows the connection between land and sky must only be there for a split second but it seems to last forever. She sees it all in minute detail, the way the lightning's jagged edges seem to cut through the air itself. It feels as if she has hours to study the angular, angry corners.

She certainly has time to notice where it strikes.

For a moment, Karrekoth's rock is lit up so brightly that Isla is sure she can see every clump of barnacles, every nook and cranny. Strangely, despite her own somewhat precarious position, she finds herself filled with worry about the rock exploding and crumbling. That would be a great deal of history getting washed out to sea.

Miraculously, it stays intact. The lightning releases its hold on its craggy peak and disappears.

And just like that, almost as if its purpose has been fulfilled, the storm calms.

Isla waits for a moment, eyes fixed on the sky. She knows that storms are tricksters and she's not stepping back onto the exposed beach until she's absolutely sure it's finished.

It's while she's staring up that she hears it; a heavy, wet-sounding crack. It reverberates across the beach, in an entirely different way to the thunder. This isn't from the sky, this is from the ground below her, or rather the rocks around her.

Legs shaky from being curled up in the cave, Isla stumbles up onto her feet. The cracking sound is bouncing eerily around her, but she doesn't really notice it. Her eyes are fixed on Karrekoth's rock.

A scorched scar now runs all the way down one side of the rock and, as Isla stares, a warm light begins to glow through it. Almost as though the lightning has opened up the rock and revealed a secret den of fireflies within. Isla finds herself moving closer, stepping out from the safety of the cave. She can't help but be entranced.

The closer she gets, the wider the scar seems to grow. Until suddenly she's right in front of it and she knows that she could squeeze through it if she wanted. She doesn't want to at first, of course she doesn't. Isla's somewhat irrepressible logic argues that there's no sensible reason to go inside a lightning-scorched rock. But now she's right next to the rock, she can hear sounds coming through the gap. She hears the crash of waves, the joyful screech of seagulls. Then a whooping, carefree laugh in the distance.

It's easy to step through the gap then. Isla's not heard that sound for a very long time but she would recognise it anywhere. So Isla follows the impossible sound of her sister's joyful laugh. And steps into the stone.

Five

Light blinds her. For a moment all she can see is brightness. Then it's gone, and she feels the dampness of stone pressing against her fingers. She realises her eyes have screwed themselves shut to try and defend themselves against the glare and so she opens them slowly, tentatively.

The beach lies in front of her, bathed in glorious and uninterrupted sunshine. The sea is a glassy pond, the sky could be its reflection. Isla sees a fishing boat bobbing in the distance, practically feels the gentle rhythm of its rocking. Everything is calm.

Then there's that laugh again. Isla practically *feels* that laugh, skipping through her veins. Desperate to find its source, she peers out from behind the huge stone, into the sunlight. The beach is fully revealed to her now and immediately she spots her sister. She's lying on one of the huge flat rocks, a good twenty metres away. But her laughter travels across the wind with ease.

It takes Isla less than a second to realise that the Morgan she's looking at is not the Morgan she's just stormed away from. This Morgan has short hair and braces, this Morgan is still shorter than her. This Morgan wears school uniform in her own unique way with a hint of pride at her own creativity. This Morgan laughs like she hasn't yet learnt what the world can do.

This Morgan has not yet lost her mother.

Isla wonders if she should be more shocked. Maybe even panicked. Apparently she has just stepped from one time into the other. Such things should definitely cause distress. But she's numb. Perhaps anaesthetised by her sister's laughter. Or perhaps her mind is just far too well practised in protecting her from the unbelievable and the unthinkable.

Morgan's laughter seems to be being caused by the book she's reading. Isla remembers that; remembers how her sister would immerse herself entirely in the world of a story and revel shamelessly in its joy. Even at this age, with adolescence clearly on its way, she does not care about laughing loud enough for the beach to hear. Not that there's anyone around to judge her; the beach is utterly deserted, which must mean it's term time. A sunny day like this in the school holidays would bring the visitors down without question. Isla remembers how her father would chase unwitting tourists out of their garden with his fishing rod when they'd accidentally wandered down the wrong coastal path.

'Morgan!'

It takes Isla a second to recognise that voice. Of course it does, she hasn't heard it in nine years. And, for a moment, Isla is terrified. Terrified to turn in case she's wrong, in case after all these years she's truly forgotten what she sounds like.

But she can't resist for a second longer. She looks towards the cliffs and sees her mother for the first time in nine years.

Marina Pembroke is coming down the path from home, wrapped in a white cardigan. Isla remembers that cardigan, how its intricate tassels used to get caught on every splinter and every exposed nail in the house. How her mum would curse the house as she untangled herself, before patting the wood as if she was worried she'd offended it somehow. She walks confidently across the rocks, avoiding the foot-trapping trenches

44

and slippery seaweed with an expertise that only comes from growing up by this beach.

'Morgan!' she calls again, finally drawing her daughter out of her book. Morgan sits up, closing the book once she's folded over the corner of the page she's on. Then she glances at her watch, winces to herself before standing up.

'Sorry! Coming!'

'I told you, back for five o'clock. You missed Isla.' Marina's words are only gently reprimanding and Isla knows that she'll never really be cross at Morgan for getting lost in a book, not when her room is filled with haphazardly constructed skyscrapers of books, ready to tumble down every time she chooses one to read.

'Shoot. Forgot she was going to call …' Morgan's reached her mother by now, book tucked under one arm as she automatically slips her other arm around her mother's waist. 'Was she mad?'

Marina tucks her daughter's hair behind one ear, revealing her face a little more. Yes, Isla remembers, she did do that. Every time. 'Oh yes, furious. She's told me she might not come back at Christmas now, she was so offended by your absence.'

Morgan rolls her eyes, detangling herself from her mother so she can hop carelessly from one rock to the next. She never could stay still for long on the beach, unless she was immersed in a book or her painting. 'What did she really say?'

'She said that university is going great, freshers' week almost broke her and that her lecturers range from dull to insane. Oh, and she's not rescued any whales yet.'

Isla smiles to herself, because she remembers that phone call. Wrapped up in the cocoon of her blankets, battling a cold but feeling incredibly proud that she'd managed her first laundry wash without breaking anything. More distantly, Isla remembers

how carefree, how light she felt back then. The world was opening up in front of her and potential was thick in the air.

For a few more weeks, anyway.

'No whales? How disappointing.' Morgan chuckles, pausing to
crouch low and examine the innards of a rock pool. She's twelve
years old at this point, perfectly poised between childhood and
adolescence. Still young enough to find wonder in a rock pool.
'She might as well give up now, then.'

Marina rolls her eyes at the instinctive need for mockery,
joining Morgan beside the rock pool. 'She sent her love but
maybe I should have just told her to send a mocking sentiment
instead.' She gives Morgan's side a gentle prod and Isla finds
her own hand drifting to her side; she'd forgotten the way their
mother would do that when she was teasing them, how it always
felt far more comforting than she was sure it was meant to.

Morgan ducks away from her mother's reach. She traverses
the rocks with the same confidence of her mother, a confidence
that is miles away from the uncertain young woman Isla watched
storm across the beach just last night – or rather years in the
future. 'If I didn't mock her, she'd only worry that I was unwell
or something. So really, I'm doing a service.'

Marina doesn't get a chance to respond to that, though her
grin would suggest she's not bought her daughter's reasoning
in the slightest. Another person has joined them on the beach,
striding across the sand and cursing loudly when he steps in a
pile of kelp. Isla doesn't recognise him for a moment and, when
she does, she feels hot tears stinging in the corners of her eyes,
until she brushes them away with her usual impatience.

Jasper Pembroke looks as different to his older self as this
sunny beach looks to the storm-wracked world Isla has left
behind. There's no forest of frowns permanently rooted to his

brow, there's no haze of confusion wrapped around him like cotton wool. His shoulders are sturdy, not stooped.

Isla can't help but feel as if she's seeing two parents brought back from the grave.

'What is the point of having that house if it's never occupied?' Jasper grumbles by way of greeting, as he finally makes it to the same cluster of rocks as his family. 'Every time I come home, there's never anybody bloody there.'

'Shouldn't have let us live by the beach then,' Morgan replies, back to examining the rock pool. 'Besides, when we are home you only complain about us leaving mess everywhere.'

From her spot half-hidden by the stone, Isla can see Marina's poor attempt to hide her smile. Jasper clearly sees it too because he shoots his wife a mild look of accusation.

'What? She does have a point...' With a laugh (oh, how Isla remembers the melody of her laugh!), Marina wraps an arm around her husband's waist. 'How was Bobby?'

'His trailer is rusty, he may need therapy. How was the post office?'

'Busy. What my dad would have called a three-pint day.'

Morgan straightens up, eyebrows quirked. 'Didn't Grandpa call most days that?'

With a snort, Jasper nods. 'Very true, Mogs.'

Marina gives her husband's arm a smack, tutting slightly. 'You can hardly talk. How many pints did you have last week with your fishing lot before you staggered home and woke the whole house with your inability to walk properly up the stairs?'

Sniggering, Morgan nods her agreement. 'You were proper loud, Dad. Anyway, what's for tea?'

Marina smiles and Isla feels herself sharing that smile. Morgan's appetite was so all-consuming sometimes that all other conversation would be thrown unceremoniously away when she was hungry. That will go too, Isla knows. So many things will go from her family when her mother does.

'Dad promised me fish pie this morning, and we all know your dad never breaks his promises when it comes to fish pie.'

'Wouldn't dare,' Jasper mutters, before jerking his head in the direction of the house. 'Home?'

Marina makes a noise of agreement, taking Morgan's hand. They begin the journey back towards their coastal path, perfectly synchronised in their steps from one rock to the next. Isla feels her own feet shuffle forward a little as she feels the temptation to follow dragging at her ankles. But what if she gets seen? That would be so typical of her luck to find a time-travelling stone and then promptly rip apart the universe.

So she stays frozen, watching from behind the stone as her family cross the sand and then start down the path home. She feels their confidence at the unchanging nature of their world and she also feels how it makes her own heart seem to crumple with yearning.

Once they're out of sight, Isla steps out from her hiding place. She comes forward until she's out of the stone's shadow, and can feel the sun against her skin. It feels a lot more comforting than usual, almost as if it will spend the next nine years collecting up all the sorrow from the Pembroke family, chilling its shine in the process.

Isla's feet move of their own volition until she finds herself on the precipice of the footprints left behind by her family. She sees the imprints left behind by her mother's sandals and wonders how long they will stay there before getting washed or blown away. Will they last beyond her mother's death? Isla can't quite remember how many more days are left; those heady, free, but limited days she got at university have blurred into one distant and hidden memory.

Suddenly, Isla finds herself on her knees. Kneeling on the ground with her fingers coming to press against the edges of one footprint, as though she might find some precious secret in the sand. But there's nothing, and once more Isla feels the stinging of tears until she brushes them away with instinctive urgency.

Across the beach, the sound of screeching seagulls gets loud enough for Isla to pull herself away from the footprints. She looks up, frowning as she catches sight of one lone crab doing its best to avoid the beaks of three seagulls. Its tiny claws are doing a sterling job at defending but Isla knows it's only a matter of time until the seagulls get their meal.

And perhaps it's the effects of time travel or the feeling of the seconds ticking away for her mother, but Isla finds she cannot kneel there and watch this crab die.

'Bloody pathetic,' she mutters to herself, not quite believing that she's just spent a day feeding various crustaceans to other aquatic animals and now can't let one crab get eaten. But, again, her feet have made the decision for her and before rationality can catch her, she's running towards the clump of squawking seagulls. 'PISS OFF!' she bellows, and the birds obligingly lift off into the sky. Which is a positive start, as Karrekoth seagulls are notoriously stubborn.

Isla grits her teeth and scoops up the still-outraged crab, hoping that the creature can't sense how many of its relations she fed to the jellyfish just a few hours ago. Doing her best to avoid the claws, she hurries towards one of the deeper rock pools. The seagulls have taken off towards the cliffs but Isla doesn't trust them to give up that easily.

She crouches down by the rock pool and carefully drops the crab into the water. It manages one sharp nip at her finger before it leaves, drawing a soft curse from Isla. The crab shoots towards the bottom of the pool before scuttling away into the shadows. Safe.

A warm feeling of satisfaction rushes over Isla as she sits back on the rock, catching her breath. She has no idea how she has ended up in this pocket of time (or if indeed this isn't a symptom of some prolonged breakdown) but at least she's managed to do something productive.

A drop of rain arrives, cool against the nape of her neck. Then another, and another. Isla glances up with a frown and sees only blue sky. Yet the rain is growing in ferocity. Her clothes rapidly become soaked again, her curls quickly return to being pressed against her cheeks and ears.

When Isla looks down from the sky, the crab-harbouring rock pool is gone, along with the sunshine. Instead she's sprawled by the stone once again and surrounded by the night. Off in the distance she hears a rumble of thunder but right here, on this beach, there is now only rain.

She's back. Her trip to the past is over. It takes her a moment to find the strength to stand up but she manages it, stumbling a little. Her hand grips onto the stone for balance and she feels heat under her fingers. Isla turns back towards the stone and sees that the lightning has left a permanent, twisted scar in its side.

As she's staring at this scarred surface, Isla feels a slight stinging sensation in her finger. When she glances down, she spots the small cut that the crab's claw has left.

'It did happen then,' she mutters aloud, deciding that talking to herself is really not her greatest concern right now.

This perturbing thought is suddenly interrupted by a soft glow that Isla realises after a moment is coming from the stone. Its scarred side spills this almost inviting light across the sand, a silent reassurance to Isla that it hasn't finished its impossible work just yet.

*

And, as Isla looks back to her cut finger and thinks of the crab that she helped escape its fate, she can't help but wonder what else the stone is inviting her to do.

She can't help but wonder who else she can save.

Six

The house is dark by the time Isla gets back. The kitchen clock tells her she's been gone for a couple of hours, which is a first for her. After all, disappearing for hours (or years) has always been Morgan's thing. It's with a touch of guilt that she notices a bowl of slightly congealed pasta waiting for her by the sink, wrapped in cling film. The dinner she didn't get round to making, instead choosing to shout at her sister and then storm out of the house.

Isla takes a closer look at the bowl and is rather forcibly reminded of why she took over cooking for herself and her father. Who knew a person could get pasta and pesto so wrong? And yes, she knows she should be grateful he's even capable of cooking these days, but it doesn't make the food any more appetising. She eats it quickly, before her stomach can really notice what it's taking on board. Then she creeps upstairs, past her sister's firmly shut bedroom door, which seems to glare at her as she walks by.

It's only once she's in bed, damp hair roughly towel-dried and wet clothes steaming gently on the radiator, that her brain allows her to fathom what's just happened. It sends a rather violent shiver down her spine, and she shuffles further down under the covers, trying to find solace in the warmth. Maybe this is it, the moment she finally loses it. Because rocks don't open up and let you back into the past; that's a fact. She's fairly sure she would have heard about that before if it was the case.

And yet, she can feel the ache in her muscles from crouching behind the stone. She can feel the sting of the crab's claw on her finger.

Isla has forgotten her mother's voice; that's the next somewhat unwelcome realisation to arrive. The warmth, the unashamedly Cornish accent, the dry sense of humour that always seemed to linger there. All gone.

That was the cruelty of losing someone. You kept realising the things that were gone. Even nine years later.

Another shiver comes and Isla rolls over, closes her eyes. Sleep. She just needs to sleep. Then perhaps everything will make sense again.

It becomes clear to Isla around lunchtime the next day that 'everything making sense again' is another unattainable aim to add to the ever-growing pile. She's spent the morning drifting about the aquarium in another daze (and Isla can't help but be distantly offended that nobody has noticed her lack of concentration) and the only thing she has been able to settle within her brain is the certainty that last night definitely happened.

Unfortunately, this certainty brings with it a whole load of doubt and questions. How has one stone managed to do all this? Can she do it again? And, of course, the one question that she's reminded of every time she catches sight of the small cut on her finger.

If she can save the life of one crab in the past, what else can she do?

Isla's seen enough science fiction over the years to know that it cannot be quite as simple as it seems. She knows that rescuing one small crustacean from seagulls is an entirely different matter to saving a person.

And yet she can think of nothing else.

She's deep down in the depths of this persistent thought when Dylan Burroughs appears once again. Isla has to wonder if he has some sort of radar that allows him to find her at the worst possible times. On this occasion, she's busy sorting out various food buckets for the afternoon feeding time. Her hands are covered in fish guts and her brain has not yet properly returned from the beach and its impossible rock, but Dylan ploughs right on with his conversation anyway.

'Need any help?' he asks, as he steps into the room. Isla takes a moment to register that he's speaking and then another moment to rewind back and take notice of what he actually said.

'Oh, it's fine. I'm sure you've got better things to do.' She doesn't mean to sound bitter but Isla's fairly sure resentment sneaks in anyway. Damn.

'Not really,' Dylan replies with a laugh. 'I did try telling the professor that nothing of interest happens around here, including in the sea ... but apparently there's a rare form of seaweed that she just *has* to have me investigate.'

Isla pauses, the dead sardine in her hand slopping back into the bucket. 'Oh, Cornish Floating Moss?'

'You've heard of it?'

Isla suppresses the urge to say something sarcastic, an urge she suppresses on an almost hourly basis in this place. 'It's hardly rare. Most fishermen round here bring half the stuff in with their nets. The floating aspect makes it interesting but also a right pain because it just gets tangled around everything.' She takes a moment to be somewhat impressed at her own ability to speak in full sentences before restarting her food sorting.

'I guess it's rare in terms of not really being found anywhere else. Professor Sawyer thinks it might have some interesting properties that could be used in medicine.' Dylan's words become a touch more like white noise now that Isla is trying to continue her work again but she makes what she hopes is an appropriate sound of interest. 'To be honest, it doesn't interest me in the slightest. I got into this job for fish, not seaweed...'

The bucket in Isla's hand slips from her grasp and clatters loudly to the ground. She knows Dylan won't have meant his words to hurt her but they do. She'd give anything to be out exploring the marine world, even if she was just exploring seaweed. But that's not his fault. Still, when he takes a step forward to help her, she shakes her head.

'It's fine,' she says, wincing at how often she has snapped those words in an attempt to make them feel true. 'I'm fine.' Ice cubes and slush mixed with fish guts oozes slowly across the floor but Isla is just relieved that this can serve as an excuse to stop this conversation. 'I should get on with cleaning this up.'

'Of course,' Dylan mumbles and, by the time she's grabbed the mop and bucket from the corner and turned back round, he's left the room.

Morgan is hovering a little nervously in the hallway when Isla gets home. Isla can tell she's nervous from the way she plays with her necklace, fingers tangling around the worn silver chain and thumb rubbing against the small anchor pendant. Her tenth birthday present from her parents.

'Hey.'

Isla quirks an eyebrow at the first word her sister says. 'Hey?' she echoes, voice a little stony. She's not forgotten last night's argument, funnily enough.

'You look like shit.'

'Wow. Have you considered becoming a professional greeter?

You do it so well.' She can't quite resist a glance across at the small hallway mirror, however. Morgan is right; her hair is exploding outwards from her scalp and the clearly restless previous night has left her looking pale and exhausted. She probably has fish guts permanently stuck under her fingernails as well but at least that's not quite so visible.

Sighing, Isla turns back to her sister. 'Was there something you wanted?'

Morgan hesitates, then slowly nods before moving to sit on the bottom step. 'I wanted to apologise,' Morgan finally murmurs. She says each word like it's heavy, and unwelcome in her mouth.

Isla crosses her arms. 'Apologise?' She hopes she doesn't sound completely disbelieving.

'Yeah, for last night.' Shifting on the step, Morgan briefly traces her finger along the bottom of the nearby wall. 'I didn't mean to … make you storm off into the night.'

Isla can hear an almost smugness in her sister's voice. A silent satisfaction that it was Isla being the one storming off for once. It's enough to convince her that this apology isn't entirely genuine. 'But you meant what you said, right?' Her voice is calm, perhaps because she's too tired to be anything but. Inside she still feels the seething sense of injustice that sent her out into the storm in the first place.

Morgan's eyes look anywhere but at her sister. As Isla rolls her eyes and starts off towards the kitchen, Morgan sighs and hurries after her. 'I just meant it can be a bit exhausting being the little sister of someone who won't accept that there are things in her life she's not happy with.'

'Is that what you think? Seriously?'

'I mean, apart from the obvious things … yeah. You always pretend like working in a shitty aquarium and looking after your father aged twenty-eight was the plan.'

Isla bites down on her lip, holds back the obvious response: *how would you know?* She doesn't want to keep fighting with Morgan, not if she's actually sticking around. 'I'm making the most of my situation, Morgan. I don't think that's a crime.'

She watches Morgan sigh again. It's she who looks exhausted now. Isla's seen this before, this tired frustration at not being able to get her point across. Usually it's followed by her leaving and, despite everything, Isla doesn't actually want her to do that. So she decides it's time to change the subject.

'Let's just leave it, okay? Now . . . do I at least get to know how long you're staying for?'

Morgan's expression is steady when she looks across to her sister. Perhaps this is one question she does know the answer to. 'I'm not planning on going anywhere any time soon . . . if that's okay?'

Isla nods automatically, without really thinking about whether it actually is okay. She can hardly refuse, can she? Even if she's sure her father has retreated into himself even more since Morgan's got back. Even if she doesn't quite know if her wages and her father's odd jobs will be enough to cover three people living here. Morgan is still her little sister; she's not about to turf her out.

'Thanks, Isla.' Morgan makes to leave the room, but Isla stops her with a hand raised.

'Um, so it's coming up to the anniversary, in a month or so. Dad and I still go visit Mum's grave if you're interested?'

Morgan looks understandably baffled. After all, why would Isla need to know this so far in advance? Isla has to admit that she's had better attempts at segues but her recent visit to the past has left her with an insatiable desire to find out more.

And perhaps this time Morgan will actually tell her something.

'Um, sure. It's not as if I'm planning on having something

better to do…' Morgan's eyes narrow, sensing a trap. 'What are you getting at, Isla?'

'Do you ever think about that day any more?' Isla feels the stupidity of her question before she's even finished saying it but she can't back out now. Morgan stares at her for a moment, then shrugs.

'Sometimes. I try not to.'

Isla is pleasantly surprised by the lack of sharp words she's received. It bolsters her to go on. 'That makes sense.'

Morgan hesitates, but appears to get the gist that her sister's not quite finished with her yet. 'Do you?'

'It was a little different for me,' Isla replies, deliberately keeping her eyes off her sister to avoid making her feel trapped in a spotlight. Dealing with Morgan often feels like dealing with a wild animal. As long as she knows she can escape, she won't try to.

'I guess.' Morgan's expression becomes a little distant as she stares out the window.

'Did you know? Like, before it happened – did you know something was wrong?'

Morgan shakes her head, eyes still fixed on the garden beyond the glass. 'I don't think so. And even when it started going wrong, I didn't feel that it was happening to me. Like … even when it's right there in front of you, you still don't think it's real. That's not your mother, that's not your kitchen floor she's collapsed on. That's not your house the ambulance is parked outside. I never realised how good the brain was at tricking you…'

Isla is silent for a moment, slightly shocked. She really wasn't expecting this much from her sister. She can't exactly remember the last time they had a conversation about 'that day' but she remembered Morgan's lips being pressed together so tightly that she wondered whether they'd become permanently fused. Clearly

Morgan notices this surprise because she laughs, a tad shakily. 'You caught me off guard,' she says by way of explanation.

'Right,' Isla replies, then pushes on with a determination to make the most of this opportunity. 'I get it though. I remember thinking that maybe you were joking, when you called me on the phone.'

'Bit of a shit joke.'

Isla makes a noise of agreement, sitting down at the table and finding solace in this strange moment of peace. When she looks over to Morgan, she recognises the signs of her sister closing up once more. There's only so much more she's going to get from her. But Morgan manages one more moment of honesty. 'To be honest, it wasn't the worst part, being there when it happened.'

'What was?'

Morgan's eyes are back to being hollow, drained. 'The days after. When she was gone.'

Isla watches her sister put back the final brick of the wall she has so carefully constructed around herself, then leave the kitchen without another word. It always seems to be that their conversations end up like this. Ordinary questions leading towards a heavy conversation which in turn leads to Morgan fleeing. That, or one of them storming out.

But perhaps Isla doesn't need Morgan to give her the answers she's looking for. She can find all she needs in the past, as long as she can get the stone to work its impossible magic once more.

She stands suddenly, leaves her bag by the kitchen table and hurries out of the back door. Recklessness seems to course through her very veins and she feels it acutely, feels the fact that she hasn't even spent a moment checking on her father. There's potential in the air, for what she's not quite sure yet, but she can't ignore it.

Moments later, the beach sprawls out in front of her. And the stone stands tall. Waiting.

Seven

Isla used to pretend that Karrekoth's stone was a mountain, so tall that you could catch the clouds from its peak. As a child, she would stand at the bottom, hands splayed across its surface, and look up. Something about its great height from that angle was strangely comforting. She was tiny, insignificant compared to that rock. And Isla liked that feeling a lot.

She's never quite lost that feeling. Even when she was a teenager, piggy-backing her sister across the sand to traverse their personal mountain. Comfort could always be found in the shadow of something that had utterly no concern for her and her progress through life.

Perhaps this is why Isla finds it a little disconcerting to see her mighty mountain cracked down one side. Even when the stone continues to stand strong, unmoved by its injury, Isla can't help but feel like she's seeing one more dream from her childhood slip away. Even colossal stones cannot last forever.

Isla pulls herself from her thoughts, forces herself to focus. She's been standing staring at this stone for long enough now; it's time to see if she can actually make use of the lightning scar in its side. She glances around, checks that there's nobody close by. A dog walker strolls leisurely along the tideline down the far end of the beach but Isla's sure they won't see anything from all the way down there. So she steps forward, until her nose is inches from the stone. The crack is right there in front of her, traversing down in an angry, jagged line. But it's dark, there is no light glowing from within.

For a moment, she wonders if perhaps she really did imagine it all. Perhaps everything has finally caught up with her, perhaps all these years of coping 'just fine' have taken their toll. She hesitates, then places her fingers along the edge of one particularly sharp corner, feeling the utterly ordinary stone against her skin.

Almost instantly, she feels heat spread across her fingertips. Light spills from the crack, as if it's been waiting for her. Perhaps it has. Noise follows light; she hears the clattering of a door shutting, the crackling of a radio with a slightly patchy signal.

When the light fills her vision, Isla doesn't close her eyes. She's ready this time, and she doesn't want to miss anything. It's bright enough to make her squint but she keeps looking forward determinedly, until the light begins to dissipate and shows her exactly where she is.

It's the kitchen that she stood in just moments before but there are clear differences. The almost regimented tidiness that Isla has enforced upon it in the past few years is nowhere to be seen; instead there's the recklessly scattered piles of crockery and other items (all with varying degrees of relevance to the kitchen) that Isla remembers as her mother's process of organisation. She spots the pile of Morgan's art supplies that would constantly be shipped up the stairs, only to come right back down again. Isla has to smile as she sees Morgan's collection of mosaic tiles and accompanying bag of grout; how many times did she leave those scattered across the sitting room floor, ready for Jasper to step on?

The back door opens and Isla instinctively backs up against the wall. It's an illogical and pretty shoddy attempt to hide but it becomes clear as her mother enters the room without a second glance in her direction that hiding is not necessary. This becomes even more evident as her father comes through from the hall, directly opposite Isla, and does not immediately express alarm at the sight of his daughter, years older, crouched down by the sink.

It would seem that she is invisible, then. Isla is aware that this new realisation enters her mind without much resistance. Apparently once time travel is accepted as possible, Isla's brain will take any other impossibilities as if they're thoroughly ordinary. In fact, Isla finds herself far more focused on why she is invisible this time when she wasn't before, rather than how incredibly unusual this situation is.

Cautiously, in case she suddenly becomes visible, Isla takes a seat on the chair that is most pulled out, so she can avoid trying to move it. Her eyes drift between her parents, as they come together like two clouds in the sky; a casual, gradual meeting with the confidence of time being unlimited for them.

That confidence makes Isla's heart twist.

Marina is carrying a basket of clothes collected from the washing line outside, which Jasper raises an eyebrow at as he takes the basket from her. 'Isn't it raining?'

'It wasn't when I put it out, was it?' Marina huffs, pushing her own damp curls from her face. She switches off the still-crackling radio with a heavy sigh. 'I swear those rainclouds hide behind the cliffs and wait for me to hang the clothes out.'

Jasper tentatively lifts a pair of trousers from the basket and watches the steady drip of water from its legs. 'Start again?' he asks, grinning across at his wife.

Marina makes a noise of agreement. 'Just don't tell Isla. She'll have our heads if she knows we've been using the washing machine two times for one load. She's still trying to convince me to try hand-washing.'

Isla feels herself smiling at that. She remembers when that was something she seriously suggested to her parents, after reading an article about microplastics in laundry reaching the ocean. And before she took on the household laundry and realised how much time the washing machine saved.

Jasper snorts. 'I'm sure she's not going to ring from university to check.' He carries the basket over to the washing machine and loads it up with the rain-soaked laundry. Once he's finished, he comes to sit opposite his wife. Their hands meet in the middle of the table naturally, fingers tangling together. It's silent for a moment, except for the hum of the washing machine, but Isla can almost hear the unspoken conversation going on between her parents. They were always scarily good at those.

'Did you work out what they wanted done at the pub in the end, then?' Marina asks finally. 'You seemed fairly irate when you popped into the post office for the paper.'

'Oh, eventually. It's those new owners, trying to be all upscale. I told them that that building has weathered more storms than they've had haircuts which does mean that it won't take too kindly to a full-scale remodelling. I also told them that my remit was more quick fixes not bloody interior design. Anyway, they settled on me having a look at the dodgy-sounding toilets and that was that. At least they paid generously.'

Marina grins, helping herself to one of the apples in the nearby fruit bowl. She just about avoids knocking over a pile of Jasper's gardening tools in the process. 'I heard they were from London; they probably thought it was highly reasonable.'

'As long as they don't London-price my pints, that's fine,' Jasper responds gruffly, though it's with a good-natured grin.

Isla feels herself getting lost in this conversation. There's so many reminders of things lost here; the relaxed atmosphere of a household with two healthy parents running it, the way her father would joke around so naturally. Her mother and the flash of colour and warmth she seemed to permanently carry with her.

However, she can't just sit here, in the sanctuary of this past moment, can she? Surely the stone had a bigger plan for her than just that? Except that stones don't usually have the ability to make plans, Isla reminds herself. After all, hasn't she been trying to use the stone to find out what she can change? And instead it has just brought her to a tender but seemingly unhelpful moment between her parents.

But then Isla watches as her mother rests her hand on her chest with a small grimace and feels potential for change electrify the air. Like lightning has invaded the kitchen. Chest pains; isn't that what the doctors asked time and time again about? They asked all of the remaining Pembroke family members if Marina complained of chest pains and they all said no. Because she did not.

Or so they thought. Yet here she is, hand resting against a heart that is mere weeks away from failing.

'You all right?' Jasper asks, frowning. But Marina chases the frown away instantly with a smile and a nod.

'Just indigestion, I'm sure.'

Isla feels an urge to scream building inside her, like the way a wave gathers itself before curling over and crashing down. If she could just do *something* to warn them, to make her parents know that this isn't a symptom to brush aside. But what can she do? She's invisible, a silent witness to the beginning of the end for her family.

Isla's hands reach out towards the nearest pile of things on the table; a stack of driftwood that Marina must have collected from the beach. She pushes at them with all her might, feeling an added weight to them which she presumes comes from being invisible (as if she understands the intricate science behind being invisible). It takes a moment longer than usual but soon the driftwood is clattering over and off the table, crashing onto the kitchen tiles below.

Isla doesn't really know what she's hoping to achieve from this. It's not as though falling driftwood has become a universal symbol of impending doom. She knows her mother isn't going to look at it and realise instantly what it's trying to convey to her. But Isla needs to try *something*.

Indeed, Marina and Jasper both let out noises of surprise at seeing the driftwood scattered across the floor but neither leap to get Marina to the hospital. Instead, Marina tuts and hops up, discarding her apple and moving over to clear up the mess.

'Must be that ghost again.' She chuckles as she forms a new and equally haphazard pile on the table.

'Oh yes, the ghost. Nothing to do with the sheer volume of crap on this table?' Jasper stands with a grin and Isla is sure that that grin makes him seem at least three feet taller.

'Excuse me, half of this so-called crap is your crap,' Marina retorts, gesturing at the nearby stack of tool boxes. 'How many damn tools does a toilet fixer need anyway?'

'Toilet fixer, really? Not sure I can let you get away with that . . .'

Isla is just thinking that this conversation is heading towards a suggestive tone that she doesn't particularly want to witness, when the slam of the front door breaks the moment apart. It's an altogether familiar slam and it still sends a slight shiver through Isla, even when this slam is not one she has to directly deal with.

It's clear that Jasper and Marina recognise the slam and its implications as well. They share a look, another silent conversation. This one, though, Isla thinks she can decipher. *Whose turn to talk to Morgan?*

Jasper shakes his head, smiling at his wife with that now

extinct sense of confidence. 'I've got it,' he says, as the thuds of furious footsteps travel up the stairs. 'You carry on trying to contact the cliff ghosts.' The mischievous smirk on his face sets his eyes twinkling, as he edges round the table and presses a kiss to Marina's temple. Then he squares his shoulders and starts after his daughter.

In the silence, Isla feels a wholly unwelcome sense of frustration towards her sister. She knows that teenaged Morgan hasn't deliberately destroyed this tender moment between her parents, but nonetheless it feels like something has been spoiled. And Isla can't help but feel that maybe she could have found a better way to warn her parents if she'd been allowed one more chance.

A wind races through the room, full of sea salt. Isla feels it ruffle her hair but the back door remains closed and the rest of the room stays still. This wind is just for her, she realises. Time is up.

The moment she thinks it, it happens. The kitchen fills with evening sunlight and the sound of her mother's absent-minded humming fades away, to be replaced by crashing waves, gusty breezes and seagulls.

Isla lurches as the chair she is sitting on disappears into seemingly thin air, and she lands on the slightly damp sand at the foot of the stone. Her hands drift to the ground, fingers worming their way down as she tries to find some solace in the cool, damp sand.

But there's none to be found, unsurprisingly. Only the itching sensation of sand under her fingernails and missed opportunities.

It takes Isla a while to find the desire to stand. Even with the past gone once again, it feels a lot closer when she's sat in the shadow of the stone. She can fool herself into thinking she can still hear her mother's humming and the confident tread of her father's feet.

The present seems a whole lot less inviting when those things still feel within reach. But it's waiting for her nonetheless, so Isla tugs herself onto her feet and takes the first step back towards her home.

As she starts the journey back to a very different version of the home she has just visited, Isla tries to find solace in the sound of driftwood hitting kitchen tiles. She did that. She changed something again. Nothing substantial, but a change nonetheless.

So as Isla reaches her back garden and tugs open the weather-warped gate, she lets one thought root firmly in her head. She will find a way to save her mother.

Eight

Isla's sleep is patchy that night. Bursts of blissfully dreamless moments that intersperse with dark, angry dreams where her mother stands on a stormy beach and won't listen to her shouts of warning, so gets swallowed up by the sea, or gets whisked away by the wind. When morning comes at last, Isla awakes with skin sticky from sweat. An air of exhaustion hangs heavy from her, like her own personal fog.

'Christ, you look a sight.'

Isla has only been in the kitchen for two seconds before she regrets getting out of bed. Jasper peers at her over his newspaper, eyebrows raised with concern. 'What happened to you?' he asks, when she doesn't reply to his initial greeting.

'Nothing. Just slept badly.' She still feels dazed, despite being awake for ten minutes now. Her words seem like treacle, sticking to the roof of her mouth.

'Bad dreams?' Jasper's still watching her with concern; she must look pretty terrible, then. Normally her father doesn't even notice when she's had a haircut.

'Yeah, I guess.' Isla moves around the table, puts the kettle on. As she's waiting for it to boil, she presses her fingertips firmly against her palms. Grounding herself back to reality, to the present. 'How are you, anyway?'

'Hmm? Oh, fine.' Jasper's started to drift back into his newspaper. 'Think I did my knee in fixing that damn bench in the church yesterday. Are you working today?'

Isla finds solace in the normality of this conversation, comforted by the process of checking the calendar by the fridge. Normally she knows her schedule off by heart but today the answer doesn't come quite so easily. 'Not today. Day after tomorrow.' For a moment she wonders why her father is asking and there's a few seconds of mad hope that he's asking because he has plans for them, normal plans like normal families might have.

But that's not it, of course. Instead, Jasper makes a thoughtful noise from behind his paper. 'I think we're running low on dishwasher tablets. I tried to put the dishwasher on last night but the bloody thing wasn't working ... Anyway, I noticed we were running low. I was thinking, you could ask Morgan to go with you to get some.' He's sounding casual, eyes fixed on his paper. But there's a desperate hope lingering beneath the words that Isla doesn't like. She doesn't need him getting his hopes up because she knows how dangerous it can be when they're dashed upon the ground.

'Maybe, Dad.' She briefly touches his shoulder and Jasper reaches back to squeeze her hand, just for a moment. A hundred words pass through that contact before he breaks it to turn the page of his paper. Isla just wishes he'd say them out loud sometimes. There's only so much mind reading she can manage.

Still, there is now the far more exciting prospect of dishwasher tablets. Isla checks the cupboard and does indeed find the box almost empty, which surprises her a little. Usually she keeps a firm handle on supplies in this house because she knows how anxious her father can get when routines are disrupted, but it would appear that this time she's let it slip. Something that Isla is never particularly comfortable with. So she neatly packages up the swirling mess of her head, puts it to one side, and goes to the shops.

It turned out, when Isla looked around the kitchen properly, that there was quite a few things they needed. So she ends up at the dreaded big supermarket in the same town as her aquarium, where the strip lighting is always a little too bright and the queues are always filled with holidaymakers buying seventeen variations of barbecue food. Even now, when summer is definitely on the way out.

Isla stands in the dishwasher-tablet aisle and scowls at the choices. There's no real reason to scowl and it certainly has nothing to do with the tablets on offer, more to do with the lingering headache that appeared sometime after her fourth nightmare-induced wake-up last night. Or perhaps it's to do with the fact that she couldn't even face asking her sister along and now she feels as if she's made another mistake in relation to Morgan.

Either way, the scowl is persistent. And only shifts a little when she looks up from her final choice and sees Dylan frowning at a box of dishwasher tablets at the other end of the aisle. The frown seems in line with her own, which is perhaps why Isla finds herself dropping her box into the basket and then approaching him.

'Hey,' she says, a little tentatively. This is hardly her style but then rocks have been opening up for her recently so perhaps now is the time to try something new.

Dylan glances up and immediately transforms his frown into that crooked smile of his. 'Isla!' he exclaims and Isla is surprised by how genuinely pleased he sounds to see her.

'Are you okay? You were looking concerned about dishwasher tablets …' Isla asks, once she's got over his exuberance.

'Oh, yeah … I was looking for one that isn't full of phosphate.'

'Because of algal bloom?'

Dylan looks up from his current selection, eyebrows raising with some surprise. 'Uh … yeah. Exactly.' He stares for a little longer than Isla would like, before chuckling. 'I should have guessed you'd understand.'

Isla shrugs with a small smile, not quite sure how to respond to that. In the end she doesn't and skips right on to the problem at hand. 'Uh, you want those ones. They're pretty pricey but they get consistently high ratings in terms of being environmentally friendly.' Isla finds her gaze lingering on the box for a moment longer than necessary; now she's trying to make ends meet on two pretty meagre salaries, being environmentally friendly has become a bit harder to achieve.

'Oh, sweet. Thanks.' Dylan drops the box into his trolley with a nonchalance that Isla finds a little difficult to stomach. 'So, no aquarium for you?'

Isla shakes her head as she adjusts her basket to sit more comfortably against her arm. 'It's my day off … my two days off actually. Weekends pay more so I tend to take my weekend in the week instead.' Isla brings her sentence to an abrupt halt, lips pursing together. She's a little in shock at how much she's just shared. 'Sorry. Overshare.'

'Hardly. It's nice to know something about you. Other than your love for octopuses.' Dylan begins to push his trolley out of the aisle and, inexplicably, Isla finds herself following him. 'You're a bit of a mystery, Isla Pembroke.'

Isla laughs, the sound hollow as it bounces off the shiny floor tiles. 'Really?'

'Yeah, people at the aquarium don't seem to know anything

about you. Other than the fact that you *really* care about the fish.'

'Shocking for someone at an aquarium to like fish, I know…'

Dylan grins that same grin of his. 'I did point that out.' He falls silent and they drift along the central aisle, neither able to commit to a particular direction. 'How's the family?' he asks finally, which brings the same instinctive wince that Isla always feels when people ask her that question.

'Fine,' she replies. The same answer she always gives regardless of how much truth it holds. 'We're fine. Managing.'

Dylan pauses at the start of the aisle for frozen food. 'That's really good to hear. I know you guys had it tough, what with your mum and…'

'Morgan disappearing for four years?'

Something akin to shock flashes across Dylan's face. 'Four years?' he echoes. 'God, Isla… I didn't know—'

'We're fine,' Isla interrupts, a little sharply. The usual defensiveness has reared up inside her and there's very little she can do to calm it again. She's about to apologise, as usual, but Dylan moves on before she has a chance.

'Cool. I'm glad. And… uh, I'm sorry. When I heard the news, I wanted to do something to help, somehow, but… I guess I never quite knew what to say.'

It's a sentiment she's heard more than once and yet Isla still finds herself taken aback by it, perhaps because of the true sincerity in his words. But, sincere or not, the sentiment is still impossible to respond to adequately. What is she meant to say? That it wouldn't have made a difference? That she didn't notice him not being there, just the way she didn't notice anyone else not being there?

When your mother is gone, it's pretty difficult to notice anything else missing. Not until your sister goes too, of course.

But then Dylan surprises her again with his next words. 'I guess it didn't matter much though, right?'

Isla shakes her head quickly, before her instinctive need to protect others' feelings can catch up and stop her. 'Not really. I mean, I'm sure it would have been great to have your help, but I can't say I was walking around fuming about not having it. I was a little busy.' Dylan nods and there's a twinkling of understanding in his eyes. 'You ... You've lost someone too, haven't you?'

Dylan shifts a little, spending a few seconds unnecessarily sorting things in the trolley. Then he nods. 'Uh, yeah. I went travelling in between terms at university, must have been a couple of years after your mum. Anyway, I went with one of my friends from university. We were doing all the usual adrenaline junkie stuff. You know: rock climbing, scuba diving ...' Dylan pauses and Isla can see how he's gathering himself for his next words. 'He wanted to go hiking one day, in these mountains in India. I was wrecked so I decided not to go and ... well, he never came back.'

Isla feels a chill that has nothing to do with the freezers they're stood beside. 'Christ ...'

Dylan grimaces his agreement. 'Anyway, when I came home I was a bit of a mess and apart from my family nobody really jumped to the rescue, not until I was starting to sort myself out a bit more. And then there was lots of apologising about it, as if them not ... you know, offering to take me for a distracting trip down the pub was the main cause for my despair.'

This time Isla's laugh feels entirely natural, which in turn feels like a breath of fresh air. 'Exactly! That's exactly it! My friend Cora, she always goes on about how awful she feels for not being there at the exact moment I found out about Mum and, well, I usually have to gently remind her that having someone there made very little difference to the fact that I'd just lost my mother.'

*

Dylan nods almost fanatically and his grin seems broader, less crooked. Isla feels distant shock at how much she's revealed but it's mostly drowned out by the sense of shared understanding that she feels passing between them.

When she starts to sense a reddening of her cheeks, though, she knows it's time to leave. 'Um, anyway. I should get going. I'll ... see you soon, I'm sure.'

'I'm sure,' Dylan agrees, nodding. 'Take care, Isla.'

She hurries away then, before Dylan can notice the flush to her cheeks. And before she can think too hard about why it's there.

Later, when the sun is just beginning to dip down towards the horizon, and Isla is trying to sort through the pile of washing for the week, Morgan comes downstairs. It's the first time she's done that other than for a meal or to leave the house, and Isla has to force herself to keep matching socks as if this is all entirely normal. She then has to force herself to actually listen to Morgan's words when she begins to speak, which makes her realise just how distant her mind currently is.

'...so if there's anything I can do?' That's all Isla catches. She glances up from the socks, frowning.

'Sorry ... say that again, Morgan? I was miles away.'

Morgan gives her an impatient look. 'Yeah, no kidding. What's up with you?'

She says this gently, there's almost concern in her voice. But that still doesn't stop Isla from going straight into defensive mode. 'Nothing. I'm just tired. I've not been sleeping very well what with ...' She trails off, because she's not quite sure how to phrase her next words without just sounding accusatory.

'What with your sister coming home after four years?'

Isla is relieved when she sees Morgan smiling her understanding. Placing down the now matched pair of socks, she smiles back. Even if the action seems to strain every muscle around her mouth. 'I guess that might be it. Sorry, start again. What was it you needed?'

A laugh from Morgan this time. 'Nothing. I was asking if there's anything *you* needed. Like help. Now I'm back, I don't want to just be ... loafing around, doing nothing.'

Isla tries to concentrate, she really does. She manages to hear the whole sentence and even manages to consider an answer for a moment. But it doesn't last. Just as it has all afternoon, her mind has started to drift back to her parents sitting here in this very kitchen.

'I was thinking, actually,' Isla suddenly begins, looking to Morgan with her best attempt at a nonchalant expression. 'What would be really helpful is if you could tell me a bit about that day?'

Morgan immediately stiffens and Isla sees the small step she takes back. It should make her feel bad, it should make her back off. But she can't. She keeps seeing her mother's hand on her chest, the wince of pain flickering across her face.

'I know it's hard,' Isla tries, keeping her voice as gentle as she can. 'But I think it's important for us to talk about it.'

Morgan looks like she'd rather stick her head in the oven than talk about it but, to give her some credit, makes no move to try and escape. 'What did you want to know about it?' she asks finally. Her voice is small; in fact, Isla could easily be tricked into thinking she's gone back in time again and this is no longer a twenty-one-year old Morgan in front of her.

'I – I guess I wanted to know if you could have done something differently, or someone else could have done something differently ...' Isla's fixed her gaze on the laundry basket but she can feel Morgan's incredulity radiating across the room, can feel how nonsensical these words are sounding. Part of her is sorely tempted to just spill the truth in case that makes everything make more sense.

Doubtful.

'I know, this makes no sense,' she finally says, forcing a laugh that sounds entirely unnatural. 'I've just always wondered what you would do if you could change things. Like, for example … if I'd have been there to help.'

Isla risks a peek at her sister and is pleasantly surprised by the lack of defensiveness. Bemusement, yes. But Isla can live with that.

'I guess … I'd just want her to not die.' Morgan shrugs, sniffing a little. 'When you're a kid you think that ambulances and doctors are superheroes. That they can fix *everything*, no matter what. And, yeah, they did an amazing job, of course … but they didn't fix everything. I remember when they arrived they were wasting time trying to work out what was wrong with her and I just wanted to scream at them to just save her.'

'They didn't know …' Isla can feel the cogs in her mind whirring into action, can feel an urge to run building in her legs.

'Well, no. Of course not. I mean, none of us knew, did we?'

Isla steps back from the table, no longer really listening to her sister any more. Because she thinks she knows what to do.

'Isla?'

'Sorry, I … I'm just going to get some fresh air. Feeling a little light-headed.'

Morgan stares at her as if she's sprouted an extra head. 'Oh. Right.' Isla hears disappointment in her voice but, for once, she cannot worry about that. 'Want me to come?'

Isla shakes her head. She's already heading towards the door, as though she can feel the potential to change things ticking away every second she stands still in this kitchen.

'I think I just need some space; I'll be back in a bit.' Each word seems to take an age to say. Isla pulls open the back door, shoots her sister a slightly apologetic look, as if that might somehow make things better and less confusing.

And then she's gone. Hurrying towards the beach as if a life depends on it. Which it does.

Nine

'I'm ready. I know what to do.'

Isla stands in front of the stone and glares at its craggy surface as if it's expressing some doubt in her abilities. As if it's openly disbelieving of the words she's just uttered. But, of course, the stone remains entirely impassive and unmoved by her declaration. She still feels better saying it though.

The wind whips around her like her own personal tornado, seeming to egg her on. Yes, rocks can time travel and wind can offer personal support. That seems in line with Isla's current experiences. Before any more elements of nature decide to get involved, Isla finds the crack in the stone and rests her hand atop it.

When the light erupts from beneath her fingers, Isla tries not to let its blinding brightness distract her. Because this time she knows exactly when and where she wants to go, and she needs the stone to know this. Somehow. So she closes her eyes, blocks out the light, and focuses as much as she can on where she wants to go. She stays like this for ten seconds, maybe more. Until she cannot wait any longer and opens her eyes.

The beach seems completely identical, of course it does. Like the stone living on its sands, it has always been solid and unmoving. But in the distance, Isla spots her mother and her sister, walking back towards the house. Marina's wearing that same cardigan; her sister is carrying a stack of oil pastels under one arm and a sketchbook under the other.

We'd just come back from the beach. I'd been using my new pastels. How many times did Morgan have to relay that story? To the paramedics, to the doctors, to her father, to Isla. She remembers how Morgan tipped the whole box of pastels into the bin a few weeks later, eyes hard with rage, as if they were somehow the cause of her mother's death.

But she can't focus on that now. She's here, she's got time. She needs to make the most of it.

Isla takes one final look at her mother and her sister. Then starts running towards the village.

It's a somewhat haphazard route to Karrekoth from the beach, involving a scramble over a ridge of rocks onto the main beach. But Isla has navigated it plenty of times before so, despite an urgency which has sent a slight trembling to her legs, she is on the main beach and racing towards the town in no time at all.

Again, the village seems utterly unchanged. Isla can't be sure that the graffiti on the beach toilets isn't the same as it was when she drove past it to the supermarket earlier. She can see Bobby Mercer's boat floating in the harbour, identical. She can see the same bus heading towards the same bus stop on its usual schedule.

But there's no time for reminiscing about that now.

She races to Karrekoth's single and all-purpose corner shop and checks the newspapers stacked by the door. 20th October 2011. She's right. She's done it. Somehow the impossible stone has heard her request and fulfilled it.

For a second, Isla is stumped by the reality of her situation. A rock has not only transported her back in time but has transported her back in time to where she wanted to be. The day of her mother's death.

A shuddering breath rattles through her, making her shiver. Her heart is pounding relentlessly, making it hard to concentrate. But she needs to. This can't be a coincidence, it can't be. Somehow, she has been given an opportunity to save her mother. And she can't mess this up.

She pulls out her phone, as the skeleton of a plan begins to form inside her head. Isla's not sure why she's expecting anything different but it's still a disappointment to see zero signal being displayed on the screen. Apparently, time-travelling phone signal is a step too far.

Sighing her frustration, she pockets the phone. Isla glances towards the shop she's still standing in front of, hesitating for a second as she considers whether anyone will recognise her as a nine-years-older version of herself. But Isla can feel time ticking away relentlessly and decides it's worth the risk.

A moment later, she practically bursts into the shop. 'Can I borrow your phone, please?' The door has barely shut behind her before she asks the question. There's no time to stall.

It's Matt Kingston behind the till, which Isla takes as a good sign. The boy is three years younger than her and is not known for his observation skills. Isla remembers the time he tried to sell her a box of oranges after she asked for peaches. He shouldn't recognise her. Indeed, Matt seems more concerned with his car magazine than his latest customer. He barely looks up as he fishes for the phone beside him. 'Make it quick,' he mutters once he's plucked it from its cradle and handed it over. 'Not meant to let customers use it.'

Isla considers explaining that it's an emergency but decides against it. No time. She dials 999, takes a step back towards the refrigerated section and places the phone to her ear. If she can just get the ambulance here faster, she can make a difference. If she can give them all the facts now, she can save them precious minutes and they can save her mother.

The moment she connects to the ambulance service, she lets her years of heartbroken researching take over.

'Ambulance service, is the patient breathing?'

'Hi, my mother's having a heart attack caused by a spontaneous coronary artery dissection. Trust me, I know that's what it is.'

'Uh ... right, okay. What's your address?'

'Birch Cottage, we're just off South Cliff Road in Karrekoth. TR12 9JH.'

There's a pause on the line. 'Oh, you know what ... it looks like someone's called this in already. Help is on the way, all right? Now, are you with the patient?'

Isla can't find the words to say any more, so she hangs up. She doesn't want to waste this person's time when she's sure they have plenty of emergencies to be dealing with.

With the phone clutched in her hand, Isla frantically racks her brains. There's got to be something else she can do. She sifts through all the facts she's gathered over the last few days and, indeed, years. Facts that she's always carefully stowed away because they felt like heavy rocks in her head. Morgan always said that the ambulance took ages to get there but she also admitted that maybe it just felt like ages. Isla knows that Morgan had to do chest compressions until the ambulance arrived. She knows that their mother was resuscitated by the paramedics when they arrived then resuscitated again in the ambulance. She knows that she was already non-responsive again by the time they got to the hospital and that they couldn't get her back after that.

Letting these facts back into her mind feels a bit like letting a hive of angry bees into her head. She feels the phone slipping out from her grasp until she forces her fingers to grip again. This isn't the time for falling apart, she tries to tell herself. There's still time to fix things.

Isla smacks the phone back onto the shop counter and leaves without another word. She stumbles back into the sunshine, squinting a little as she tries to get her thoughts together.

She hasn't actually thought of an idea before she starts running. She just knows that she wants to be at her house, doing *something*. Maybe the paramedics can do more if Isla's there to explain everything she knows about her mother's condition. And her sister's only twelve, maybe she can't do the chest compressions properly. Maybe she's too scared to hurt her mum. Maybe Morgan just needs Isla to be there to help, even if that means seeing her sister years older than she should be. Even if that somehow breaks all the rules of time travel, Isla doesn't care. She just needs to do something. Before her mother is put into an ambulance that she won't leave alive.

She gets to the end of the harbour road. Then she hears the sirens. The sound wriggles down the narrow streets of Karrekoth, bouncing eerily off the buildings and bringing people to a halt. After all, when was the last time they heard that sound in their village? Isla's fairly sure she's never seen an ambulance or police car here, and only one fire engine, back when the church roof got struck by lightning when she was eight. This is an extraordinary event for Karrekoth and the people of the village have come to a halt out of respect for this change to regular proceedings.

The ambulance careens around the corner and into the harbour. She watches it speed towards her and, for one moment, wonders if she should stop it; perhaps if her mum never gets into the ambulance, the end result will be different? But instantly she dismisses the idea as the desperation-fuelled madness that it is. The ambulance doesn't kill her mother, the heart attack does.

The blue lights and caterwauling sirens whizz past her, and all she can do is race after it.

Isla was on all the running and swimming teams at school, but that doesn't mean she can keep up with an urgent ambulance. She's only at the beach toilets when the ambulance takes the turning up to her home. Still, she doesn't give up. Her breath is beginning to sting at the back of her throat but she pushes on, half-stumbling up the hill as panic turns her legs to jelly.

By the time she's reached the top, the inevitable realisation that this plan will not work arrives. The ambulance is parked, the doors are thrown open and two paramedics are already rushing inside. Isla hears Morgan calling for them to hurry and even from where she's standing, she feels the utter panic in her sister's voice.

Isla can't move. She's frozen, glued to the road. Besides, she thinks bitterly, there's no need to move any more; what can she do? She has come all this way back in time to see a moment that she can't change. Even her phone call to the emergency services seems pointless now; will them knowing why her mother's heart has stopped make it any easier to start it again? She knows the facts around what killed her mother; she knows deep down that the moment to save her would have been months ago, when an artery silently developed a tear and started a slow chain of events that would lead to her heart stopping today.

Here and now, it's too late. That becomes all the more obvious when she sees the paramedics hurrying from her home a few minutes later, carrying a stretcher between them. Isla's mother lies horribly still with a mask strapped to her face but Isla finds herself strangely focused on the fact that she's still wearing the cardigan. It reminds her in an excruciating sort of way that this is a woman who barely twenty minutes ago was talking to her daughter on the beach, wearing that cardigan and an expectation that today was going to be thoroughly ordinary.

Morgan seems even younger when she steps out of the house. Maybe it's the fact that she's grabbed a coat that no longer fits her. Maybe it's because there's still oil pastels smeared over her fingers. Maybe it's just the wild fear radiating from every inch of her.

She's on the phone, fingers trembling over the door handle as she tugs the door shut. 'We're going to the hospital now. I don't know, Dad – they haven't said. Just hurry up, please!' It's only when the door is shut that Morgan realises she's now walked out of the house with the house phone. Isla watches her sister try to contend with a problem that doesn't fit in this situation at all. Morgan stares at the phone for a second, then drops it on the doormat and stumbles into the ambulance.

Nobody notices the young woman staring at this whole scene as if waiting for the channel to change and give her something better to watch. The ambulance doors shut; the engine starts. Immediately, the sirens drown out the crash of waves and the screech of seagulls. Isla has just enough time to stumble off the drive before the ambulance hurtles past. She watches it bump down the hill, swerve round the corner. Then disappear.

Isla feels the grass tickling at her knees and realises suddenly that she's no longer standing. Somehow her legs have ended up crumpled beneath her. Unsurprisingly, she doesn't care.

All she can focus on is the relentless passing of time. Each second seems to scratch against her chest. How many more does her mother have? How far into the journey until the paramedic knows, even if she won't say it aloud yet, that this is a hopeless case? Isla wants the world to freeze, to stop and to mark the exact moment that her mother leaves them. This is not business as usual; so why does the ocean continue to wash back and forth against the sand miles below these cliffs? Why do the seagulls continue to circle the Pembroke chimney, looking for their usual spot to settle for the evening?

She knows she should cry but she can only feel shock chilling against her skin. She wants to scream but her throat is empty, hollow. She's got nothing. Her head drops low, her back curls over, until her forehead is pressed against her knees. Waiting to feel *something*.

She does, eventually. But it's not what she's wanting to feel. There's the shifting of the grass beneath her legs as it becomes sand, the changing direction and speed of the wind. When she pulls her head up once more, it's with no sense of relief that she sees the beach has returned. Light spills onto her from the fissured rock towering above her once more, chasing away the gathering darkness of the evening.

But there's no relief to be found in its glow. All Isla feels is frustration, building inside of her like the beginnings of thunder.

'WHAT IS THE POINT OF YOU?' The words erupt from her so suddenly that it makes her chest burn. But she doesn't care. The stone must have known, somehow, that her plan was futile, that taking her to that day wasn't the answer. And yet it let her try and fail anyway. Isla stumbles to her feet, finds her fingers digging into the crevice of the stone as if she might somehow find an answer in there. 'WHAT IS THE POINT IF YOU WON'T HELP HER?'

Silence crashes heavily around her. Even the waves seem to hold off, even the seagulls seem to stop squawking. They apparently couldn't manage it when her mother was dying but now, when she needs a distraction more than ever, it's all too easy to keep quiet.

And, of course, it doesn't help. It just makes the weight of failure feel ever more crushing.

Isla feels her hand slide away from the stone as defeat saps away the anger that had briefly erupted from her. The moment her fingers disconnect from the rock, Isla spots the glowing from within. Gentle but persistent, as though it's trying to remind her of what it can do.

But Isla only hears fading ambulance sirens and the flatline of a heart monitor. There's nothing left for her here.

Ten

Isla tries to act normally when she gets back to the house. But she knows it's futile, knows she might as well try leaping off the cliffs and flying. Morgan is already suspicious after she ran off so suddenly, and keeps casting brief looks at her sister over a silent dinner, while even Jasper gently asks if she's feeling okay.

All she can do is keep pretending that she's fine. What else is there? Explain that she's dismayed by a stone's failure to save their long-gone mother and wife? Right, because that would go down wonderfully.

Eventually, she manages to get rid of both Morgan and Jasper by trying to talk about Marina. That's enough for Morgan to hurry off to 'rest' and for Jasper to suddenly remember he has a television show to watch. Soon enough, Isla is alone in the kitchen. It doesn't make her feel any better, but at least she has space to try and tidy away the feelings swooping around her head.

She should've known. That's the most persistent thought. She should've known that bringing her mother back would never have been possible. She should've known that nothing would ever be able to do that, not even a time-travelling stone.

Miracles can only go so far, after all.

Isla tidies the kitchen and finishes the laundry sorting then goes to bed, knowing that sleep is something she won't see for a long time. She huddles under the covers and tries to block out the sound of those damned ambulance sirens. And, when that doesn't work, she turns to watch the gradually changing sky through the gap in her curtains.

Morning comes grey and overcast, the clouds heavy and oppressive. It feels a little bit like they're trying to push through her window and invade her bedroom. Perhaps that's why she eventually gets out of bed and heads downstairs, even if there hasn't been much sleep achieved.

It's with some surprise that Isla finds Morgan in the kitchen already. After all, it can't be much later than seven and Morgan has never been one to enjoy early mornings. But here she is, sitting at the kitchen table with a cup of coffee clutched in her hands like it's her life support.

Isla hesitates on the threshold, considering whether she should still go in. But eventually the need for caffeine wins out. Besides, isn't avoiding difficult conversations Morgan's forte, not hers?

'You're up early,' she comments as lightly as she can manage, stepping into the kitchen and heading for the kettle.

Morgan jerks a little, apparently lost in a reverie that takes some effort to retreat from. 'Oh,' she says, rubbing at her eyes. 'Yeah, I didn't want any more sleep apparently.' Her tone suggests she's not entirely pleased by her own body's decision and Isla shoots her a sympathetic grimace. Bodies refusing to sleep; now that she can understand.

'Well, you look like you could use some more.'

Morgan snorts, taking another drink of coffee. Isla notices a slight fumble in her fingers that almost causes the cup to drop. 'And you wonder where I learnt my crappy bedside manner.'

'From the best, of course.' A hesitant grin is shared between them before silence falls once more. Isla lets it sit comfortably while she makes her tea but once she has sat down, she chases it away with a somewhat awkward clearing of the throat.

Morgan gets her question in first, however. 'Are you feeling better?'

'Hmm?'

Morgan's eyes narrow a little and Isla feels her examining gaze zero in on her. 'Yesterday. You suddenly felt light-headed and had to run outside ... for like three hours.' Her suspicion is as clear as glass, and just as sharp.

'Oh, right. Yeah, fine. I think I'd just inhaled too many fish guts or something.' Isla forces a casual laugh that she hopes sounds more convincing than it does in her head. From the look on her sister's face, she's fairly sure it doesn't.

'Uh huh ...' Morgan looks at her for a long moment and Isla is sure there's going to be more interrogating coming her way. But it doesn't. Instead, Morgan turns back to her coffee, eyes getting lost in its depths. Isla wants to feel relieved for being off the hook but instead she just feels worried. Morgan has always pushed for truth with the persistence of an octopus breaking a shell. And Isla knows when an octopus is no longer interested in shell-breaking, something is wrong.

'Morgan?' Isla says her name without really knowing what she wants to say. So when her sister looks up, she finds her mouth dry, empty.

Maybe it's fortunate that Jasper enters the kitchen at that moment. Isla is far from surprised to see him awake this early but she's a little disappointed that his arrival brings whatever conversation she was about to start with Morgan to an abrupt halt.

'Morning, Dad,' Isla prompts gently, as he almost makes it across the kitchen without a word. It pulls Jasper out of whatever thought was clouding his awareness of reality and he looks at his two daughters with slight surprise.

'Oh, morning, you two. This is early ...' There's concern in his voice more than anything, which Isla recognises; a concern that routines have changed because something bad has happened.

'It's fine, Dad. We both just woke early,' Isla explains with highly-practised reassurance.

'That's right,' Morgan agrees and Isla can hear the same tone in her sister's voice, which brings a further hollow feeling to her chest. Isla was meant to protect her little sister from knowing that their father needed such careful reassurance. Just another thing she didn't quite manage, apparently.

Jasper's shoulders slump in obvious relief. 'Right, of course.' He starts making his own drink but Isla finds herself more interested in watching Morgan, who is surveying her father warily, as if she expects him to explode at any moment. Isla can't exactly blame her for that. He's never lashed out at them, even at his worst moments, but that hasn't stopped the emotional breakdowns from being traumatic.

Of course he remains entirely unaware of Morgan's cautious observation. 'I'm going to take a look at some of the fishermen's boats today. A few of them are complaining of weird sounds in the engines so I thought it would be better to just do them all at once. Then the garden bench could do with repainting ...'

'Sounds great, Dad. A busy day.' Isla doesn't know if it's her tiredness today that makes her more acutely aware of the sickly saccharine encouragement infusing her voice. Whatever it is, it makes her feel a little ill. And Morgan's somewhat disbelieving expression doesn't help.

It's only when her phone starts ringing that Morgan tears her eyes away from her father. Isla watches the way she jumps as if she's just been electrocuted, the way her fingers tremble so much over getting the phone out of her jumper pocket that she almost drops it on the floor. Her eyes settle on the screen and Isla sees recognition followed swiftly by foreboding.

'I – I need to take this,' she mutters, barely audible. She doesn't wait for any sort of response from her family, already tripping out of the room. Isla can't quite believe that those clumsy feet are the same ones that used to climb Karrekoth's rock with such confidence. 'Hello? Yes, this is Morgan Pembroke.' The words drift down the hallway but Isla isn't able to catch any more as her sister hurries upstairs.

'That sounded important.' Jasper sits in Morgan's hastily vacated chair, eyes on the door that his daughter has just left through.

'How can you tell?' Isla asks, pleasantly surprised by her father's apparent insight.

'It's that tone of voice, you both do it. When you're on the phone to your boss, when Morgan was talking to her teachers and not trying to get a detention.' Jasper takes a sip of coffee. 'Your mother used to do it when the vicar came into the post office.'

'Why? Mum didn't go to church …' Isla knows that's hardly the most important part of this conversation but her father speaking about her mother these days is about as common as going a day without hearing a seagull.

Jasper chuckles softly at that, eyes hunting for solace in the bottom of his mug in an eerily similar way to his youngest daughter. 'No, but she still knew that if you wanted to get ahead in this village, you kept the vicar sweet.'

Isla smiles to herself, because now she remembers her mother explaining that logic. She certainly knew the complicated inner workings of Karrekoth and how to exploit that when necessary.

But the smile doesn't last long. Inevitably, thinking about her mother only reminds her of her failure to save her.

'I should get on. Stuff to do,' Isla mumbles and even her father looks somewhat dubious at her words. Hardly encouraging.

By the time she gets upstairs, Morgan is just hanging up her phone call. Isla pauses in the hallway and watches how her sister holds the phone a few inches away from her ear, seemingly frozen in a moment. She's turned away from Isla but Isla can see from the slope of her shoulders that whatever that phone call was about, it's rattled her.

'Mogs?' Isla prompts as she takes a step towards the door.

But when Morgan turns around, her expression is set in neutral, hardened in place. 'It's fine,' she says automatically, clearly anticipating Isla's next question. She pockets the phone, moves towards the door. 'I should get dressed, stuff to do.'

It's about as convincing as when Isla tried to claim the same thing to Jasper. But Morgan doesn't give any chance for further investigation. She's stepped forward and closed the door before the words have barely left her mouth.

Isla doesn't see Morgan after that. The front door opens and closes as Isla's stepping out of the shower and a quick look into her sister's empty bedroom confirms her suspicions. Her sister has left and all Isla has to reassure her is the suitcase still lying in the corner.

With the mysterious phone call and the still-heavy sense of failure on her shoulders, Isla wishes that this wasn't her day off, though it's not the first time she's wished that. It's not as though a day off for her ever actually means a break. It's still hard work, it's just without the distraction of fish.

Still, it is at least a little harder to think about time-travelling stones when she's trying to work out how her father has managed to spend a precious fifty pounds on white boat paint when his old boat is pea green (and hasn't even been painted in years). It turns out he added too many cans of the wrong colour to the basket on the website and hadn't thought to ask her how to fix it, and had just put the extra cans in the shed for 'a rainy day'. By the time she's sorted that out, picked up her father's medication, cleaned the bathroom and asked Jasper to stop trying to help her clean the bathroom (she's not having him do his back in again), most of the day is gone.

Along with Morgan, still.

'She's been gone since eight this morning – what the hell could need doing in all that time?' It's late afternoon now, and Isla has run out of willpower and can no longer resist bringing up her gripes with her father.

Jasper pauses in his careful painting of the bench in the back garden, glancing up at his eldest daughter. 'She is twenty-one, Isla. I mean, we haven't known where she is for years. This shouldn't be that much of a change, surely?'

'This is different, Dad …' Isla spots the small frown on her father's face. She can't tell if it's from concern for Morgan or from concentrating on the paintbrush. 'Why has she come back after all this time? Where has she been? What does she want from us?'

Jasper makes a non-committal grunt, a sound that Isla is all too used to. Sometimes she wonders if her father would choose to speak only in grunts if he could. He pushes the paintbrush into a particularly tight corner, silent for a moment. It's such a long moment that Isla starts to think he's deemed the conversation finished. But then he finally speaks again, words slow and measured. 'Judging by this morning, it sounds like she's come back to talk.'

'What?'

Slowly, Jasper stands up. He's got paint all over his trousers and Isla finds herself momentarily distracted by deciding how best to try and get those stains out. But then he's speaking again and she forces herself to focus. 'This morning when I walked into the kitchen it sounded as if you two were having a good chat.' Isla raises an eyebrow, because she's not entirely convinced that this morning qualified as a chat, let alone a good one. Jasper shoots her a wry look at that. 'It's at least a lot better than the radio silence we've had for years, Isla – let's not be *too* high in our expectations. So maybe she's ready. To talk. But she just needs some space to find the right words.'

'Wow,' Isla says, taken aback. Then she smiles, a little wryly. 'So you *do* know about emotions?'

Jasper sniffs, jabs his paintbrush in her general direction. 'Careful.' But he's grinning. She wishes she could bottle that grin. It's become so rare but it's still so comforting. The grin of the man who used to carry her on his shoulders all the way down to the sea, then jump over the waves with her until their ankles throbbed.

'Anyway, Morgan has always taken a little longer to get her head round her feelings. You know that better than anyone, bud. Takes after her old man, I guess... Your mother always knew exactly what to say to get her out of that – that cloud of hers.' Predictably, Jasper's grin has gone now that he's found himself remembering his wife. Instead there's a small, almost pained frown. It still hurts him. Isla isn't sure the memories will ever stop hurting her father.

'Dad?' Isla prompts, fearing that she's losing her father to that deep fog of his again.

He sits at the end of the bench that he's yet to paint, rubbing at his chin. 'I knew I was doomed with Morgan, the moment I saw her in the hospital – on that day. It was like seeing an old photograph of her. As though she wasn't real, not our Morgan any more. Just a bad copy of her.'

Isla stands frozen, because she doesn't want to disturb this moment. The fact that her father is opening up like this is borderline miraculous, and she wants to make the most of it. 'How do you mean, Dad?' she finally asks, ever so gently. Like building a castle of cards.

But Jasper shakes his head, blinks himself away from the moment. 'Long time ago ...' he mutters, picking up the paintbrush again. 'I should get on, bud. Try not to worry too much about her, eh? She'll come back for dinner, I'm sure.'

Isla watches as her father carefully pieces himself back together again. Almost identical to the way Morgan built up her defences earlier. Two peas in a thoroughly dysfunctional pod.

'Right, sure.' She knows there's no use arguing the point further; her father has retreated into his own thoughts and she knows from experience that not much will bring him out of those again.

But perhaps her father doesn't need to tell her.

'I'm ... going to the beach. Just to get some fresh air.' Isla is fairly sure her father has stopped listening past the first sentence. He makes one of his grunts of acknowledgement, eyes fixed on his paintbrush. Switched off from the world once more.

Isla takes the beach path slowly, as if it might swallow her up with one wrong step. She can see the peak of the rock poking up from beyond the thick heather lining the path, almost like a beckoning finger. It fills her with foreboding, completely opposite to the pointless hope she had last time she approached it.

What is she doing? She's already proven to herself that this stone can do nothing other than bring more disappointment. And yet, something in her father's words has brought her back to it. Because it's made her realise that it's not only her mother that Isla is missing. It's the sister who leapt from rock pool to rock pool with blazing confidence, who would curl up beside Isla and talk her through every intricate detail of her newest artwork, eyes aglow.

The stone is suddenly there, in front of her. Waiting. And Isla knows that she can't give up on it just yet.

A minute passes, filled with silent seconds of indecision, then commitment, then more indecision. Until finally, light flashes across the sand and the beach lies empty once more.

Eleven

The stone sucks her away instantly, as if it's been waiting for her. Perhaps it has. Noise immediately follows the usual bright light; she hears the squeak of wheels on lino floors, the cacophony of dozens of voices, the beeping of machinery. A cloying scent of disinfectant hits her nostrils, and Isla begins to realise where she is.

St Francis Hospital's accident and emergency department throbs with urgency. Nobody seems to notice that a young woman has appeared from nowhere, though the stone has had the apparent foresight to drop her into a corner of the room. Though Isla does have to wonder when she decided it was reasonable to give stones the ability of foresight.

She's in a long corridor, doors everywhere. There's a large sign, confirming that this is indeed the A & E department, hanging above a large square desk. There's a variety of people clustered around the desk, both visitors and medical staff. Isla feels a thick lump of fear in her throat as a stretcher is wheeled past her, automatically averts her eyes. Hospitals; she really doesn't like them. Unsurprisingly.

Pushing that fear away with practised efficiency, Isla moves down the corridor, past the desk, following the signs for the waiting room because she knows who to look for and she knows where to find her. It's full of noise, with people filling every inch of the room. The sound of pained and impatient people is jarringly familiar from an agonisingly detailed memory of a life-changing phone call.

The moment Isla remembers this, she spots her. It's a wonder, really, because Morgan is trying her hardest to blend right into the wall. Isla finds herself drifting into one of the few spare seats, two rows away from her sister. She's fairly certain her sister wouldn't notice if the Queen herself sat down beside her, but Isla doesn't want to make her sister even more distressed by revealing her presence. It becomes increasingly clear, however, from the lack of interest from anyone around her, that the stone has apparently made the decision for her to be invisible once again. Isla doesn't know the reason for that decision, but she's glad. Being invisible makes it a whole lot easier to pretend this is nothing more than a dream.

Still, she tries not to stare. Even when invisible it feels rude, but Isla can't really help herself. She remembers her father's words, about her sister seeming like a dodgy copy. Now Isla knows exactly what he meant; as if this is the knock-off version of her sister, trying to pass for the real thing. Empty eyes, tightened jaw, shoulders held straight but with the tiniest tremor running through them. She's holding it together because she has to but she won't last long. Isla can tell that from her sister's fingers, the way they've curled into her palms. She can only imagine how hard her fingernails are digging into the skin.

Does she know yet? She must do; she must have seen something in the paramedics' eyes as they worked in the ambulance. Isla wants to scream at someone because why has she been left on her own? Her little sister, who at this point in time still sleeps with the door cracked open so she can hear her parents' voices downstairs, left alone to make sense of a world that's just changed entirely.

'Morgan Pembroke?'

Isla's head turns along with her sister's, towards a doctor hovering at the edge of the waiting room. Morgan doesn't stand at first and Isla doesn't blame her. The doctor has a distinct air about her, the air of someone tasked with an unenviable job.

'Morgan Pembroke?' she calls again and Morgan sighs, clearly realising that she cannot hide forever.

'I'm here, that's me.' Isla watches Morgan stand slowly then carefully pick her way through the crowded rows of chairs. The doctor begins to escort her down the corridor. Part of Isla considers just staying rooted to the chair but that's not the point of her being here, is it? If she's been given this opportunity, then she has to try and be there for her sister. Without actually being *there*.

'Morgan, you probably know already that your mother was very unwell when you called the ambulance,' the doctor is saying, as Isla catches up with them down the hallway.

'Just tell me. I don't want … I saw them give up in the ambulance so … just tell me, please.' Morgan's voice is defiant, like it was when she would try to insist that the teacher was entirely in the wrong when they gave her detention. She's fooling nobody and she must realise that because the façade disappears almost instantly. Shivering, shoulders drooping. 'She's gone, isn't she? You couldn't save her, could you?' The accusation in her voice is clear and Isla feels an instinctive urge to reprimand her, to remind her that doctors are not miracle workers. Then almost immediately feels guilty for it because doesn't her sister have every right to be as angry as she wants?

'We don't need to do this out in the corridor, let's step in here, sweetheart—'

'Will that make it any less awful? Really?' Morgan rears back from the doctor, arms wildly flailing to try and get as far away as possible. 'She's *dead*! My mum is *dead*! And you think it makes any difference whether you tell me in a corridor or a poxy little room?' Her shouts are loud, loud enough that Isla is fairly sure she would hear if she was still in the waiting room. And maybe that would have been better, then she wouldn't have to see the way her sister crumples suddenly. All the defences she's been painting on wash away in an instant and she's on the ground, crying furiously. Because she is furious, Isla can tell. She's furious at the injustice of it all, that it is *her* mother gone.

Someone rushes past Isla, close enough for Isla to wince instinctively. Then she catches a whiff of paint and engine oil that is entirely recognisable. Her father. Jasper stumbles to a halt beside her sister, hovers a hand just a few inches away from her back in case she's somehow electrified. 'Morgan?'

Morgan scrambles up as she hears her father's voice, falls against him with a cry of both relief and pain. 'Dad ... I'm sorry! I'm so sorry!'

'Sorry?' Jasper manages to keep them both upright, arms wrapped tightly around his daughter. A confident strength that Isla knows will be completely gone within days. 'Morgan, what are you talking about?'

The doctor, who is look mightily relieved at having someone here to control Morgan, steps into his sight line. 'Mr Pembroke?' she asks and receives a brisk nod in response. 'Please ...' She opens the door to her right, gestures for him to step inside.

Isla can see from her spot, half-pressed against the wall, that her father does not want to step inside. Perhaps if he was Morgan's age, he would have followed in her footsteps and dropped to the floor. But, for now, he has the understanding that he can't. He gathers Morgan to his side, kisses her forehead briefly. 'Come on, Mogs ...'

Then he brings them both into the room.

Isla was sure that the stone would send her back after that. It seemed like the natural moment for her little trip to end, especially when Isla could not bring herself to follow them into that room. But it didn't. And an hour has passed, in which Isla can only sit in the waiting room and, well, wait. There's a distant panic that perhaps she is now trapped here but she won't think properly about that, not now. She just waits for her family.

It's another ten minutes before they appear. Isla remembers a magic trick she once saw at a friend's party, where the magician's assistant walked into a box and was transformed into a completely different glittery lady. In a way, seeing her father reappear from that room is just like that. Except there's no applause and whichever magician performed this particular act needs to be banned from ever doing it again. Because he has been transformed in all the wrong ways.

Jasper leads his daughter by the hand but Isla can see he's not really aware of what he's doing. He's glazed over, looking at an entirely different scene. But Isla can see how much concentration it's taking to just put one foot in front of the other.

'Dad?' Morgan is so quiet that Isla feels herself leaning forward a little to catch the words.

'Morgan, I need you just to sit here a minute, okay? I need, I need to just ... You just need to sit here a minute.' Jasper gently steers her towards a seat, a few along from Isla.

'You need to what? Dad? I don't want to stay here. I don't want to be alone.'

'Just a minute, Morgan. Please!' Jasper's voice has risen a little, drawing the eyes of others waiting. 'I'm sorry, love,' he says a moment later, hushed again. 'Just a minute.'

He doesn't wait for her answer, perhaps because he knows it won't be good. After all, he's said the same sentence pretty much on repeat. Morgan watches, stumped, as her father leaves her alone in the midst of chaos.

Isla feels herself shudder, because she didn't know. She didn't know that Morgan had been left alone minutes after having the worst news confirmed to her. Why didn't she know? Why didn't her sister tell her? Was it because it was just the first of many times that her sister got let down by her father? Or was it something else? Was Morgan trying to protect her, just the way Isla has been trying to do all these years?

After a moment, Morgan pulls her mobile phone from her pocket. She stares at it blankly, as if she's forgotten how to use it. Finally, after another long moment, she opens the phone and finds the number she wants.

Isla realises a second too late what's coming. And it takes her another precious second to realise this isn't something she wants to see. It was bad enough hearing it down the phone the first time, after all.

And now she's seeing it, right in front of her. Isla wants to run from the room because this is a moment she has carefully packaged away for years and she doesn't want to know what will happen when it gets unwrapped. And yet she can't find the will to actually stand up. Almost as if her staying here, however unseen, means her sister isn't alone for the hardest phone call of her life.

'Isla? It's Morgan. You ... You need to come home. Something happened. Something happened to Mum.' Morgan's voice stumbles over each word and Isla wonders how she didn't know straight away what her sister was trying to tell her.

Morgan's free hand is clenched tightly, fingernails digging deep into her palm. She brings her knees to her chest. 'It's really bad Isla,' she whispers, voice hitching in her throat. '*Please*, you've got to come back, right now.'

Isla closes her eyes, feeling sorrow rising within her chest. She remembers each and every one of those words, how they didn't seem to make sense to her on the other end of the phone. How she stood up slowly from her desk, felt the room tipping beneath her as if she was back on one of Karrekoth's fishing boats. *What do you mean, really bad? Morgan, tell me. What's happened?*

Morgan lets out a sob that seems to crack the air around it. 'Mum's gone, Isla!'

Three words. Just three words to change everything and Isla was sure it was more. How could it only have been three words?

Isla counts the seconds of silence, feels the twist of the road caused by those words. She remembers thinking about going to get some food before that phone call. Her biggest concern simply whether the shops would be shut already.

Then boom.

Morgan, hang on. I'm coming. Isla can almost feel her own lips mouthing these words, can almost feel the chill of her keys that she picked up from her desk. She felt that her heart slowed, stilled. Calmed its beating as an attempt to help her concentrate, to make sense of what she was hearing from her sister.

'I'm sorry, Isla. I don't know what to do!'

Isla remembers that this is the moment her sister loses the ability to speak. She opens her eyes, glances over. Watches as the phone slips from her hand as Morgan brings her head down to her knees and lets sorrow take over. It was terrifying to hear her sister crying like that then and now it's no different.

Isla sees her father coming back in from wherever he's been. She watches how he stumbles to a halt, watches the tiny, almost imperceptible step he takes back. She takes in the wide eyes, sees the panic and grief. By the time she gets back from university and finds her family, that panic and grief will have become a dreadful numbness.

'Morgan?' He sounds so frightened, as if he's approaching a starving bear.

But Isla doesn't get to hear or see what her sister does next. That now very familiar salty wind rustles the magazines in the corner, unnoticed by anyone but Isla. Time to go.

In an instant, the hospital is gone. Snatched away and replaced by the sand and the sea and an almost pleasant sunset. Not that Isla can focus on that right now, not when the twisting, cruel pain of grief is slowly worming its way through her chest. A grief that she has allowed herself to pretend she has forgotten about. But now it's right there, in the forefront of her mind. A needling, persistent pain.

Isla slowly becomes aware that she's crying. She feels the tears dampening her cheeks, chilling her skin when the wind blows past. Instinct kicks in and she takes a deep breath, forces herself to pull the tears back down inside. She sits with her back against the rock and her head in her hands, tries to let the darkness found in her palms bring a vague sense of calm back.

Finally, with shaky legs, Isla manages to pull herself upright. She rests one hand on the stone, draws in a controlled breath. Funnily enough, she's quite good at those.

Her eyes drift up to the distant cliff, and the precariously balanced house atop it that she has always called home. And her thoughts drift right back to her sister.

Morgan never really told her what it was like at the hospital. She never admitted to Isla that she yelled at a doctor because she was so thickly encased in fear and sorrow. She never told Isla that their father left her alone in the waiting room, minutes after finding out that her mother was gone. So Isla can't help but wonder what else her sister has not told her. And what part those untold words played in sending her sister away from them. She looks to the stone again and, almost instantly, it glows. A silent response to an unasked question.

She hesitates, fingers resting on the edge of the stone's fissure. Is there really anything to be done in the past? After all, she tried to stop her mother's death and failed outright.

Isla knows, deep down, that she's already made her decision. That when it comes to helping Morgan, she will always try.

So Isla decides to do just that. And steps back into the stone.

Twelve

This time, Isla's more ready for the transition from present to past. Not something she ever quite imagined being ready for, but she's ready nonetheless. The beach is whipped from beneath her feet and almost instantly replaced with grass but Isla does not stumble. Instead, she puts one hand out to steady herself, her fingers brushing against worn and splintered wood.

After a moment, Isla has got her bearings. Her hand is resting on the somewhat ramshackle fence that runs alongside her house, which stands directly in front of her. She's back home, which fills her with slight relief. Anywhere's better than the hospital, with its frantic corridors and scent of bleach stinging her nostrils.

The wind is howling around her home, making it seem even more dramatic than usual. She can hear the creaks of the worn window frames, the whistling as the wind spirals down the cavernous chimney. Those sounds might scare others but to Isla they're almost like a lullaby. Comforting.

Not so comforting is the sound of a car engine, rapidly approaching. Normally Isla wouldn't be so alarmed by that sound but she's not in her time and the owner of the car is most likely to be someone who will recognise her. And she has no idea what state of visibility the stone has deigned to cast over her this time.

Isla curses to herself, glancing around for somewhere to hide. It's heading towards dusk; the shadows are growing. But not enough to give her adequate cover alone. It will have to be the bushes, she realises with some regret. These bushes are the sturdy, prickly kind that cover the coastline around here. Great for surviving the elements, not so great for providing comfortable hiding places.

But it will have to do. The sound of crunching gravel and a complaining car engine is getting louder. Isla scrambles away from the front drive of her home and squeezes behind the nearest bush, wincing as she immediately feels thorns digging into her arms. It seems she's got there just in time though, as seconds later a car comes to a halt right in front of the bush. It's a white car that she doesn't recognise, until she sees her own feet step from it, wearing her old, faithful pair of plimsolls with a felt-tip octopus doodled on the side, courtesy of her sister.

'Thank you … that's fine, keep the change.' She hears her own voice, muffled as she presumably talks to the driver. Isla realises that this must be a taxi. And then a second later she realises that this must be *the* taxi that picked her up from the train station when she rushed back from university.

Isla shifts a little behind the bush, needing to catch a glimpse of herself for a reason she can't quite explain. Perhaps it's vanity, perhaps it's curiosity. She cautiously peers through the thorns, watches her past self drag her suitcase towards the door with trepidation. The first time she had ever felt scared to approach her home. Isla wishes she could say it was the last time, but she knows that's not the case.

The door opens before she gets there. Isla can't see properly from her hiding spot but she can remember. Morgan must have been waiting by the door or watching from a window, that's the only way she could have got outside so quickly. Isla hears the rush of feet, then the clunk of a dropped suitcase.

Even with the wind whistling around the cliffs, Isla can still hear her sister's sobs. Or perhaps she just remembers them. Her sister, almost as tall as her and yet entirely childlike in that moment. Isla wrapped her arms around her and almost lifted her off the ground, so determined to protect her from the world she was anchored to. And Morgan's sobs shook right through to the core of her bones. Desperate, furious and utterly terrified.

Isla feels a shiver pass over her, entirely separate from the chill of the wind.

The stones crunch again as feet stumble inside, suitcase dragged in behind them. The door slams a second later and she's left with the elements. Before, Isla wanted the world to stop and pay its respects to the tragedy unfolding. Now, she finds its blissful ignorance almost comforting. The dark shadow of grief and loss can almost be ignored out here, buffeted away by the breeze.

But Isla knows there's no use in her sitting behind a bush and just waiting for something to happen. The stone must have brought her here for a reason and that reason can't simply be watching seagulls roosting around her chimney. So she throws caution to the wind, comes out from her hiding place, and strides towards the door.

She opens it with ease, which should be impossible considering it's locked. But at least it reassures Isla about what the stone is wanting her to see. Surely this must mean she's also invisible again? Only one way to find out…

She steps into the kitchen, bracing herself for screams of fear. But there are none. The two sisters occupying the room have absolutely no awareness of her being there.

Morgan is holding on to her sister so tightly, it's as if she's worried that gravity may stop working any moment and drag them apart. Isla remembers how she left this house barely more than a month ago and yet it seemed entirely unfamiliar. Little things such as the shoes being in a different-shaped pile, the hallway light not being turned on. Isla watches as her younger self pulls her sister towards the kitchen, pausing when she sees that the table has been shoved to one side, the chairs tugged away. The salt and pepper shakers, shaped like little postboxes, lie stricken on their sides.

Morgan hovers at the threshold, shifting her weight from one foot to the next. Like a bird about to take flight. 'I had to move stuff, for the paramedics.' A simple sentence but loaded with so much weight that Isla can practically hear it crash to the floor.

'Where's Dad?' Isla can't help but notice how distant her younger self's voice sounds in this moment, almost disembodied.

'He's sleeping upstairs.'

The younger Isla nods, says no more. That one question was all she could manage, Isla remembers, perhaps because Morgan's answer brought out a whole flock of other questions and she just didn't know where to start. The sisters stand side by side in silence, staring at the empty space where the table once was. An empty space that can't be more than a metre squared and yet seems like a yawning chasm.

'We should put the table back.' Isla shrugs off her jacket, hangs it on the usual peg, tries not to touch her mother's coat as she does so. 'It's just in the way.'

'Isla?'

'We won't be able to do anything with that table like that.'

'Isla?'

'It's lucky it didn't scrape the floor.'

'Isla!'

Isla can see how her own fingernails are digging into her

palms, how she has to force herself to look at her sister. She didn't want to because she knew that her sister's eyes would reflect exactly how she was feeling. And Isla remembers how she wouldn't let herself feel like that, not yet. Not when she's got things to do. 'Morgan, help me move the table, okay? Then ... then we'll sort stuff out.'

Morgan stares at her sister, her expression bottomless. Then she nods. They drag the table back into its spot, tuck the chairs under. The younger Isla carefully rights the postboxes, dusts away the small spillage of salt and pepper. Everything takes a little longer than necessary, just in case that can halt reality for a moment.

But eventually the table is sorted and they have no choice but to sit at it. Morgan drops into her usual chair, her sister next to her. There's a gap between them but Morgan makes no move to close it, feet curled around the legs of the chair and hands gripping tightly to the sides. From her spot by the doorway, Isla resists the urge to step into the room and intervene, somehow. Though what on earth would she do? Make some sodding tea as usual? As if that will help.

'Do ... Do you want to know what happened?' Morgan's voice is trying its hardest to be steady but it turns out small, fragile.

Isla didn't know the answer to that question. Which is why a moment later, the younger Isla shakes her head. Isla remembers how it just didn't seem to matter how it happened, just that it did. Her mother was gone. She had plenty of grisly images floating around her mind; she didn't need any more. But the invisible Isla catches her sister's shoulders slump a little, almost disappointed. It goes unnoticed by the other Isla though, who can only frown at the table as if it might suddenly reveal the next step for her.

The sisters slip back into silence, reality pressing in from all corners of the room. Funny, even now Isla can remember how it felt like that bit in *Alice in Wonderland*, when she drinks the potion and finds herself shrinking to the size of a pencil. Her once comforting home morphed into something that no longer seemed to fit her.

The smallest sob escapes Isla's lips a moment later. She was trying so hard to be strong for Morgan, whose gaze is burning into the side of her head, but there was no stopping it. Isla watches as her younger self places a hand to her mouth, closes her eyes.

'How can this be happening?'

The words tumble from her mouth and Isla hears the creak of Morgan's chair, watches her shift away a little. Isla had felt a dreadful guilt at that, because she was meant to be helping her little sister, not scaring her. Forcing her eyes open, the younger Isla swallows the lump of sorrow clogging up her throat. It felt like swallowing paste.

'Sorry, Mogs. I just ... I don't understand.'

Morgan sniffs and Isla watches her sister carefully shrug her words away, notices how her shoulders seem too stiff, like a puppet on strings pulled far too taut. Was it so obvious, even then? How scared her sister was? And yet Isla has the all-too-conscious awareness that she didn't notice it at this moment, not properly. 'Nobody does,' Morgan mutters. 'People at the hospital kept saying how unusual this is, for someone her age ... like that's meant to help somehow. But it doesn't, of course it doesn't. It just makes us even more unlucky ...'

'They're trying to help, I guess.'

'It doesn't.'

Isla sees fire in her sister's eyes burning fiercely and feels a flutter of foreboding, even all these years later. 'Morgan, this isn't the time to get angry. We've got to – pull together.'

Morgan snorts, resting her chin atop the table and glaring mutinously ahead. Isla's seen this look so many times, ever since her sister learnt the word 'no', and how to use the appropriate muscles to create a frown. Ever since she learned that anger is a lot easier to feel than fear.

Her mother could coax a smile out of that frown with ease. With a little joke or a gentle tickle behind her ear. But neither of those options would quite cover this situation.

Isla has settled for a hand on her sister's arm. Morgan pulls her head further down, until her forehead is resting on the wood and the rest of her face is out of sight. 'Why her?'

'I don't know, Mogs.' Isla can hear a prickle of impatience in her own voice, harsh and unwelcome. She thought her sister should know that such questions are pointless or at least that Isla, of all people, wouldn't know the answer.

'Why didn't she realise sooner? She must have felt something before, she should have told someone.'

'Morgan, you know that's not fair ...'

Morgan's shoulders scrunch up by her ears and Isla hears a heavy sigh from somewhere beneath her sister's arms. There's exhaustion radiating from her and Isla wants to scoop her up, tuck her into bed. She could do that now; she's got the strength unlike her younger self. She could find a way to bring them back even further in the past, to when they would cuddle up under the covers and Morgan would make up her own ghost story, torch propped up under her chin. And they would never get scared, even when her imagination grew wild and unruly, because they knew that this house was their fortress, impenetrable.

Isla knows deep down that none of that will do now, though. Not really. And as she watches the younger Isla rub her sister's back and hold her own sadness behind strong harbour walls, she wonders if there is really anything that would make it better now.

'Maybe we should sort out some food.' Morgan glances up at her sister's words, murmured so quietly it's almost as though she isn't conscious of saying them.

'Food?' Morgan splutters. 'Now?'

Isla gives her sister a firm look. 'When did you or Dad last eat? Properly?'

'Does it matter?'

'Of course it matters, Morgan. You need to eat. You need to look after yourself right now, even if it feels tricky.'

'I can't think of anything I'd rather do less than eat.' Morgan lowers her head again, scowling at the table. 'And you certainly won't be able to get Dad to eat. I just want to sit here and – and work out what we do next.'

'Mogs. It's not for *you* to work that out. You just need to focus on looking after yourself. I'll focus on everything else.' Isla can't quite remember saying those words but she clearly did, the evidence is fairly undeniable after all. She certainly doesn't remember how the words caused her sister's scowl to grow even deeper, even darker.

Yet it has. Morgan shakes her head. 'I don't want any food,' she mutters, though it is increasingly clear to Isla from all these years in the future that that isn't really what her sister wants to say. 'I just want space.'

She stands up abruptly, followed almost immediately by her older sister. 'What do you mean – space?' Isla asks, the foreboding clear to everyone in the room.

'I mean, I'm going out to get some space and some air because I – I don't want to be in this room any more. I *can't* be in this room any more.'

Morgan sounds as if she's trying so hard to be grown up,

was that really how she said it? Isla only remembers her being typically moody and adolescent, even if, technically speaking, at twelve years old she wasn't quite adolescent yet.

'Mogs, you can't just go out. You're a child.'

'So are you,' Morgan snaps back. 'You're not an adult, Isla. Just because you've been at university for one stupid month. You're not an adult.' It's so obvious what she's trying to say in those words now. *You're not Mum.* And yet Isla doesn't remember hearing anything other than her little sister lashing out at her for no apparent reason.

Morgan doesn't let Isla say anything further. She whirls away from the table and storms down the hallway. A moment later, the slamming of the front door echoes through the house. The kitchen feels so silent and empty then. The younger Isla stands frozen, suddenly alone with a crushing sense of being utterly out of her depth. Until Jasper calls from upstairs, a tentative voice shouting her name. Isla watches the way she puts herself back together then leaves the room, stiff and almost robotic.

But the invisible Isla doesn't need to see that moment again. She remembers all too well how her reunion with her father goes. What she doesn't know is what happens next with her sister and, somehow, that feels most important. So she stumbles down the hallway, slips out the front door and hurries after her sister.

Morgan's bolthole has always been the beach, but this time it's different. After following at a distance, Isla finds that her sister has disappeared into the park opposite their primary school. It bewilders Isla because this was a place that they never really bothered with; what fun was a park when you had the beach?

But now, as Isla watches from the nearest corner, Morgan climbs expertly over the closed gate and slips into the shadows.

Isla is about to follow her, already has one foot in the road, when a car suddenly roars towards her with an angry beeping. She leaps back, just in time to avoid being hit and to catch the look of irritation being cast her way by the driver. It causes Isla to pause, confusion racing through her. Since when did she become visible? She glances around, suddenly feeling a little vulnerable. Though what she's looking for is beyond her; the stone following her and casting a magical spell of visibility over her with a giant, stony wand? Hardly likely.

Besides, with dusk now firmly settled over Karrekoth, the park is succumbing to the darkness. Isla can only just make out the ghostly silhouettes of trees, the winding path and the playground. It looks somewhat unnerving in the dark; empty and abandoned. Whether she's visible or invisible, Isla can't lose her sister. She crosses the road, just in time to watch Morgan drop down onto a swing and curl her legs up beneath her.

She's probably fifteen metres away, but she can still hear her sister cry. Isla makes a decision then, to throw caution to the wind. She slips around the edge of the fence, following the perimeter of the park until she's directly alongside the playground. Now Morgan is only a couple of metres away and, by crouching low, Isla is fairly sure she's hidden behind the trunk of a tree standing right by the fence. More importantly, Isla can now see her sister a lot more clearly.

The anger from the kitchen has disappeared completely. All Isla sees now is a terrified, heartbroken young girl. Morgan is curved over, head in her hands. Every inch of her seems to tremble as she cries, so much so that Isla is worried she might shake herself right off the swing. Somehow, though, she manages to keep herself upright. The minutes pass and Morgan does not lift her head, does not move. Just cries and cries, lost to her own fear and sorrow.

Isla feels every muscle in her body itching to move, to climb this fence and get to her sister. Because this is the Morgan she can help; she's always known how to stop her sister crying. It was when she stopped crying and stopped talking that the problems started.

Except she didn't stop crying, she just hid it away. And Isla missed it. Her sister sitting crying alone in this park and what did Isla do? She made bloody pasta and silently fumed about her sister's apparent immaturity. Even when Morgan came back for dinner, Isla didn't do anything to help her; she just went upstairs and sat in her room and ... well, Isla really doesn't care to think about that.

Guilt prickles against her skin. She promised to look after Morgan. And in this moment, at this first hurdle, she failed.

It's this all-consuming guilt that stops her noticing her foot slipping. Until it's too late. Her crouch collapses beneath her and she lands on the ground. It doesn't hurt, but it does make a noise. A small crunch of the leaves beneath her but the sound seems to bounce wildly from shadow to shadow, travelling across the park with ease.

Isla hears Morgan's crying stop abruptly. Then the clink of the swing's chain as her sister stands up. 'Hello? Is ... someone there?' Morgan tries to sound brave but there's a telltale tremble. Unsurprising, really.

Isla stays frozen, hoping that if she stays still, her sister won't spot her. There's deafening silence, even the air seems to hold its breath to see if Isla can hide successfully.

'Hello?' Morgan calls out again, this time sounding a little further away. Isla dares a peek through the fence, sees her sister standing on the edge of the playground, looking towards the other side of the park.

Slowly, ever so carefully, Isla pulls herself onto her feet. She winces as the material of her shoes seems to bellow its creaks, as her dress's swishes seem as loud as a howling wind. Isla's eyes are fixed on the back of her sister's head, so she spots it instantly; the moment when Morgan turns towards her.

'Is that—'

But Isla never hears the end of that sentence. The wind picks up around her, the ground softens beneath her feet and the park in front of her dissolves into light. Perhaps she's imagining it, but she's sure she hears her sister shout. For all she knows, this blinding light has flashed in front of her too.

Then comes the inevitable sensation of falling down, sand shifting beneath her hands and the sound of waves crashing back into her ears. The stone towers above her. She's home.

Isla stumbles to her feet, watching as the crack in the stone fades to darkness once again. Beyond the stone, the sea is steadily approaching. The tide is coming in; she needs to move. But Isla can't find the will to do so, lost in her own tidal wave of feelings.

'I should have followed her.' Isla forces herself to say the words out loud, even when the sentence sends a churning, sickening feeling through her. The words seem to be carried upwards by the wind, and Isla has a terrible fear that those words will be whipped through the town. That they'll swirl down the narrow streets and squeeze down chimneys, into the ears of everybody in town until they all know that she let her sister down in the moment she needed her most.

That must be why she left in the end, Isla realises. Morgan just didn't want to be let down any more.

But perhaps Isla can do something about that. Perhaps if her mother's death is unchangeable, the stone has other things in mind. It has taken the time to show her the mistakes she's made with her sister, after all.

So maybe this is her chance to fix them.

Thirteen

The kettle clicks, water bubbling violently and almost spilling out of the top until Isla tugs it off its stand. Strange, even with a blissfully undisturbed night of sleep, the real world is still proving difficult to concentrate on the whole time. Like she's left half of her brain down on the beach.

But she's got work to do.

Isla quickly makes up two mugs of tea, expertly stirring in half a teaspoon of sugar for her sister and ensuring she only adds milk to her own. How her sister drinks her tea without milk, Isla will never know.

It's a little difficult to knock on the door when she's holding two mugs, so she goes for a gentle kick with her foot. Part of her is itching to skip waiting for a response but in the spirit of retaining their fragile peace, she waits. A moment later, she's rewarded by the door opening.

'Oh, morning.' Morgan wears her tiredness in a distinct shade of grey that Isla can't help but be concerned by. But she decides to tackle the easier things first.

'I brought you tea.'

Morgan looks at the offered cup with slight suspicion, before finally taking it. 'Thanks ... I could use it.'

Isla watches as her sister carefully places it on the bedside table, noticing that the bed seems fairly unslept in. But she forces herself not to comment, not to ask where she disappeared to all of yesterday. She's hardly one to talk when it comes to disappearing, after all. 'So, I've got work today but wondered if you wanted to come along and help out? Could be fun.'

'Fun? What's fun about dirty fish tanks?'

Isla shrugs. 'The fish?' she offers.

Morgan tucks her hair behind her ear, frowning a little as she considers the offer. Isla can practically see her shrewdly inspecting it for traps. 'Are you going to ask me difficult questions?'

'No comment.'

Morgan can't seem to help grinning at that, rolling her eyes heavenwards. 'I swear you should have become a lawyer or something... you're wasted on fish...'

Isla smiles, but says nothing. Waits it out.

After a moment, Morgan sighs dramatically. It's a little too dramatic to be believable, so her next words don't come as much surprise. 'All right, fine.'

'Cool. Ready in half an hour?'

'Half an hour.'

Dennis takes very little convincing from Isla to allow Morgan to help out today. He's nursing a cold and looks as if he might be about to convince her to just take the whole aquarium off his hands. So any help is welcome apparently, and soon Isla has Morgan feeding the freshwater fish section while she cleans the tanks on her list. To be honest, the cleaning is where the help would be most appreciated but Isla wants to keep Morgan in a good mood and, well, keep her from running out of the aquarium without another word.

'Does it seem different?' Isla asks, once she's sure the silence they've settled into is comfortable enough to be broken. 'Being back home?'

Morgan snorts, shoots her sister a rueful grin as she sprinkles pellets of food into the angelfish tank. 'Are you kidding? I swear, Karrekoth never changes. Pretty sure the boats in the harbour were in the exact same formation when I left.'

Isla grins a little as she considers this. It's most likely true. 'Well, you know how Bobby Mercer gets about his boat.'

'Christ, Bobby Mercer. Forgot about him. Remember when he tried to tell Mum to paint the front of the post office because it looked too boring?'

Isla laughs aloud at that, feeling a weight lifting from her chest as she does so. She always feels that way, in the rare moments when someone speaks about her mother without any reference to her death. A nice reminder that her mother did more than just dying.

'Mum called him a cackbrained tit...' She muses as she scrapes a particularly stubborn bit of grime from the tank glass.

Morgan nods appreciatively, leaning against her current tank with a small smile. 'Cackbrained... she had such a way with words. Nobody could deliver a one-liner like her.'

'Hmm, think you come in a very close second, Mogs.'

Morgan shrugs, clearly not ashamed by it. And Isla doesn't blame her for that; there's no compliment quite like a comparison to their mother, even if it's comparing a less-positive aspect. Isla always felt such a glow of pride when people said how much she looked like her. 'So, what did you want to ask me?'

'What?'

Morgan laughs, shifting so she's facing her sister more directly and placing the tub of fish food down on the side. 'Isla, you're about as subtle as a rhino in stilettos. Since when have you just casually invited me to work? So let's cut the bullshit and we can both go back to our day.'

Her sister doesn't sound particularly annoyed which gives Isla the confidence to go on. 'Well, other than the obvious questions about where you've been ...' She pauses, watching as Morgan's lips purse just a little, before hurrying on. 'I was thinking about that night ... when I came back from university.'

'Why?' Morgan has transformed in an instant from relaxed to tense. It's like watching a cat suddenly realise there's an intruder in their garden.

Isla shrugs. 'I guess you coming back has made me think a lot about ... what happened.' Morgan doesn't look entirely convinced and Isla sighs, placing down her sponge so she can bridge the gap between them and squeeze her arm. 'I just wanted to ask, when you stormed off that night ... did you wish I came after you?'

She's reached the crux of the matter now, the whole reason she woke her sister with a bribing cup of tea and invited her here. The only reason why she managed to sleep last night, because sleep was a lot easier when there was a plan hatched in her mind.

For a moment, Morgan's silent and Isla has to settle with listening to the gentle buzzing of the tank filters and the distant chatter of visitors on the other side of the tanks. She tries not to stare at her sister, tries not to zero in on any potential clues for her reaction.

Finally, Morgan sighs. 'I don't know,' she admits. 'I mean ... it was a really long time ago. I was only twelve. So at that moment in time I think I just wanted to be alone and wallow in ... everything.' A pause, and Isla can see that Morgan is gathering enough bravery to go on. Her voice is a little quieter when she continues, almost like she's hoping Isla won't hear her. 'But I guess it would have been nice, to not be alone. Which makes no sense, I guess. If I didn't want to be alone, I should have stayed with you.'

Isla chews at her lip, feeling a hundred different possible answers fluttering in her throat. 'Maybe. But, like you said ... you were only twelve.'

'I guess.' Morgan drops back into silence for a moment. Isla lets her mull over her thoughts, focusing on the group of tourists taking photos on the other side of the glass. The water in the tanks distorts their image a little but Isla can still see that there's a heady excitement about them, as they point to the brightly coloured fish darting between the seaweed.

'I almost ran away that night, you know.'

Morgan's words are blurted out in a rush but Isla just about catches them before they're lost. She looks to her little sister, takes in the faraway look on her face. 'You did?'

'I felt so trapped. After she ... left. The house felt as if it was shrinking around me, changing. Remember that time we went to the funfair and went in that mirror hall?' Isla nods. She hated that place but Morgan dragged her inside and then promptly got them lost for twenty stressful minutes. 'It was like that. Everything was different and I didn't like it. I felt like if I stayed a second longer, I'd be stuck. Lost in a mirror image of the world I knew ...'

Instinctively, Isla moves to take her sister's hand. Morgan's fingers twitch for a second, like she's thinking of yanking away. But then she allows their fingers to tangle together. 'But you didn't. What stopped you?'

Morgan sniffs. 'You're going to think I'm crazy ...'

Isla thinks about the stone on the beach and the inexplicable doorway to the past it holds within. 'Try me.'

'I was sitting in the park, thinking about where I could go ...

when I heard this sound and when I looked over ... she was there. Just for a second.'

Isla can feel her heart thudding hard against her chest. 'Who ... Mum?'

She nods, chewing on her lip. 'I mean, it was super dark so I couldn't really see ... it could have been some creep for all I know. But it definitely looked like her. Curly red hair and everything ...'

'And then she was gone?'

Morgan nods. 'Exactly. And, I don't know, it felt like a sign. Like that was Mum's way of telling me that she was looking out for me ... and that I needed to go home.'

Isla knows she's got to say something but right now her mind is reeling. Her sister saw her. And, not only that, but her sister thought she saw some vision of her mother. Isla doesn't know whether to feel guilty or glad; her sister has been living with this lie for nine years but, on the other hand, it stopped her running away aged twelve, which would have been a whole lot worse than her running away at aged seventeen as she ended up doing. Had that been her, and the stone's magic, all along?

'Isla?'

'Sorry.' Isla blinks rapidly, forces herself to focus. 'I was just – thinking.'

'About your sister being a nutcase?'

'Of course not. Besides, I'm fairly certain I knew that already.'

Morgan rolls her eyes at that. 'Cow,' she grumbles, but there's not much feeling behind it. In fact, it's almost fond.

Isla smirks, falling silent. There's something exceedingly healing about being with her sister and just chatting. Swapping insults, laughing together. In that moment, Isla could pretend that she never left, and that there wasn't the big unanswered question of what brought her back hovering over everything.

Or the somewhat bigger unanswered question of what exactly Isla had achieved with her time-travelling trips.

The sisters work in companionable silence for most of the day after that, only sharing brief comments about what the fish are doing or, usually more interestingly, what the visitors are doing. Isla finds it hard to start any more serious conversations when she's got so much on her mind and Morgan seems perfectly content not to start any of her own.

Still, it's with a much more settled feeling in her chest that Isla drives them home. Morgan has her head rested against the window for most of the journey, looking comfortably weary, but, as they come into the town and Isla slows down behind a bus, she lifts her head up suddenly.

'Oh shit,' she groans, which brings Isla rather abruptly out of her own thoughts. She follows Morgan's gaze and immediately spots the cause of her sister's swearing: Louisa Moore, who runs the beach café and lives vicariously through everybody else's gossip, is making a beeline for them, waving at the car in a way that doesn't really allow for Isla to keep driving. Not without potentially causing a car accident and certainly not without causing a village scandal.

'Shall I tell her you escaped from a cult?' Isla whispers, drawing a small smile from Morgan, but she can see that her sister is now incredibly nervous. 'Hey, it's fine. I'll get rid of her.' Patting her sister's leg, she brings the car to a halt at the side of the road with an expertly fixed smile in place. 'Hi, Louisa,' she says as politely as she can muster once she's rolled down the window.

'Oh, I thought so!' Louisa practically coos. 'I said to Di over at the café – I'm sure I've seen Morgan round and about, and I was right!' Louisa's eyes are glittering at the prospect of this new gossip as she focuses on Morgan who has sunk down into the seat as much as she can. 'It's so nice to see you again, love.'

Isla glances back to Morgan, shoots her a meaningful look to play along, before glancing back to Louisa. 'Yep, she's back!' Her voice sounds ridiculously saccharine but it seems to fool Louisa. 'Back from her travels.'

Morgan hesitates, then slowly shuffles herself a little more upright. 'Uh huh, was great.'

Isla catches Louisa run an almost inspecting gaze over her sister and feels an almost primal urge to get out the car and push her into the harbour. But Morgan stays strong, lets the gaze bounce off her.

'Well, that's just wonderful. Where were you travelling?'

Sister exchanges glance with sister; silent words are shared in seconds. Then Isla turns back to Louisa. 'Mexico.' Isla hears Morgan cough beside her but forces herself not to react.

'Mexico. Wow ...'

'Yep, very hot. Very interesting,' Morgan manages to reply in a slight mumble.

'Anyway,' Isla begins, taking hold of the worn handle for rolling up the car window, 'we're heading back now, actually. You know ... gotta get dinner on and all that.'

Louisa gives them both that sympathetic smile that never fails to make Isla's stomach churn. 'Oh, of course ... do give my love to your dad, eh?'

It's only once they're driving back out of the village again that Isla feels Morgan relax. She carefully adjusts her position in the seat, shooting her sister a smile that Isla can spot easily out of the corner of her eye. 'Nice lying. Thank you.'

'It's fine. Just make sure you've done some research on Mexico ... she'll be quizzing you next time.' With that said, Isla gives her sister a brief smirk. 'And hey, now I know you weren't in Mexico.'

'Great sleuthing there, Sherlock.'

They share a laugh and Isla can almost see it stitching together a few more of the tiny frayed threads in their relationship. There's a long way to go; she knows that. But it's a start. And it seems that Morgan has noticed it too because a moment later, as they're coming up the hill to their house, she speaks again.

'I was in London.'

It's a short sentence but it's surprising enough to make Isla brake a little sharply as they reach the driveway.

'Jeez, Isla … no need to take it out on the brakes.'

As Isla turns the car engine off and looks across to Morgan, she sees the slightly sheepish smile on her sister's face. She knows, then, that Isla's abrupt braking is somewhat her fault.

'London?' Isla echoes, determined not to let that particular nugget of information slip through her clutches. 'What … what were you doing there?'

Morgan raises an eyebrow with a small smirk, popping open her door. 'Don't push it,' she says simply and, with that, she's out the car and heading back towards the house.

Isla rolls her eyes, but it's with a smile. Because it's something. And she can work with something.

Fourteen

There's no real need to go to the stone that evening; Isla knows that deep down. But she can't help it. It seems to call to her in the kitchen, no matter how hard she tries to drown it out with the sound of the tumble dryer or the radio.

Part of her worries that, if she ignores it, she'll miss something important. Something else that the stone desperately needs to show her. The visit to her first evening back home did help after all, even if it hurt in a way that Isla isn't sure she's fully allowed herself to face up to yet.

She rushes through making a shepherd's pie for dinner, leaves it cooling on the side with a note beside it. *Gone for a walk, help yourself. I x.* It's not the most informative of notes but it's no worse than what she usually gets from her other family members; that's her excuse, anyway.

The stone is glowing before she even gets to it. The light casts somewhat unnerving shadows across the sand and rock pools but Isla doesn't give herself any time to worry about that. She's not planning on staying on this beach for much longer, after all.

The moment she rests her hand on the gleaming cracked· surface of the stone, she feels an almost violent tug, pulling her inside. As though it's desperate to start its work.

It spits her out into a murk of fog. It's the thick, soupy kind that slithers in from the sea and sits oppressively over a town until the sunshine finally succeeds in burning it away. The sort of fog that Isla's mother used to call 'mermaids' hunting weather', because of an old folklore she'd heard about mermaids coming out to stalk ships in the fog. Isla remembers how Marina would gather her daughters to her side and pretend to check for secret scales on their arms and legs, grinning at their giddy laughter until she pretended to be satisfied and release them.

Isla never thought fog would become something painful to think about. But she has quickly learnt that grief can twist any ordinary, everyday occurrence into sharp, persistent thorns.

The fog has transformed what Isla thinks is South Slope Road into a murky, blurred scene. It's almost like her village has been dropped underwater. The buildings shift and warp in front of her, but she can just about make out the familiar roof of her old secondary school. It almost looks like the mast of a haunted ship.

As Isla takes a tentative step into this moment in time, she becomes increasingly aware of other people around her. They're walking with the reluctant purposefulness that teenagers going to school often have, wearing variants of the navy-blue uniform that she distantly remembers wearing herself, all those years ago. She finds herself following the crowd in an almost instinctive manner, easily swept into the current.

It's as she's approaching the gates that she spots a distinctive head of red curls. Isla pulls the hood of her coat over her head to hide her own hair and comes to a halt beside the fence; she's close enough to hear the conversation but has enough fog cover to go unnoticed until she can determine what state of visibility the rock has bestowed upon her this time.

Her past self is standing by the gates and Morgan is hovering beside her. Her sister looks like she's doing her best to disappear into the mist, with her back right up against the gate's brick post and her head down.

'Why couldn't we come later?' Morgan mutters to her sister. 'Everyone's going to see me.'

Nineteen-year-old Isla looks exhausted; there are dark shadows beneath her eyes and even her freckles seem to have paled away. At Morgan's question, she sighs. 'I told you, Mogs – it's the only time Mr Murray could do. And this means I can leave Dad asleep without worrying.'

Morgan frowns and Isla can see from her position that she doesn't find any comfort in this reasoning. 'Maybe Dad could have come with us ...'

She receives a sharp look from her older sister for this. 'You know he's not up to that, Morgan.'

'He's our *dad*, he should be.' Morgan's voice cracks, and she turns away before anyone can see her face. But Isla can still catch her plaintive words. 'It's my first day back ... he should be here.'

Isla watches as her past self grips her hands together tightly and she can imagine the deep grooves she's leaving in her palms. Then she gently takes her sister's shoulders and turns her round to face her again. 'Morgan, I know this is shit, okay? I *know*. But I need you to help me. I'm going to get Dad back to normal; I am. But he needs time. And we need to get on with things, like getting back to school.'

'Get on with things?' Morgan echoes, and the watching Isla winces. Those words sound so careless, callous almost. 'Mum's gone, how can we get on with things?'

'You know what I mean ...'

Morgan swiftly disentangles herself from Isla, as she tries to place a placating hand on her shoulder. 'I don't think I do, actually. I don't think I know what the hell "getting on with things" means. I don't know what you're talking about!'

'Morgan, for Christ's sake!' Isla wears a frustrated glare now, as she takes a step back. 'Can you stop being difficult for one damn minute?'

Silence. From the shadow of fog, Isla winces at her own past impatience and how it transforms her little sister. Morgan's face drops. Without the anger that her past self has, Isla sees clearly how disappointment radiates from her sister, how it almost glows through the fog like a lighthouse.

Morgan shakes her head and turns to leave. 'Fine, whatever. See you later.'

'Morgan…'

But Morgan does not turn round. She trudges off into the murk, arms wrapped around herself as if she might keep out the world that way. Isla watches her little sister (and at that moment she really is *little*), before looking back to her younger self.

It's hard to work out who seems smaller.

Isla jolts herself out of that particular thought; the stone has sent her here and there must be a reason for it. There must be something she's supposed to do to help, just as she had stopped her sister from running away aged twelve. Isla racks her brains, trying to think. Then she remembers a snatch of conversation from this very day, how it had caused her confusion all those years ago.

'Thanks for the jumper, Isla. It helped.'

'What?'

'The jumper you left in my locker.'

'I didn't leave a jumper in your locker, Mogs. What are you talking about?'

'You didn't? But… Mum's jumper, it was in there.'

'That's not possible, Mogs. It must have been someone else's.'

Isla had been baffled but she remembered feeling a great sense of gratitude at how the strange occurrence had brought her sister out of the morning's sulk. Perhaps it had been her all along. And with that thought lodged in her mind, Isla waits for her past self to trudge towards the headteacher's office for her meeting about Morgan, before turning and running in the opposite direction.

St Clare's secondary school is on the west side of Karrekoth, only a fifteen-minute walk away from the Pembroke house. Usually fine, except if you're racing home to try and fix a particular moment in the past and know that you have only a limited amount of time until your past self returns.

By the time Isla gets home, the fog has begun to lift just enough to allow a bitter wind to pester the village and Isla's hands are red raw with cold. It's therefore no surprise that it takes her a precious minute to fumble for her own house keys in her pocket and get the door open.

Almost instantly, the wind snatches the handle from her hand and slams the door open. The resulting bang echoes excruciatingly loudly throughout the house and Isla hovers on the threshold, breath held and ready to flee. But the bang fades away and silence resumes. The house is still. She closes the door as quietly as she can, wincing at every creak.

Isla stands thinking for a moment, mentally rewinding back to these dark days. Then she slips cautiously down the hall and over to the threshold of the sitting room, avoiding the squeaky floorboards with expert precision.

The sitting room is shrouded in darkness, curtains still pulled firmly closed. The only light comes from the television, which is muted and playing some mindless daytime show. On the sofa, unmoving and unaware of the half-intruder to his home, is Jasper Pembroke. He's asleep, but Isla can make out the frown permanently etched into his brow.

The sight is unexpectedly jarring. She'd forgotten that the

father she complains about now is worlds away from the father she had on this day. The father who would leave the sofa to go to the toilet and little else, because his legs were like jelly and his house was filled with landmines of memories.

She quietly pleaded with him that morning to go with Morgan to school, kneeling on the floor by the sofa and one hand scrunched into the folds of his jumper. He had looked at her as if she was a stranger before shaking his head and mumbling weary excuses.

Isla stares and, for a moment, is overwhelmed with the desire to shake him awake and scream at him. *They need you, you stupid, stupid man.* But she knows it will do no good. She knows her father, the man who would shoo monsters from her cupboard with the bravery of a knight, is currently lost. And Isla knows it will take nine years just for the faint outlines of that man to return.

It's time to move. She hasn't got time and she hasn't got the courage to look at her father's shell any more. Isla turns and leaves him to sleep, heading up the stairs as quietly as she can. She passes her own bedroom and then her sister's closed door, then steps into her parents' room. It still smells overwhelmingly of her mother's honey shampoo and the tea tree oil she rubbed on her wrists, and Isla can't really blame her father for not wanting to step in here. It's a little like stepping into a wasps' nest.

Nine years' worth of time forms a bit of a shield, though, and that's enough to get Isla across the threshold and towards her mother's wardrobe. She pulls open the stiff door and bites down on her lip as the onslaught of familiar scents seems to double. For a second, she's nine years old and trying on her mother's shoes while Marina watches from her favourite seat by the window.

And then it's gone; Isla shakes the memory away before it

grips on too tightly, kneels down and carefully roots through the boxes of clothes stacked in one corner. She started packing her mother's things up the weekend before Morgan returned to school, in an attempt to start some transition towards 'moving on', that nonsensical term people bandied around after a death. She managed two boxes.

In the top box, however, Isla remembers one thing she did manage to pack. It all makes sense now; Morgan's rambling about finding her mother's jumper in her locker and said jumper strangely transporting from this box to Morgan's bedroom. Isla always assumed Morgan took it out herself and made up that strange story about it being in her locker. Her sister has always had a vivid imagination, after all. But now Isla is beginning to think differently.

She lifts the lid and hunts through the carefully folded clothes until she finds her mother's grey-and-white-striped jumper, the one she wore when it got too cold for her favourite white cardigan. It slips over her fingers, soft and comforting. This jumper has given her countless enchanting hugs over the years. She can only imagine how magical it must have been for Morgan to see it in her locker.

She folds the jumper under one arm, hurries down the stairs to her own room. It's still mostly packed up because Isla did not accept that university was finished for another few months. Standing on the threshold, Isla tries not to become overwhelmed by the misguided hope the room seems to radiate. Her laptop's open on the desk, halfway through her first assignment. Did she really believe she'd get to go back one day? Did she really think everything would eventually slot back into place and she'd be safe to leave?

Isla feels her eyes sting with threatening tears, overcome for a moment by the weight of loss. But there's no time for that. She can't fall apart.

Luckily, she's well-practised at sweeping sorrow away. Isla allows herself a shuddering breath, then wipes at her eyes and gets back to her task. She leaves her bedroom and heads back downstairs.

'Isla? Is that you?'

She freezes on the bottom step, foot hovering in mid-air, as her father's voice comes from the sitting room. 'Uh ... yeah. It's me!'

'Was she okay?'

'Oh ... I think so.' Isla finds her voice shaking a little and one hand grips the banister. She remembers that she got so cross with Jasper for not asking about Morgan's first day, though she didn't have the energy to actually confront him about it. But now it seems as though he just asked the wrong Isla.

'That's good, thank you, bud. For going.' Jasper's voice is distant, as if he's already falling back to sleep; it's enough to get Isla moving again. He's grateful and, even if she's hearing it nine years delayed, it still helps.

Isla races back to her school with a renewed determination in her chest. Jumper clutched close, she goes round the back of the building, finds the dodgy fence that she remembers Jessica Henley proudly telling her about back in Year 12. Apparently she would sneak out through it to meet her boyfriend from the nearby MOT garage at lunchtime. Isla never expected that particular bragging tale to come in handy ...

She gently pushes aside the rotten plank of wood and slips into her old playground.

It's easy enough to find Morgan's locker. The school isn't big and her locker is adorned with a handmade *Welcome Back Morgan!* poster. Morgan's school friends were always intensely well-meaning and kind but Isla knows this poster will have caused her sister even more stress. She will have wanted to slip, invisibly, back into school life and not be infamous because of her loss. But this poster, with the numerous collected signatures at the bottom, makes it clear that that will not be possible.

Isla is sorely tempted to remove the poster but knows she can't; she's meddling in the past enough as it is. Instead she takes the sleeves of the jumper and carefully threads them through the dangling padlock on the locker and secures them with a knot.

She stands back to admire her handiwork and nods to herself, satisfied. A little piece of comfort for her sister on this difficult first day back in school has been secured so, when a breeze suddenly begins to whirl around her ankles and she glances down to see a thin layer of sand skimming over the slightly tattered lino tiles, Isla is ready to leave.

When she looks up, the school is gone and the beach is back. As Isla steps out from the shadow of the stone, she makes out a dim moon beginning to climb into the sky. The wind has died down and the sea laps calmly at the nearby ridges of rock. Peace drifts across the breeze hesitantly, waiting for a stronger gust of wind to snatch it away.

A small smile settles onto Isla's face, the feeling a little unfamiliar to her muscles. It's a smile of achievement, because the jumper helped, her sister said as much. Isla knows it won't stop her sister running away five years after that particular day, because it already happened. But now, with two fulfilments of past events completed, Isla can't help but wonder if there's more she can do.

If she can make sure certain memories stay true, perhaps she can also make some new ones.

She doesn't get very far with that thought. As she gets halfway up the path back home, she's met by her father. Isla can't remember the last time she saw Jasper this near to the beach so it takes her a moment to actually realise that it's him.

It takes her another moment to realise that something is dreadfully wrong.

'Dad? Are you okay?' she asks, trying her best to keep her voice steady.

'Oh, Isla, there you are. Thank God . . .' He trails off, eyes a little wide as he seems to realise that now he has to tell her what's the matter.

Seeing that he's struggling, Isla places a hand on his shoulder and gently squeezes. 'It's all right, Dad. Just tell me what's wrong.'

Jasper clenches his eyes shut and Isla can feel him shaking. 'It's Morgan. Something's happened to Morgan.'

Fifteen

Something's happened to Morgan.

She's heard that before. The teacher at parents' evening, looking pointedly at the empty chair where Jasper should be and gently explaining to the nineteen-year-old substitute that her sister isn't doing well at all. Or a whisper between parents, unaware of their elder daughter's flapping ears as she makes a bedtime drink. *Something's always happening to Morgan.* Isla snapped that at her mother once, when their trip to the aquarium in Newquay was interrupted by a phone call from Morgan's drama club after she managed to trip and cut her forehead open. Her chest filled with bitter frustration that day, and even her mother's look of disappointment did nothing to stop its swell.

And yet when she hears her father say those words, all Isla feels is fear. A dreadful, shadowy fear that she has become all too acquainted with in her relatively short life. She pictures her sister clutching her chest as her heart crumples inwards, or her sister in a broken pile at the bottom of the stairs. Isla skips ahead past miles of rational reasoning and is already trying to manage the fallout, when her father speaks again.

'She won't let me in her room but she's crying, really loudly. And she just kept shouting for me to get you. She said she needed you.'

Isla's silent panicking slows to a halt. Her sister's not dead, she's speaking, she's crying.

Her sister's not dead.

Steering her father back up the path, Isla tries to fathom his words. How long has it been since her sister has admitted to needing her?

'Did she say anything else?' Isla asks, forcing herself to focus. The path feels wobbly beneath her feet, the rocks set in the sand seemingly coated in ice. Like that dream when you're no longer able to run.

'No,' Jasper replies, hovering just a step behind her as they stumble up the path, both as clumsy as each other. 'She just kept crying.'

Morgan's door is still shut when Isla reaches it and for a moment she hesitates, alone in the corridor. Jasper has retreated to the kitchen, mumbling about putting the kettle on in case that might fix the problem. And Isla is once more on her own and wondering if she can do this. It's not the first time she's comforted a crying sister, of course, but has she ever actually helped? After all, she didn't stop her sister running away…

'Mogs?' Isla knocks on the door very gently, almost tentatively. She hears a soft whimper from within and that's enough for Isla to stop worrying about her own capabilities. She pushes the door open and steps in.

Only Morgan's head is visible, protruding from beneath the duvet. Her eyes are scrunched shut and there are angry blotches of tears scarring her cheeks. As Isla steps across the threshold, Morgan curls up until the duvet's almost twisted into a tight spiral. In this moment of movement, another small whimper comes from her mouth. Pained.

'Morgan, what's going on?' Isla hears her own apprehension

because Morgan hasn't let her sister see her this vulnerable for a very long time.

Somehow that question is enough to make it impossible for Morgan to be brave any more. She shakes her head, stumbling to breathe over her own tears and suddenly she's sobbing. Then she pulls back the covers and reveals a mattress stained with angry streaks of red. 'I'm sorry, I didn't know what to do, I'm sorry.'

Morgan isn't making any sense to Isla. It's almost as if she's skipped ahead, missing out the key part where she actually explains what has happened. But Isla sees the blood on her little sister's sheets and immediately decides that now is not the time to find out.

'Tell me what I need to know and tell me what you need me to do.' Her voice is steady, as she forces herself to pretend that this is just a standard Morgan panic, that there is no blood.

Morgan tries to sit up, arms shaking. She gets semi-upright, arms snaked around her torso. Isla can't help but notice the trails of blood growing down her sister's pyjama trousers. 'I didn't mean to, Isla ...'

'You didn't mean to what?'

Morgan's trembling fingers find her sister's as she comes to sit beside her. 'I didn't mean to lose the baby.'

She says those words so quietly, as if she's afraid the walls themselves will hear and cast judgement. But Isla just about catches them.

'Morgan, I don't ... I don't understand what you're saying. What baby?'

A sound comes from her sister, one she's never heard before. It's almost like she's being cracked in two. 'My baby, the baby ...'

'Do – do you mean a miscarriage?' Isla tries to say the word as delicately as she can but it still feels brutal and heavy out in the open.

Morgan's red-rimmed eyes find her sister's. Isla sees a haunted young woman in them, but also a terrified girl. 'Yes, I mean a miscarriage,' she whispers, each word seeming to cause her physical pain. 'I had a miscarriage – a month or so ago. And now ... this ... I think something's wrong!'

Isla has the distinct sensation of being in the midst of a storm. She knows any step could take her further into the howling gales. Every possible response feels wrong, dangerous. And her sister is waiting, desperately, for *something*.

'Okay,' Isla finally says, forcing herself to sound calm. 'Okay, let's sort right now out first. Then we'll sort out the rest.' She places a hand on her sister's cheek for comfort. 'Morgan, if it was a month ago ... this is probably just your period ...'

Morgan groans, her face crumpling again. 'You're right,' she sobs, as she drops her head down onto her sister's shoulder. 'And that means ... it's gone. The baby's really gone. I know it's stupid, I know it's been gone for weeks but ... I just hoped, maybe ...'

Isla falls silent as Morgan trails off, lets her sister rest practically her whole weight against her. She's not equipped for this; she doesn't know anything about miscarriages, why would she? But then when has she ever known anything about the trauma she's suddenly had to handle?

Gently, Isla shifts away so she can meet Morgan's gaze. 'Let's deal with the little stuff first, okay? Then we'll do the big things. Cramps?'

Morgan sniffs, so small in this moment that Isla half expects to hear her asking for Calpol. Then she nods. 'Cramps, really bad cramps.'

'Okay. I'll get you some ibuprofen, and ... and a hot-water bottle.' Isla stands up, buoyed along by her list of actions to complete. Then, stepping a little tentatively over to her sister's suitcase, she digs around until she finds what looks like another pair of pyjamas. 'Put these on then go into my room. There's no use you lying in stained sheets. I'll wash them and your other pyjamas later. There's plenty of sanitary pads in the bathroom if you need them, in the box by the sink. I'll be back in five with medicine and hot-water bottle, all right?' She hands Morgan the pyjama trousers, hesitates before crouching down beside her sister again. 'Mogs, it's all going to be okay. This is something we can get through, I promise.'

She almost looks convinced. 'Okay,' she whispers, and allows her sister to help her to her feet. 'I'm sorry.'

Isla isn't quite sure what she's apologising for but she decides that now is not the time to find out. So she just smiles, presses a slightly hesitant kiss to her sister's forehead and leaves the room.

It takes Isla the agreed five minutes to get the supplies. Jasper watches her collect the right dose of painkillers, fill up a hot-water bottle and get a glass of water. Then he quietly makes a cup of tea with Morgan's half a teaspoon of sugar and places it on Isla's tray. When Isla catches his eye, he looks away.

She knows he's scared to hear the true reason his daughter is curled up sobbing in bed. She knows he's petrified of finding out that something is terribly wrong with her. So, even though frustration at his silence simmers away inside, she takes a moment to place a hand on his shoulder as she leaves the room. 'She's going to be fine, Dad.'

Jasper nods, lips pursed tightly together. He says no more, apparently lost in thoughts that Isla has never had a hope at understanding. Besides, she's got more important things to handle.

By the time she gets back upstairs, Morgan has dutifully changed her pyjamas and moved into Isla's room. She sits in the dead centre of the bed, trying to take up as little space as she can.

Rolling her eyes, Isla smiles weakly as she steps into the room. 'You're allowed under the covers, you know.'

'I don't want to mess up your sheets as well…'

Isla picks up the pills and the glass of water, hands them over. 'Take those now, then get under the covers.'

'Yes, Doc.'

Isla smirks at her sister's retort but says no more, lets her distract herself with the jibe. Once Morgan has taken the medicine and drunk the water, Isla peels back her duvet and gestures pointedly. Sighing, Morgan crawls under the covers, propping the pillows up behind her so she can sit upright.

'Hot-water bottle,' Isla says, handing it over. Morgan wrinkles her nose at the somewhat threadbare ladybird cover but takes it with no further complaint. 'Cup of tea because obviously Dad wanted to help,' Isla continues, putting it on her bedside table.

'Obviously.' Morgan carefully places the hot-water bottle on her lower abdomen then rests her head back on the pillow. 'Thank you,' she murmurs a moment later.

Isla moves to sit at the end of the bed, her back resting against the wall and her legs draping over Morgan's. 'You're welcome.'

The sisters fall silent, lost in their own different thoughts. In the end, it's Morgan who speaks first. 'Do you remember the first time I got my period?'

Smiling a little, Isla glances over to Morgan. 'You were about to go on a sleepover… you didn't tell me at first, tried to sort it yourself.' A soft laugh escapes both sisters' chests in harmony.

'The bathroom looked like a murder scene…'

Isla grins, remembering how her sister had stormed into her room, radiating fourteen-year-old petulance. *Help me, would you?* she'd snapped, as if Isla had been watching her struggle, eating a box of popcorn the entire time. 'You were so cross with yourself for not sorting it out. Always so damn stubborn.' A moment of hesitation, then Isla reaches across to squeeze her sister's hand. 'Surprised you didn't just tell your period to piss off, probably would have and all.'

'Nah, stern words are your speciality.'

It's probably true, Isla reflects. 'We were a good team that day. Got you to your sleepover on time. Got the bathroom sorted.'

'Got me all plugged up.'

'Gross, Mogs.'

A small but wicked smirk flickers briefly across her sister's face. She reaches for her tea, sips it very carefully. It is still hot most likely but Morgan always drinks her tea at a temperature that risks scalding. Once she's returned it to its space beside Isla's pebble collection, she heaves a heavy sigh. 'I guess you'd like some explanation.'

'Only if you think it will help.'

Morgan picks at the edge of Isla's duvet. 'About three years ago, I got this job with this charity in London, providing shelter for homeless young people. When I first arrived in London, they helped me out when I had nowhere to go, then offered me the job ... apparently they thought I was good at listening to people's problems. I did some art tutoring for the residents, and I painted a mural for them on their garden wall. Shit pay, but accommodation and food so I took it. It was nice, I enjoyed helping people who were like me.'

'I can imagine you being good at that.'

Morgan accepts the compliment with a small smile, shrugging slightly. 'It's a lot easier than dealing with your own problems. Anyway, I got close to one of the proper members of staff there, called Max. We got on really well; he was nice and funny and ... well, I'm sure you can work out the rest.'

Isla's mouth is dry as she looks at her sister, tries to imagine her in a homeless centre. Vulnerable at first, but then easily strengthened by the feeling of responsibility. She can picture Morgan painstakingly sharing her love of art with others, can see her delivering the no-nonsense advice she's always been so good at. Unfortunately, she can also imagine her sister becoming enchanted by a kind guy with a good sense of humour. Morgan has always craved love. Isla remembers how, as a toddler, she'd fight for sole ownership of their mother's lap, how she couldn't sleep without a parent there to hold her. Times never changed that much. All that changed was the damage such a need could cause.

'You … you got pregnant.'

A long sigh comes from Morgan and Isla sees how her expression has clouded. 'Yeah. So *stupid*. You know how to stop it from happening, you hear it thousands of times growing up and still … it all goes out the window.' She brushes a tear from her eye, shakes her head. 'I thought maybe it would help me. Like … if I had someone to care for, who relied on me … I would be okay. And, yeah, I kept thinking about all the things a child needs, how I've not had a mum for a long time so where would I even start … but I thought maybe I could do it, like maybe this would be the thing I was good at.' Morgan kneads at her eyes, drawing her knees up to her chest even though this seems to make her grimace with more pain. 'And then … I lost it. Six weeks in … A whole life gone, just like that. A whole set of future days and moments and potential lost. Again.'

'What about Max?'

Morgan snorts, shakes her head. 'Oh, he told me he wanted nothing to do with it from the start. Told me he wasn't being selfish because he was just thinking of all the people he wouldn't be able to help if he was just looking after me and a baby …' Her voice is light but Isla can feel the bitterness lurking underneath.

'So yeah, he turned out to be a dick. Wouldn't even come with me to the hospital when it happened. My business, apparently.'

'You went alone?'

Isla's voice must betray her feelings because her sister looks up abruptly, eyes wide. 'Don't get cross, Isla … please … I'm fine.'

Isla pulls back a frown she didn't realise was there, thinks of her little sister, who wouldn't even get injections without a great panic, going all on her own at such a terrifying moment for her. 'It's just … You must have been so scared.'

Her sister's hand trembles as she toys with the edge of the duvet. 'I guess I was, yeah.'

'I wish you hadn't had to do that, Mogs.'

Expression distant, Morgan shakes her head slowly. 'It's happened now. Nothing to be done. Nothing for you to feel guilty about.' She shoots her sister a mock accusatory look, meant to bring a smile to Isla's face presumably. But Isla can't stop thinking about the stone standing waiting patiently amongst the piles of kelp. Maybe this is it; the thing she'll actually be allowed to change.

'Isla?'

Jolted from her reverie, Isla finds Morgan watching her closely. 'Sorry, just thinking about … time.'

'Nice and specific there.'

Isla finds instinct taking over for a second and she smacks her sister's nearby foot. For a second she panics; her sister's in pain, what is she doing hitting her? But then Morgan kicks her leg back in return, grinning. Normality swells around them. They could be kids again, trading insults until Morgan's younger level of patience ran out and she resorted to wrestling. Isla would find her ticklish spots with practised ease, making Morgan squeal loud enough to cause Jasper to yell at them from somewhere inside the house.

But now's not the time for complete normality, not yet. 'I just meant that there's so many small moments in time that I wish had gone differently.' She's tempted, for a moment, to tell Morgan about her extraordinary discovery. But then she decides against it. Her sister has enough on her plate, after all. Besides, there are ideas cracking open in her head like awakening shells and the ideas aren't exactly ones she thinks Morgan would like.

'It's fine, Isla,' Morgan says. 'Besides, it brought me home.'

'It did?'

Morgan nods, picking at the edge of the duvet again. 'I guess... the expectation of being a mother for just a moment made me think about the family I'd left behind, how I couldn't do it on my own any more. And when I lost that... well, I *definitely* didn't want to do it on my own any more.'

Isla smiles at that, finding a great comfort in the words. Then she reaches across and squeezes Morgan's hand. 'I'm going to take the day off work tomorrow, okay? I want to make sure you're okay.' Isla stands, holds up a hand to stem any possible complaints from Morgan. 'Don't bother arguing; it's happening. You can hole up in bed away from us all day, that's fine. But I want to be here if you need anything else. You sleep here tonight; I'll take the sofa.'

Morgan looks at her for a long moment, expression unreadable. But then she nods her acceptance. 'Okay. That would be nice.' She shuffles down under the covers, closing her eyes with a suddenly exhausted sigh.

In that moment, she could be thirteen again. Or even younger. And Isla can't help but think how much easier that would be.

Sixteen

The rain has found a way to cling to everything in the street. The lamp posts glisten, adorned with thousands of tiny droplets. The pavements steam gently, casting strange clouds around the feet of passers-by, and there's a steady rhythm of splashes as cars drive through the puddles belligerently loitering at the side of the road.

Isla can't be certain but she's fairly sure this is London. There's something about the incessant throb of life around her that feels distinctly like the capital city that she hasn't visited since she was a child. Besides, when she stumbled away from her makeshift bed on the sofa in the middle of the night, sleep a distant possibility, and made for the beach, she had only one moment in her mind.

And now, standing under the shelter of a shop awning, Isla is fairly sure the stone has heard her tumultuous thoughts. It seems to be getting good at that. So now she's here, in the place where Morgan fled to and hopefully in a place where Isla can do something to prevent her next hardship.

Because she's determined to prevent it.

There's a feeling of a buzzing, almost angry anticipation growing within her as she lets the seconds slip by. It's as if she can feel the clicking motion of the cogs that are trundling endlessly towards this one moment where her sister will make a decision to spend the night with a man and unwittingly bring herself a whole new trauma. And each moment that passes, uninterrupted and unchallenged, makes her feel more and more like screaming.

A flash of dark hair passes her and maybe Isla's senses are heightened because she's certain she catches her sister's perfume, the same she's had since she turned fifteen. A sharp scent of mandarin and lime that Isla always found a little overpowering.

But right now it's highly appreciated, as Isla immediately ventures out from her shelter and follows after her sister. Morgan walks with a purposeful step along the street, apparently blissfully at home in this damp, haphazard-seeming city. Isla certainly doesn't feel so comfortable. There's something highly alarming about being so far away from the sea, from being cocooned by people all around her. It's a far cry from Karrekoth.

Isla follows Morgan all the way down the street, until she reaches a small coffee shop, whose windows spill a warm, welcoming glow out onto the pavement. Here Morgan halts, glancing into the shop before her face lights up with a smile. Whoever she's seen, it's made Morgan gleam with happiness. It's probably the happiest Isla's ever seen her for a good while. She tries to ignore the twinge of jealousy that causes. Morgan pushes open the door and steps into the warmth without a backward glance, leaving the rain and crowds of London out in the cold.

Coming to a halt, Isla presses against the coffee shop's wall and peers cautiously through the window. She watches as Morgan squeezes past small tables and squashy armchairs, until she reaches one table in the corner. It's occupied by a young man who Isla presumes is Max. He looks a little thinner than perhaps healthy and Isla can see his clothes aren't in the best of condition. Disapproval simmers in her stomach, thick as porridge. She knows she shouldn't judge a book by its cover but this is her little sister and she knows what's coming, so she'll judge this book however she damn pleases.

So it's with a tight-lipped expression that Isla watches this Max stand and kiss Morgan's cheek, one hand snaking down her back with an arrogant confidence that her skin is his to explore at will. Morgan doesn't complain, though. Isla can't help but notice that. She pulls him in for a proper kiss on the lips, grinning as she moves to sit down. Their table seems to shine brighter with the excitement radiating from her, because Morgan's joy has always had the inexplicable power of chasing away the gloomiest, heaviest of storm clouds. If only that joy was as common as Karrekoth's storms.

The time seems to drift by in slow-moving patches then, as if the clocks have dutifully slowed their ticking just for this pair. Isla can only stand in the drizzle and hope not to be spotted as she watches Morgan and Max laugh their way through their coffee. She can only wince as Max's fingers skate over her sister's, as she loses herself in his gaze. Isla is reminded of a snake and its charmer she once saw on the television. She wonders if that snake's family ever watched in horror at how totally bewitched it became.

The night draws in completely around them, chasing away the last clouds of rain and leaving a sky that is devoid of stars and glows with an almost angry orange. London, a different planet.

Finally, the coffee shop begins to close and its shelterers are spat rather unceremoniously back onto the street. Morgan and Max don't seem particularly bothered, as they pull their coats back on and step outside once more. Isla has shrunk back into the shadows but she gets the feeling that they wouldn't notice her anyway. Or at least the one who matters wouldn't notice. Morgan seems to drift a few centimetres off the ground, as if she's far too happy for this world. Max, on the other hand, seems firmly attached to the pavement. She floats, he stalks.

Perhaps she's being unfair. Perhaps her overprotectiveness has clouded her view slightly. But she can't help but look at Max and imagine him telling her little sister that the problem they both created is only hers to solve. She can't help but see their entwined hands and imagine his pulling away, imagine hers left empty as she waits in a hospital room, terrified.

'So I guess I'll see you tomorrow? It will be nice to stay over...' Morgan is saying, as Isla hovers a few yards behind them as they come to a halt at a crossroads. The street is emptier now; she knows she's playing a riskier game and might be spotted at any moment. But she can't stop herself. She needs to hear every word of this exchange.

'Yeah, definitely. I gave you my address, right?' Max cradles her cheek, thumb skimming over her lips. He smiles, drawing her close with one hand and nuzzling his nose against hers. 'Our first night alone ... finally.'

Morgan grins, kissing him fervently, almost desperately. 'Finally,' she murmurs, once she's pulled away. Now it's Max who seems enchanted by her gaze, as she presses one hand against his chest. Then she takes a step back, shooting him one final grin before starting off down the left turning. Isla can see, even in the gloom, that there's a spring in every single one of her steps.

She also can see that Max is watching her leave with an almost hungry expression. Isla is forcibly reminded of a shark. Desperate to snap his gaze away from her little sister, Isla finds herself moving past him and bumping her elbow against his side.

'Oops, sorry,' she mutters, not looking at him. She hears him mutter something irrelevant back, then his footsteps as he finally begins to move. A brief glance back and she can see that he's started off down the right turn of the crossroads.

A fleeting moment of consideration and she's started off after him.

She doesn't know what she's doing, not really. She just knows that she has to follow him. There's no plan in her mind, just a roaring beast of protectiveness. Look after Morgan; that's always been her goal. A lot of pain she has failed to keep her sister from. She couldn't stop their mother dying, she couldn't stop that tearing her up inside. But maybe she can stop this bastard from giving her sister something else to have nightmares about.

What's your plan, Isla? She doesn't know. Maybe she's going to tie this idiot up and leave him in an alleyway somewhere. The thought doesn't bring her any guilt, just a savage sense of satisfaction. Her sister would be safe then; what would it matter if he spent a few cold hours in the darkness?

Or maybe she can just tell him. Make him see that if he ever goes near her sister again, she'll rip him apart. Isla has no doubt in that moment, in the coppery darkness that counts for night-time in this city, that she would do it.

'Excuse me!' Her voice comes stumbling out into the silence before she can stop it.

Max turns, expression set with suspicion already. 'Yeah?' he asks, shoulders squaring. This is a man who has spent his whole life defending himself, that's clear. This is a man who doesn't get spoken to by strangers for any good reason.

But Isla isn't intimidated by that, not when her sister's cries of pain are stuck on repeat. 'You're Max, right?'

Immediately, Max's expression hardens. 'How do you know that?'

'That girl, you were with.' Isla pauses, glancing behind her. She's sure she heard the whoosh and crash of a wave but there's nothing except a dark street. When she turns back to Max, he's stepped a little closer.

'What about her?' His eyes flick up and down her body, a cursory examination that Isla finds repellent. He smirks. 'You jealous, love?'

A rumble of thunder shatters the silence, so loud that Isla instinctively covers her ears. But Max doesn't react in the slightest, except to frown at her with bemusement. 'What … what is up with you?'

'I'm fine,' Isla says through gritted teeth, watching as lightning flashes in the distance. 'That girl … you need to—'

The lightning erupts around her before she can get another word out. It envelops her, fills her vision with hot white light and for a terrible moment, Isla is sure that she's dead. But she's not giving up yet. 'YOU NEED TO LEAVE HER ALONE!' she screams desperately into the abyss of heat and light. 'LEAVE MY SISTER ALONE.'

Her words are immediately caught by a wind and sent spiralling into the sky. She feels herself being knocked back by an invisible force until fortunately soft sand cushions her fall. The light is gone, the beach is back. Above her the sky is inky black and clear; there's no sign of any storm clouds. So where did the lightning come from? And why did it steal her away from a chance to save her sister?

That thought drives Isla across the sand, back towards the stone. It's still glowing a little but it seems weak, almost residual. And, as she gets even closer, the light winks out completely.

But she's not giving up just yet.

'Let me back,' she growls, fingers stumbling over the rough surface. 'I need to go back.'

Then she realises that the scar is gone.

It takes her a few seconds to know for sure. A few seconds of frantic, desperate searching, fingers scraping painfully against the unforgiving stone. But there's no cleft, no glow of heat. The stone is whole again. And the past has been locked up with it.

Isla drops down onto the sand once more, feeling dejection rising up within her. This can't be happening; she can't have lost this extraordinary doorway, this impossible opportunity to change things in the past.

But maybe that's just it. She thinks about those angry words she screamed at Max, thinks about what good they could have done. Would he really have changed his plans just because some enraged woman bellowed demands at him in a dark street? Would Morgan really have let him go just like that?

And there's a terrible, selfish thought lingering in Isla's mind too. If Morgan had never got pregnant, if she'd never had the miscarriage, would she have ever come home to them at all?

The stone towers above her in the darkness, casting a silent judgement over her. But Isla thinks she gets the message. She pushed too far. She came too close to changing something that would have repercussions, repercussions that she would not have liked at all.

'Okay,' she whispers, stumbling to her feet. 'Okay, I get it. I pushed too far; I can't change too much. I understand. Please … please let me back in. Please let me keep trying.'

But the rock stays sealed. And so the past stays closed.

Seventeen

Morning comes around far too quickly after that. Somehow, Isla makes it back to the sofa before dawn erupts across the sky but it's a close one. And then of course sleep is nowhere to be found. Isla lies with a blanket pulled up to her chin but all she can smell is the wet pavements of London and her sister's perfume. And all she can think is that she's failed, yet again. She couldn't keep Morgan safe and now the stone won't even allow her to try any more.

Her fingers still feel frozen from the night-time air and are covered in grazes from her desperate searching for a crack that no longer existed. They throb a constant reminder to her that she messed up *yet again*.

When she hears the sounds of her father stumbling about to make coffee in the kitchen, Isla knows she has to get up, even though part of her just feels like skipping this day entirely.

But she can't. There's a house relying on her, even if Isla currently feels that she's as reliable as a hole-ridden boat.

So, finally, Isla shuffles out from under the covers. She pulls her dressing gown tightly around her pyjamas, digs her hands deep into the pockets. A protective armour of sorts. She heads upstairs but finds her bedroom empty, bed neatly made and window cracked open for airing. Trying not to panic, Isla steps out into the landing and crosses over to her sister's door.

'Morgan?' she asks, gently knocking.

'Come in!'

Isla opens the door, hesitating on the threshold as she watches her sister practically buzz around the room. 'You're … up?'

Morgan nods, barely glancing up from her purposeful unpacking of her suitcase. 'Yup, good eyes there, sis.'

'Are … you sure you should be up?'

Isla catches Morgan's eye-roll as she straightens up, folding a t-shirt over her arm. 'It was just cramps, Isla. I'm not an invalid.'

'Well, yes … but there was a bit more to it than just that.'

'I'm fine.' Morgan sounds entirely certain but there's an unmistakeable tremble in her fingers as she plucks another t-shirt from her suitcase.

'Morgan,' Isla begins, recognising the signs of her sister building up a wall once more. 'We're not going to just sweep this under the ever-growing carpet, are we?'

Morgan shrugs, dropping the top into her drawer. 'We might be. What does it matter? Thinking about it or not thinking about it doesn't change that it happened.'

'But it can change how it affects you, moving forward.'

Another shrug. She doesn't say anything in response, which Isla takes to mean that Morgan knows she's right. Of course, that doesn't mean she's going to actually do anything about it. With a slightly more savage energy behind her, her sister carries on unpacking.

'Morgan, please just rest. Just today. I'm just about to call in work and take the day off; we can just … relax today and get you fully better. There's no need to rush into anything.'

Morgan slams her drawer closed, jaw tightly clenched as she rounds on her sister. 'Isla!' she snaps. 'Stop. I am not a child any more. I don't need a sick day or a blankie or a fucking sippy cup of orange juice. I need normal life to continue. So back off, okay?'

Isla almost does what she says. Almost. But even with the stone closed off to her, she still has the memories it's recently refreshed for her. And one thing is clear. Her sister is never more angry than when she is terribly sad.

So Isla stops herself before she can leave the room properly. 'Okay ... okay, I'm sorry. But let's compromise. I won't treat you like a child if you won't treat this the way you always treat difficult things – by getting angry and ignoring it.'

Morgan narrows her eyes but Isla just raises an eyebrow, daring her to deny it. It's been a while since she's been quite so upfront with her sister like this, but Isla finds it alarmingly easy to slip back into this role.

A second passes, a silent stand-off. Then Morgan drops down onto the bed, latest t-shirt clutched to her chest. Her eyes lose their sharpness; defeat settles around her.

'Sorry,' she murmurs finally, which brings a small noise of surprise from Isla before she can quite stop herself. Morgan clearly hears this because she rolls her eyes at her sister. 'It's not that much of a rarity, surely?'

'Hmm ... no comment,' Isla replies but her voice is warm and devoid of blame. Anything to keep this conversation on the positive path it seems to be following. 'Look,' she begins with a sigh, sitting down beside her sister on the bed. 'I'm not saying you need to tell me everything. I probably don't want to know everything. But I am saying that there's no way you can deal healthily with this with just denial. I think we've both seen how little that achieves ...'

Morgan sniffs an agreement but that's enough for Isla, for now. She pats her sister's arm bracingly. 'So, if you don't want to be treated like a child ... do you want to come do some more work at the aquarium? I think Dennis was quite impressed, y'know.'

A snort this time. 'I get the sense that your boss is not entirely difficult to impress, Isla. I watched him forget the name of a clownfish.' But when Isla doesn't say anything, just leaves her offer still dangling in the air, Morgan sighs with defeat. 'Okay. Fine. But I'm still not cleaning any damn tanks.'

It's that ease of getting Morgan to agree that should have flagged to Isla that there would be a catch, somewhere. Nothing was ever that simple with her, was it?

And the catch comes when they walk into the staffroom for lunch and find Dylan Burroughs already sitting there. Isla pauses on the threshold for a millisecond before remembering that she's with Morgan and Morgan is damn good at spotting changes in her behaviour.

Indeed, Isla catches the curious grin sent her way as her sister squeezes past her and makes a beeline for the man sitting before them. 'Dylan Burroughs, from Isla's class!' she states with a somewhat alarming and perplexing force to her voice, pointing a finger of recognition in his direction. 'Morgan Pembroke. Isla's sister.' She's holding out a hand to Dylan before he's even finished his mouthful of sandwich, which is perhaps why he looks so startled at the sight of her. Something flashes across his face and, when Isla looks to her sister, she sees a similar expression being quickly wiped away. It's too brief for Isla to read properly and a moment later, Dylan has his somewhat lopsided smile back in place as he shakes Morgan's hand. So Isla has no choice but to dismiss it, for the moment.

Once he's swallowed his sandwich, he gives a slightly better smile. 'Morgan Pembroke. You're the one who turned Isla to the company of octopuses.' Isla feels her cheeks warming as both Dylan's and Morgan's eyes turn to her. Her sister's smile is now sickeningly triumphant.

'I told you already,' Isla mumbles. 'You can't extrapolate a conclusion about that just from one incident.'

'Oh, Christ,' Morgan groans, rolling her eyes as she makes her way to sit down. 'This sounds like a conversation I need to phase out of.'

'Not an octopus fan yourself, Morgan?' Dylan asks, obligingly pushing his usual stack of papers out of the way as Isla sits herself down also.

'I could have been. But my sister probably scarred me for life with all her talk of … tentacle patterns.'

'Not a thing,' Isla can't help but mutter, which causes Morgan to shoot a rather smug look at Dylan.

'I mean, she is right. They're not a thing.' Dylan seems to consider taking another bite of sandwich then decides this is more important. 'An octopus's tentacles are like our legs. You don't see doctors having conversations about leg patterns, right?'

Morgan's eyes raise heavenwards. 'God … who knew there were two of you in the world?'

Isla knows the question is rhetorical but still feels a strange sense of pressure to say something. She glances at Dylan and is immediately perturbed to find herself meeting his gaze. He looks away first, though there's a smile lingering in the corner of his mouth, amongst the leftover crumbs of his sandwich. Without another word, he takes a bite of his sandwich.

The conversation is short-lived after that. Dylan and Morgan both seem intent on asking Isla as many questions as possible in an almost dizzying way, which Isla doesn't quite understand. There's a strange intensity in both of their stares and so Isla is somewhat relieved when, soon after, Dylan packs up and politely wishes them a good afternoon before leaving.

The door has barely shut before Morgan has pounced. 'Christ,' she declares, once more. 'What was *that*?'

Isla tries to find a few spare seconds of time in carefully closing her Tupperware box, as if that might help her find an answer. It doesn't.

'What do you mean? It's just Dylan from school.'

'Yes, I got that far, thank you.'

'He's just working with a professor and he's doing some research for her here while she's travelling, or something.'

'"Or something". Nice.'

'Meaning what?'

Morgan tears open her packet of crisps with savage triumph. 'As if you don't know everything you can about him already.'

Forcing her expression into something that she hopes one could call neutral, Isla shakes her head. 'I have no idea what you're talking about.'

'Isla, he is clearly smitten as fuck. Didn't you see how he was smiling at you every other second? And backing you up on your ridiculous octopus tentacles shit?'

'Maybe he just doesn't like scientific inaccuracies.'

Morgan snorts, waves the comment away for the meaningless piece of evidence it apparently is. 'Do you like him?'

'Morgan . . .' But her sister holds up a hand with a stern expression, bringing whatever protests she was about to make to a halt.

'Answer the question.'

Isla is silent for a moment, mainly because she doesn't actually know what her answer is. It doesn't help her thought process to have Morgan watching her like a hungry shark, so it takes a little longer than Isla cares for. 'I ... I think so. I mean, it's hard. I haven't ...'

'Haven't what?' Morgan presses, when Isla finds herself trailing into silence once more.

'I haven't really thought about that sort of stuff ... for a while. I haven't really had the time and, well, Karrekoth hardly has the largest pool of choice.'

Morgan makes a noise of agreement and for a moment Isla wonders if perhaps she's off the hook. But then her sister goes on. 'So, here's your chance. Dylan's always seemed nice, and he clearly likes you.'

'How would you know if he's nice or not; you've never spoken to him properly before today?'

Something unreadable crosses Morgan's expression once again and she suddenly becomes very busy with tidying up her lunch. 'I can just tell,' she finally says, a little impatiently. 'Just ... ask him for a coffee and see what happens. You deserve a bit of fun, Isla.'

Isla considers it for a brief second, then shakes her head and drops her remaining bits of lunch into the nearby bin with a sense of finality. 'It's hardly the time for me to be worrying about coffee with a guy. Besides, we're thinking about you at the moment, remember?'

Her stern look at her sister isn't entirely serious, but it still seems to cause a negative reaction in Morgan.

'Don't think there's a chance of me forgetting,' she murmurs, before hopping up. 'I'll go see if they need any help in the gift shop, or something.' Then she's gone, before Isla has any chance of saying anything further.

And while she's perfectly cordial towards Isla for the rest of the day and the journey home, Isla still gets the sense that somehow her refusal to ask Dylan out for coffee has caused

Morgan to begin building up her defences again. This makes no ruddy sense to Isla and she feels frustration growing; what does it matter to her sister if she goes out for coffee with Dylan Burroughs or not?

The car has barely rolled to a stop outside their house before Morgan has hopped out, called a rushed 'thanks' to Isla, then raced inside the house. Perhaps that is why Isla does not follow her inside, or perhaps she's just unable to give up on her secret miracle yet. Either way, she drifts down to the beach.

She stands in front of the stone, eyes scanning its surface with desperation. But the surface is unbroken, unscarred. There's no proof anywhere that it ever possessed the ability to let her travel back in time.

A dreadful fear that Isla has been ignoring all day blossoms in her chest, icy and uncomfortable. It's a fear that this isn't a blip, temporary and fixable, but instead a permanent closure. She's had her chance to fix the past and she's spoilt it, so that's that. No more tries.

And if that's the case, what else is there? What does she do next?

Isla rests one hand on the stone, wincing at how cold and extinct it feels. There's certainly no impossible magic beneath her fingers any more.

A crunching of stones draws her from this unpleasant thought. She turns, hand snatching away from the rock rather abruptly.

Isla's expecting it to be Morgan, or her father. Someone coming to find out why she's not come into the house yet.

But it's not. It's Dylan, looking just as perplexed as Isla feels.

Eighteen

'What are you doing here?'

The question comes out of their mouths in perfect unison. It brings a laugh from Dylan but Isla is too shocked for that. Or, if she's being honest with herself, too suspicious for that. After all, what possible reason would there be for him to be on this beach, unless he's somehow followed her all the way from the aquarium without her noticing?

Perhaps Dylan picks up on this suspicion because he hastily answers the question a second later. 'Uh, your sister invited me round for what she suggested was a thoroughly well-planned and expected coffee with you. But clearly that's not the case...'

Isla steps away from the stone. 'You... you seriously thought I had planned coffee with you and then asked my sister to ask you for me? As though we're sixteen again?'

Despite the slight chill of the beach, Dylan's cheeks redden a little. 'Uh... yeah, I guess I did.' He rubs the back of his neck, that wonky smile returning. 'How much of an idiot do I look right now, then?'

With a thoughtful noise, Isla allows herself a small smile. 'Better an idiot than a stalker, which was my initial concern.'

Dylan seems to sag slightly with relief then, before biting

his lip as he casts his eyes around the empty beach. 'So ... how about that coffee?'

Isla considers it for a moment, probably longer than is comfortable for Dylan. But if he is going to blindly follow the suggestions of her little sister, then she thinks it's only fair he gets a decent amount of squirming time.

Finally, she lets him off the hook. After all, there is something rather comforting in the thought that, despite everything, her sister went out of her way to sort this date out for her. She can't throw that all away now. 'Okay, fine. One coffee. But it can't be long, I've got dinner to do.'

The coffee turns into a shared box of chips on the harbour, when it becomes increasingly clear that they've both lost track of time and forgotten that Karrekoth's single café shuts after six so that Louisa doesn't miss *Emmerdale*. In a way, Isla is glad. She's not sure she could enjoy a coffee with that elephant-eared woman nearby, taking notes for her gossip phone calls later.

It's not quite the weather for enjoying chips on the harbour wall. The clouds are dark and there's a persistent wind buffeting against them, trying its hardest to knock them back into the grey, frothing ocean behind them. But, as residents of the village, both Isla and Dylan are well-versed in resisting a coastal wind.

Dylan takes a chip from their box and lets out a sigh of satisfaction. 'Now that's something I always miss. No other country does chips like us. And no other village does chips like Karrekoth does chips.'

Isla sniffs her amusement, shooting him a disbelieving look. 'I think a number of other countries and certainly other seaside towns might have something to say about that.'

Dylan shakes his head with a grin. 'I'm not saying we're the best at it, not by a long shot. But there's something to be said for the slightly over-enthusiastic way we throw ourselves into making them. Knowledge and expertise be damned. Though perhaps it's just because they taste like home.'

'Do you miss home, when you're away?'

Dylan considers it for a moment, legs swinging absentmindedly while his brow furrows. Isla feels a strange sense of approval to see him taking this question so seriously. 'I don't know,' he concludes at last. 'I don't think I miss it when I'm away, but when I come back I realise that perhaps I was missing it after all. Does that make sense?'

Nodding, Isla gives him an encouraging smile. 'Sure it does.'

'What about you, do you miss home when you leave it?'

Suddenly, the chips that have been sitting comfortably in her stomach begin churning anxiously. She feels the instinctive tension in her feet, preparing her to run. Because surely she can't admit to this adventurous marine biologist that she hasn't left home since she tried to go to university. And even that was only Exeter. How can she tell Dylan that whatever he thinks he knows about her family, there's so much more to it? Because she knows it will just bring on more sympathy, which always feels like being dipped in the iciest of seas.

'Why do you do that?'

Dylan's voice breaks through her slightly panicked thoughts and Isla looks up with a frown. 'Do what?'

'Whenever I mention home – or family – you go somewhere.' There's a strange sense of concern in Dylan's voice. 'Look, I know there's ... stuff with your family. But I hope you know you can always share it with me?'

It's a very lovely sentiment, but it doesn't make the answer any easier to explain. 'It's ... a little complicated.'

Dylan's crooked smile returns. 'Families tend to be. Want to talk about it? Properly, I mean. I feel as if everyone in this little village likes to think they know it all already but I'm sure there's a lot more to it than what some bored café owners think...'

Isla grins a little at that; apparently her relief at seeing the café shop closed earlier hadn't been quite as subtle as she'd thought. But she's still not expecting the nod of her own head, the apparent acceptance of Dylan's offer. For a moment, she's frozen in surprise. Then words spill from her mouth in a tidal wave. 'Mum died nine years ago and, yeah, everyone thinks they know what happened next. Everyone thinks because they saw Dad wandering lost about town in his dressing gown that they know exactly how everything fell apart. Everyone knows that Morgan ran away so everyone thinks they know how hard that was...' Isla can feel her head screaming to stop, with its instinctive need to keep everything to herself, but the message doesn't quite reach her mouth. She keeps going. 'The truth, Dylan, is that I don't miss home when I'm away because I'm never away. And I don't know what it's like to eat something and be wonderfully reminded of home because... it's always there. The furthest I ever get to go away from it is that shitty aquarium.'

Her mouth dries up then, as though her head has finally managed to switch it off. Which is all well and good, except now there's just silence. Even the bloody wind seems to stop, just to let her squirm a bit more.

'I... I didn't mean to offload on you, sorry.' Isla murmurs after a second, when the silence gets too much.

Dylan shakes his head. 'It's fine. I'm glad you did.'

'Really?'

'Sure. I mean, now it makes sense.'

'What does?'

He shifts a little and Isla senses some discomfort in him, which makes her brace a little for whatever he's about to say. 'Isla, you've always been crazy bright and you clearly know your stuff when it comes to marine biology, even if you didn't finish your degree.'

Cheeks reddening, Isla shrugs. 'I just read a lot…'

'Whatever the reason is, I guess I was a little baffled when I came back and found you still here, in that aquarium, because it didn't make sense for someone like you to be permanently working at that place. And sure, I knew about some of the stuff you've been going through with your family but it's as you said – nobody could ever know the whole story. Nobody could ever know all the things that kept you here.'

Isla frowns a little at the past tense he uses, because it's not like it's all fixed now. Sure, her dad is going out to do little jobs and generally knows what day of the week it is but Isla's still sitting with her phone on the harbour wall beside her in case there's a problem and someone calls. Things aren't fixed, not yet.

'I don't mean that as an insult,' Dylan hurriedly clarifies, clearly seeing her frown and misreading its cause.

'Oh no, I know. You didn't insult me, promise.'

Slumping a little with relief, Dylan then takes a deep breath. 'You should really go for the professor's internship, you know. You'd be great. I know there's still things going on here but…' He reaches across the small gap between them, hesitates, then pats her hand. It's a little awkward but not unpleasant. 'There's a whole lot of ocean out there and I really think you need to see it.'

'The internship… right,' Isla murmurs, vaguely remembering him mentioning it before. 'What is it again?'

Dylan laughs, rolling his eyes as he digs about in his rucksack, which has been balancing precariously on the harbour wall the whole time (and causing Isla great amounts of unease). 'It's in Hawaii. Investigating and researching shark sanctuaries. It's six months, unpaid but Professor Sawyer's company pays for accommodation and will give you a living allowance. Internships like these are often how people end up working for the professor, and I'm sure she'd take a shine to you straight away.'

Again, Isla has the strange sensation of her mind getting ready to say one thing and her body doing something else. Because it sounds amazing, of course it does. Six months in an entirely different country, a world away from Karrekoth, studying sharks? But she's already got her reasons ready for why it just wouldn't be possible. She's ready to shake her head but, instead, she finds herself nodding. 'I'll think about it, I promise,' she murmurs.

Dylan's grin is full of excitement which Isla finds a little baffling. Why should he care so much, after all? A moment later, he finds what he's looking for in his bag and hands it over. A slightly crumpled, stapled pack of papers. 'Here, a spare application form. I printed some off after Dennis looked very confused at the prospect of an online application system...'

She takes the form with slight trepidation, feels the weight of the potential it holds. The front page has Professor Sawyer's research company logo in the corner. She's seen that on countless research papers she's read. Could she really be involved with a company she has admired for so long? That sounds like the sort of dream opportunity that other people get.

But she puts it into her own bag all the same (resting safely on the ground and not the bloody wall), taking care not to crease the corners despite the haphazard storage it's clearly already had. 'Thank you, Dylan.' She sounds stiff; she knows she does. He looks pleased all the same, though.

'No problem.' He hops up then, almost scattering the box of chips into the ocean behind until Isla comes to their hasty rescue. 'So, what now? We could go for a freezing paddle?'

Isla begins to laugh at that, because she hasn't paddled in the ocean for years. But then a rumble of thunder rolls lazily across the sky above her, and any remaining threads of laughter die in her throat. Dylan's still speaking, she thinks, but his words fade to a fuzzy blur of white noise, as Isla casts her eyes up at the sky, then across towards the distant cliffs that have her beach below them. She sees how the clouds are darkening, how they seem to twist around each other like furious snakes. The wind picks up, fussing around the edges of her coat and disturbing the nearby seagulls. They take off into the air, screeching their outrage at the situation. A storm is coming.

The moment she thinks it, the lightning appears. It's right out on the distant horizon, casting the sea in an eerie glow for a moment. Just a small flash in the clouds. But it's coming this way, she's sure of it.

'Dylan,' she blurts out. 'I'm sorry. I've really got to go.'

Understandably, Dylan looks a little nonplussed. They had been halfway through a fairly pleasant evening after all. 'Oh, right. Sorry, look at me rambling on. You did say you had to get back for dinner ... and guess we don't want to get caught in a storm, right?' There's obvious disappointment in his voice and Isla feels a pang of guilt. But that pang is chased rather rapidly away when the next rumble of thunder echoes across the sky.

'Right,' Isla says, without really thinking. She can't stop watching the clouds, can't stop tracking the progress of lightning flashes. Dylan seems to notice, glancing round to stare at whatever is capturing her attention. Isla seizes this opportunity and slides off the wall, grabbing her bag from the ground. 'This ... this was really nice, Dylan,' she manages to say, her words a garbled mess. 'I'll see you around!' she calls back, already hurrying towards the beach. Isla doesn't look round, because she's pretty sure she doesn't want to see the sight of him standing, abandoned, by the harbour. Just in case it makes her stall. Because she can't stop now, not when the stone may be about to open up once more and give her another chance.

So she keeps running; she chases the storm across the harbour and back towards the beach, not slowing even when the rain begins to lash down, even when she can feel the wind whirling ever more viciously around her. All she can think about is getting to the beach. The lightning is creeping steadily closer to land and she can hear the thunder directly overhead, louder with every echoing boom.

It has to hit the stone again, it has to. And she has to be there. She doesn't even know *what* she wants from the stone, just that she has to have another chance to do something.

The beach has already become strangely marsh-like by the time she arrives, the sand thoroughly rain-sodden. It sucks at the bottom of her shoes but Isla will not allow herself to slow down. Even when she almost loses her footing, she only allows herself a half-second to get her balance again before she's hurrying on.

The waves are crashing against the nearby band of rocks, a little too close for comfort. In her haste, Isla has completely forgotten about tides. For a moment, it stops her. She knows the tide won't fully cut off her path home but there's still something unnerving about having a storm-stirred sea roaring at her from such close proximity. It's enough to bring a moment of rationality, to make her think that maybe she shouldn't be here, in the middle of a storm, on the off chance that one stone gets hit by lightning.

Of course, as is often the way with these things, her moment of doubt is immediately followed by exactly what she's here for. Lightning crackles through the air, bringing goosebumps to Isla's skin, as she watches the spindles of light rush from the sky and attack the stone. She hears a now quite familiar crack of ancient rock and she knows it's worked, that the impossible doorway has returned.

Unlike last time, the storm does not suddenly dissipate as if its work is complete. The wind continues to moan, the rain continues to fall and thunder rumbles on. But Isla doesn't hesitate any longer. She picks her way across the beach, determination crackling around her like her very own lightning as the wind seems to perfectly mimic the sound of her sister's sorrow-filled cries as she lay amongst blood-stained sheets. Because she may be seemingly okay but Isla knows that can't be completely true. So she needs to find out the truth.

The stone smells of sulphur and steam drifts off its surface, only to be whisked away almost instantly by the wind. Isla sees how the deep scar is once again visible, feels herself smile as a light glows from within.

'Let me help her this time,' she almost growls to the stone, determination rearing up inside her as her hand becomes bathed in the light. From within she hears a slam of a door, the familiar stomping of feet up stairs.

Smiling with grim triumph, Isla steps into the light and disappears once more.

Nineteen

First she hears another slam of a door, louder and more jolting now there's no stormy wind to muffle it. Isla hears that before she sees anything except the stone's light, before the world has once again reappeared around her. She should be used to it by now, but it still makes her wince.

When the light finally does clear, Isla finds herself on the upstairs landing, outside her and Morgan's bedrooms. Immediately, she notices how tightly Morgan's door is closed, and the way the posters covering it are still shivering slightly. A different type of storm has passed by them recently and Isla can guess who was responsible for it.

She takes a tentative step towards the door but she finds herself pausing almost instantly as footsteps come trudging up the nearby stairs. There's not enough time to hide or panic about being seen, and Isla finds herself freezing, as if that might somehow help her. She can only pray that the stone has made the right choice for her, and when her mother appears a second later and spares no attention to the frozen older version of her daughter standing in front of her, Isla knows it has.

Again, Isla is momentarily stunned by the appearance of her mother. Marina looks almost identical to the day she died, even though Isla is fairly sure this is some time before. Jasper always used to joke that his wife had some magical immunity to the effects of time. Isla desperately wishes that was true.

Swallowing that unpleasant thought, Isla forces herself to focus on her mother's progress across the landing. She pauses outside Morgan's door and hovers her hand inches from the wood, ready to knock. It's odd seeing her like this, with hesitation freezing her movements. Isla only remembers her being completely certain and confident in her actions, almost super-human in her decisiveness. But now Isla can see an utterly human frown upon her face as she silently plots her next move. It's nice to know she's not the only who has found Morgan's fury-cocooned sadness hard to deal with.

Finally, Marina decides against knocking and simply pushes open the door instead. Isla hears a highly familiar growl of frustration coming from within and immediately follows the sound and her mother into the room.

Morgan is sitting under the desk with the chair pulled in tightly against her legs, as if this will somehow protect her, as if all her family members have an inexplicable weakness against wheeling furniture. Isla can just about make out her sister's scowling face from the shadows and guesses that she's about eight years old. She's still wearing her hair long and in plaits, so she can't be much older than that; Isla remembers quite distinctively how nine-year-old Morgan came swanning home from the hairdresser's one day with a proud smile at her new short hair.

With a grunt of effort, Marina lowers herself to the floor and places herself next to the desk, with just enough distance to not freak out Morgan while still being able to see her. Textbook. Except Isla sometimes feels that she can give her sister all the distance in the world and it still does no good.

'Morgan?'

'Go away.' Morgan's voice is shaky but still defiant. She gives the chair an angry push with one foot but Isla can see how careful she is to not actually kick it into her mother.

'Tell me. What happened?'

'Why should I? You can't fix it.'

'How do you know?' Marina affects an expression of shock and outrage. 'You don't know what I can't fix. I fixed Dad's shoes, didn't I? And they were busted good and proper after that dog got to them.'

Morgan puffs out a breath of pure exasperation. 'Because, Mum, that was shoes! You can't use super glue and ... sewing to fix a group of nasty cows.'

'Language. Unless you're taking about Hector's actual cows.' Marina quirks an eyebrow, shifts a little closer. 'Are you talking about Hector's cows?'

Morgan tries her hardest not to smile, but she can't quite suppress the reluctant giggle. 'No,' she murmurs a moment later. 'I was talking about the nasty—' she hesitates, giving her mother a wary look '—idiots? At school.'

'Hmm, moderately better. Which idiots?'

Morgan sighs, wriggling until only her head is poking out from under the desk. It requires some rather impressive contortions but she manages it. 'The kids in my class. I got told off for talking in class even though I *needed* to and then at break they wouldn't leave me alone, kept saying how I was the naughtiest person in the class and that Miss was going to get me thrown out ...' At this point, Morgan pauses and even from her spot a few steps back, Isla can see her sister's demeanour change from self-righteousness to shiftiness.

'And then what?' Marina prompts with extreme gentleness, though there's a glint in her eye that suggests she knows what's coming.

Morgan groans, rests her head against the floor. 'Then I kicked Drew and got in trouble. Miss said that nice girls shouldn't use violence to get their point across. Then I said what about Boudicca because we was learning about her in History and she definitely used violence … and Miss told me I was answering back and I had to spend five minutes inside at lunch.' With her story complete, Morgan lets out a final rather dramatic noise of frustration before hiding her face in the carpet.

Silence settles into place and Isla finds her attention falling back onto her mother. She knows what her mother will be thinking about Morgan's teacher's idea of what 'nice girls' should be doing; Marina had, after all, brought her girls up with the stories of Emmeline Pankhurst and Rosa Parks, and the message that girls did not owe anybody their smile unless it had been earned. But Isla can't quite work out what she'll tell Morgan about her opinion of her teacher. After all, Morgan had a bit of a reputation for repeating her parents' words indiscriminately to others. Isla could still remember the infamous time when Morgan had told her Reception teacher that her mum thought she was 'overdue an operation to remove the stick out of her bottom'. That had been an exceedingly awkward pick-up time.

'Mogs, come here …' Marina says after a long moment of quiet.

'Are you going to tell me off for kicking Drew?'

'Eventually, but that can wait.'

Isla can see her sister carefully deliberating this, can see the cogs of her brain whirring into overdrive as she makes her decision. Finally, she appears to concede to the idea, wriggling out from under the desk a moment later and flopping down onto her mother's lap.

'You know what I'm going to say …' Marina begins, after a moment of tenderly freeing her daughter's hair from its plaited confines. 'What have you forgotten?'

Morgan sighs, pushing a stray strand of hair away from her face with great impatience. Yes, the drastic haircut is definitely around the corner. 'You're always on my side,' she mumbles.

Marina nods, tilting her head so she can look at her daughter a little more directly. 'Even ...?' she prompts.

Another sigh from Morgan, this time full of inevitability. 'Even if it doesn't always feel like it.' She's silent for a moment and Marina leans back against the desk, giving her a little more space. 'So I should have just told you instead of storming out of the car and up here?'

'Ladies and gents, we have a winner!' Marina exclaims with a chuckle, giving Morgan's side a gentle prod until she squirms away. 'But you know that goes for your teacher too. Miss Bradley was right to tell you off for kicking, though I'm not entirely sure what it has to do with you being a nice girl ... but you should have just gone to her first instead of assuming she'd be against you. Am I right?'

Morgan sticks her bottom lip out, deepens her frown. Isla remembers that look, the look for when Morgan knew she had to admit to being wrong and was trying her best to avoid it. But she gives in relatively promptly, giving her mother a rueful look before nodding slowly. 'Yes ...'

Marina smiles with approval and, Isla notices, slight relief. Isla can understand that; it wasn't always this easy with Morgan after all. Sometimes the under-desk hiding could go on for hours.

'Well, that's that sorted then. I suggest we waste no more time on this floor and you come help me in the garden. There's a whole load of weeds that need your savage pulling skills.' Morgan considers this for a moment, then lets out a small, rather fiendish-sounding chuckle.

'Can I use Dad's big shears on the tricky ones?'

'Will you promise to keep all your fingers?'

'Ugh, you're no fun.' Morgan's eyes are all light now, as she presses a kiss to her mother's cheek, then scrambles out of her mother's lap and out of the room.

For a moment, Isla is left alone with just her mother. It's strange to stand there, invisible, and watch the way she lets this rare bit of solitude settle against her shoulders and ease the tension out of them. There's just a split second where Isla sees vulnerability and worry flit across her mother's face. It's so different from the confidence she always wore in front of her family, wrapped around her like a familiar scarf. She's human once again, not just a mother with the tools to fix everything.

But this moment is gone almost instantly. Morgan shouts for her to hurry up and Marina blinks herself back into mother mode and leaves the room. Isla wants to follow; she's desperate to see more of how Marina wrangled Morgan out of her sulks. She remembers now, how much Morgan thrived on feeling helpful and useful. She doesn't get a chance though; she manages one step forward before the sea breeze returns to whip around her ankles and tug her from this moment. Isla tries to resist, tries to dig her feet into the carpet of Morgan's bedroom but the wind pays no attention. The room disappears and the sea is soon crashing furiously around her once more, oblivious to the impossible time travel happening on its beach.

But Isla doesn't hang around. It's still stormy after all, but it's more than that. This little visit has given Isla plenty to think about and she knows what to do. Buoyed by the past words of her mother, she sets off back home.

Morgan's door is, of course, closed when Isla reaches it. She can still see the speckled scars of the Sellotape that stuck her posters to the wood, even if said posters are long gone. But somehow those scars give Isla the confidence she needs; they remind her that this is still the same room, that this is still the same Morgan she just watched her mother successfully help. Older and more complicated, yes, but still the same person.

So with that thought bolstering her, Isla takes a deep breath and pushes open the door. Her sister may no longer be wearing her hair in plaits or hiding under desk, but Isla hopes that this more direct approach of her mother's might still do the trick.

Morgan is sitting at her window, hot-water bottle back in place and sketchbook spread open on her lap. Though Isla can't see much sketching on the page just yet. The moment Isla opens the door and steps across the threshold, Morgan snaps the book shut. Isla notices an almost urgency in the way her sister then discards the hot-water bottle, as if she might somehow succeed in hiding her lingering pain from Isla.

'That door was shut.' It's not quite a 'go away' but it's certainly not far off.

'Well, now it's open.' Isla keeps her voice as non-confrontational as she can. It seems to work. Morgan continues to frown but doesn't try to force her out of the room yet. A small victory that Isla will certainly take.

With the caution of a zookeeper working in the lion enclosure, Isla sits down at the very far end of Morgan's bed, as far away from Morgan as she can manage.

'Thank you,' Isla finally says, after a few seconds of heavy silence.

Morgan slowly sits back by the window. Isla can see how every one of her limbs seems rigid, defensive. 'Thank me ... for what?'

'For tricking Dylan into coming over.'

Morgan's cheeks flush. 'Oh. He told you?'

'It was pretty hard for him to explain how he ended up on

our beach otherwise, not without coming across as someone who needs police attention ... When did you ask him?'

Morgan shrugs, eyes fixed on her feet. 'Before we left the aquarium. I guess I knew already that you never would make the first move and, well, he doesn't strike me as the sort to either. So I helped you guys out.'

Isla hesitates, before standing up and coming to sit beside her sister on the windowsill. Morgan budges up to make space, but Isla notices that she's not overly desperate to get away from her. That's a positive sign at least. 'And that's why you were being weird in the car?' she asks gently. 'Because you were being super weird, you know.'

Morgan sighs, resting her head back against the window. 'Yeah, I know and ... I guess so. And because you did that thing again, in the staffroom. That thing when you're just ... too kind,' Morgan finally says. It's not exactly what Isla is expecting and it would seem this is obvious from her expression, because Morgan goes on a few seconds later. 'I know that sounds nuts.'

'Just a little.'

'But it's just ... I'd had this horrible thing happen and you just went straight to looking after me and I wanted to repay you, but you never let anyone do anything for you because ... Well, I don't really know why.' She glances across to Isla. 'I guess I was just frustrated that you never let me help you.'

Isla thinks back to the conversation she witnessed on this very bedroom floor, and on the way her sister's eyes immediately lit up when she was given an opportunity to help her mother. It can't be that simple, can it?

Shifting until she's more directly facing her sister, Isla smiles steadily. 'Well, I need your help now.'

Morgan's expression is full of surprise. 'Really? What about?'

'I ... sort of left Dylan quite abruptly on the harbour. I needed to get back here and sort stuff, like dinner,' Isla catches the suspicious look in Morgan's eyes and hurries right on past that particular lie of hers, 'but I don't want him to think I didn't have a nice time because I did, I really did. So … what should I do next?'

'You just left him?' Morgan rolls her eyes. 'You're an idiot. Dad and I are perfectly capable of making dinner. Well, I am. What did you say?'

'Just that I had to go and that I'd had a really nice time with him.'

'Wow, dreamy. Well, you'll have to message him or something. So he knows you actually meant it. Find him on Facebook or whatever old-person thing you use, then he'll know you put some effort into it as well. And reiterate that you had a nice time and that you're sorry you had to run off.'

'Really? That simple?'

Morgan shrugs, picking at a flaky bit of paint on the windowsill. 'Sure. It was only a first date, if we're even calling it that. He's not owed anything else from you. Remember what Mum always said? A woman does not need to explain herself to anyone, especially not a man.'

Isla feels her smile tickle the corners of her mouth. 'Dad used to get driven mad by that, especially when she said it that time there were ten live crabs swimming around the bath …'

Morgan giggles at that, a sound so rare that Isla's heart always swoops a little hearing it. 'Did we ever find out why she had those in there?'

Isla shakes her head slowly. 'They were gone by the time we got back from school the next day and she never mentioned them again …'

Smiling, Morgan shakes her head. Then she reaches across the tiny gap between them and takes her sister's hand, squeezing gently. It surprises Isla so much that it takes her a moment to return it. But she does, feeling the warmth spread right from her fingers to her chest.

'I wish she was here ... *so much* sometimes.' These words come after a moment of silence and, when Isla glances at her sister, it's as if Morgan isn't looking at her bedroom any more, but an entirely different scene. 'I mean, I miss her all the time, of course, but it's a bit like ... an eternal bruise. Always there but not always painful, until something knocks it and the pain comes flooding back.' Her free hand starts to pick at the already ravaged paintwork around the window again. 'I keep thinking about how she'd know exactly what to say to all of us right now. She'd get Dad back to normal and you out of that stupid aquarium and ... well, who knows where she'd start with me.'

Isla hesitates, then wraps one arm around her sister's shoulder and draws her in close. 'She'd say thank you for coming back.'

Morgan stiffens against her and, for a moment, Isla has the sensation of hugging a statue. Then her sister softens a little, head resting on her shoulder. 'That simple?'

Isla considers the question for a moment, considers how dark and lonely this house has felt for the last four years. It's easy then to nod her agreement. 'That simple,' she replies and, for once, feels confidence in each word.

Twenty

Marina Pembroke used to read to her daughters every night, even when perhaps they were both too old to really need it any more. Neither daughter ever complained about that, though, not when their mother's voice had the ability to drown out even the most caterwauling of storms. Not when her arms would wrap around them like two sturdy harbour walls and the sense of safety would feel so complete, so unshakeable that Isla would feel that she could take on anything waiting for her beyond their front door.

And especially not when she read from *that* book. *Coastal Tales for the Adventurous*, treasured greatly by their mother from her own childhood and beyond. Its leather-bound spine was intensely battered and the painted illustration on the front was faded to almost invisibility, except for the stubbornly vibrant tentacles of a giant squid reaching out from beneath the faint outlines of waves.

There were thirteen stories in that book and each Pembroke family member had their favourite. Morgan loved the one about the haunted lighthouse, Marina always chose the tale about the spirits of the wind and sea, while Jasper begrudgingly enjoyed the story about the foolish pirate and his false treasure. As for

Isla, she was fascinated by the tale of the giant squid and the lonely whale.

But now, as the morning sunshine kisses the top of the stone, making the still-damp surface glisten almost magically, Isla finds herself reminded of one story in particular. She can see the illustration spread out on the page, as clear as day. The seething and unavoidable whirlpool that sucked unwitting boats into its depths, broke their masts neatly in two and scattered unfortunate sailors into the mouth of the hungry sea. As she stands in front of this rock once more, knowing that she doesn't *really* need to be here, she can't help but wonder if she's being sucked down a whirlpool of her own.

Why is she here, after all? Morgan spent the previous evening around Isla and Jasper with a truly warming look of content on her face the whole time; Jasper even had the energy and wherewithal to help load the dishwasher. Her family is making tiny but important steps towards normality without any time-travel magic.

And yet, Isla can't help but think that those steps could be a lot bigger if she came back to the stone. So here she is, standing in the shine of a barely risen sun, wondering if this stone won't be quite so obliging as to let her come back home this time and will slurp her down into the depths of time for good.

Perhaps sensing her hesitation, the stone begins to shine out in a rather persistent way. Isla feels its potential to help seeping out onto the sand and how can she resist that? Like that unfortunate ship, she is slurped right back in. She feels the beach disappear. There's the usual few seconds where all she can see is white, then the world returns.

Isla gives herself a moment to blink the spots away from her vision, before taking in her new surroundings.

It's immediately obvious that she's gone back to another

moment after her mother died. She can tell this easily from the disorganised piles of laundry scattered around their family kitchen. Her mother was a little scatty, yes, but her chaos was always organised in some way. But now the laundry lies in turmoil, strewn across the table as if the washing machine has spat it out of its own accord. The smell of damp fabric hangs in the air. This is the kitchen of a Pembroke family still stuck firmly in the pit of despair.

The house seems quiet, empty. But as Isla steps from room to room, she begins to make out the faint sound of crying coming from upstairs. She recognises it as Morgan almost instantly; that sound has become entirely ingrained in her memory, funnily enough. And, like some sort of sniffer dog, she's compelled to follow it.

She finds Morgan upstairs, sitting on the next flight of stairs that went from the first floor to their parents' bedroom at the top of the house. In typical Morgan style, she has managed to twist herself into the smallest possible shape and fill the tiniest fraction of space. Isla approaches cautiously, though she's becoming increasingly sure that she is once again invisible. Whether Morgan would notice her anyway is dubious; she is crying full pelt with her face buried in the crooks of her arms, though that's not enough to fully smother the desperate cries.

But Isla doesn't know why her sister is sitting alone crying with nobody to comfort her. Where is everybody? It's not as though Jasper left the house often during this time, if at all. And even he would hear this sound amongst the fog of his own despair, drawn by the battered remnants of fatherly instinct to try and help her, however fruitlessly.

Then Isla sees the haphazard garland of paper snowflakes on her own bedroom door and realises what day this must be, realises why her sister must be alone.

'Christmas shopping,' Isla whispers. She went Christmas shopping but Morgan refused to come, arguing that it felt fake and pointless. Jasper, on the other hand, was having one of his rare 'good' days and was surprisingly easy to convince once he was reminded about the hardware store. So they went out and left her sister at home for a couple of hours. Isla can still remember the adolescent scorn Morgan doled out when Isla checked she would be okay on her own. *'Ugh, I'm twelve, not three.'* So much for that.

She was fine when they got back though, Isla's sure of it. So what happened?

The answer comes floating down the stairs just seconds later. An open window or an exposed crack has let in the perfect breeze, just right for carrying a ripped page of yellowing paper down the stairs.

It comes to rest at Isla's feet, almost as if it's wanting to be seen by her. She gets a glimpse of shimmering scales on the other side, before it settles fully to the ground. A foreboding creeps into her bones, instantly chilling them. She knows those scales; she knows what this ripped piece of paper is from.

Picking her way around her still-crying sister, Isla starts an almost urgent journey upstairs. Every step feels precarious, unsteady. As if the floor is about to collapse and send her crashing down to the foundations. But she keeps going, until she reaches the top floor and sees the carnage her sister has caused.

Their mother's old storybook lies in pieces. Isla sees whole chunks of stories torn out in one go and left in somewhat intact piles, but then there's also clusters of tiny fragments of paper, piled up like autumn leaves. The leather-bound cover lies upside down, spine crippled and crumpled, by their parents' bedroom door. The carefully inked illustration of the unrelenting whirlpool is in four pieces by the top of the stairs. It looks as if it is completely destroyed.

'Morgan ... what have you done?' Isla hears her own whispered question distantly, like it's coming from the next room. There's a thick cloud of shock and confusion wrapping around her, blurring the world. Why would her sister do this? She adored this book, more than anyone. And how has Isla gone all these years without knowing what she did?

The answer to that second question comes stumbling up the stairs behind Isla, tripping over her own feet as her continued sobbing knocks her off balance. Morgan comes to a halt inches away; Isla could reach across and touch her if she wanted to, but Isla's not sure she would trust herself to do that right now. She might end up shoving her instead. There's an almost blinding rage beginning to build inside her, thick as tar, the more she sees of the destroyed book. Her sister had no right, no right to take this precious artifact and decimate it. It was *their* book. No, it was their *mother's* book. It was never just Morgan's.

But, despite the fury, all Isla can do is watch. Watch as her sister drops to the floor and stares at her handiwork. Isla watches her shoulders hitch higher and higher, feels a savage satisfaction at hearing Morgan's crying get more and more hysterical. Her usual instinct to want to help her is long gone, stuck beneath layers of anger and dismay.

Until she hears Morgan's voice, frail and quivering. 'I ... I didn't mean to ...'

Isla is floored then. She's heard that sentence so many times from Morgan over the years, almost like a catchphrase. It shouldn't cause her so much surprise. But it does. Because she's heard it so many times and never really believed it; never believed she didn't mean to snap Isla's favourite pen when she was seven or didn't mean to ruin her birthday treat by having a tantrum at the entrance of the London Aquarium. But she can't accept that Morgan would have deliberately destroyed the book she loved so dearly. So maybe she didn't mean all those other times either. Maybe she didn't mean to leave her family and break their hearts all over again.

There's a chink in her anger now; she can't help it. She can't help but see this wreckage as nothing but a terrible error caused by a dreadfully hurting girl. She can't help but see Morgan's running away in a new light, where she didn't want to hurt them, perhaps didn't even really mean to go.

All this is enough to make Isla kneel down beside her sister and watch her with concern rather than anger. She feels the rage simmer down until there's only all-too-familiar worry for her sister.

Morgan's hands hover over the remnants of the book, transfer from one ripped page to another. Until finally she finds the page with the twirling spirit of the wind leaping joyfully over the smiling spirit of the waves. Marina's favourite story. Morgan scoops it up, presses it to her chest as if she might be able to absorb it right into her heart. She can't of course, but it seems to give her the strength she needs to scoop up every broken bit of the book. Isla sees the tenderness in her fingers, the way she smooths out the crinkles in a somewhat futile attempt to fix this mess. It cements Isla's belief that Morgan really didn't mean to destroy this book. And, as Isla follows Morgan around the landing and then down the stairs with her pile of pages, Isla can't help but wish she could reverse this mistaken destruction for her sister. An impossible task, though perhaps not so much now.

Her sister carefully stows the remnants of the storybook at the back of her wardrobe then leaves her bedroom rather abruptly, as if she's more likely to forget about it the less time she spends with it. Her head dips low and her arms are wrapped tightly around her torso, a protective posture against her own actions. Isla supposes she'll spend the next few hours carefully putting herself together again, ready to pretend to her returning family that nothing out of the ordinary has happened.

Isla takes a tentative step forward and opens the wardrobe, staring at the carefully hidden carcass of her childhood. But there isn't anger any more. Just a hollow sorrow that her sister was so broken that she had to destroy something so precious to her, and then hide it away all this time.

How much did that guilt eat away at her insides? Did that play some strange part in her leaving? A secret so heavy that she could no longer hold it in, so she just had to run away?

Tentatively, as if the pages are interwoven with explosives, Isla reaches into the wardrobe and pulls out the destroyed book. There's a brief moment where she worries that being able to touch these pages means she's now visible but then Isla decides there's no time to worry about that. She creeps from the room and into her own bedroom, nudging the door shut behind her.

With that done, she spreads the pages out on the bed. She panics for a second, as she's suddenly overwhelmed with the enormity of her task. Can she really fix this? Yes, she decides, she can. Or she can give it a damn good go. She grabs the Sellotape from her own desk, silently thanking her past self for keeping the same stationery organisation as she does now. Then she gets to work.

Isla isn't sure how long it takes her to finish fixing the book, but she does notice the darkness starting to draw in as she tapes together the final page. The house has stayed silent the whole time she has worked and she can only imagine where Morgan has gone to ensure there's no inkling of this event in her expression when her family return. Probably the beach, which doesn't fill Isla with that much comfort, as she looks out at the wintry evening taking hold.

But there's nothing she can do for that Morgan. Not without presenting herself to her sister and causing another trauma in her younger life. So Isla gathers the haphazardly mended book against her chest and comes to stand in the middle of the bedroom. For a moment she stands waiting, feeling a little foolish. The stone has always yanked her away at its own leisure (and usually a tad prematurely if Isla ever got the chance to offer some feedback to said stone), but now Isla is ready to go back and she feels nothing; no wind, no sand at her ankles. Typical.

To make matters worse, as Isla stands waiting she begins to hear the thudding of approaching footsteps. She tries to convince her panicking mind that it's probably just Morgan coming back to her own bedroom. But a moment later Isla hears her own voice:

'I'm just going to put these bags in my room, Dad! Then I'll make us a tea!'

Of course.

Isla casts her eyes around the room, desperately considering where she can hide. There's the wardrobe, which is exactly where her past self will put those bags, and there's under the desk. Neither is anywhere near useful.

She's just taking a desperate step towards the desk, which feels like the best out of the two options, when the much-awaited feeling of wind around her begins.

'Took your bloody time,' Isla snaps at the sand now tossed about her feet. In what seems to be a response, the room rather abruptly disappears, just as she sees her bedroom door beginning to open.

A moment later, she is face to face with dark, rain-slicked

rock. The glowing light from within its core burns at her eyes then slowly dissipates, leaving her in the gloom of a no longer sunny morning.

Isla stumbles back from the stone, head feeling a little groggy. But there's also triumph, still warming her insides despite the blustery wind around her, as she glances down at the leather-bound book clutched against her chest. Granted, the daylight makes it look even more tattered, but it's still their old book. It's got to mean something.

She smiles at the thought, turns round to leave.

And spots Morgan, standing three feet away. She's staring at Isla, eyes wide and almost luminescent with their surprise.

'Isla? Where the hell did you come from?'

Twenty-One

'Isla?'

It's been too long already. Isla knows it's been too long already. Her sister is staring, waiting, and already the pause has been too long for Morgan to be brushed off, to be fooled into thinking this is an ordinary encounter.

But still the words won't come.

'Isla! Have you turned to stone yourself?'

Morgan steps forward, jabs her sister's arm a little forcefully. It seems to do the trick for Isla, and she shakes her head. 'What are you doing here?' she finally asks, deciding that ignoring her sister's question is the best decision for now.

'Looking for you. You didn't show up for breakfast. Dad was freaking out … what the hell are *you* doing here?' Morgan's staring at her incredulously, and Isla can't blame her. Though part of her, a little uncharitably perhaps, can't help but feel satisfied that now Morgan knows how it feels to look for a missing sister.

'I … came for a walk.'

'You just stepped out of the rock.'

'No … I didn't.'

Morgan skirts around her sister, eyes fixed on the stone with an almost wary disbelief. 'You absolutely did. You stepped out of that rock, which was glowing … Isla, what is going on?' She turns back to Isla, a defiant glint in her eye. She's daring Isla to lie. But then her eyes land on the book gripped tightly in her sister's arms and she immediately frowns.

'Is … Is that …' Her voice is soft, yet somehow audible over the sea breeze. 'That's Mum's book. How do you have Mum's book?'

'It's complicated.' Isla steps away from the stone, as if that might tempt her sister to follow. It doesn't. Morgan stares at her sister as if she's speaking a different language.

'But that's impossible. You … you can't have that.'

'Why not?' Isla feels the sharpness of her words and winces a little, guiltily watching as Morgan stumbles back.

'Because …' she begins, and there's a definite shine to her eyes now. 'Because I …'

'Because you ripped it up,' Isla finishes, somehow managing to keep her voice a good deal gentler. It still brings a flinch from Morgan. 'Mogs, it's okay, really.'

'How can you know that?' Morgan's voice is a shocked croak, before her eyes flick back over to the stone. She darts around Isla, carefully runs her hand over the stone, her fingers finding the thin fissure almost immediately. Instantly she recoils, expression full of understandable shock.

'It's hot … Why is the stone hot, Isla?'

Isla feels her mouth open and shut uselessly like a fish out of water. 'Morgan,' she begins, 'it's just a rock—'

'Isla! Come on! You're being super weird lately! You've been out even more than I have, you've missed cooking dinner more than once which even I know is unheard of for you, and you keep randomly running off without any proper explanation!' She steps forward, her fingers gently jabbing the book in Isla's arms. 'And now you have a book that I know for a fact should be ripped up and at the bottom of my suitcase, not Sellotaped together in your hands!'

Gritting her teeth, Isla looks back towards the shadowy silhouette of the stone, just about visible in the gloomy morning. 'Fine, *fine*. I ... I found something in the stone.'

Morgan rolls her eyes, irritation blooming from her. 'What did you find, a lion and a witch?'

Isla decides to ignore that probably warranted sarcasm, though it doesn't particularly help her confidence in telling the truth. She knows it's going to sound insane. 'A ...' Isla hesitates on the precipice of the truth, feeling a fear fluttering in her chest.

'A strip club? A toilet? A what, Isla?'

Glaring at her sister and her impatience, Isla shakes her head. 'It sounds crazy but ... I found a way to the past.'

Morgan is silent, allowing Isla's panic to grow nicely. Her sister's not going to believe her, her sister's going to notify the appropriate authorities and it's going to be a terrible, awful mess.

'Right. Of course you did.'

Groaning, Isla steps forward and holds the book out. 'I promise you, Morgan! How else would I have got this? I've ... I've been using the stone to go back in time and it took me to the day you tore this up and I – I fixed it!'

She can see a glimmer of something in Morgan's eyes, something that might be close to acceptance. But her sister shakes it away. 'That's fucking insane, Isla! Stop this. You clearly just went through my suitcase and found it and fixed it or – or something.'

'Or something, right. Or I did it in the past and brought it back here.' Isla takes a deep breath, as her brain frantically scans through her stone experiences and latches onto something that could be proof. 'Morgan, I know that Dad left you alone in the hospital.'

Morgan is still, so still that even the wind seems to somehow skirt around her. 'What?' she says finally, voice hushed.

There's a lump in Isla's throat now, as she remembers that awful, lonely sight of her little sister sitting in a hospital waiting room all on her own, because their father couldn't handle their new reality. 'You never told me that he left you alone, you never told me that when you phoned me, you were sitting all by yourself in a hospital ... you never told me, but I *saw* it. The stone let me see it, Morgan.'

Morgan watches her for a long moment, looking every bit as small as she did in that hospital. Then, slowly, she glances back to the stone. 'It's like the story ...' she whispers, as she takes a step closer.

Isla is stumped. 'What story?'

Rolling her eyes, Morgan's gaze snaps back to her sister. 'Honestly, did you not listen all those times we read it?' She tosses her hair out of her face rather imperiously, before stepping forward and taking the book from her sister. Isla feels her arms instinctively tighten around it for a second, until she forces herself to remember that she brought it back for her sister in the first place. She has to trust her not to destroy it all over again.

Morgan sits down on the nearest rock, carefully turns the pages until she finds what she's looking for. Isla sees the upside-down yet still vivid illustration of lightning striking sand. 'In here. There was that story about the wind and the ocean ... and the lightning.' Morgan's voice sounds a little smaller, as it often does when she starts talking about the past. Almost as if she's trying to shrink herself back to that age. 'The ocean's sister is struck by lightning and in her grief she carves the stone ... and if lightning strikes the stone—'

'It opens a door to the past,' Isla finishes. Morgan nods, somewhat dazed. 'But Morgan, that's a story ...'

'And yet here we are.'

*

Sister surveys sister, both apparently unaware of the dark clouds descending, or the wind still whipping around them. Realisation, thick like fog, wraps around them.

'Shit...' Isla finally says, the word seeming pathetic and tiny on her tongue. But there's no alternative coming to her.

Morgan laughs, the sound tremulous and shaky. 'Yeah, shit. So, when do I get a turn?'

The abrupt change of direction takes Isla by surprise for a moment. But then she frowns, turning away and starting back towards the house again. 'You don't. It's not a game, Morgan. And the stuff you see is... tough.'

Morgan catches her up with ease. Distantly, Isla feels some relief that clearly her cramps have got better. 'I didn't say it was a game. I'm not a child, Isla. If you get to go see the past, then why shouldn't I?'

The house slides into view as they round the corner. Isla can see the kitchen light glowing out like a lighthouse but she turns away, facing her sister fully again. 'It's not about being a child.'

'What is it then?'

'Morgan...'

'Tell me, Isla. Tell me why!'

'Morgan. You ran away for four years because you couldn't handle the reality of what happened to us so what makes you think you can handle seeing it again?'

Morgan's almost excited gleam in her eyes snuffs out immediately and Isla knows she's said too much. But it's the truth, isn't it? How can her sister expect to cope with real-time experiences of their past when it's still haunting her present so cruelly?

'That's not why I ran away,' she snaps.

'Well, you've never told me otherwise.'

Morgan grits her teeth, pushes past Isla and, without another a word, storms off towards their house.

Isla watches her leave, suddenly exhausted by the feeling of an opportunity passing her by. The back door slams shut ahead of her, the sound resonating eerily through the gusts of wind, and Isla can only follow it.

She's a whole hour late to work by the time she's got inside, got properly dressed and got herself over to the aquarium. Nobody seems to notice and Isla knows she should be relieved by this but instead she just feels irritated. What is the point in her being here if people don't even care if she's not?

Dylan is hovering around the Pacific Ocean section, apparently waiting for her. It's a testament to how much has happened in the past twelve hours that it takes her a moment to work out why seeing him fills her chest with a new pang of guilt. Then she remembers, rather abruptly.

'Dylan!' she blurts out, as she places a box full of various supplies down on the nearby counter.

He looks a little taken aback, which is entirely understandable. She has just somewhat shouted in his face, after all. 'Uh, hello.'

'Are you okay? You look as if you're waiting for something.'

Dylan laughs a little. 'I was waiting for you, actually. I just wanted to check you were okay after your sudden, desperate need to cook dinner last night...'

Isla feels her cheeks warming and she just hopes the lights from the tanks are dim enough to hide this. 'Oh. Right. Yes, I'm fine.' She stops, lips pursing together as she tries to consider how she can apologise for running off without having to explain why she did it in the first place.

Dylan surprises her though, by apparently being satisfied enough by her words to move on entirely. 'Cool. That's good. So, did you think any more about that internship?'

Shit. The internship. In the rush of two visits to the past, a discovery by Morgan and then a subsequent argument with Morgan, Isla has completely forgotten about that. Well, that's another worry to add to the ever-growing pile, she thinks bitterly.

'Um ... not really, no. I mean, I got sort of busy.'

'Right. Dinner is very distracting,' Dylan replies, grinning now. It's entirely light-hearted and Isla tries to smile but it feels like trying to move concrete across her face. Apparently this shows because Dylan tilts his head, eyebrows furrowed. 'Isla? Are you okay?' he asks, before holding up a hand to bring Isla's immediate response to a halt. 'And I mean, are you *actually* okay, not just whether you're pretending to be.'

That stumps Isla; nobody ever wants to know whether she's *actually* okay. Only if she's okay enough to do whatever they need her to do. Swallowing, she finds herself sitting down on the small chair beside a tank full of golden butterfly fish, who immediately scatter away from her.

'I had a bit of a fight with my sister this morning.' The words tumble out of their own accord, which seems to be a bit of a habit when she's around Dylan.

Dylan shifts until he's resting against the small area of tank-free wall in this room. 'Ah ... what was it about?'

He sounds genuinely concerned; perhaps that's why Isla finds herself able to answer. Though even her suddenly over-keen mouth manages to omit certain key details. 'She asked to do something with me and I said no ... It's just that she's not ready and I don't want to make things worse for her. But obviously she doesn't see it that way. Still, it's fine. She'll just have to get over it.'

There's a long silence and Isla can see from Dylan's frown that he's mulling over his next words carefully. That settles a slight foreboding in her chest. 'What?' she prompts, a little sharply. 'Do you think I should have let her?'

'Well, it's a little hard to comment when you've given me literally zero details about anything, but isn't it her choice, to decide whether she wants to take the risk?'

Isla shakes her head rapidly. 'It's not ... it's not that simple, you don't know Morgan. She'll never be able to cope and then we'll be right back to square one.'

'And wouldn't you rather she did that beside you?' Dylan sighs, pushing off the wall and moving until he's stood a little closer to her. 'Look, like you said, I don't really know Morgan but from the little I *do* know, she strikes me as the sort of person to not let her sister stop her from doing what she wants. So, if this mysterious thing is going to be so potentially damaging for her, wouldn't you rather be there to help her?'

Isla snorts a little at that, feeling a slight pounding starting in her head that has nothing to do with the somewhat fluorescent lighting in the room. 'Morgan doesn't let me help her; that's the problem.'

'Do people who don't want help come back after being away for four years?' Dylan's question is asked innocently, but Isla can see in his eyes that he knows he's got her there. Perhaps that's why he backs off slightly a moment later. 'Look, Isla, I'm certainly in no position to really offer any advice. But I'd hate for Morgan to get herself into a scrape without you there to help her out of it.' He briefly rests one hand on her shoulder, then rather suddenly turns and heads for the door. 'I've got to get on. But maybe just think about it, yeah? And don't forget that internship! Hawaii's sharks need you!' he calls back as he leaves.

Then he's gone, leaving Isla with the fish, the fluorescent lights, and a dilemma.

*

Morgan comes thudding down the stairs the moment Isla's closed the front door behind her. She's dressed for a windy walk on the beach; leggings, boots, a thick fleece. Perhaps she's just being practical but Isla can't help but take it as a show of defiance.

'Good day?'

Isla surveys her sister with open suspicion at her sudden interest. 'The usual,' she replies, a little slowly. 'Yourself?'

'Yes, fine.' Morgan follows Isla down the hallway and into the kitchen. There's a steely edge to the gaze she sets upon Isla and Isla thinks she can guess what's coming.

She's not disappointed.

'I thought about it. All day,' Morgan states with an almost savage satisfaction, glowering at her sister. 'And I want to go through the stone.'

Isla puts the kettle on before answering, turning to face Morgan with arms crossed. 'And presumably you've got a way to convince me? Something better than just storming off?'

Morgan's jaw tightens but Isla can see she's refusing to let herself be riled. Damn, that would have made things easier. 'Yes. If you don't let me go with you, I'll just go on my own.'

Isla can feel Dylan's imagined triumph radiating into the kitchen like a sunrise. 'That's it?' she mutters, trying to shrug away Morgan's point.

Morgan shrugs, shining out with the confidence that Isla is currently lacking. 'It's all I need. Or are you really going to just sit back and let me go to God knows when ... on my own?'

There's an exceptionally smug look on Morgan's face and, unfortunately, it's not entirely misplaced. Dylan already knew it, and deep down so does Isla. She knows that her protectiveness will always trump everything else.

'I'm guessing your silence is surrender?'

Isla grits her teeth, switching the kettle off with a resigned sigh. Clearly tea isn't going to be a possibility any time soon. 'Fine,' she says finally. 'On one condition.' She turns back round, faces her sister head-on. 'I brought back the book for you because I know you didn't mean to destroy it. But if we're going to do this, I need some honesty from you. Starting now. So tell me: why did you rip it up?'

There's a long silence but Isla can wait, especially when she can see Morgan is taking the question into serious consideration. Her brow is deeply furrowed and her gaze is a little distant; Isla can imagine she's looking upon a very different scene. Probably one involving a decimated storybook.

'I wanted it to help. I went to look at it and I wanted it to help so much... but it made things worse. I kept turning the pages, over and over, trying to find one story that would make me feel... *something*. But all they made me feel was sick and scared and... furious. I got so mad and then suddenly I'd ripped a page. After that it was like I'd opened up these floodgates. I couldn't stop. I just kept ripping and tearing... until it was all gone. All broken.' Morgan sighs, pressing the heel of her hand into her forehead. 'I didn't know what to do. I couldn't let you see what I'd done so I... hid it. And you never asked.'

Isla has to concede that Morgan is right there. She never did ask; she hadn't really thought about the book for years. It was just another painful memory that she didn't have time to get stuck in.

She's aware that Morgan is staring at her, almost desperately. Presumably waiting for some sort of response from her. If only Isla knew which one was right.

So Isla decides it's just easier to move on, to accept that her sister made a mistake and that the stone has now allowed her to fix it. 'Have you put it somewhere safe? That's not your suitcase?' she asks. Once Morgan nods, Isla sighs her acceptance. 'Good.' Taking a deep breath, she moves round the table and back towards her sister. 'Okay, we can go to the stone. But you do exactly what I say, right?'

Morgan hops up straight away, triumph gleaming from her eyes and all traces of worry gone, for the moment. 'Yes ma'am.' She races round the table and pushes open the back door, sending the elements whooshing inside. Her eyebrows raise expectantly as she looks to her sister and Isla feels like a fish trussed up in a net. Nowhere to escape.

She sighs, steps towards the door. 'Okay. Let's do this.'

Twenty-Two

Isla thought she was used to the light from the stone but, as she waits for it to fade from her eyes, she can still feel it smarting, almost burning. She knows she could close them but she's got her sister next to her and Isla is determined to keep an exceedingly close eye on her. Morgan hovers like a hummingbird, full of anxious energy. It's the sort of energy that sent her buzzing right out of Karrekoth before. So Isla watches her, closely.

The light fades and Isla sees their kitchen emerge, a real-life picture slowly loading in front of them. It's subtle, the differences. And perhaps if Isla didn't know they were back in the past, she wouldn't notice them. But she's on high alert, so her eyes are drawn to the fire already stoked in one corner, and her nose is drawn to the way the kitchen smells of fresh fish instead of cheap surface cleaner, because Marina firmly believed that if you lived in a harbour, you supported your local fishermen. She saw her own father struggle to make ends meet, after all, so it's not too much of a surprise to see a washing-up bowl full of mussels in the sink.

And this means, in this moment, their mother is alive. Isla isn't sure how she feels about that; she hadn't consciously thought of any particular day to travel to (where would she start with that, after all?) but being here, surrounded by an almost smothering amount of evidence of a living Marina, Isla can't help but worry how her sister will cope.

Her sister steps forward, frowning at the scene. 'My school sketchbook,' she murmurs, fingers skating across a worn ring-bound book resting on the table amidst a pencil case, a blazer and a purple file with 'Geography' intricately doodled onto it in black felt-tip. Strange relics that Isla hasn't thought about for years and yet remembers clear as day.

'Morgan?' Isla prompts gently. 'You doing okay?'

Morgan nods slowly, casts her eyes around the room once more. 'Yeah … yeah, I'm fine, I think. Where is everybody?' she asks, voice hushed. 'I mean … this is all my stuff, Isla, but where am I?'

Isla shakes her head slowly. 'I don't know,' she replies as she moves towards the window. The sky outside is gloriously blue; the tree in the garden is gleefully dropping its leaves to the ground. Autumn.

'It's autumn,' she relays to her sister, as she turns back round. But then she sees Morgan, frowning at the wall just beside the fridge.

'I can see.' Morgan nods to the wall and Isla looks obligingly, spotting immediately what she's been frowning at. The family calendar; she's forgotten they had one of those. But that's not the problem.

'It's October,' Morgan continues, her voice shaky. 'And that's the stupid fish-pun calendar sold at the church that year … Oh my God, Isla, is this—'

She doesn't get to finish. Isla hears voices behind her, turns rapidly and looks out the window towards the source. Immediately, she spots her mother and a younger Morgan heading in their direction. She sees her mother's white cardigan, sees the oil pastels tucked under her sister's arm.

'Shit.'

Isla doesn't give herself any more time to think. She crosses the kitchen in three broad strides, takes her sister's arm and tugs her to the stairs. Part of her expects Morgan to complain but maybe she's also spotted who's coming and makes the wise choice to stay mute.

They crouch on the tenth step, Isla acutely feeling the ridiculousness of the situation. It's like being six again, trying to listen in on her parents' conversations after she was supposed to be in bed, as if she might catch them revealing something extraordinary.

Then the door opens and Isla feels her sister grab her hand beside her. 'Isla ... this is ...' She can't find the words, gulping for air. But Isla knows what Morgan is trying to say. The truth is glaringly obvious.

Below them, in the kitchen, their mother has sat herself down while the younger Morgan roots through her discarded rucksack by the fridge. Neither of them pay any attention to the intruders hiding on the stairs, but Isla isn't taking any further risks. She grabs Morgan again and tugs her up to the landing, wincing at every tiny creak that their feet make.

'We need to leave,' she whispers. 'We can't stay.'

Morgan frowns, shakes her head rapidly as if she's trying to dislodge a hive of angry bees from her head. 'No, I'm not going. I'm not leaving her.'

'Mogs, trust me. We can't change this, the stone won't let us change anything too big, I've ... I've tried. And you don't want to see this.'

Morgan's eyes are stormy with defiance as she shakes her head again. 'I don't care, I won't leave her. What's the point of coming back if we just run away?'

Isla feels frustration and panic welling up inside her but she doesn't get a chance to say anything further. Their conversation is interrupted by a crash downstairs and a shout of shock that Isla recognises instantly as her sister's.

'It's happening,' Morgan whispers from beside her, face stark white in the gloom of the landing. 'She stumbled and knocked over the chair… then she fell down… and I shouted.'

Isla notices the way her sister's feet are drifting back towards the stairs. She shakes her head abruptly to try and stop her but it doesn't work. Of course it doesn't work. A second later, Morgan turns and creeps back down four steps. Reluctantly, Isla finds herself following until she's squished up beside her sister. She doesn't want to look but she also can't keep her gaze away. Doesn't she owe this to Morgan, anyway? Her sister had to do this alone, the least she can do now is witness it through a gap in the banisters.

But Isla spots her mother curled on the ground in pain and immediately wants to scrunch her eyes tightly shut. Marina looks tiny, almost childlike, so that the Morgan knelt beside her looks practically giant, though Isla is sure a giant has never worn an expression of such terror before.

'Mum? Mum, what's wrong?' Morgan is asking, one hand on her mother's shoulder. Marina doesn't answer except for a terrible noise of agony, as if her very ribcage is splintering. 'Mum?' Morgan shakes her head, lets out a small whimper. Then jumps to her feet. 'I'm… I'm calling an ambulance, okay? Hold on!'

Isla can feel her sister's leg trembling beside her and when she looks to the older Morgan, she sees stiffened shoulders and hands tangled together. One fingernail is being relentlessly picked at, the movement rhythmic and picking up speed as the seconds tick by. Down in the kitchen, Isla can see the same fingernails stumbling over the buttons on the phone.

'It's going to be okay… just, just hold on, please…' Morgan

murmurs as she places the phone to her ear, her free hand resting on Marina's head.

'Do her chest,' the older Morgan hisses beside Isla, shaking her head. 'She's having a heart attack, do her chest.' Isla frowns at the almost derision in her sister's voice, and how it's directed relentlessly at her younger self. In an automatic motion, Isla reaches across and takes Morgan's hand. Immediately, she feels her sister's fingers wriggle until they can grab on tight.

Isla wants to tug her away, far away. She hates the way her sister's eyes are narrowed with disappointment as she watches herself. Isla never once dreamed of her mother's death being anyone's fault except her own; she's the oldest, she should have been there to save the day. The thought of Morgan feeling that same weight of guilt makes Isla feel sick.

'Mogs. We don't need to watch this.'

Morgan doesn't answer, lips remaining firmly pressed together. Her younger self is fumbling her words down the phone, one hand still gripping onto her mother's shoulder. She looks like she's ready to defend her against anything. If only it was that simple. But there's no monster to fight away. All Morgan can do is hold her mother's shoulder and tell her it's going to be okay, then begin to follow the instructions being given to her down the phone. Each second is stretching out impossibly, and Isla can feel her sister's fingers dig into her own hand, harder and harder.

Morgan pulls her ear up from their mother's mouth and nose a moment later. 'She's not breathing! I can't hear her heartbeat! Please, please hurry! I can't do this on my own!' Morgan's cheeks are damp now as she listens to the person at the other end of the line and Isla sees panic seething inside her eyes. She lets out a small sob, before nodding her head. 'All right, I need to put the phone down to do that, though … Okay …'

Morgan drops the phone to the ground, pleats her hands

together. Isla realises what's coming and decides a second later that she can't watch this. She stands up abruptly, tugging her sister up with her. But Morgan is frozen, cemented to the stairs. 'Morgan, *please*, we don't need to see this. You don't need to see this, not again.'

Her words might as well have been in a different language, for all the good they do. Isla hears a small grunt of effort as the younger Morgan begins chest compressions and she closes her eyes, desperate not to have another traumatic image seared into her brain.

But then she feels Morgan's shoulder move away from her grip, hears the creak of the stairs as feet start down them. The worry for her sister is enough to snap her eyes open once more, just in time to see Morgan starting down the stairs with purpose radiating from her.

'Morgan!' Isla groans as she starts after her. 'Morgan, you *can't*!'

Morgan doesn't listen, though. She keeps storming down the stairs, then starts towards the kitchen. Isla catches up with her at the threshold of the doorway, yanking her back. 'Morgan, *stop*! You have no idea what might happen!' Her voice is hushed, because the younger Morgan may not have looked up in their direction but who's to say that she's just too focused on her mother to notice them?

'Does it matter?' Morgan snaps, rounding on her. 'Does it matter if the whole fucking world crumbles apart if she gets to live?'

Unsurprisingly, those words are enough to make Isla falter. And that's all Morgan needs. She tugs her arm free, explodes into the kitchen.

'Let me help, I can help.' Her words are shaky yet clear as day.

But nobody notices her. The younger Morgan continues to

press desperately on her mother's chest and Marina remains unconscious. A sickening scene that won't stop for anything, certainly not a young woman who has been cruelly forced into invisibility, no matter how desperate said woman is.

'PLEASE, I CAN HELP!' Morgan bellows it this time and rushes forward, arms out ready to shove her younger self out the way. Isla watches with dreadful foreboding and yet can't bring herself to stop her. Because what if she somehow manages it? What if her mother's life couldn't be saved by Isla, but can now be saved by Morgan?

Of course it's not that simple. Isla should have known that, should not have let her hopes rise for even a second.

Because the crushing disappointment when the wind snatches them from this time and deposits them back on the beach is enough to make Isla feel that she may just collapse into the sand.

But she can't. She's never allowed to just collapse, is she? Not when her little sister needs her. Morgan stands inches from the stone, hands still stretched out to intervene in a scene no longer present.

'What … what happened?' she finally whispers.

She sounds like a child who has just watched the most disappointing magic trick. And Isla knows she has to answer her, that she has a responsibility to help her sister make sense of this. But she doesn't know what to say.

Morgan rounds on her, eyes already shining with dreadfully furious tears. 'What happened?' she demands and this time her anger is enough to drag words from Isla's mouth.

'The stone … if it doesn't want you to change something, it won't let you. It will bring you back. I did say.'

'What the hell is the point of it then? What does it want us to do? What else would we possibly want to do other than save her?'

Isla shrugs, feeling utterly helpless in the face of her sister's anger. Or, more accurately, despair. 'I don't really know yet. It lets me change the small things, like fixing the book. But... I don't know.' She draws a deep breath, forcing calm upon herself as she steps forward. 'Morgan, I'm sorry you had to see that. If I'd known that it would take us there...' Isla begins, feeling the painful uselessness of her words.

'Which time?' Morgan's voice sounds faraway, as though it's floated out to sea.

'What?'

Morgan turns back to Isla, eyes hollow as already her anger turns to that terrifying blankness of hers. 'Sorry I had to see it just now? Or then?'

'Both, I guess.'

Her sister's face is inscrutable. She sniffs, nods and turns away. 'Me too.'

'Morgan, we need to talk about this.'

But Morgan doesn't hesitate in shaking her head. 'I can't, Isla. Not now.' And she's walking away before Isla can say another word.

It's the crack of dawn when Isla gives up trying to sleep. She's tried since midnight, which was the time she reached before running out of excuses to stay up. She didn't want her father to worry, not after he watched both her and Morgan troop back into the kitchen with drawn expressions and nothing much to say about where they'd been. So she pretended it was fine, forced a smile for Jasper's sake and went to bed at a somewhat reasonable time. Business as usual.

Except now, as Isla feels another hour of wakefulness dragging by, she decides it's not fucking business as usual after all. Heaving herself from her bed, Isla wraps herself in her dressing gown and moves to scowl out the window at the still-dark sky and the shadowy sea, lit only by the sinking moon. As if she might somehow find the antidote to her restless mind in the dips of the waves or the heaviness of the clouds.

There was a moment, a brief moment, when Isla thought that Morgan was right, that it was a good idea to bring her with her to the past. She had thought that maybe it would open some sort of communication between them. But now Isla can't stop thinking about what her mother would have said. *You let her see what, Isla? What were you thinking?*

The imagined questions make her stomach churn. What was she thinking? That her sister would somehow find strength and healing in seeing her mother's death all over again?

Right. Logical.

Her door opens shortly after Isla stops staring at the sea and starts staring at her wall instead. It creaks cautiously, hesitantly, and so she doesn't hear it straight away. But then there's an awkward clearing of a throat and Isla realises that someone is in her bedroom.

It's a bit of a surprise to see Morgan there. Isla thought (and feared) that she wouldn't see her sister for hours now. But here she is, looking as exhausted as Isla feels, though with a defiant look in her eyes that is part comforting and part unnerving.

'I could hear you stomping around in here, figured you weren't sleeping either.'

'I was hardly stomping.'

Morgan shrugs, closing the door before moving to sit on Isla's bed. 'How long did you sleep then?'

'A few hours. Two or three, give or take . . .'

'Congrats. I managed two.'

There's an almost pride to Morgan's voice which Isla can't quite understand. But she doesn't comment; it's really not important considering just how much Isla doesn't understand about her sister.

'Are you okay?' Isla asks, after a moment of silence. Morgan has sunk back against one pillow, bringing the second pillow round to hug against her chest. She has the pursed lips of someone desperate to say something, but she shrugs noncommittally at her sister's question.

'Mogs, I'm fairly sure you didn't come into my room at ...' Isla pauses, glances at the clock on her desk '...quarter past six in the morning just to try out my pillows. And I'm really not awake enough to be Sherlock bloody Holmes.'

Morgan sighs heavily, chin resting atop the pillow. 'You were right,' she murmurs at last.

'What was that?'

'You heard. You were right, don't go on about it.' Morgan lets out a huff, eyes flicking across to Isla. 'I was just so ... desperate. To change it. Because that's when it all went wrong, right? After she died. But it was stupid to think it could ever be that easy.'

Isla hesitates for a moment, before moving to sit beside her. Morgan budges up obligingly, but Isla notices that she doesn't make too much effort to widen the gap between them. That's encouraging. 'The first time I went through, it took me to a few days before. And – and I saw this crab about to get eaten by some seagulls so I saved it. After that, I kept thinking there must be a way to save her because I'd managed to save this crab. I'd changed time. Each time I went back, I was looking for ways to save her. But then when the time came, when my chance arrived ... it didn't work. And just like you, I was furious. So cross that I'd been given this opportunity and I'd failed.' Isla feels a lump in her throat, swallows it away. 'But I guess there are some days that are too ... big to be changed. I mean, just think how it would change all the days that came afterwards, how different today would look, if she was alive?' Isla shakes her head, frowning at the magnitude of that question. 'So I think the stone wants us to find the other ways to help. Like fixing the book, or leaving Mum's jumper in your locker...'

Morgan looks up sharply at that. 'Wait, you did that using the stone?' she asks. When Isla nods, Morgan's face lights up with a brief smile. 'I always thought that was a little bit of magic. Guess I was right.'

'Guess you were.' For a moment, Isla considers telling her sister about the night in the park as well but then decides that the gradual approach is probably going to be better here. 'See, there's things we can do, Morgan. I know we'd love to be able to save Mum but as we can't, we'll have to settle for being a bit more creative. Finding the little things to change.'

There's a soft laugh from Morgan and Isla feels her head come to rest against her shoulder. 'Only you could make a surprise trip to the past seem like completing a shopping list.' She yawns, jaw nudging against Isla's arm. 'So, which day do we fix first?'

Isla hesitates, then wraps an arm around her sister and pulls her a little closer. 'How about we just do tomorrow first. I think we both could use some time to recover, all right?'

Morgan sighs, but then makes a noise of agreement, somewhat begrudgingly. When Isla looks down a moment later, it's clear that her sister has fallen asleep against her shoulder. Isla can't remember the last time she did that and it brings a faint smile to her face. Then she carefully shuffles herself into a somewhat more comfortable position and closes her eyes.

And with her sister's soft breathing tickling against her ear, it's not too much of a surprise to find that sleep soon envelops her as well.

Twenty-Three

It may not have been the recommended amount of sleep, but it's enough. Though perhaps it's enough simply because the sleep is done with her sister's head rested against her shoulder and one hand rested on hers. Isla has a suspicion that she could have only slept for half an hour like that and it would have felt adequate. There's a surprising magic to be found in the embrace of a sister, powerful enough to chase away the lingering exhaustion and make the morning seem just a little brighter.

Isla wakes sometime after nine and leaves her sister curled up in her bed. She looks too peaceful to disturb, though in the end she follows Isla downstairs less than half an hour later. Isla's busy emptying the dishwasher when Morgan sidles into the room, a tentativeness hovering around her like mayflies.

'Isla?'

Isla pauses in her plate stacking, sensing an importance in Morgan's words. 'You okay?' she asks.

Morgan nods, before seeming to reach a decision and stepping further into the kitchen. 'I was wondering... whether I could maybe see about getting a job at the aquarium. Properly.'

Isla feels her eyebrows rising. This is a step towards something like an acknowledgement of the fact that her sister is here to stay, for now at least, and Isla tries not to let the significance of that show too much in her expression.

'I'm not trying to, y'know, tread on your toes,' Morgan goes on hurriedly, perhaps misreading Isla's silence for something else. 'I know crabs and seaweed are your thing, but it's something, until I get myself on my feet. I want to contribute. And, well, the other day after… everything.' She pauses to gesture at her stomach with a grimace. 'Well, it was a really good distraction.'

Isla finds her sister's shiftiness strangely endearing. She thinks about the proposal for a moment, as she wipes away a leftover smear on one plate. 'It would probably be in the café or the gift shop. I know there's no space in the actual aquarium at the moment.'

Morgan nods rapidly, wide-eyed. 'Oh sure, I mean totally. That's fine. I don't want to clean up shark shit anyway.'

'That's not… Never mind. Come in with me today and we'll see what we can do, okay?'

'Cool. Brilliant.' Morgan pats the nearest bit of table to Isla in an entirely unnecessary gesture that screams awkwardness. 'Thanks, Isla.'

She leaves soon after that, hiding a smile behind her hair without much success. A smile that she wears more outwardly when Dennis calls her in for an interview later that day (if you can call Dennis's five-minute chat about his thoughts on *Jaws* an interview), and a smile she beams out proudly when she gets the job. Isla watches her leave Dennis's office with her head held high and feels something that she thinks might be relief. She hasn't felt that in a while.

'So, somebody looks as though they've been accepting help from their sister…' Dylan comes to a halt beside Isla as she stands in the aquarium's foyer, watching Morgan get hustled off towards the café.

Isla glances over at Dylan, rolling her eyes at his all-too-obvious smugness. 'This wasn't the thing she was asking for help about,' she responds, 'so there's really no need to look that smug.'

'Well, again, in the absence of any other information from you ... I have to make my own conclusions.'

'How unscientific of you. I'm sure Professor Sawyer would be heartily disappointed.' There's a comfortable enjoyment in this conversation and Isla wonders if it's because, for the first time since Dylan re-entered her life, she doesn't have anything else distracting her.

Until Dylan speaks again. 'Talking of Professor Sawyer ...' He leaves the sentence hanging but Isla knows what he's getting at and she feels herself wince. The internship; she keeps forgetting about that. Hardly surprising considering what she's been up to in between her conversations with Dylan. And now Dylan has brought it up again she feels the all-too-familiar sensation of having something playing on her mind.

'I haven't really had a chance,' Isla mutters. 'And *don't* mention it to Morgan.'

Dylan frowns. 'Why?'

'Because it will freak her out if she thinks I'm about to leave her.'

That crooked grin slides up Dylan's face. 'What? Even now, when she's got this highly prestigious job to get on with?'

'I'm serious, Dylan. You can't mention it to her yet, not until I've worked out ... how.'

Holding up his hands in surrender, Dylan nods. 'You have my word.' There's a pause, then Isla feels him nudge her arm gently. 'Sounds like you might have made a decision, though.'

Those words bring a jolt of surprise to Isla. Now he's pointed it out, she can't deny it. Why would she be so keen for Morgan to find out in an appropriate way if she wasn't seriously considering it? After all, if it was just a case of turning down the offer then there was no harm in Morgan knowing.

Some of this must show on Isla's face because Dylan's looking at her with almost gleeful excitement. 'Just don't forget the sun cream when you're packing. I hear Hawaii sun is brutal.'

With a wink and another friendly nudge, he's left her. The foyer is empty then, just Isla and her thoughts and the irritating whale music that gets played on a loop in this room. Rain is lashing against the glass of the entrance doors, enough to put people off leaving their homes at all, even to visit the sheltered aquarium. It's going to be a quiet day. Isla would usually take that as an opportunity to do a stocktake of feeding supplies or health check the occupants of the larger tanks.

But today she finds herself drifting to the staffroom and extracting the application form from her rucksack. She spreads it flat on the table, stares at it for a few minutes. Funny how one stapled set of papers can feel so daunting, especially when it's so bloody blank. Isla scrawls her name into the appropriate box in case that helps.

It doesn't really. But now it has her name on it, the thought of the stack of unanswered questions being traced to her is enough impetus to get Isla to carry on. So she flips the page, takes a deep breath, and begins to write.

Perhaps unsurprisingly, it takes Isla the majority of the day to finish the form. It's slightly more surprising that nobody appears to ask why she's not doing any of her usual jobs, but appreciated nonetheless; the form's questions are relatively standard and yet Isla still has to think carefully about exactly *why* she would be suited for the role. It's hard to consider herself a serious contender for a prestigious international internship when sitting in a staffroom that has a 'funny fish photo competition' board in one corner.

But she finishes it eventually. Then stows the form in the bottom of her bag, because there's no chance of her handing it in until she's spoken to her family about it.

Still, there's an almost hopeful sense of change in the air as Isla goes to find Morgan and drive them home. Her sister seems to have the same sense because she seems almost too big for the car, her excitement and pride filling her up like a less spiky version of a puffer fish.

'…and then Mitch said he'd never seen someone make such a realistic octopus out of salad before so I should definitely consider going for a more managerial role in the café. I told him that he was technically my only superior so that would mean taking his role away from him, which he actually didn't seem that bothered about…' Her words wash over Isla in waves but they're warm, comforting. Tropical waves rather than stormy Cornish ones. There's real happiness in her voice, and it's enough to make Isla grin until Morgan notices and reprimands her.

'Honestly, you look like some doting grandmother with that smile. Can't you ever just be normal?'

As she forces the car up their hilled driveway, Isla smirks. 'This from the girl who made an octopus out of lettuce…'

Perhaps Morgan would have argued back against this, perhaps not. Isla never gets the chance to find out because as they reach the top of the hill and their house comes into view, it's clear that something is wrong.

The front door is wide open, and a thin trail of smoke billows out from inside, curling up into the sky until the wind catches it and sends it scattering. Isla feels foreboding, oh so familiar, rush back into her chest.

She brings the car to an abrupt halt, ignoring the angry

crunching from the brakes. Morgan is calling something to her but Isla doesn't hear, not over the thudding of her own fearful heartbeat. In that moment, all she can think about is the other occupant of the house and what's happened to him. *Not again. Please, not again.*

Isla rushes into the house. It's freezing, which is one good sign. Clearly whatever is making the smoke isn't enough to chase the chill out. She follows the smoke, ignoring how it immediately fills her nostrils and aggravates the back of her throat.

'Dad?' she calls out, following the word with a hacking, painful cough. Too much smoke. 'DAD?'

No answer. She's in the kitchen now and the smoke is thicker in here, and dark. She quickly spots how it seems to be billowing from the oven and runs over before she can think too much about it. The moment she opens the door, a wall of acrid-smelling smoke rushes at her. Her eyes immediately sting but she blinks it away, determined to find the source of this chaos. Determined to bring order back into her home.

Inside the oven sits a casserole dish, the blue-spotted one that her mother got from some market in France. Inside the dish is the charred, smouldering remains of something that Isla thinks was meant to be edible. But that opportunity has long since passed and now it's just black, shrunken, ruined.

Fingers trembling, she turns the oven off, grabs the oven gloves and tugs the casserole dish out. It's still searingly hot through the thick material but Isla holds firm as she carries the casserole dish to the sink and switches the cold tap on. Angry sizzling immediately erupts from within the dish, accompanied by another cloud of smoke.

Morgan stumbles into the kitchen at this point and Isla just about manages to point her towards the back door before she's crippled by another fit of coughing. Distantly, she hears the door smack open and a moment later, there's relief as the smoke is dragged out by the wind and oxygen gradually returns to her lungs.

'What is that?' Morgan gasps, pointing to the dish now overflowing with smoke-stained water.

Isla shakes her head. 'Nothing good.'

Morgan bites her lip, all levity gone from her face. She can't seem to drag her eyes off the smouldering dish, at least not until a sudden thump sounds above their heads.

The foreboding prickles again. 'Stay here,' Isla murmurs to her sister, squeezing her arm as she moves past her and heads up the stairs. Somehow she knows what sort of scene is awaiting her and she doesn't want Morgan to see.

Her sister doesn't try and argue. Perhaps she already knows exactly what Isla is trying to protect her from.

Upstairs, at the top of the house, she finds him. His bedroom door is closed but Isla has long since stopped seeing that as a deterrent. An invitation, if anything.

'Dad?' She keeps her voice soft, tries not to let it shake as she steps into the room.

Jasper is sitting by the window on the old rocking chair that had belonged to Isla's grandfather. The cause of the thump becomes clear almost instantly, as Isla spots a pile of books that have been swept off the top of the nearby bookshelf to lie in an untidy heap on the floor.

'Dad?' Isla says again, but Jasper's not actually moved since she came into the room. His head remains down, cradled by hands that seem a lot older than the ones she left doing the washing-up that morning. As if he's spent the day carefully stitching deep wrinkles into his fingers.

She crouches down beside him, places one hand carefully on his knee. It still manages to startle him, though. He jerks his head up abruptly with a muffled sob that has fear deeply woven through it.

'Just me,' she says, well-rehearsed patience and calm slipping into her voice. 'What happened, Dad?'

Jasper's face crumples like wet paper and though he tries to hide it in his hands again, Isla stills sees every crease of despair. She keeps her hands on his legs and lets him cry, hoping that he can't feel the way fear is sending tremors down her fingers. Why is she scared? Why isn't she entirely used to this by now?

Maybe there are some things you're just not meant to adapt to, she thinks.

After a long few minutes, he lifts his head again. 'I'm sorry,' he croaks. 'I didn't want you to see ... I wanted to be better than this for you.'

'What happened, Dad?' she asks again. 'You were absolutely fine this morning.' Not that that means anything, she knows. Her father's calm can be disturbed by the smallest of things.

'I – I was going to make you dinner ... I started making fish pie. Remember how good I was at that once? And – and I thought it might help cheer Morgan up and feel better ...'

Isla smiles. 'You do make good fish pie,' she agrees, deciding it's best not to mention what state his current attempt is in. 'But ...?' The prompt is gentle, seasoned with years of practice.

Jasper looks away, eyes drifting to the window. 'But who am I kidding? As if one poxy fish pie is going to make a sodding bit of difference to her, after what she's gone through with the baby. That's all I could keep thinking and then I came up here and ...' Shaking his head, Jasper seems to lose the words and falls into heavy silence.

For a moment Isla is lost in her own thoughts. She feels a distant sense of amazement that her father has managed to work out what has happened to Morgan, because she's fairly sure her sister hasn't told him, but that's soon lost amidst the heavy concern she feels for her father's state of mind.

'And it all got too much?' Isla prompts, when it's clear Jasper isn't going to find the end of his sentence. She receives a slow nod in response. 'That's fair, Dad. And … well, it's great you even thought about cooking for us. That's progress, right?' A shrug this time. 'Dad?'

He heaves a sigh, looks back to her. 'I know, I know … It's progress, sure. But it's not enough, is it? Nine years, I should be able to make a stupid pie. I should be able to do my job and be more than an embarrassment to this town, to my family.'

'You're not an embarrassment to anyone, Dad. Nobody thinks that for a second. You're just someone who's had a difficult time and it's made things harder for you to cope with. And that's all right; nobody would blame you for that. Nobody would dare with me around, hmm?' She shifts a little, so she can pull him into a tight hug, as if that might somehow protect him from the dark, invisible thoughts that seemed to have taken hold of her father's mind once more. He rests one hand on her arm and she tries to draw comfort from that. There's been times when hugging her father has been like hugging a block of wood.

But it's hard to find much solace in a single hand on her arm. Especially when she doesn't manage to get much more from him other than an agreement to a cup of tea. It's hard to be truly comforted when she goes downstairs, finds Morgan hovering anxiously at the door to the kitchen, and is unable to give her much good news beyond their father's safety. There's nothing consoling in the familiarity of the routine of making tea, taking it up to the bedroom, finding Jasper unmoved from his seat.

Isla makes dinner but she's not quite sure why she bothers. She's certainly not hungry and Morgan spends about fifteen minutes pushing the food around her plate before excusing herself. When Isla takes a plate up for Jasper, she spends twenty minutes trying to convince him to try some before leaving the plate on the bookshelf. Later, when the moon is the only light in his bedroom, she comes back and takes the untouched plate away downstairs.

The house stands silent. She sits in the kitchen with the scent of smoke still hanging in the air and the moonlight casting a ghostly glow over the table. At some point, when sleep starts to drag at the corners of her eyes, she remembers the form in the bottom of her bag and bitterness burns in the pit of her stomach like acid.

Because she knows that Hawaii is an exceedingly long way away from her reality. Because she knows that she will never leave this lonely house on this lonely cliff.

Because she knows that somebody is always going to need her.

Twenty-Four

She wakes with a start when someone gives her shoulder a rough shake. With a jerk, she straightens up and winces as her cheek rips away rather painfully from whatever it is she's been sleeping on so soundly.

The kitchen table; as she blinks away sleep, Isla becomes increasingly aware of the fact that that is what she's been sleeping on. Not exactly the behaviour of someone in control.

Even worse, it's Morgan who has woken her up, and who now stands beside Isla, arms crossed and eyes narrowed with concern. Just perfect.

'I'm fine,' Isla says automatically, giving her face a vigorous rub. 'Just nodded off.'

'It's morning.'

'What?'

Morgan heaves a sigh, moving over to the kettle and switching it on. 'You've slept here all night; it's the morning. So don't give me the "I'm fine" nonsense.'

Isla shakes her head, then instantly groans at the stiffness that has taken over the muscles in her neck. Inevitably this earns her a smug look of triumph from Morgan.

'See? Not fine. Opposite of fine.' Morgan crosses her arms again and Isla can feel her watching her closely as she staggers to her feet. 'You don't need to pretend with me, Isla. Not any more. Not a child, remember?'

'I know. I'm not … pretending. In the grand scheme of things, spending a night asleep at the kitchen table is not really that big a deal.'

'Compared to Dad.' Morgan's voice is quiet, almost drowned out by the bubbling kettle as the water comes to a boil. She shrugs as Isla finds a reply not instantly available. 'That's what you mean, right? Compared to almost setting fire to the kitchen and hiding upstairs, it's not that big a deal.'

'Mogs, it's—'

'Please don't say it's fine,' Morgan interrupts and there's real pleading in her voice. '*Please*, Isla.'

She's never heard her sister sound that way before, but it doesn't quite stop Isla from wanting to protect her from the truth. She skirts around Morgan so she can get the supplies for tea. 'But it *is* fine, Morgan. He's been a lot worse than that. Maybe you've just forgotten.'

She doesn't mean that to sound like a criticism but she can tell that Morgan has taken it as one. It's clear from the way her sister frowns and looks away, arms hugging round her chest.

'Mogs, I'm sorry. I didn't mean it like that, I just meant … it's easy for us all to forget how much he's changed.'

'I think we should go to the stone.'

'What?' Isla stares at her sister, at the words that have just tumbled from her mouth in a hasty rush.

'I think we should go to the stone. It's like you said – we've forgotten how much he's changed. So let's remind ourselves. And – and it might help us find a way to help him again. Together.' Morgan says that final word with heavy meaning, eyes defiant as she meets her sister's gaze.

'And what if it just makes us feel worse?'

Morgan snorts, casting her gaze around the gloomy kitchen that Isla has just spent the night sleeping in. 'I think that's worth the risk.'

As Isla looks around the room as well and takes in the permanently burnt casserole dish still drying on the side she can't help but see her sister's point.

'Okay. Let's try.'

The stone waits, impassive as ever. Isla has often thought that when climate change has decimated humanity, this rock will still be here, unmoved by it all. She remembers saying that to Jasper once, on a rare walk along this beach. He gently told her to be a little more positive, which she found highly ironic.

On the beach, the early sunshine is completely blanketed by the thick clouds, and Isla can feel damp seeping through her socks from the puddles she tripped into on the way down. Apparently this couldn't wait until the weather improved. Morgan barely let her get changed out of yesterday's clothes.

'It's shitting freezing. I can't believe you were going to come out in your slippers.'

Morgan rolls her eyes from her spot beside her and mutters something that sounds a lot like 'Yes, Mum', before trying to be as surreptitious as possible in her zipping up of her coat.

'So I just put a hand on the cracked bit, right?' she says a moment later, as she steps into the relative shelter the stone provides from the wind.

Isla nods, not particularly enjoying how confident in the process her sister seems already. She's fairly sure it won't be too long until Morgan decides she doesn't need a sisterly escort any more. 'Then wait for the glow. And we go through, together. Okay? And you need to think really carefully about exactly what you want to see ... that usually works ...'

'Sounds like you've got the scientific process sussed there, sis,' Morgan mutters, grinning a little.

'Hand, stone, now. Before I change my mind…'

Morgan obliges and, almost instantly, the glow starts. It's searingly bright in the gloom of the overcast morning and both sisters find themselves shielding their eyes. But then Isla feels Morgan grab her arm and tug her forward sharply, into the light. It's a relief to feel its warmth wash over her skin, just for a moment. But it's slipping away before she can enjoy it too much.

She recognises the hallway of their home instantly. Isla glances to Morgan questioningly but her sister shrugs. Either this isn't quite where she was expecting or she's being deliberately secretive about her plan.

Both options are irritating.

Morgan's the first one to step forward, picking her way cautiously towards the kitchen. Isla follows, spots a line of polished black shoes by the coat rack and immediately feels a rush of foreboding.

'Mogs!' Isla hisses and, when her sister turns around, she points at the shoes. 'This day? Really?'

Morgan stares at the shoes, fingers instantly tangling together. 'The funeral?' she whispers. 'I … I didn't think anything to do with the funeral, why the fuck are we here?'

Isla shrugs, feeling frustration bubbling inside. 'Because it's a shitting stone, not a sat-nav! And now – now we've got to see this shit-turd of a day?'

'Will you keep your voice down? Your bloody bat ears will be picking us up in a second if you're not careful!' Morgan snaps back, jabbing one finger up towards the ceiling and the bedrooms above.

Isla grits her teeth as Morgan looks towards the stairs

momentarily, checking they're still alone, before turning back to her. 'It's fine. We're fine.'

Then Isla sees herself walk from the kitchen and right towards them.

Immediately both sisters freeze which, in hindsight, is ridiculous. Isla knows she's not part-dinosaur; it's not as if she only senses things by movement. But then the younger Isla, dressed in a smart black dress, walks right past both sisters and up the stairs without a glance in their direction.

Both Morgan and Isla watch her go upstairs, before letting out twin sighs of relief.

'We're invisible again, then?'

Isla nods slowly. 'I think the stone decides when it's best for us to be invisible or visible. I guess this is another time when it thought we should be invisible.'

As if to prove their conclusion is correct, the younger Morgan then thunders down the stairs and past them.

'Yep, definitely invisible. I notice everything.'

Isla has to laugh at this. 'You didn't even notice when Mum painted your bedroom.'

'I was six, Isla...'

Isla smirks, feeling a warmth from this small exchange of almost light-hearted banter. It feels a little jarring standing next to a line of funeral shoes, which is perhaps why the smirk is only short-lived. Besides, Morgan is swiftly followed down the stairs by Isla again, and the older counterparts both find themselves more focused on stepping towards the kitchen.

In the kitchen, the younger Isla is already putting the kettle on and tugging bread from the bread bin. There's an air of almost frenetic energy about her, and the Morgan sitting at the kitchen table is watching this with exhaustion. It's been two weeks since they lost her, Isla calculates from her spot by the door. She remembers how the days went so quickly, no matter how hard she tried to stop them; she didn't want time to pass by, to leave her mother in the distant past.

So much for that.

'Where's Dad?' the younger Morgan asks after a second, as she digs one fingernail into the wood of the table.

'I don't think he's up yet.' Isla's voice is soft and painted with an unbearably false lightness.

'Don't we have to leave in, like, an hour?' Morgan glances to the clock, then back to her sister. The worry is clear as day on her face.

'Yes. But it doesn't take him long to get ready. It will be fine, Mogs. Do you want jam or honey?'

'Oh, I'm not hungry.'

Isla looks for a second as if she's going to try and argue this point. But then she sniffs, dropping the bag of bread back on the counter and sitting down beside her sister. 'Yeah, who am I kidding. We're not eating anything.'

Morgan laughs a little at that. It's a weak laugh, but it warms the kitchen anyway. A fire lit from the sisters' moment of agreement; Isla remembers the powerful warmth that could provide.

'It would be a shame to miss out on the food later though. Apparently Mrs Myrtle is making scones to feed the entire village.'

'Mrs Myrtle thinks scones fix everything,' Isla murmurs as she packs away the untouched bread.

From the other side of the doorway, the older Morgan reaches across the gap and tugs on Isla's sleeve. She feels her sister's fingers shaking a little as she scrabbles through the material of the jumper. Isla glances over to Morgan, who nods down the hallway. Once Isla has obligingly followed her nod, she sees what her sister has spotted and feels her stomach lurch like an unruly wave.

Jasper Pembroke has made it downstairs. He is, technically speaking, dressed but he's certainly not ready for a funeral. If one can ever be ready for a funeral.

His shirt is buttoned incorrectly, half tucked into his trousers which seem a little too long around his ankles. Grief must have shrunk him because Isla is sure they fitted him when she helped him buy them. His tie is currently untied but that, at least, he is attempting to fix. He stands in front of the hallway mirror, which is just large enough to show a person's head but nothing more, which is perhaps why the tie is still not tied.

Although the violently shaking fingers are probably more to blame.

Isla itches to help him. And she can't work out if that's because she wants to help her father or if she wants to protect the girls in the kitchen from this sight.

Except it's too late for that. The Morgan in the kitchen has spotted her father as well and comes barrelling past the invisible sisters a second later.

'Dad! You're up!' There's palpable relief in her voice. Isla remembers what that felt like; the early days when both of them thought that it would be okay as long as their father was there. Until that idea got smashed, savagely, over and over again.

Morgan comes to an unsteady halt as she finally sees her father, properly. He hasn't turned around or acknowledged her at all. The sisters watching by the door are sadly unmoved by this reaction but the younger Morgan is frozen, eyes wide, fingers tangled.

'Dad?' Isla has followed her sister from the kitchen. Already, Isla can hear that her younger self is developing the special tone of gentle patience required for her father.

Jasper jerks out of his tie-knotting reverie and looks towards his daughters. 'You both look lovely,' he croaks, every syllable sounding like an ordeal to say.

Morgan looks to Isla, uncertain. Then she turns back to her father. 'Thanks. Not really my style but I thought Mum wouldn't appreciate me turning up in jeans…' It's a tentative attempt at humour that falls flat at her feet. Jasper tries his hardest to smile but it appears that he cannot manage more than a grimace. A second later and one hand comes over his eyes to hide what must be the arrival of tears.

Isla can see that this horrifies her little sister. Apparently her younger self spots it too because she's already intervening. 'Morgan, can you get Dad a coffee? Think the kettle's just boiled.'

It seems that Morgan does not need to be told twice. She nods and backs down the corridor and into the kitchen without another word. Her older counterpart watches her go with a frown. 'You know I had never made coffee before, right?' she mutters across to Isla.

Isla has to laugh at that, despite everything. 'I'm sure Dad wouldn't have noticed if you gave him boiled slugs,' she points out, nudging her gently with one elbow.

Morgan smiles, but then her gaze is pulled back to her father. As is Isla's, albeit with some reluctance.

'Dad, come sit down.' The other Isla gently guides Jasper to the stairs and helps him sit down. Then she sits down beside him and with remarkably steady hands manages to tie his tie.

'How did you know how to do that?' Morgan whispers.

Isla shrugs as she watches her younger self set to work on her father's wonky buttons. 'I… I don't know. Maybe Mum taught me? Or I just worked it out because I had to… like the coffee,' she says, nodding to the younger Morgan as she carefully carries a mug of what looks to be fairly ordinary coffee past them and to her father.

'Oh, you're a star, Mogs, thank you.' Isla takes the mug from her sister and places it rather firmly in her father's hands. Jasper doesn't really register it, until Isla gently tips it up towards his mouth. 'Drink, Dad. It will help.'

Jasper finally lifts the mug to his mouth and takes a gulp. If Morgan's first coffee is not quite right, he certainly doesn't register it. 'My girls . . .' he murmurs, a little distantly. 'What would I do without you?'

Isla smiles, then turns to Morgan. 'Can you run upstairs and get the sewing kit? It's in the biscuit tin under the hallway table.'

Morgan frowns. 'But you don't know how to sew?'

'Well, I'm sure now's a good time to learn.' Isla gives her sister a gentle nudge in the right direction and watches as Morgan scrambles up the stairs. Once she's gone, she turns back to Jasper. 'Dad? Are you going to be able to do this?'

Jasper kneads at his eyes with his free hand, takes another slurp of coffee. 'I hope so. I have to. I will.' He rests one hand on Isla's cheek for a moment and, as she watches from her spot by the door, the older Isla can almost feel the comforting warmth that gesture always provided. Even when her father was at his worst, his hand on her cheek somehow always made her feel better.

'Hand on the cheek . . . classic,' Morgan murmurs from beside her and Isla can't miss the wistfulness in her sister's voice.

Morgan comes stumbling back down the stairs, tin clutched to her chest. 'This tin?'

Isla glances up briefly from trying to fold up the hem of her father's trousers. 'That's it. We need a needle and some dark thread.'

Morgan drops down beside Isla, cracking open the tin and rooting through the somewhat haphazardly arranged supplies. 'This is when I wish Mum was more organised . . .' she mutters, before immediately freezing as her own words hit her.

Isla has frozen too, looking at her sister with an expression that even the older Isla cannot interpret.

'I didn't mean ...' Morgan begins, and everyone in the room must be able to hear the tears choking up her throat.

But, by some miracle, it is Jasper who comes to the rescue. He lets out a soft, slightly barking laugh. 'She was the most disorganised person I knew ... couldn't even pair up her own damn socks.'

The kneeling sisters stare at their father and, from the doorway, Isla feels their relief beginning to blossom. A sudden moment of realising that the things they always laughed at about their mother are still there and can still be laughed at.

Isla shakes her head with a soft laugh, Morgan giggling beside her. 'And she used to get our school uniform mixed up all the time, even when we were in different schools.'

'There was that time she sent me to school with Dad's sardine sandwiches and Dad got my Cheestrings and Penguin bar ...'

Another moment of shared laughter, before the kneeling Isla hurriedly clears her throat. Back to business, though there's a touch more lightness to her than there was a moment ago. 'Let's sew these trousers then, eh, Dad?'

Jasper sniffs, nods. 'Don't worry too much about keeping it straight ... your mum always said that was the hardest part about sewing, and nobody's going to be looking at my ankles ...'

Isla takes this advice with a businesslike nod before taking the needle and thread her sister has now found. Silence drops over the small group as Isla focuses on the task at hand, while Morgan rests her chin on her sister's shoulder in a rather unhelpful way of watching her work.

'Was that really necessary?' Isla murmurs from the doorway.

Morgan shrugs, grinning unabashed. 'For such a weirdly triangular person you have surprisingly comfortable shoulders.'

'Nobody knows how to deliver a backhanded compliment quite like you, Morgan Pembroke.'

'Cheers.'

The invisible sisters fall silent once more, easily drawn back into the scene before them. A scene with a sense of familial togetherness that Isla knows will disappear before too long. The trousers get sewn and Morgan ferries the box upstairs without a word from Isla, before hurrying back downstairs a moment later with her father's suit jacket. Both sisters help Jasper into it and Morgan then gets all three pairs of shoes ready in front of their respective feet. It's a slightly futile act, considering the shoes were barely two feet away anyway, but everybody can see that Morgan just wants to feel useful.

It's not long after that the doorbell goes. The three Pembrokes all know that beyond the door will be the first step towards a funeral that none of them are truly prepared for, which is perhaps why they make no move to answer it just yet.

'Just one moment!' Isla calls out, before taking both her sister's hand and her father's. 'What's that quote Mum used to say, Dad? About storms?'

Jasper looks as if his thread of control is about to disappear again but he clutches on grimly. 'The fishermen know that the sea is dangerous and the storm terrible, but they have never found these dangers sufficient reason for remaining ashore.'

'Van Gogh,' Morgan murmurs from their makeshift circle, smiling softly. 'The first artist she taught me about ...' As Isla watches from the door, she can almost hear her mother saying that quote. Wrapped up together in a blanket after a terrible day at school, hands deftly tugging the knots from her unruly curls.

'Well then,' Isla says, and the tight squeezing of her family's hands is clear even from the doorway, 'into the storm.'

Twenty-Five

The stone does not keep them long after that. They stay long enough for them to watch Isla ferry her pasted-together family out into the world, long enough for the sound of car engines to rumble through the house then slowly fade away. They stay long enough for the crash of waves to reclaim the silence for its own.

Then the waves grow louder and Isla knows their time is up.

They're greeted by a now beautiful morning back in their time. The clouds have finally relinquished their hold and there's a rare, blissful view of blue sky and calm sea. Low in the sky, the sun is trying its best to warm up this corner of the world and, for now, the wind is calm enough for it to have a chance at succeeding.

Isla looks to Morgan. Her sister steps from the shadow of the stone and basks in the sunshine for a moment, and Isla is reminded of the cat she sometimes sees sunbathing on the wall by the harbour; it's the same look of relief at having a moment of warmth and light to enjoy.

'We were a good team back then,' Morgan finally says. Glancing over to Isla, Morgan shoots her sister a small smile. 'Team Trousers.'

Slowly, Isla sits down on one of the small ledges jutting out of the stone. The exhaustion from the previous day's trials seems to fill her very bones with cement but she manages to return the smile. 'That's a terrible team name. But yes, we were.'

Morgan flops down beside her. After a moment, her legs tangle around her sister's and Isla finds the sensation to be oddly comforting. An act from long ago, from a pair of sisters greatly different to the ones on the beach now. 'I forgot how well we could work together.'

'Me too.'

'Why did we stop?'

Isla's silent; understandable considering the difficulty of her sister's question. But then Morgan has always been uniquely skilled in getting to the crux of the matter, no matter how painful it might be.

'I ... don't know,' she finally replies, gently digging one foot into the floor of pebbles and sand. 'Maybe we just got distracted. We had a lot on our minds.'

Morgan makes a thoughtful noise. It doesn't sound entirely convinced. When Isla glances across at her, she grimaces somewhat apologetically. 'It's just ... I don't think it's that. I think you stopped letting us work together. Or stopped letting me help.' She reaches across, squeezes Isla's arm in an attempt to ward off whatever she's expecting Isla to say. 'I'm not blaming you. You were trying to protect me.'

'I was,' Isla agrees softly. A steady trickle of memories sneak into her mind no matter how hard she tries to block them out. There's a lot of scary days she's kept her sister from witnessing fully. 'You're my little sister, Morgan. I would have protected you from everything if I could.'

'I know.' Morgan's head comes to rest on her shoulder and she laughs softly to herself. 'Yep, still comfy ...'

It's not until the crunching of footsteps comes a moment later that either sister moves. Even then it's somewhat sluggishly, until a voice accompanies the sound.

'Oh, this is where you are…'

Isla's head jerks around rapidly then, eyes wide. 'Dad?' she splutters, not quite able to believe that her ears could be correct. But it's him, looking a little worn around the edges but here, on the beach nonetheless. She can't quite remember the last time that happened.

'You're here, on the beach… and dressed.'

Jasper sniffs his amusement as he comes to stand beside their makeshift seat. He's wearing only a small smile but Isla is quick to notice how it manages to reach his eyes and send a flicker of light through them. 'No flies on you as usual, eh?' Then he nods towards Morgan, who has been uncharacteristically quiet beside Isla. 'Morgan decided to give you a break this morning; apparently you looked far too comfortable asleep at the table so she came upstairs with some breakfast and tea and some much-needed chat.'

'She did?' Isla looks down at the head still resting on her shoulder. She can't really see Morgan's face but the pride radiating from her is all too clear.

'She did,' Jasper reiterates.

'I told him why I came back…' Morgan murmurs quietly, fingers picking at the edge of the stone. 'I'd lost something huge in my life and there were only two people I knew would be able to help me through that, him included.' She shrugs, her shoulders digging a little into Isla's chest as she does so. 'I also told Dad that one burnt fish pie does not a failure make.' Lifting her head up at this point, she scrutinises her father carefully. 'I didn't think you'd actually listened though.'

'I always listen. Eventually,' Jasper replies, looking so serious for a moment that Isla feels that pathological need of hers to lighten the mood.

'Mostly is perhaps a more accurate word,' she retorts, shooting her father a good-natured grin. Jasper snorts his agreement at that, and Isla feels a flood of relief that her father has not allowed last night's blip to consume him entirely. Apparently all because Morgan refused to let Isla take it all on her shoulders.

'Anyway, it's freezing down here. And you two should make sure you eat breakfast as well.' Jasper tugs his jacket around himself a little more tightly, jerking his head back towards the house. 'Coming?'

Morgan hops up almost instantly. 'Yeah, definitely. I'm growing sodding icicles here. Isla, coming?'

Isla is about to stand up, about to follow what feels like an almost normal family back home. But there's a sharp jolt of electricity that seems to travel from the stone beneath her and into her leg. A sudden, sharp shock of warmth trying its best to get her attention. She just doesn't know why.

What she does know is that she's apparently not quite ready to leave yet. The stone wants something from her and, as tempting as breakfast with a repaired father and returned sister feels, she can't ignore this call.

'I'll be along in a sec, just going to get a bit more fresh air, get rid of the cobwebs.'

Jasper nods his acceptance, but of course Morgan is watching her with intense suspicion. When their father turns away to head back up to the house, Isla gives her a sister a quick shake of the head. A silent reassurance that she has nothing to worry about.

Isla waits until they're out of sight before standing and turning to the stone once more. 'What is it?' she asks softly, way past being above talking to solid rock.

The stone glows almost immediately. There's an eagerness to it that makes Isla hesitate a little. For a moment the light reminds her strongly of the glowing tip of an anglerfish and she wonders if this is some sort of trap.

But it's too late. This particular lure entangled her weeks ago and she has not yet been able to resist it.

Four years is a long time to wonder about something. Forty-eight months, two hundred and eight weeks. Even with everything else that occupied Isla's head, it was still a long time to consider the complex question: why did Morgan run away?

She never told them properly after all. She only told them eventually that she was safe, then kept that reassurance up with relative frequency. But nothing else. Isla has always had her suspicions of course. And though she never voiced it for fear of what guilt it would cultivate, she always thought that the loss of her father, in an entirely different way to the loss of her mother, was one step too far; that his withdrawal chased her sister away. Isla failed to fix her father sufficiently so her sister had left to find a life not filled with the cracks of grief. She only has to think about Morgan's sixteenth birthday for that belief to be firmly cemented. It was over a year until Morgan would disappear, but that was surely the first steps towards her running away.

So when the light clears and she sees the birthday cake on the table, complete with sixteen candles waiting to be lit, Isla can only assume that the stone thinks so too.

She's in the café, the one owned by Louisa. Isla had managed to convince her to let them hire it for a discount if she put some flyers for her café in the aquarium foyer. A somewhat dodgy deal considering Dennis hadn't been asked but of course he never noticed. And it was Morgan's sixteenth birthday, so Isla was determined to make an effort.

The café is empty; nobody's here yet. Odd because Isla remembers that she was here with the cake and the food before anybody else. The cake's here; she can see the sandwiches stacked up in the corner. But she can't see her younger self anywhere.

Until she catches sight of herself in the window reflection. She's no longer dressed in the half-outfit she'd thrown on that morning to accompany her sister to the stone. Instead, she's wearing a navy-blue party dress. Her curls are no longer scraped into a bun but properly tamed and styled. There's even sodding make-up on her face ...

'Oh God ...' Isla whispers, understanding beginning to creep up the back of her neck. The final realisation comes a second later when Cora Myrtle totters up to the front door, wearing those ridiculous heels she bought the week before and waving at her brightly, as if this is all entirely normal.

'Don't panic, I'm here!' she says with a laugh the moment she's stepped into the cafe. 'Christ, it's cold, think my toes might freeze off on the way home but worth it, eh? Don't these shoes make my legs look *insane*?' She's babbling in her usual way as she deposits two bottles of brightly coloured cocktail mixes by the birthday cake. 'Cute cake, you said it was shit, what are you like? It's great!' By this point, some of Isla's dumbfounded silence seems to have registered in her friend because she pauses, hands on her hips. 'Isla? What's wrong?' Cora's carefully penciled eyebrows raise heavenwards. 'You're not still worrying about the playlist, are you? Morgan won't care, she'll be chuffed by all the effort you've put in.'

I need to speak. Say something. Isla's brain is urging her mouth into action but her mouth is proving stubborn, to say the least. It's only when Cora takes a step towards her with a deeper concern in her expression that Isla finally manages to get some words out.

'I'm fine,' she half-splutters. At least her voice sounds the same. 'Sorry, I was just miles away for a second.'

'Well, get switched on, love. You've got company.' Cora laughs, gesturing towards the front windows behind Isla. When she turns around, Isla is greeted by the sight of a great gaggle of Morgan's friends coming towards the café. Half of them already seem too drunk for proper walking.

'Christ,' she mutters, remembering the mess that some of these particular teenagers would cause later.

But that's not what the stone has brought her here for, that much Isla is sure of. Especially when the stone seems to have gone a whole extra mile by turning her back into the twenty-three year-old who organised this party. So what does it want her to do?

It's not until the café is filled with people and the music is loud enough to make the windows shake that Isla works it out. She's watching her sister on the other side of the room, watching how she has her group of friends encircling her like a strange, drunken shield. There's a heady excitement and joy radiating from them but Isla, without the need to worry about whether there's enough sausage rolls, can see what she didn't notice last time. The way her sister's eyes drift around the room every few moments, how they linger on the door until she forces herself back into the party. Isla thinks she can guess who she is looking for; there's one key person missing after all.

And Isla knows that Jasper won't ever appear at that door. Isla knows that he is sat at home in a gloomy sitting room, trying to lose himself in television to distract himself from the fact that he's not managed to go to his own daughter's sixteenth-birthday party. Isla knows that he spent all day to-ing and fro-ing between the decision to go or not, until a few hours before when it got too much and he just dissolved into exhausted, hopeless sobs.

She told him to stay at home; she told him that Morgan would understand and he didn't need to feel bad about it. And, at the time, Morgan seemed to have understood. Isla remembers how impressed she was with her sister's apparent mature response. But it didn't last. The day after had seen one of the worst arguments she would ever have with her sister.

And now Isla is sure that that argument was the first stone on the path to Morgan's departure. Now Isla is sure that her sister is pretending to be having a great time while nursing the wound of an absent father.

'He needs to be here.' She whispers the words to herself and the music dutifully drowns them out. But Cora still gives her a strange look.

'Did you say something?' she shouts, despite being right beside her.

'Uh, never mind.' Isla puts down the drink she's been handed at some point this evening, touches her friend's arm to get her attention. 'I'll be right back; make sure nothing gets trashed, okay?'

Cora looks suitably bemused but nods. 'Sure thing!'

Isla squeezes through the crowd and out of the café, keeping her head down as much as she can to avoid anyone else noticing her leaving. The fresh air outside hits her, cool and relieving after the sticky heat of the café. But she hasn't got time to revel in that now. She's going to fix her sister's birthday, whatever it takes.

Isla tugs off her heels, loops them round her wrist. They may not be quite as tall as Cora's but they're still not going to be helpful for running in. And running is exactly what she intends to do right now.

*

The second she closes the front door, crushing silence settles around her.

Yes, she remembers this silence. She remembers how it crept about the house until it felt more like a funeral parlour than a home. She remembers how she had to force down the churning sensation that she just wanted to scream into the crushing abyss of hush until something changed.

The house is dark; nobody has turned enough lights on. But then why would they? The only person home can't even get to their daughter's birthday party. Putting lights on is clearly too much of a stretch.

Isla steps through the gloom, half trips over the pile of shoes in the hallway. In the kitchen she finds the leftover mess of her party preparations; baking trays piled by the sink, a discarded balloon on the floor. She resists the urge to start tidying and instead heads for the sitting room where she can make out the flickering light of the television.

'Dad?' she calls as she steps into the room. Her father is barely visible in the gloom until she finds the nearest light switch and flips it on.

Immediately, Jasper jerks out of a half-sleeping state. He squints towards the door, frowning at the sight of Isla. 'Is … it over already, love?' he croaks, rubbing at the wild bristle on his chin as he shuffles into a more upright position.

'No.' Isla feels the sharpness of her response cut against her tongue but there's no going back now. 'Dad, you need to be there. She needs you to be there. I don't care if – if you're too tired or too sad or … whatever. She *needs* you. You are breaking her heart and I can't let you do that any more, not to Morgan.' Her throat feels tight, sticky. Jasper's looking at her with complete shock; of course he is. She's never spoken to him this way before. But she can't stop now. 'So I need you to get up and get dressed and come to the café and celebrate your daughter's bloody birthday!'

There's a long silence that Isla feels every second of. Jasper won't meet her eyes and Isla knows she's probably gone too far. She's gone into the den of the wounded bear and given him an extra kick, but what was the alternative? How many times has she put her father's depression before her sister?

Jasper looks down at the floor, a deep frown of thought travelling across his face. Finally, he pulls himself to his feet. He stumbles slightly but then he's upright and steady. 'You're right,' he croaks. 'Of course you're right. I'm being selfish. As always.'

'No … that's not what I'm saying, Dad,' Isla sighs impatiently because she can hear the dark tendrils of depression still worming through his words. 'I'm just asking you to please … try.'

He steps towards her, presses a hand to her cheek. He's been curled up on the sofa all evening and yet he still feels cold. 'I know. And I will. I will try. Give me a second to get dressed properly. Then I'll come with you.'

Jasper leaves the room, walking with a hesitancy that Isla can forgive him for. After all he's going to try … and that's all she ever wanted him to do. Has it been this simple all along? A case of just asking him? Perhaps. Except Isla can't help but feel a slight twist of foreboding. The two things she's changed before in her sister's life were things that had already happened; Morgan seeing her shadowy form outside the playground and the jumper in the locker. Isla merely ensured they happened, albeit without much awareness at the time. But this; this is different. Isla knows for a fact that her father never came to her sister's sixteenth birthday party. She's changing something, properly. And she just has to hope it's for the better.

*

When they return to the café forty-five minutes after her initial departure, Morgan practically runs from the opposite end of the room to her father's side. 'Dad!' she exclaims, wrapping her arms around him tightly. 'You came!'

Jasper staggers a little from the force of her greeting but he's smiling. A real smile. Isla wonders when her little sister last saw one of those. 'I came,' he murmurs. When he steps back from her, Isla can see the effort it's taking him to keep everything together. It reminds her a little of the fishing boats struggling against a gale force wind but she forces herself to remember that they usually make it back safely. This is going to be okay.

'Let's get a drink, eh, Dad?' Isla says, coaxing her father towards the table laden with various bottles. 'There should be something suitable and not jammed full of sugar and totally ridiculous colourings.'

Jasper nods and starts his slightly hesitant journey towards the table but Morgan catches Isla's arm before she can follow him.

'You got him here – for me?' she asks, voice soft so nobody else can hear the vulnerability there.

Isla nods. 'I know you said it was fine but ... I thought it might not be.'

A small, slightly sheepish smile flickers across her sister's face. But then she's looking a little more serious, almost sombre. 'He will be okay though? Here? I don't want him doing something he's not ready for.'

Isla glances over to her father, watches him as he chooses a can of lager and then scans the room. He is obviously a little uncomfortable in this highly social situation but that's not too different to his normal state. He's never been the life and soul of a party.

'He'll be okay,' she assures her sister a moment later. 'Now, will you please enjoy your party? I spent a long time getting all

this ready for you so go, enjoy, get stupidly drunk or whatever.'
Morgan gives her a slightly odd look at that, one that Isla can't
quite interpret. But then she's gone, heading back to her friends
with a spring in her step. She's happy, Isla cautiously concludes
and feels satisfaction spread through her limbs like the warmth
of a bath.

She's ready then, when the wind whips around her ankles a
few seconds later, and the stone tugs her back to her time. Isla
has to just trust that the stone has made her disappearance less
obvious than it feels, that the real past Isla has taken her place
seamlessly. She doesn't remember anybody being particularly
alarmed at the party and claiming to have seen her vanish, so
she'll just have to trust this impossible rock once more.

A tentative sense of elation settles against her shoulders as
she begins the walk back home. Clouds have covered the blue
sky and it's become a little overcast but that can't dampen Isla's
mood. Because this time she's sure. She's certain that this time
she's helped her sister and perhaps even her father.

The house seems fairly quiet when she arrives but as she steps
further into the kitchen, a shadow shifts in the doorway of the
sitting room and her sister appears.

'Hey ...' Isla begins, feeling a rush of excuses surging up her
throat. 'I was, uh—'

'It's fine, I know where you were.' Morgan cuts her off, shaking
her head. There's a strange tone to her voice, almost accusation.
It immediately makes Isla bristle with defensiveness.

'I don't always have to go to the stone with you, you know.'

'I know.'

Isla frowns. 'Then what's with the funny look?'

Morgan shifts, a little awkwardly. 'I ...' A pause, then a heavy
sigh as she moves to the kitchen table. 'Well, you were gone a
while and I was kinda worried you were going to be late for

work so I went looking to see if you had the number for the aquarium in your bag and...' She trails off, nodding to Isla's bag sitting on the table, innards half-tumbling out. In pride of place, for both sisters to see, sits the crumpled application form for the internship.

Morgan's voice is quiet, but loaded with a concrete-hard accusation, as her eyes flick from the form to her sister. 'When were you going to tell me about this?'

Twenty-Six

Marina used to say to her daughters that fighting between sisters was normal, as long as they always told each other that they loved each other afterwards. Isla can remember how she would scoop both girl against her side, ignore their squirming and tickle them until they said those all-important words. Isla has a fairly clear memory of her doing this right up to the week she went to university, and even though both she and Morgan could probably squirm free if they wanted to, neither ever did.

There, Marina would say once both girls had relented, *now you can be mad with each other but know that if anything happens, you didn't make a terrible mistake.*

Now, with Morgan frowning at her and an internship almost glowing incriminatingly from the middle of the table, Isla wishes for perhaps the millionth time that her mother was here.

'Isla? An answer sometime soon?' Her sister doesn't sound angry exactly, but she also doesn't sound pleased.

'I wasn't going to do it.' Is she lying? Isla isn't sure but the words have fallen out of her mouth all the same. 'Dylan gave it to me to think about but obviously I wasn't going to do it.'

This doesn't seem to placate Morgan in the slightest; in fact it seems to make things worse. She runs a hand through her hair, huffing a noise of irritation. 'Aside from the fact that it's pretty fucking filled in for someone not doing it... I didn't ask that, Isla. I asked when you were going to tell me.'

'Why does that matter? If I wasn't going to do it?'

'Of course it matters! We could have talked about it!'

Isla finds herself snorting at that, the exhaustion of everything that's happened recently shortening her patience significantly. 'Right. Talked about it. There's nothing to talk about. It's in *Hawaii*, Morgan. That's not just a quick jaunt down the motorway. It's in another country. In what sort of fairy-tale world would that be something that I could do? Just look at yesterday evening with Dad!'

'Yeah, and look at this morning! I'm here now, I can help Dad... we could manage, Isla! If you talked to us about it we could have worked something out.'

'Enough, Morgan. I'm not talking about this any more.'

Morgan's hand slams against the table, hard enough to make the spilled contents of Isla's bag shiver. 'No. Enough, *Isla*. Why do you always get to decide when a topic is worth talking about? You have a go at me for never telling you anything but who do you think I learnt that from, Isla? The two people I have left in my life don't tell me shit! Dad would rather discuss shipping forecasts and you can only confide in... in a sodding rock!'

Isla feels anger radiating from her sister in thick waves that feel that they could knock her down at any moment. For a moment, she's stunned into silence. 'Why has this made you so angry all of a sudden?' she finally whispers.

Morgan shakes her head, her shoulders stiff with a rage she is clearly trying to hold back. 'I'm angry because Mum always told us to be honest, above all else. And you won't stop lying. To me and to yourself.' She takes the form, pins it to the kitchen noticeboard savagely. 'You know I think there's a reason you like that shitting stone so much. You're both stuck in the past.'

'Morgan.' But Isla doesn't get any further. Her sister has left the room before she can say another word. And, of course, Isla wants to follow. It's just that she can't, because she doesn't actually know what to say. No words of defence have leapt into her mind and so all she can do is stay rooted to her spot by the kitchen table, until her sister's bedroom door slams somewhere far above her.

Morgan stops speaking to her after that. She carefully builds up a wall again and doesn't let it come down, not for anything or anyone. Isla tries at first. She knocks on her bedroom door in two-hourly intervals, waits hopelessly for an answer that doesn't come. She tries to start a conversation over dinner but Morgan picks up her plate and goes to eat in another room without a word. By the time their next shift at work comes round, Morgan has found a bus route that will get her there and has left the house long before Isla comes to ask if she wants a lift.

After three days of this, Isla stops trying. She knows she should be the grown-up here but her sister's ability to completely ignore her has always managed to rile Isla up beyond reason and maturity. So she stops trying. She leaves her food on the side and stops trying to eat dinner with her. She stops knocking on her door and she stops asking if she wants lifts to work.

The wall goes up on both sides. The recently stitched together threads of a sisterhood are once again yanked apart. Isla sees how her father looks between the two of them with quiet disappointment and it's almost enough to make her try again. Almost. Then her sister will enter the room with her plainly misjudged fury and Isla's resolve unravels into the air.

All of a sudden, without anybody really keeping track, a week passes and rolls them right into the middle of October. And the Pembrooke house braces itself as the 20th inches closer. The day that they all quietly wish would somehow be skipped out of the calendar.

Jasper's waiting for her when Isla gets home from work that day, wearing his smarter coat and a stony expression. As soon as he sees Isla coming through the door, he's striding towards her and meeting her in the hallway.

'Where's your sister?' he asks, picking his keys up from the hooks set into the wall.

Isla sniffs, rolls her eyes. She's still infuriated by her sister's behaviour. 'She's walking up the hill. I tried to offer her a lift from the bus stop but …'

'Well, we'll pick her up on the way.'

'Dad?'

Jasper steps around her, heading for the door. 'It's her day. We go see her on her day. Whatever else is going on. Get in the car.'

Isla winces as she turns around and follows him. It's not as if she's forgotten; of course she hasn't. She's just tried not to think about it too much, and the logistics of navigating this moment of remembrance when all she can feel right now is anger. 'Right, of course,' she murmurs.

Morgan's halfway up the drive when they meet her. Jasper brings the car to a rather abrupt halt and rolls down the window. 'In you get, Morgan.'

Morgan's hollow gaze flicks from her father to Isla in the front passenger seat and her eyes narrow. But she knows where they're going and it seems even her stubbornness won't stoop to refusing this. So with a sigh she gets in the back, throwing her bag onto the seat next to her with rather unnecessary force.

Of course, the car ride is silent. Isla watches the mutinous-looking sea whizz past the window and feels her sister's eyes on the back of her head like two laser beams, and finds solace in the fact that at least the journey is short.

Karrekoth has one small graveyard in the village's church but Marina never liked that place, so they chose a cemetery a mile or so out of the town. It was on top of one of the many hills around their village so there was always a wind whipping across it but it also brought the smell of the sea, which they all knew Marina would have enjoyed. Isla always used to worry a little that it felt too isolated and exposed on top of its own hill, but now she has grown to love the wildness of the place. There is no particular order to the gravestones and plaques, no neatly groomed paths. Trees sprout from the uneven ground with complete disregard for the surroundings and some of the gravestones have tipped haphazardly over the years, making them seem more like rocks on the beach than hallmarks of death.

Her mother's stone is in one corner, near a wizened old tree that has been bent into an almost right angle by the wind. It always reminded Isla of an inside-out umbrella. There's a bench sheltering by the tree's trunk, which the three Pembrokes now sit themselves upon.

Jasper is squeezed in the middle between his two daughters and Isla can feel him casting glances between them every few moments. But nobody says anything. Isla stares at the chalk-white stone in front of them, tries to connect the words on them with her mother. But, as always, she mainly just feels numb. Her mother isn't here. She doesn't know where she is, but it's not here.

'Right, I'll start, shall I?' Jasper finally says, his voice sounding a little fraught. 'My memory for the year is this one . . .' He draws a deep breath, looks between both girls again. Isla sees a sharpness in his gaze that she hasn't seen for a long time and she should be encouraged by it but instead it makes her feel a little nervous. 'When you, Morgan, were four years old, you wandered off from us at the summer fayre in the village. One moment you were looking at the cake stall, the next you were gone. And Marina was shouting your name over and over, so loudly that they couldn't hear the raffle announcements going on. But it wasn't Marina who found you, and it wasn't me who found you. Isla, you did. Because you took yourself off and you thought carefully about where your sister would go and you found her. By the hook-a-duck, because you'd remembered how she really wanted to win a stuffed tiger toy. And you dragged her back to us and you were so cross with her for scaring us but Marina held you both so close and said that it didn't matter where one of you went as long as the other one was looking out for you.' Jasper sighs, the sound shaky and tossed about by the wind. 'Then we went to get ice cream. And you two argued over who got the bigger scoop . . . until Marina pushed them both onto your noses and made you laugh . . .'

He trails off, leaving them in silence. Isla feels herself surrounded by the memory, shocked by her father's vivid storytelling. Usually it is her telling the long story and it is Jasper giving her the one-liners. But now she can practically smell the strawberry ice cream, hear the echoey speaker calling out the raffle numbers. Isla can almost feel the stickiness of her sister's hand when she grabbed her from the hook-a-duck and pulled her away.

'Except we don't do that any more. That would require *communicating* which is apparently impossible.' Morgan's voice is quiet, but has enough hardness in it for Isla to hear. 'Right, Isla?'

Isla doesn't get a chance to respond; Jasper jumps in first. 'No, you don't. And that's why I'm sharing that memory today. Because I don't know what to do with you two. Your mother raised you to be a *team* and, yes, I know that I haven't helped. And I feel the shame of that every day. But I thought that you two working together was one thing I could always count on. And when you left, Morgan, I always kept hoping that one day you'd come back and it would be the same as always. You two, being a team. And it has been and that's been wonderful. But now, for whatever reason, it's as if you're fighting over the ice cream all over again and you just won't sodding stop.'

Jasper stands up, pinching the bridge of his nose. 'So. I'm going to go home and you two are going to sort this out, now. Because this has gone on long enough. Call me if you need a lift, together. Otherwise don't bother.' Isla watches in silence as he rests his fingers briefly against the top of his wife's gravestone, sees the way he lingers for a second. Then he shoots both Isla and her sister a firm look of disappointment, before turning to leave.

Isla hears the sound of his feet on the muddy grass getting softer and softer, until they're just left with the wind and the rustling of the trees.

'He seems better,' Morgan finally says, fingernails digging into the arm of the bench. 'Almost like he would cope if his daughter went to Hawaii for an internship…'

Isla feels herself tense, her instinct to snap back riling up instantly. 'Stop it, Morgan, please,' she finally murmurs. Because really, she's just tired. Tired of having to pretend that the decision to ignore the internship is so easy and obvious. She's been pretending to Dylan all week, after all. *I just don't think it's for me. Really, it's fine. Thanks for the offer though!* She's almost forgotten what her real tone of voice sounds like.

Morgan falls silent and, when Isla looks over, she sees her sister sliding off the bench and coming to sit beside the gravestone. 'She'd tell you to go.'

That's the final straw for Isla and she finds herself standing up, moving a few steps away. 'That's sort of besides the point, Morgan. If Mum was here to tell me to go then of course I would go. But she's not here and that's the whole shitting problem! I can't leave you because she's gone! And somebody has to do all the things she can't do any more! And I can't do that if I'm in bloody Hawaii! So don't you *dare* try to use Mum against me like that! When I am just doing what she told me to do – to look out for my family! I am not going to leave you alone! And so I cannot go. I have to do my job! I have to look after you!'

Raising her hands in the air, Morgan shakes her head. 'You just... just don't get it, Isla. I'm already fucking alone. I was alone the moment my mother dropped down dead in front of me. And that won't change just because you're around to cook me damn pasta! This isn't just on you. This isn't just *your* family.'

'I'm not saying it is! But somebody has to do all those things Mum did, somebody has to keep us together. And it's not going to be Dad and you're... you're barely around long enough for it to be you. So I have to do this, I have to help!'

'The way you did at my sixteenth?'

Isla stops, frowning. 'What?' she whispers, a little hesitantly. Though of course she's heard every word.

Morgan looks away, sadness dragging at the corners of her eyes. 'I know that's where you went the other day. I felt it... the memory changing...'

'Yeah, for the better,' Isla interjects, but there's a churning feeling in her stomach now. 'It... it was for the better, right?'

'Do you know what I remember about that party, Isla? Before you changed it? Yeah, I can remember what it was like before as well. Your precious stone has made damn sure of that.' Morgan takes a shuddering breath, brushing at her eyes furiously. 'I remember that my sister went to all this effort to make my birthday brilliant and for one glorious moment I was happy. Now... now I remember that my sister left my party and forced my severely depressed father to attend. I remember that my friends spent the whole evening pretending not to notice his trembling hands when he greeted them. I remember that when he had a complete ... freak out and you took him home again, you wouldn't accept that you'd made a mistake. Because you know better, Isla. You *always* know better, right?'

Words have left Isla. All she can feel is the disconcerting sensation of one memory being unravelled and replaced with another. She sees her father fumbling over his beer until it clatters to the floor and makes everyone glance over before hastily looking away once more, pretending not to notice. She sees the moment when she finds him in the toilets, tears running in twisting rivulets down his face. She can practically feel his almost claw-like grasp on her arm as she helps him out and takes him home. Morgan's sixteen-year-old frustration floats through her ears. *Why did you bring him? Why would you make him come to this of all things?*

Isla can hear what she said back then, as clear as day. And the words slip out again now. 'I was only trying to help ...'

Morgan shakes her head. 'You're *always* trying to help, Isla. That's the problem. You spend so much time trying to help that you never actually stop and think whether you should.'

Panic is rising in Isla, an unstoppable movement that brings with it a sickening realisation that she has made things worse. Again. How many times has she tried to get things right, to make things better, only for it to come back to haunt her? Isla can feel frustration itch against her skin, can feel heat rising up the back of her neck despite the October chill.

'I couldn't just leave it, Morgan! I couldn't just not try anything! You're my little sister!'

'So you've reminded me, over and over again. But I don't always need you to come to my rescue! I don't always need a fucking … guardian angel, changing my past! I can manage, I *did* manage for four years, on my own!'

The itching, burning frustration is getting too much. Isla can feel it taking over every part of her. Perhaps that's why her words turn cruel in her head and perhaps that's why she does nothing to stop them coming out. 'You didn't manage though, Morgan! You got fucking pregnant! That's about as far away from managing as you can get!'

It's easy to see that she's gone too far. She senses it before the words even leave her mouth and now, as she looks at Morgan's ashen face, she knows it for sure. For a moment there's just terrible, weighty silence. Then her sister speaks, voice dreadfully, painfully quiet.

'Well. I guess it's a good thing I lost the baby, isn't it.' Each word sounds robotic, clunky. And when Morgan stands up, she's stiff, rigid. Isla thinks that for a moment she sees a glistening of tears in her eyes but Morgan has blinked them away almost instantly. 'I'm going for a walk. Alone, Isla. I need … I need to be alone.'

Isla wants to say something else; she doesn't want Morgan to leave with those dreadful words of Isla's ringing in her ears. She wants to apologise or explain or *something*. But her mouth is dry and her head is empty. She's got nothing. All she can do is watch her sister leave her alone with her thoughts and her mother's gravestone.

She feels that there should be tears from her too. Everything's hopeless enough for there to be, right? But as she sits back on the bench, she feels nothing. Only numb, the same numbness she has felt since she answered that phone call from her sister all those years ago and had her world irredeemably changed.

So, in the absence of tears, Isla just stares at the wind-worn gravestone, at her mother's name, and tries to work out what on earth she's meant to do.

Morgan's words float back into her head after a moment, quite uninvited. *I was alone the moment my mother dropped down dead in front of me.* All these days she's visited and tried to fix to help her sister but really it was never going to work. Not until she's fixed that one moment, that one dreadful, lonely moment. And she knows she can't change her mother's death, but that's not the only part of that day that broke her little sister.

Isla stands suddenly as determination crackles through her like her own personal lightning. She knows what she has to do.

There's a moment though, when she pauses. When another set of Morgan's words force themselves into her head. *I don't always need a fucking guardian angel changing my past.*

But Isla shakes them away. And starts to run.

Twenty-Seven

Isla's muscles are screaming their complaint by the time she scrambles down the last set of stones and onto Karrekoth beach. She's run the entire way from the cemetery, despite the treacherousness of some parts of the coastal path. Ridiculous really; it's not as though the stone is going anywhere.

But then it's not the stone she's worried about.

So here she is; slightly out of breath and leg muscles almost trembling as she strides briskly across the beach and towards the stone. There's been a strong wind bombarding the coast since she was last here and a growing wall of sand has been thrown up against the side of the stone, to the point that their usual sitting ledge is almost at risk of being buried.

The cracked side is still visible, though. And that's all that she needs.

'Please work,' she whispers, partly to herself and partly to the faceless stone before her. She scrambles up the sandy verge, rests her hand on the rock. Closes her eyes and thinks as hard as she can about what she needs to do. The stone hasn't always been the most reliable at listening to her thoughts but she has to hope that this time it will. She has to hope that it hasn't decided that someone who utters such cruel words to their sister shouldn't be allowed this extraordinary doorway to the past.

For a terrible moment there's nothing and Isla groans softly to herself as desperation makes her shoulders sag. *Please, let me help her.*

Maybe it's coincidence, maybe it's not. But as she feels that desperate thought leave her, she feels the ground shift and the wind disappear. She feels the light sear against her closed eyelids.

The moment Isla senses that she has arrived, she wastes no time. Eyes snap open and she briefly takes in the scene before her, getting her bearings. Then she starts running. Karrekoth's buildings and roads slowly take over from the beach she arrived on and soon Isla is stumbling to a halt outside the corner shop.

She scans the newspapers stacked outside for the date, feels a rush of something that could be triumph, but could also be panic, when she finds it – 20th October. Ten years ago.

Isla wheels around until she's facing Karrekoth's tiny church and squints at the clock face set into its tower. Half one. If she's remembered and calculated correctly, she has four and a half hours. Long enough, but only just.

Isla stands in the autumn sunlight bathing Karrekoth harbour for a moment, forcing her heart to slow down enough for her brain to be able to think. She just needs a phone with signal in this time period (unlike the one in her pocket). Easy enough, surely. Except she's also got to do it without anyone recognising her, which is easier said than done in a tiny village.

She's just considering risking asking Matt Kingston in the shop again, when she sees her father walking up the nearby harbour steps and towards the café. For a moment she is floored by the confidence in his stride and the ease with which he carries the thick coil of rope he has. Nine years has certainly not been kind to Jasper Pembroke. Isla can feel a growing temptation to follow him, to get lost in the last moments of a father unaffected by grief, but she can't. She's not here to help him.

Besides, she knows her father has a phone on his boat and has just left it unattended to go to the café. Which means she has at least twenty minutes while he drinks his coffee and avoids being asked to look at the café's toilet plumbing for the hundredth time. A perfect opportunity.

She waits, poised, until the café door has shut behind him. Then Isla hurries to the harbour steps and tries not to slip on the kelp-covered stone in her haste to reach the bottom.

Despite her rush, Isla can't quite battle back the lump of emotion at seeing her father's boat in such good condition. The paint is pristine, the windows glisten proudly in the sunlight. Everything on the small deck is exactly where it should be. A thousand miles from the sad, peeling specimen it is in her time. She tried to help Jasper keep up with the maintenance but at some point it slipped by the wayside, overshadowed by more important things like keeping the house standing.

Swallowing away the lump, Isla carefully steps onto the deck of the boat and ducks under the low roof, into the bulkhead. The miniature room is mainly filled with fishing paraphernalia but hooked to one wall is the satellite phone that her mother made Jasper get after he came home two hours late from a fishing trip.

It takes Isla a moment to remember how to work it and another moment to remember how to call directory enquiries. Funny how such things have disappeared from her head now she lives in the world of mobile phones and search engines.

Soon she's got the number she needs, though. The dial tone rings painfully slowly as Isla keeps her eyes glued to the harbour steps in case she spots her father's feet, but finally someone answers.

'Exeter University, student services. How may I help?'

'Oh, hi. I'm trying to get an urgent message through to Isla Pembroke, I'm her ... sister. She's a first-year marine-biology student, she's in James Owen Court … I can't quite remember her room number.'

'Right, that's fine. I can find her easily enough on the database. What's the message, please?'

Isla draws a deep breath, forces herself to think for one more moment until she's absolutely committed to her decision. Then she speaks again, voice managing to remain somewhat steady. 'Her mother's fallen seriously ill. She needs to get home immediately.'

'I see. Right, well, I will get that message to her straight away and ensure she's able to get herself home, don't you worry.'

'Th-thank you, I really appreciate it.' Isla hangs up then, not wanting to waste any further time now she knows her job is done. Fingers slightly slippy, she fumbles with placing the phone back in its cradle before scrambling off the boat and back up onto the main street of Karrekoth.

There's no sign of Jasper but Isla still doesn't hang around. She makes her somewhat shaky way back to the main beach, finds a secluded spot away from all the dog walkers that frequent the stretch of smooth and golden sand during the day, and sits down. Despite the sunshine, it's still October and Isla can feel the chill of the coastal breeze already setting into her bones. But she can't move, not yet. Adrenaline is still coursing through her body from the thrill of a successfully completed task but, as it starts to seep away, Isla feels the weight of what she's done beginning to take its toll. She's made a change, something that was clearly small enough for the stone to allow it to happen, but something that she hopes might make a significant difference.

Now all she has to do is wait.

Somehow the hours slip by, in strange patches of speed and then dismal sluggishness. Isla spends a good portion of the time sitting on the beach but, as the sun begins to lower, she starts to head up towards her home. Nobody pays her any attention as she makes her journey, not even the irrepressible chatterbox Maude out for her evening walk to ease her arthritis. So Isla is fairly sure the stone has figured out her need to check that her plan has worked, and has obligingly made her invisible once again.

She stands outside her home and tries to ignore the sensation of time ticking away for her mother, because it feels like being trapped at the bottom of a sand timer, slowly drowning in sand. There's nothing she can do for her, she forces herself to remember. This is about Morgan.

Isla thinks it must be around half past five when a taxi pulls up in the driveway and comes to a halt outside the house. She watches herself half fall out of the car, hurriedly throw some cash at the driver then race towards the door. She yanks open the front door, just in time to allow Morgan's shout of shock to escape into the evening air.

And though part of her really can't face seeing this scene *again*, she has to know that it's worked. So with reluctance weighing down every step, she follows her younger self into the house.

As she stumbles into her hallway, Isla can feel the memories twisting and changing inside her, can remember now how the whole way home from university she felt a dreadful fluttery sensation in her chest, as if a butterfly was trapped in there. She didn't know what exactly was waiting for her, not until she came barrelling into the kitchen and saw her mother's prone form on the floor, saw Morgan huddled next to her.

Now, her sister's fear is so potent that it slithers right down the corridor and attacks the new arrivals viciously. Even the ones that cannot be seen.

'Morgan! What's happened?' The younger Isla skids to a halt in the kitchen with her invisible older self close behind. Her sister's head snaps up, and her eyes cloud with confusion for a moment but then relief takes over.

'Isla? You're ... you're here? What ...' She shakes her head, focusing on the real problem at hand. 'I don't know what's happened to her!' Morgan's voice cracks on the last word, an egg dropped to the floor. As Isla drops down beside her, Morgan's fingers worm into the material of her cardigan and cling on tightly.

'It's okay, it's okay.' It's not okay but maybe her words will make it so, Isla remembers fruitlessly hoping. Or at least make her sister breathe.

'Have you called an ambulance?' she asks, and then when Morgan shakes her head, the younger Isla settles on this course of action. 'Okay ... Get the phone, call an ambulance. She needs an ambulance.' Isla watches her younger self squeeze her sister's hand as firmly as she can, before gently disentangling it from her cardigan. 'Now, Mogs.'

Morgan squeezes her eyes shut for a second, tears dribbling down her cheeks. But then she jumps up obediently, runs for the cordless home phone and starts to call 999. Her older sister watches her for a second to check she's doing it right, then turns back to her mother. She didn't want to really; Isla feels that new memory settling into her head; how she'd been able to force herself not to look properly so far by pretending that all her attention had to be on Morgan. But now she has to look, has to notice how the colour has drained from her mother's face like the tide disappearing from the beach; has to notice the way her eyelids flutter and her breath comes in occasional, painful-sounding bursts.

'Mum?' Isla tries, taking her mother's hand. From the door,

the older Isla finds herself glancing at her own hand. She can recall now, how her mother's hand felt both clammy and freezing at the same time, how she didn't know what that meant. 'Mum, can you hear me?'

There's the softest noise of what could be acknowledgement but it's so quiet that it could simply be a particularly laboured breath. Isla can feel the younger Isla's terror spread throughout the room, chilling the air impossibly.

Morgan drops down beside her sister, phone clutched to her ear. 'She's not breathing really, no. Um ... I don't know ...' She turns away from the phone, looks at her sister. Her eyes are wide, clutching onto Isla's like she's her life raft in the middle of a storm. 'They're asking if she's got a pulse.'

'Right,' Isla whispers, then carefully picks up her mother's arm and places her fingers on her wrist. Marina doesn't react at all. Was there a pulse? Isla feels the new memory forming in her head, feels the rhythm of a fading heartbeat on the edge of her fingers; one little flutter then silence. The silence was crushing, enough to make her own heart surge into a sprint of desperate, panicked beats.

Slowly, the younger Isla shakes her head. 'I heard one heart-beat but now there's nothing.'

Morgan relays her words, tears dropping from her chin to the floor in large spots. 'Right. I'll see if she can.' Looking back to Isla, she carries on, 'They said the ambulance is coming as quickly as it can but we need to do chest compressions until then. Can you do those?'

Isla winces from her invisible vantage point. Can she do those, right. It sounds so incongruous, like being asked if she can make a fucking boiled egg. Isla spent a few summers before this year working as a lifeguard at the beach and had learnt how to do them then. But that's not the same as doing them on a real

263

person. And it's certainly not the same as doing them on her own mother.

But the younger Isla pleats her hands together all the same and places them on her mother's chest. Marina looks like a limp doll beneath her daughter's palms, and when Isla begins to press down on her mother's chest, her body jerks sickeningly. It's enough to make the watching Isla's stomach twist.

'You can do it, Isla,' Morgan whispers, obviously noticing how her sister's hands falter a little. 'You *have* to do it, Isla. They're coming. It won't be long now.'

Her sister sounds utterly uncertain but it seems to help. Isla starts the compressions, counting along to try and keep time. Or perhaps it's just to distract from the reality of what she's doing.

Isla is almost hypnotised by the scene before her, unable to draw her eyes away from her own hands trying to start her mother's heart up again. Unable to focus on anything but the tugging sensation in her brain as these new memories replace old ones.

At some point the ambulance crew arrive and Morgan hurries to let them in. It felt like mere seconds and, at the same time, hours. Sturdy hands take over on her mother's chest and Isla can see her younger self's almost reluctance. She knew rationally that they were the hands of paramedics, real experts, but she still had to resist the urge to fight them away. It's her mother, after all. Surely she should save her, nobody else.

'No pulse, Greg.'

'I'll get the defib.'

'Girls, can you push back this table? We're going to need some space.'

It takes the younger Isla a long second to realise that the paramedic is speaking to her. It had sounded a bit like the woman was on the other side of a high, thick wall. Finally, though, Isla nods and stumbles to her feet. Morgan is hovering behind Greg the paramedic but Isla grabs her arm and tugs her away.

'You don't want to see this,' she mutters. 'Help me move this table, okay?'

Morgan doesn't argue, which is perhaps a sign of how tightly panic has woven around her. They push the table against one wall, away from the limp form that's supposed to be their mother. With the job done, Morgan turns back towards the paramedics and her mother but as the defibrillator begins counting down to a shock, Isla instinctively tugs her sister back to her. With a second left, she hugs Morgan tight to her chest with one hand pressed firmly to the back of her head.

From the doorway, Isla watches her mother jerk like a broken puppet and knows she will never forget that sight now she has forced herself to see it. Twice. But at least she knows her sister hasn't had to.

Morgan wriggles free once Isla allows her to, shoots her sister a fiercely accusatory look. 'That was not your decision,' she whispers, eyes burning. But then she's crumpling like soggy paper and falling right back against Isla's chest. Her crying is quiet, unobtrusive. Nothing like the young Morgan's usual dramatics. The sound of it wriggles right under Isla's skin and burns.

'I've got a pulse, just about. It's very weak though,' Greg confirms to the other paramedic.

She nods, moves to grab the stretcher they brought with them. 'Let's go.'

It's a flurry of activity and then suddenly their mother is being carried from the room and the sisters are being left behind. Isla almost wishes they would just stay rooted here in this kitchen, arms wrapped securely around each other, because at least in here they can just pretend nothing's wrong. But she knows they won't. She knows they can't.

'We need to go,' the younger Isla whispers, smoothing the back of Morgan's hair. 'Are you ready to go?'

Morgan lifts her head up, meets her eyes. Hollow green meets hollow green. Both as empty as each other. 'No,' she sighs, but steps away all the same. Her hand slips into Isla's and the older Isla can recall how she felt a brand new sense of responsibility settle over her. So heavy that it was as if Morgan's hand had been carved from stone.

She also remembers how it scared her to death.

The world dissolves soon after that. The beach of her own time returns but Isla can't move, not yet.

She isn't quite sure how long she sits in the sand with the onslaught of new memories pressing against her skull. But she knows she can't move until she's let them settle.

It feels a little bit like trying to settle a porcupine. It hurts, prickles. Her head feels heavier, burdened with a whole new trauma, as the image of her mother being shocked runs through her mind, over and over, and makes her chest tighten, her stomach twist.

There's a few terrible minutes where she has to battle against her own almost evolutionary instincts to protect her own sanity, where she has to resist the urge to just turn back to the stone and change it all back again. What if this destroys her, rips her apart from the inside out? What good will she be for her sister then?

But Isla only has to remember the feeling of her sister crying in her arms to know that she's done the right thing. Morgan wasn't alone, Morgan had her there and she didn't have to see every terrible moment. That's good enough for Isla.

Finally, after a long while, Isla pulls herself to her feet. It's time to go home, time to find out what difference she has actually made. She can feel herself shivering a little, but she's not sure if that's the cold or the new memories.

She doesn't get a chance to think about it further, though. The sand and rocks before her are suddenly lit up in bright, gold light. Light that she's come to recognise all too well. Except it seems brighter this time, more determined almost.

Isla turns back around, squinting slightly against the glare. The stone is shining once more and seems to be shining right at her, as if it's a spotlight trained directly and deliberately in her direction.

'What? What is it?' she asks out loud. 'I don't need you again. I've done all I need for now.'

The light shows no signs of faltering. In fact, Isla is sure that it gets even brighter until her eyes begin to water a little. She steps forward, hesitantly.

'Is there … something else?' Of course there's no answer. Just the light, glowing at her with belligerent persistence. Isla glances towards the sea for her usual tide check, sees no oncoming waves that could stop her getting any closer.

So she has no excuse. 'Okay. Okay.' A deep breath, an attempt to gather whatever strength she has left. 'Take me where I need to go.'

And the stone does just that.

Twenty-Eight

The Pembroke house is dark, the true darkness of a house asleep. Night presses against the window, all-consuming. Isla remembers how she used to think that, when night-time arrived, it would seem as if the house was in space. No trees to see any more, no distant strip of sea. Just shadows.

With the glow of the stone still scorched on her eyes, everything seems even darker than usual. Isla stands by the kitchen table with just stillness and silence for company, except for the gentle ticking of the clock that's showing the time as three o'clock.

'What am I doing here?' she mutters, partly to herself and partly to whatever invisible power decided she needed to come to her house in the middle of the night.

Of course there's no answer, but it turns out that Isla doesn't need one. It becomes obvious why she's here a moment later, when her sister comes down the stairs, suitcase in tow.

It's a stark difference from the Morgan crouched beside her dying mother, but it's also nowhere near the Morgan who just stormed away from her in a cemetery. Her hair seems even more stubbornly dark, and hangs heavily around her face in a thick, almost protective curtain that Morgan does nothing to push back. Her clothes match her hair in shade; Isla remembers that dark hoody that her sister lived in for months at this age, a cotton cocoon of sorts. Everything about her sister at this point in her life screams 'don't look at me', not that there's anyone around to do that just now.

So this is it. This is the night Morgan ran away. And, for some reason, the stone has decided now is the moment that Isla needs to see it.

Isla instinctively steps back into the shadows of one corner of the kitchen. Her eyes stay fixed on her sister, though, as she cautiously places the suitcase down by the door and pads stealthily over to the sink. She can see her sister's hands shaking a little as she opens the small shell-patterned tin on the windowsill behind the sink, and empties out the money that Isla always kept in there for emergencies.

Even now, with four years passed, Isla still feels the residual rage she had when she discovered that carefully saved money gone. Even now, when she can see the way her sister hesitates before putting the money into her back pocket. Nobody was forcing her to take it and run away, after all.

Morgan glances around the kitchen and Isla is confused by the almost wistfulness in her gaze. If she's so fond of this place, why did she decide to leave? It still doesn't make any sense and Isla can't help the feeling of disappointment that this moment still happened. It was a long shot, of course, that her changing of the past would in turn change this huge moment in Morgan's life, but Isla couldn't help but dream. Except now that dream is dashed against the kitchen tiles, as her sister takes one final look at the kitchen before turning to go.

Isla's feet follow her, almost automatically. It seems that some part of her is desperate to see this moment play out, even if that means coming out of the shadows. But Morgan doesn't pay her silent and once again invisible stalker any notice. She carries on down the hallway, quietly puts her shoes on and zips herself into her coat. The hesitation in her is clear, which does make Isla feel a little better. This decision always seemed so easy for Morgan, judging from the casual texts she sent her family over those four years. Isla always thought Morgan treated the whole thing like an extended holiday but now, watching the way she looks back down the hallway, it would seem that this is a big decision for her.

But there's still no inkling as to why she made it.

It's as Isla is considering this for the umpteenth time that Morgan tugs something from the pocket of her hoody. It's an envelope, a little crumpled in the corners but with obvious care taken to smooth out said crumples. Even as she takes it out of her pocket, Morgan continues to attempt to neaten the appearance of the envelope. As she's doing this, Isla catches a glimpse of the front, sees her own name scrawled on the front of it.

A jolt of almost foreboding confusion fills Isla's chest, because she's fairly sure she's never seen this envelope in her life.

But, as the seconds tick by, it becomes just a little clearer; clear as swamp water rather than clear as mud. Her sister grips the envelope tighter and tighter, until, in the silence of night, there's the audible sound of paper creaking. Then she shakes her head, rubs at her face with almost frustration, and pockets the envelope once more.

This inability to leave behind this mystery envelope seems to lock Morgan into her decision. With a heavy sigh, she lifts up her suitcase once more and turns to leave. There's one hopeful moment where the dark and the wind outside makes Morgan pause on the threshold, one hopeful second when Isla wonders if perhaps she won't go after all.

Until Morgan seems to steel herself and leaves. The door closes with deliberate gentleness but Isla still winces as if it's been slammed. Silence settles back into place but now it feels different, heavier somehow. Perhaps it's the disquieting feeling of knowing that, in a few hours, the remaining Pembroke family members will realise that their home has just splintered yet again.

And still, Isla doesn't know why. Doesn't know why her father will soon be forced to ring the police and ask for their help in finding his daughter. Why Isla will have to spend the next four years dreading each text message in case it says something she can't handle. *I'm never coming back; It's your fault, you know; I'm afraid the owner of this phone was found dead.*

Perhaps that's what drives her forward, down the hallway and out the door. The wind howls around her and, in the dark, it's spine-chilling, like the cliffs are shouting at her.

But if her seventeen-year-old sister can walk into this shadowy nightmare, then so can Isla.

She hurries away from the house, following the path of her driveway until she has caught up with her sister. Now she's confident that she is indeed invisible, Isla has no problem with walking right next to Morgan. Besides, she wants to see her properly, just in case the answers to this whole mess are written on her face.

Isla sees hollow anger and badly hidden fear but that's it. Morgan could just be going for one of her furious walks that were fairly standard at this age, if it wasn't for the suitcase and the time of night.

They walk with purposeful speed until the road curves past the beach toilets, where a car is waiting with its engine running. Instinctively, Isla wants to grab her sister and tug her away. What sort of person is waiting around in a car at this hour, after all?

The answer comes as an icy shock a moment later, bringing Isla a chill that has nothing to do with the coastal wind. As

Morgan approaches the car, the front door pops open and Dylan Burroughs steps out.

Isla feels herself come to a halt, feet suddenly freezing to the ground. What the hell is Dylan Burroughs doing here? He barely knows her sister at this point; what the hell is going on?

But everything about him suggests he's been expecting her, from the grim smile of greeting to the way he holds out a hand for her suitcase.

'Bastard.' The word slips from Isla's mouth, full of poisonous rage. How could he do this? And, even worse, how could he never tell her that he was involved? He must have known how scared she and her father were. Yet he said nothing, buggered off to do his own fancy marine-biology things just a month or so later with no consideration for the family he helped break up.

Dylan's speaking; she can hear it distantly over the wind. She knows she should listen but her anger is making it hard to focus. It's only when her sister lets out a small groan of turmoil that Isla finds the ability to listen once more.

'Are you sure about this, Morgan?' Dylan asks, taking a step towards her with a frown of concern. 'You can just turn and go back … I won't say anything whatever you choose.' There's real care in his voice and Isla shakes her head, mind buzzing with bemusement.

Morgan looks back towards her house, face barely visible in the light of the distant street lamp. It casts long shadows across her features, transforming the few tears on her cheeks into strange, twisting snakes. Doubt lingers there for a moment but then she shakes her head, turns back to Dylan. 'I'm not sure, no. But I'm not going to go for long, I'll be back after a little while. This has to be better, Dylan. This *has* to help her.'

It's Dylan's turn to look up at the Pembroke home, his brow furrowed with thought. 'And if it makes it worse?'

'Then I come back.' Morgan takes a step towards the passenger side of the car, her expression back to steely determination. 'You ... you will tell me if it gets worse, right?'

Dylan sighs, turning to get into the car himself. 'If I can. It's not like I have hidden cameras in your house, Morgan. But I'll do my best to keep an eye out, until you're back.'

He slides into the car, Morgan following suit a moment later. But Isla can only watch, rooted to the ground by a sickening mixture of confusion and resentment. Because who on earth did Morgan think she was helping by leaving? And how did Dylan expect to keep an eye on their family when he wasn't even here? The questions roil around Isla's head, almost making her feel sick.

Before she can fully recover from any of this, the car begins to move. It rumbles away from its parking spot, brake lights almost taunting her as they pull away from her. It's enough to wrench Isla from her shock and she starts running after the car, desperation ridding her brain of any sort of logic. What does it matter if she's invisible, or that she can't hope to catch a car?

Logic goes only so far when Isla's sister is involved.

She runs after the car until the harbour comes into view and the glowing brake lights get so far ahead that they become tiny pinpricks of light. Isla stops denying reality then and allows herself to stumble to an unsteady halt. Her breaths come in short, sharp gasps, each feeling as though she's breathing in a whirlwind of glass.

'Morgan ...' Her sister's name leaves her now-dry lips and is bounced around her ears by the wind, taunting her. She tries to console herself with the reminder that her sister is back safely in the present, that this won't be the last time Morgan sets foot in Karrekoth.

But betrayal has a funny way of smothering all other thoughts.

Besides, her sister might be back but right now, with Morgan barely talking to her, Isla isn't sure how much different things really are. It still feels like her sister's being driven away from her, into the night.

Isla has no idea how long she stays on this dark and dismaying road before the stone takes pity on her. She's not even sure she notices the moment that asphalt becomes sand, that middle of the night becomes beginning of an evening. The beach and the stone drift back into her awareness and she sighs, feeling the exhaustion of a day that just will not stop hurting her.

Slowly, her next steps reveal themselves to her. Slowly, she realises that there is so much more to her sister's disappearance than just an angry, confused teenager taking off into the night. *I have to help her*, that's what Morgan said. And it's only now, that she really begins to take stock of those words. Morgan thought she was helping her. But Isla just can't work out how Morgan thought her leaving would help, not when her running away has always felt as if it was meant to be some sort of punishment. And then, in the midst of all this confusion, there's Dylan. A silent conspirator who has never once thought it was time to admit the truth to Isla.

Isla knows then that she has to speak to her sister, right now. There's too many unknowns for her to accept any more. With those thoughts buoying her along, Isla stands and stumbles away from the stone. For a moment she half expects (perhaps half hopes) it to glow once more, to draw her back into another confusing memory.

But it stays dark. And Isla has no choice but to begin the journey towards home and to the difficult conversations she knows will be waiting there.

Twenty-Nine

There's a surprise waiting for Isla in the kitchen but it's not necessarily a pleasant one. Which is, in itself, not a surprise for Isla at all; other people her age were surprised with engagements or trips to Paris, while Isla was surprised with smouldering fish pies and awful family revelations.

So when Isla steps inside and finds her father deep in conversation with none other than Dylan Burroughs, she lets that slightly sickening sensation of an unpleasant shock ride over her like the familiar wave that it is.

Jasper turns as Isla shuts the back door. 'Oh, there you are,' he says with barely enough warmth in his tone to defrost an ice cube. 'I was wondering where you'd got to.'

Isla glances briefly at the clock. It's been two hours since they went to the graveyard. Shit. Too long, too long to have those hateful words of hers festering in Morgan's head.

But there's another immediate problem to solve, right in front of her. 'What are you doing here?' she asks Dylan, deciding to get straight to the point.

Dylan looks a little nonplussed so Isla guesses some of her anger at him has seeped into her voice. Unusually for Isla, but perhaps unsurprisingly, she feels no guilt for that.

'He came over to see you,' Jasper supplies, now sounding more uncertain than irritated. 'Because of the date and all.'

For a moment, Isla feels herself soften, just a touch. 'You – you knew that was today?'

Dylan shrugs a little sheepishly, still watching her carefully. Isla wonders if he's been bracing himself for the day her tone turns frosty towards him, and so knows exactly what's caused it. 'Your sister mentioned it when I asked if she was all right at lunch.'

Immediately, Isla's head is filled with the image of the last conversation she witnessed between Morgan and Dylan. For a moment, the kitchen transforms into the dark road, the nearby lamp becomes the red glow of a car's retreating brake lights.

'Oh yes, you two are good at sharing things, aren't you?'

'Isla, are you all right?' Isla can feel her father staring at her with understandable shock, for the words that have just come from her mouth are dripping with a venom she wasn't even aware of possessing.

Dylan stands, the motion careful and cautious. 'Maybe we should go for a walk?' he asks, meaning weighing heavy in his words.

'Yes, maybe.'

'You just got back,' Jasper points out, frowning. Isla can see the beginnings of anxiety in the creases of his forehead and forces herself to take a moment to placate him.

'We won't be long, Dad. Then I'll get dinner on.' She keeps it simple, doesn't try to explain. She wouldn't know where to begin after all.

They leave Jasper muttering about going out to finish one of his jobs for the day and return to the blustery world outside. Isla leads them away from the beach, not wanting to sour her sanctuary with the surely unpleasant conversation they're head-ing towards. Instead, they follow the other coastal path up onto the cliffs overlooking the beach and Karrekoth, where there's no hiding place from the elements. Or from difficult questions.

The first bench they come to, Isla gestures for them to sit. The silence of their five-minute walk has been deafening, but Isla still can't quite bring herself to speak. Because she knows that once she begins, there's no going back. The truth about Dylan will be out in the world beyond the stone and there will be no more pretending that it didn't happen.

In the end, though, it is Dylan who speaks first. 'So,' he says, eyes set on the hazy horizon in the distance. 'I'm guessing from your new... slightly terrifying attitude that you found out. About Morgan.'

Isla looks across at him, trying to find some sort of explana-tion in the contours of his face. But there's nothing. 'Yes,' she finally says with a sigh, looking away. 'I found out.'

Dylan falls silent again, which just infuriates Isla all the more. 'That's it, then?' she prompts. 'You're just going to sit in silence while I try to be a sodding mind reader and work out what the hell compelled you to drive my sister away in the middle of the night, to take her away from her family? Because if that's your plan, Dylan, I swear to God I will throw you off this cliff right here and now.'

A wince and Dylan glances at her, regret pooling in his eyes. 'I don't doubt it,' he murmurs, grimacing a little. 'I'm not planning on sitting here in silence, Isla. I'm just... trying to work out where best to start. It's sort of complicated.'

'Really? Because it seems pretty bloody simple to me. You're a damn coward. And you're bloody lucky that Morgan came back safe. She was *seventeen*, Dylan! A child! What part of that felt okay?' Isla can feel rage gathering power inside her like a tsunami, can feel it rapidly barrelling out of her control. 'And you ... you have the audacity to come back here and suggest I bugger off to Hawaii on a jolly holiday ... I guess if I wasn't here you didn't have to be reminded of what you'd kept from me, was that the plan?'

'No, not at all!' Dylan looks suitably horrified at the idea but it doesn't do much to placate or convince Isla.

'Or maybe you just want Karrekoth free of the whole Pembroke family? Is that it?'

'Isla ...'

Isla holds up a hand, stopping whatever placatory nonsense is about to come out of his mouth. 'Don't. Whatever you're about to try, just don't. I don't want to hear another word from you unless it's you telling me why you thought it was okay to take my little sister away from her family.'

Dylan looks down, eyes fixed on the weathered ground at his feet. But it's clear they're focused on an entirely different scene. 'She was very convincing,' he says finally, 'and, well, I guess I believed in her cause, and believed her when she said she wouldn't be long gone. And, well, I figured that she'd do it anyway without my help so I thought it was best that I helped her get somewhere moderately safe. Then I didn't stick around long myself after she went, and I just assumed she'd come back soon as she said. And I know, I should have checked but things got so busy once I started working for Professor Sawyer.' He stops a little abruptly for a moment, perhaps sensing that reminding Isla of the marine biologist career she has missed out on is not the best move. 'Then when I came back last month and you said she'd been gone for four years ... well, I didn't know what to do.' At this point, he manages to look up and meet Isla's gaze. 'Isla, I know it was wrong ... but surely now you must understand that she was just trying to help, that she wasn't being a stupid rebellious teenager, she was being your sister.'

Isla can feel herself staring and can feel the blankness of that stare. Dylan's desperate look becomes confused in an instant and he frowns, leaning forward a little. 'Wait ... has she still not told you why she went?'

She shakes her head, watches how that simple motion sends Dylan reeling back away from her. 'Dylan. Why did she go?'

'It's really not my place ...'

'It wasn't your place to help her run away either but you managed that okay,' Isla retorts, sharp enough to slice Dylan's hesitation into shreds.

'Look, I don't know all the details,' Dylan hastily concedes, 'but I do know she was trying to help you.'

She knows that already, she heard that snatch of conversation on the dark road. But hearing it from Dylan again doesn't help it make any more sense.

'How? How could she have thought running away would help me?'

Dylan glances around a little helplessly, as if he's hoping someone else might appear from thin air and answer for him. When they don't, he sighs with defeat and turns back to face her. 'She said that until she left, you would never be able to move on. She said that her leaving meant that you were free.'

'But ...' Isla can feel excuses immediately brewing inside her, can feel the automatic denial preparing itself. Except this time, for once, she finds the willpower to push those instincts away. 'That's what she thought?' she finally asks.

A slow nod from Dylan. 'You were going to go for an interview for the aquarium in Exeter, remember?'

It's Isla's turn to nod now. Because of course she remembers. Exeter Aquarium is huge and proper and actually well regarded amongst marine biologists, and she'd got an interview, somehow. For the first time, Isla had felt herself step towards something like an achievement in her life.

'And do you remember why you never went for it?'

Sighing, Isla presses at her forehead as if that might somehow stem the approach of that particular memory. 'Yes,' she finally mutters. 'Morgan had a panic attack on the bus to college; I went to look after her instead.'

Dylan smiles a little and there's sympathy in his gaze, the sort that makes Isla feel distinctly nauseous. 'And someone else got the job, right? And you pretended it was fine but the way Morgan explained it, that was the moment she decided enough was enough. That she couldn't ... hold your life to ransom any longer, that was how she put it.' He shrugs, eyes back on the ground. 'I wasn't sure it made complete sense but I knew from those words that she wasn't any harm to herself. And, as I said, I thought she'd be back before the end of the week. If I'd known she was going to be away for four years, of course I'd never have helped her. But she'd never struck me as someone who really thought things through ... I guess this time she had.'

A hand comes to rest on hers and Isla considers pulling away. Something stops her though, and she can't quite explain what. 'I know I should have told you the truth, Isla. I was a coward. We were getting on so well and I thought there might, you know, be something there between us. And I didn't want to ruin it, even if I knew I should.'

Isla knows she needs to speak, knows she needs to say something to Dylan; an acceptance or rejection or *something*. But her mind, for once, is utterly blank. Nothing comes to her aid and, when Dylan pulls his hand away a second later, his disappointment is clear. Yet still, there's no words she can fathom into a sentence.

The sentence still hasn't arrived when Dylan speaks again. 'Look, I understand if you can't forgive me for this. But, I guess, if it helps ... I didn't say yes this time.'

Words arrive pretty quickly then. 'What?' Isla breathes, eyes snapping back to face him. 'What do you mean, this time?'

Dylan bites his lip and Isla can see the cogs whirring away behind his worried gaze. 'She – she asked me this morning. Whether I would help her out if she decided to leave again. But I said no, I told her she needed to work this out herself.'

There's a distinct sensation of the cliff eroding away beneath Isla's feet. Morgan was planning on leaving again. She went so far as to ask Dylan, knowing full well that this time he might tell Isla. And then she came home, decision hovering over her head, only for Isla to utter such cruel words that she couldn't stand being around her a second longer.

'But it's fine, right? I mean, I asked and your dad said she came back from work okay?' Dylan's voice is a faraway sound, like the whine of a mosquito, and Isla can only find enough concentration to shake her head slowly. 'Isla?' Dylan prompts, a little more urgently.

'She came home, but we had a fight over at the cemetery and ... she ran off.' Isla swallows and the sensation is somewhat akin to swallowing sand. 'She wasn't at the house when you got there?'

This time it's Dylan's turn to shake his head slowly. 'I – I don't think so.'

A panicky sense of foreboding trickles down Isla's back, a cold chill of fear. 'I have to go,' she whispers. 'I have to find her.'

Dylan murmurs something about helping and how he's so sorry to have kept this from her. But Isla has once again stopped listening, or rather stopped hearing. Because all she can hear now is her own words, on repeat. Their sudden, sharp cruelty digs at Isla's skin as she recalls the way her sister recoiled, how her skin paled. *I need to be alone*, that's what she said.

And Isla knows that her sister will go to awfully drastic lengths to be alone.

Thirty

A home is like a living extension of its occupants. That's something Isla has learnt over the years. When her mother was alive, her home always felt warm, always smelt sweet regardless of what was cooking. It had the same feeling that she would get sat on the harbour wall of Karrekoth, watching the sunset glisten on the ocean. When Morgan was born and was first brought home, Isla remembers how the home still felt warm and comforting, but the sunset came with a little whirling wind to agitate the surface of the sea. Then, of course, when her mother died, the home just felt hollow, like that dark, narrow cave that lurked at the other end of the beach and always made Isla feel uneasy.

Now, as Isla bursts through the door of her home with her throat stinging from running the whole way back, there's only fear to be found inside. It sticks to the wall like mould, immediately and oppressively filling her lungs as she shuts the door behind her. Silence crushes down, her ears strain desperately to hear something that might give her a sign that someone is here.

But there's nothing.

'We should check upstairs, just in case.' Dylan's voice is an unwelcome interruption to the silence, because Isla told him she didn't need his help and yet here he is, insisting on sticking by her side. As if finding Morgan the second time around makes up for the part he played first time around.

She doesn't want to, but she goes to check Morgan's room. Isla rests her fingers on the door and tries to find the strength to push it open. There's no time to hesitate, after all. But the fear has spread up here as well and it seems to sap away at the muscles in her arm.

A deep breath, then she does it. And even though she's expecting emptiness, it still hits her hard.

Isla can't quite give in to reality just yet, though. Her brain supplies dozens of nonsensical reasons why her sister wouldn't be in her room. And with those reasons as fuel, Isla searches the entire house. She upturns her own room, digs around under her father's bed as though her sister is five years old and not a damn adult. Checks the bathroom, hunts through the study and the sitting room. Stands in the kitchen and waits to see if she will appear, impossibly, from thin air.

Of course there's nothing and nobody. Isla drifts out into the back garden and stands at the top of their beach path, trying to spot anything that might possibly give her hope that this isn't happening.

Nothing.

With hands shaking, Isla pulls out her phone as she retreats back inside. She calls Morgan's phone three times, stubbornly sticks it out until the voicemail each time. *Please call me, Morgan. Please don't leave us. We can sort this. Please just call me.*

'Anything?' Dylan's voice is soft as he hovers by the kitchen table. Like a fly who knows he's highly at risk of being swatted.

Isla grips her mobile phone tightly, presses it against her forehead as if she can somehow telepathically convince her sister to ring back. She doesn't care that she's leaving Dylan hanging, she doesn't care that she's making things more awkward for him.

But in the end the silence of her non-ringing phone begins to press painfully against her ears and Isla has to give up.

'Nothing,' she whispers.

There's a slamming sound of the front door being opened then forcibly closed by the wind and Isla half leaps towards the hallway. But it's only Jasper.

'Sorry, bud, popped out to do a job that took longer than expected. Bloody church's heating has gone haywire. It was like a sodding oven in there—'

'Dad,' she rasps, bringing his rambling to an abrupt halt.

Jasper pauses, looking at her properly now he's left the gloom of the hallway and entered the kitchen. 'Isla?' he asks, concern slipping into his tone. Then he glances around the room, gaze barely skating over Dylan as his own worry clearly steps up a notch. An awful realisation begins to settle into the corners of his eyes. 'Where is she?'

It's not difficult to work out who her father means. Isla drops down into the nearest chair, legs suddenly feeling weak and shaky. 'I think she's gone again, Dad.'

'Christ. Okay. Okay.' He seems to use his repeated words to steady himself, before shaking his head and moving to wrap one arm around her. 'It's okay, love ...' For a moment he stays silent, then sighs heavily. 'I shouldn't have been so hard on you two at the graveyard, it wasn't fair ...'

Isla can hear heavy regret seeping into her father's words so she shakes her head rapidly. 'No, Dad, it was something I said.'

'I mean, I probably didn't help,' Dylan mutters from his spot by the door.

Jasper's expression is one of bemusement as he looks over to Dylan but Isla is having none of it. 'You can go now, Dylan.' Her tone is firm, with no wriggle room for arguments.

'Hey, Isla, it's okay. We could use the extra help.'

Amidst the cold feeling of panic and anger, Isla can't help but feel surprised by her father's steady reassurances and sense of calm. That's usually her role. She stays silent for a moment, allows the seething waves of emotion to calm down, then fixes Dylan with a firm look. Just in case he takes her next words as a false sign of forgiveness.

'Okay. You're probably right, Dad. Did you drive here, Dylan?' Once she receives a silent nod from Dylan, she goes on. 'Good, then we can check further afield while Dad checks the village.'

'R-right,' Dylan stammers.

'I'll meet you in the car. I need to talk to Dad, alone.' Isla watches as Dylan manages a wobbly attempt at a nod before hastily leaving, then turns back to her father.

'Do I want to know?' Jasper asks.

Isla hesitates, considers it. Then decides there isn't time. 'It's nothing, don't worry.'

Jasper surveys her for a moment, clearly trying to decide if he believes her. Then, at last, he nods. 'You wanted to talk to me?' he prompts, ever so gently. It reminds Isla of the tone she's usually using on him.

'Yes ... yes, I did ...' Isla whispers, but she can't find the energy to say any more. With Dylan gone there's no anger to distract her and the familiar sense of hopelessness returns, just too heavy for her to carry any longer, for her to even know where to start with explaining this mess to her father.

'Come on, Isla,' Jasper says with a surprising tenderness, as he moves to her side and places a hand on her shoulder. 'You're our family superhero. Never giving up, even when everything felt so ... so *awful*. So let's pick ourselves up, put on our raincoats, and go find our Mogs.'

Put on our raincoats; the words coax a weary smile from Isla because it's what her father always used to say when she was a child in the midst of a despairing moment (usually about the loss of a favourite pen or the words of an irritating classmate). They'd put on their raincoats and go down to the beach to find the best rock pools, and they'd lose themselves in the miniature worlds, wrapped up against the elements and safe from real life, for just a while.

'I miss those days... when it was so easy to fix things,' Isla admits, and Jasper snorts with a weary understanding.

'Tell me about it. Now let's move.'

So Isla finds herself being handed her coat and led outside. Dylan waits in his car, pale in the glow of the setting sun, but for a moment Isla is frozen by the weight of her next decision and how it might affect their success in finding Morgan. It feels like those books she used to read, where you had to choose your own fate and one decision would send you tumbling back to the start. Except this time, she knows she can't just try again. She knows that if this goes wrong, the stone will not let her change it.

And that's why she can't go any further, not until she's said the ugly truth growing inside her. 'I... I think it's my fault, Dad.' The words taste so unpleasant against her tongue, a rotten piece of fruit.

Jasper turns sharply to stare at her, his frown fully furrowed. 'What are you talking about, you daft thing? How can this be your fault?'

'I've failed her. I have! To run away once, maybe you could blame her but two times?' Isla whispers, feeling that all-too-familiar and all-too-unwelcome lump of tears in her throat that she once again forces herself to swallow away. 'I didn't listen to her... she was obviously screaming for help again and I missed it *again*. I couldn't help her, I just made it worse.'

'And who said it was your job to help her?' Isla hears the rustle of her father's coat as he shifts closer, then pulls her into another hug. It's funny how even now, as an apparent grown-up, it still feels as comforting as it did when she was a child.

But there's still the nagging truth that she can't ignore. 'Dad … who else was going to?'

She feels his gentle wince and it brings another wave of guilt over her, but the truth is the truth.

'Look, I know I wasn't exactly the best father for you two …'

'You couldn't help it.'

'Whether I could or not, that's not the point. Not having a decent father and not having your mother doesn't automatically make you a parent, Isla. You were barely a grown-up yourself. And you know what? You did a damn good job considering. You've not failed anybody, you hear me?'

'I was meant to keep her safe … I promised Mum I'd keep her safe.'

'And you *did*. Isla, come on now. Who kept her fed, who kept her clothed and in a warm house? Who made sure that she was looked after so well that we never had to get social services involved?' Jasper's somewhat calloused hands gently take her hands and squeeze, bringing her gaze up to meet his. 'Marina was an extraordinary woman and an incredible mother. But honestly? I'm not sure even she would have been able to keep Morgan from doing what she thinks is best. Sometimes us Pembrokes just need to do our own thing.'

Isla feels a rush of affection for her father that she hasn't felt with such strength for a long time. Perhaps it's because, for the first time in a long time, she truly sees the man she grew up with before her. The man who knew exactly what to say to untwist that knot of worry she so often tangled inside herself.

'I should go,' she murmurs finally.

'Yes, you should. Go on, go find her … and sort that soft-headed fish boy out at the same time.' Jasper shoots Dylan a look of disparagement before turning back to Isla, winking. 'I get the sense he needs it.'

With a shaky laugh, Isla hugs him tightly, pressing against his chest to gather the familiar scent of washing powder mixed with sawdust.

One last moment of security, then she goes.

Thirty-One

It's a dreadful fear, the fear of losing a loved one. Isla remembers when she was little and lost her mother for a moment in the shopping centre, and how it felt like wading through the ocean only to come across an unexpected deep spot; an awful sensation of suddenly being totally out of your depth.

Isla remembers when she went to wake Morgan up for college that morning and found her bedroom empty. That time it didn't just feel like a sudden deep spot in the sea, it felt like being dragged into the centre of a whirlpool.

So tonight Isla isn't sure where to start. Once she's got into Dylan's car and he's asked her where to go first, there's a terrifying moment as her mind reels at the sheer size of the world around her. It's been at most two hours since Morgan could have disappeared. And the road from here splits into dozens of tributaries almost as soon as it's over the first hill. Dozens of possible choices that her sister could have made and, right now, Morgan's mind feels as readable as the graffiti in the beach toilets.

But she can't hesitate forever.

They head for the train station first. It seems the most natural place, because Isla has a nasty, painful feeling that her sister will want to get as far away as she can, while she can. The sky is darkening around Dylan's old Jeep as he drives them out of the village, navigates the twisting corners. Isla can see the sun's light dipping behind the hills looming in front of her. It adds an almost fiery quality to the gloomy clouds. For the anxiety-ridden Isla, it feels a bit like they're driving towards the heart of a dragon's lair. Or the stomach of a volcano. Either way, it's not good.

It's a silent drive for the first few moments. Isla can feel Dylan's occasional glances bouncing off the side of her face but she ignores them initially, until it finally becomes too difficult to concentrate.

'I'm not sure what you're hoping for, Dylan, but I hope it's not my forgiveness.' Her voice is cutting, slicing mercilessly through their silence.

'No.' He stumbles over the simple word in his haste to spit it out, shaking his head rapidly. 'Of course not.'

'Then what? What do you want?'

Dylan doesn't say anything at first, focusing on heaving the Jeep round another hairpin bend. 'I just wanted to ask if you wanted to talk about it... about what your sister said to me before she went, last time.'

Isla knows it's entirely factually correct to add the 'last time', but that doesn't stop it burning against her skin. He's talking as if her disappearance is already done and dusted, as if the countdown to another four years of no Morgan has already begun.

'No,' she says firmly. 'I don't know why my sister decided to divulge so much to you about our personal lives but I certainly won't be making that mistake.'

Isla feels a slight shudder as Dylan momentarily forgets how to steer, then hears him sigh. 'Mistake?' he echoes.

She nods without hesitation, sisterly protectiveness still raging inside her like a wildfire. 'Yes, a mistake. If you were the right person to trust, you never would have taken her away.'

Bitter certainty radiates from her words, enough to kill the conversation there and then. Dylan stops talking and stops throwing her glances, which, at first, Isla welcomes, until the still silences grow so heavy and oppressive that she has to open a window to stop the feeling of suffocation.

By the time they reach the train station, the orange has gone from the sky and there is just black peppered with a few overly keen stars. The station is the only one serving the five main villages and towns along this coastline, including Karrekoth, and it sits just a few streets away from the aquarium. In contrast to the daytime buzz that the seaside town has, it is now fairly quiet. A few people shelter from the wind beneath the station's awning as they wait for taxis or lifts, a station guard stands impassively beside the ticket machines, a taxi idles by the entrance. The two platforms beyond the barriers are sprinkled with a few people weighed down with bags but, as Isla stands and cranes her neck to look along the whole length of them, she sees no sign of Morgan.

Instantly, her mouth feels dry as panic threatens to engulf her. For a moment, Isla considers just giving up and sitting down on the cold stone floor. But it's a brief thought, spurred only by instinctive fear. Then she pulls herself together, tugs the reins of panic back, and forces herself to move again.

'Excuse me,' she croaks to the guard outside. Swallowing to try and return some of her speaking skills, she tries again: 'Excuse me, have you seen a girl with dark hair … uh, looks like this.' She fumbles about in her pocket for her phone and finds the most recent photo of Morgan she has. An ill-fittingly joyous selfie she took just a month ago, when their sisterhood was feeling the beginnings of healing. The aquarium stands in the background while they both grin proudly in their newly matching uniforms. A world away from a lonely train station at night.

The guard squints at the photo then grimaces. 'Sorry love, I haven't. And I've been here all afternoon.'

The denial is expected but it still hurts like he's slapped her in the face.

'Right. Thanks anyway.' She knows she sounds disappointed; she knows it's not his fault and she's probably making him feel bad. But she's just too tired to sound any other way.

Isla turns back towards the night and the waiting, oppressively silent car. Tries not to think about all the endless roads wriggling around her.

'Isla?'

Dylan steps out of the car, expression drawn with concern. Clearly she's not doing *that* good a job at keeping her panic stifled.

'She's not been here,' she murmurs.

'Well, that's probably a good thing, right? She can't have gone too far without her own car.'

Isla feels the steel in her gaze as she looks at him, a silent reminder that she got very far without a car last time. All thanks to him.

'Look, Dylan, you really don't need to help me any more. I can keep looking on my own. You've been working all day, after all.'

'So have you.'

It's a fairly obvious retort and Isla knows she could argue it further if she wanted to, but she finds herself stalling. Dylan leaps on this opportunity. 'Be angry with me all you like, that's fine. But you know you'll search far more efficiently with a car. So let's stop trying to fix the mess I've got our friendship into and focus on finding Morgan, okay?'

*

They drive for hours after that, because Isla can't really deny that he's right, even if it stings; she's not going to find her sister by looking around all of Cornwall on foot. Dylan gets Isla to list any place nearby that her sister has a connection to, however distant that connection might be. And they visit every single one of them. They visit both her primary and secondary school, they scour the entire cemetery with phones acting as torches. When they both come up empty, they try the other nearby beaches, the aquarium, even the other villages that they used to sometimes pop into for better shops. Still nothing.

Sometime near dawn they end up back by Isla's house. The sky has turned from black to dusty blue and the sea that has disappeared into the darkness for so many hours begins to be revealed once again, with the slowly sinking moon reflected on its glassy surface. Morning is on the way, bringing with it a further sense of panic for Isla. How long before it becomes too late? Surely more than one night?

They sit on the same bench they sat on hours earlier, up on the clifftops with Karrekoth beach spread out below them. This time, though, Isla is not quivering with rage. Instead she is slumped with exhaustion and dejection.

'She's gone,' she finally says, feeling the heavy finality of those two words anchors on her tongue. 'She's gone, again.'

A sigh from Dylan as he sits beside her. He looks as tired as she feels and he slowly turns his bunch of keys over and over in his hands, eyes glazed and shadowed. 'Isla, maybe we need to get some more people involved to help us, ask around the village a bit more … I know that might make her angrier and everything, but it will help keep her safe, right?'

That stomach-sinking thought is settling into Isla's mind when she's distracted by something on the beach below them. In the distance, just beneath the pinprick glimmers of her own home, Isla catches sight of a flash of light. Golden and warm, stark against the gathering mist of the morning. And she knows exactly what it is.

Suddenly, Isla finds herself standing up. Something has jolted her upright, almost as if she's been struck by lightning herself. But it's nothing to do with lightning. And everything to do with her sister.

Because if the stone is lighting up then she's sure it's trying to tell her something, and Isla has a horrible feeling that she knows exactly what that is.

'I have to go,' she blurts out, the words coming out in a jumbled, panic-laced mess. When she tears her gaze away from the glowing stone and back to Dylan, she finds him also frowning at the beach beyond the cliffs.

'What's that light?' he asks, standing up and taking a step towards the edge. But Isla stops him with a hand to his chest.

'Dylan!' she snaps, as firmly as her panic will allow her. 'I have to go. And you ... you need to stay away.'

That's enough to pull Dylan's attention back to her. He looks hurt but, to give him some credit, he pulls himself together a moment later. 'I understand. You need space to think. But look, call me, okay? If there's anything else I can do ...'

Isla distantly hears herself make a non-committal noise of acknowledgement. She doesn't have time for this now. Dylan's guilt will just have to wait. 'I have to go.' Third time she's said it now but at least this time she manages to move. Ducking around Dylan, Isla starts towards the beach. She can feel him watching her go, can feel his regretful eyes burning against the back of her neck.

And all she can do is speed up her pace until she can't feel it any more, until there's just the wind and the worry keeping her company. Worry that makes her feet stumble over each other in her haste to reach the beach, as if she can somehow stop her sister from doing something she no doubt did hours ago.

But, of course, by the time she has skidded her way down the coastal path and onto the sand, there is only emptiness waiting for her. The stone stands dark and blank, doing its best impression of ordinary.

'No …' Isla whispers, because the stone is certainly not fooling her. She saw the glow after all. She races forward, coming to a halt at the base of the craggy rock and worming her fingers into the all-too-familiar crack. It's still warm, confirming Isla's fear.

This time, her sister has run right into the past. And she could be anywhere.

Thirty-Two

She does not hesitate. She wills the light to reappear with such forceful determination that it's a wonder the stone doesn't explode beneath her fingertips.

And now, as the rock slurps her into the past and hopefully towards her sister, Isla feels a terrible sense of déjà vu, combined with a fear that this is one experience she's not ready to go through again. It's all-consuming, entirely thwarting her desperate attempts to focus on somehow finding her sister amongst the bright light of the stone's impossible power.

So perhaps it's no surprise that when the light clears, there's no sign of Morgan. Isla stands in the middle of what she soon recognises as the foyer of St Clare's secondary school, feeling a hollow sense of hopelessness that doesn't match the brightly lit room and cheerful chatter coming from the nearby school office.

'Why here?' Isla snaps at the ceiling, imagining for a moment that it is made of the stone that brought her here. Unsurprisingly, she does not get an answer.

A door slams open down the hall and Isla is drawn to the sound, experience telling her that it's likely got something to do with Morgan. Indeed, she spots an all-too-familiar storm of a sister stomping towards her.

This younger Morgan is followed a moment later by a younger Isla, who is carrying a large artist folder under one arm.

'Just bin it, Isla,' Morgan snaps.

'Morgan, don't be like that … I just meant that perhaps your GCSE project could be a little less … depressing.' Isla's voice is full of placating tones but it's not doing anything to soothe her sister. Morgan continues to stomp down the hallway, right past the invisible Isla who watches this scene with bubbling foreboding in her stomach. 'We live in one of the most beautiful places in the world, couldn't you have painted that instead?'

Morgan practically growls with frustration, swinging round to face her sister. She snatches the folder out from Isla's arms, and folds the whole thing in half with furious savagery. 'We were meant to create something that inspired us. This stupid village doesn't inspire me unless you count inspiring me to walk into the sodding sea.'

Isla watches her younger self wince at the sudden destruction of the folder but make no move to rescue it from Morgan. Everything about this Isla is soothing, consolatory. And it's making her younger sister more infuriated by the second.

'Okay, so the village doesn't inspire you. But did it have to be *that*? Nobody wants to see that if they can avoid it, Morgan.'

Morgan dumps the folder in the corner by the recycling bins, her scowl deepening as if somebody has taken a shovel to her brow. 'Well, we can't all avoid it, can we?' she mutters, heading towards the glass exit doors. It's said so quietly that the younger Isla doesn't hear it but the invisible one does and the bitterness hits her like a stampeding elephant.

The two sisters leave the school building a moment later, escaping an evening that was meant to be enjoyable, a school exhibition of GCSE Art projects, but that turned sour in a matter of moments. Isla thought the sourness was her sister's perfectionist attitude when it came to her artwork, but now she wonders if it wasn't that at all.

All the while, her Morgan is still nowhere to be seen. Isla knows she has to find her and yet she can't resist stepping forward and tugging open the crumpled folder. She needs to see the painting again, with Morgan's unheard words now ringing in her ears.

It spills out from its confinements the moment Isla lets it free, colour suddenly invading her vision as the paper unfurls on the floor.

A heart, anatomically correct with painstaking detail, is sprawled across the paper. It all seems ordinary at first but Isla remembers how she spotted the smaller elements and felt her stomach churn. One artery is bruised, swollen and clearly beyond repair. It leaks black paint out into the background where a house stands crumbling, its broken rocks tumbling down the edge of the paper.

Isla feels every bit of turmoil that she tried to ignore the first time she saw it. *It's lovely Morgan ... a bit bleak but, you know ... lovely.* Her words felt misshapen when she said them all those years ago and she knew straight away that they weren't fooling anyone.

But perhaps all her sister really wanted was for her to understand why that particular, dreadful moment was such an apparent inspiration to her. Isla only wishes she did understand because still, all these years later, it makes no sense.

The moment that wish enters her head, Isla feels the ground yank away beneath her feet. The school disappears in a haze of light but is replaced almost immediately by the centre of Karrekoth, sodden from a recent rainstorm.

Isla has mere seconds to get her feet steady before she is once again confronted with herself and her sister from the past.

Morgan's younger now, maybe around fourteen. But there's no storm brewing behind her eyes this time; instead she holds herself with pride while half jogging to keep up with an Isla who seems harried, rushed.

'So guess what happened at school today?' Morgan says as they breeze past the invisible Isla, who hastily moves to follow them. Morgan's eyes are alight with the excitement of whatever drama she's witnessed, but Isla barely glances her way.

'Can it wait, Morgan? We're in a rush, remember?'

Morgan bites her lip, crestfallen for a moment. Then she stitches her smile back on and catches up with Isla. 'Can't we rush and listen to my story? Trust me – you're going to want to hear this.'

Isla watches her own jaw tighten, hears the deep breath she sucks in. 'Fine. Just … make it quick, okay?'

Morgan is a little taken aback by this; Isla can tell from the way she hesitates, swallows, then carries on. 'So you know Mrs Tate, the art teacher? The one who definitely smokes pot in the supply cupboard.'

Isla nods as she roots through her bag. 'Uh huh,' she says, her tone distracted. She's completely focused on whatever she's looking for.

'Well, she came into class today in a right state, slammed her bag on the desk and stuff. And nobody knew what was going on because she's normally so chilled, and then she told us how her mum's ill …' Morgan pauses, clearly trying to assess her sister's attentiveness. It takes Isla a second to realise her sister has stopped speaking and looks over to Morgan, a moment too late.

'Keep going, I'm listening.'

'No, you're not.' Morgan's frowning now, arms crossed. 'At least tell me the truth, Isla …'

'Sorry, it's just … Dad's prescription, I can't find it.'

Morgan rolls her eyes, grinning despite her irritation. 'You put it in your pocket, you numpty. How did you forget that?' Her words are lightly teasing but they cause her sister to stiffen, almost defensively.

'Maybe because of everything else I'm trying to remember?' Isla snaps, sparing a brief second to shoot her sister a reprimanding frown. 'Try to cut people slack, Morgan, eh?'

Isla has only just finished huffing her disappointment when Morgan comes back with her retort. 'I was just teasing you, Isla. You know ... that thing we used to do all the time?'

But this rushed and distracted Isla doesn't have time to respond. She makes a brief noise that could really mean anything before cursing as she spots the pharmacy lights being turned off. It's barely graced five o'clock but Mr Harris who owns the shop has always been renowned for his somewhat pedantic timing. 'No, no – wait!' she groans, breaking into a run to get across the street in time. Urgency radiates from her in an almost blinding haze, certainly blinding enough for her not to notice how deflated Morgan seems.

Isla watches her sister's sagging shoulders and frustrated frown, and waits for a reaction of sorts; a sulk, a sarcastic comment. Something. But there's nothing except brief defeat before she stitches herself carefully back together and troops after Isla.

It fills Isla with a strange, empty feeling. She remembers this time, remembers telling Cora proudly that her sister was doing so well because in her mind the new lack of crying and arguing *was* a good thing, was a sign that Morgan was beginning to heal.

But she wasn't at all. She was just learning to hide it better, until a few years later there would be too much to conceal in this tiny village and she would have to leave.

And now she's left again, except this time it's through a seemingly endless expanse of past days. That thought jolts panic back into Isla and she looks around, desperate for any sign of her sister. However, she only gets a few seconds to do so, before the world shudders with wind and she's once again whisked away into the stone's glow.

This time, though, the light seems brighter, harsher. The wind around her is choppy and wild, and Isla sees moments of her life flitting by as though she's lost in the middle of a tornado. Except it's not just her life. It's theirs. She sees whooping sisters on a rollercoaster, the moment their mother pulled the car over because Isla and Morgan wouldn't stop bickering in the back. Sharing a blanket on the sofa and jabbing each other in the chest when they got too squashed. Morgan's last day of primary school where she stood sobbing and nobody could cheer her up except for Isla, who just hugged her until she was calm once more.

The whirlwind slows, temporarily. She sees Morgan and herself, both crammed into the tiny downstairs bathroom. Isla is in the deep throes of adolescence while Morgan is gangly, probably around ten. Despite the whirling wind and distracting light, Isla stills hears their giggling as they try to paint cat whiskers on each other's faces. Halloween. Isla remembers how they went trick or treating every year until she had to tell thirteen-year-old Morgan that she couldn't, that Isla had to stay at home and try to fix the broken boiler.

The scene disappears before Isla can even get steady, can even try to look for her missing Morgan. Giggling bathrooms turn into a swimming pool set in the hazy hills of France. A rare holiday abroad. Isla feels the warmth of the sunshine even as it begins to set, then sees the muddle of red and brown hair as two sisters sit by the edge of the pool and teach each other the rudest French words they know. The laughter bounces around the peaceful surroundings, joined by the gentle splashing as two pairs of legs wiggle contentedly in the water.

Longing swells up inside Isla and she glances around, desperately looking for another brown-haired little sister. But there's nobody else to be seen, even her parents are somewhere inside, clearly comfortable in the knowledge that their daughters can look after themselves.

'Please ... enough ...' Isla whispers to the sun-baked air, because she knows what the stone is trying to do by showing her these glittering moments left behind in the past. But what use is it if she's lost her Morgan for good? And the more she stumbles from moment to moment, the more Isla feels a hopeless sense of inevitability. Her sister is gone.

The French hills shiver and dissolve into bright light again, Isla catches a final moment of carefree laughter before it's drowned out by an all-too-familiar rumble of thunder.

Suddenly, without much more warning, Isla is on her beach in the middle of a storm. It's not quite the raging thunderstorm that brought her the stone's magic in the first place, but it's not far off. Immediately, her curls are soaked and sticking to her face unpleasantly. Spluttering a little in the sudden onslaught of elements, Isla pushes her hair out of her face and stumbles forward, out of the shelter of the towering cliffs. A furious wind immediately roars in her ears, ominously sounding like some sort of warning.

But then Isla spots the figure standing at the water's edge. In the haze of rain it's a little hard to see but a moment later, Isla is running because she's sure she would recognise those squared shoulders and stiffly crossed arms anywhere.

'MORGAN!' Her shout doesn't sound nearly powerful enough to be heard over the wind but Morgan turns all the same. Except it's not Morgan.

Marina Pembroke squints through the rain and for a moment seems confused, eyes narrowing with thought. But then she smiles, the act seeming to somehow brighten the fuming world around her, and holds out a hand.

Isla skids to a shocked halt, stumbling a little on the sand and pebbles. Because this isn't fair; surely this isn't fair? What is Isla supposed to do with this opportunity that seems so utterly beyond what she deserves? Because her mother is looking straight at her and yet when Isla looks down at herself, she's still the same Isla who ran into the stone's impossible doorway. She sees her rain-sodden aquarium shirt, spots the same faded trainers she's been wearing all day. She definitely hasn't changed, the way she did at Morgan's sixteenth birthday.

When Isla looks back to Marina her mother is wearing concern in thick layers on her face.

'Isla?' she asks, the sound just audible above the storm.

A deep breath, summoning courage and resisting the urge to simply collapse to the ground. 'Hello, Mum,' Isla finally says, and hears the words almost tremble in the air.

And, just like that, the storm is over.

Thirty-Three

Silence settles.

The beach becomes still, wind and rain immediately smoth-ered by an invisible force. Even the waves seem to hesitate in their incessant movement, before crashing against the sand with a new gentleness. Nature has muffled itself in respect of this impossible moment of surprise.

Marina glances up at the sky then pushes back the hood of her raincoat, revealing her matching set of red curls. Each movement is confident, steady. Isla had forgotten that, forgotten how her mother moved through the world ready for whatever storm she met. Isla tried to replicate that confidence after she was gone but it had been wholly impossible.

'You're soaked, Isla.' Marina finally says, tutting and reaching out to touch one of Isla's bedraggled coils of hair. 'And ... why are you dressed like that? What's going on, why are you here?' Her almost bottomless green eyes scan her daughter's face, a frown appearing on her forehead. Isla knows she's working it out, knows she's realising the impossible truth.

'Mum.' The word still feels so unfamiliar and full of such weight against her tongue that Isla feels herself stumble over it. 'I'm ...' She stops, shakes her head. How can she begin to explain? Where would she even start? Isla casts her eyes around helplessly, trying to find some sort of clue as to when this is, as if that might somehow help her answer the question.

'You're a lot more grown up than the girl I left at university last week,' Marina finally comments, her smile knowing. 'What have they been feeding you up there, eh?' Her hand drifts to touch Isla's cheek and it feels so warm, so comforting that Isla cannot help but allow a shuddery sob to escape her chest.

'Mum…' That word again, croaked and tremulous. And this time Isla cannot bear its weight any more and she stumbles forward, wrapping her arms around the woman she has not seen for far, far too long.

Isla feels her mother's arms come around her and it feels like the warmth of the sun. The familiar smell of her fancy perfume (the only thing she ever splashed out on) mixed with the salt of the sea and the sherbet lemons she kept in a jar at the post office. It's too much to take in at once and Isla feels her legs buckling beneath her, until her mother scoops her back up again and gently steps back to appraise her daughter once more.

'Hey, it's okay…' Marina whispers, rubbing Isla's back in soothing circles as she tries to gain control of herself. 'What's happened?'

Half-laughing with disbelief, Isla shakes her head. 'I can't, Mum. I can't.' She presses her knuckles to her eyes, determined not to waste this time crying. 'Just… tell me, Mum. What's the date?'

Marina raises an eyebrow. 'It's 21st October… 2011.'

Isla stares, feeling her heart thump painfully against her ribcage as if it feels the need to tell her just how monumental her mother's reply is. When, of course, Isla doesn't need anything to tell her that.

'But that's…' She stops, trails off with lips coming tightly together to stop herself from spilling a dreadful truth.

'The day after I died?' Marina looks at her with a small, sad smile as Isla feels shock wind its way across her own expression. 'It's okay, Isla. I know.'

'But that's ... how is that ...' Isla shakes her head with frustration, trying to get her thoughts straight. 'Mum, I don't understand any of this.'

Marina chuckles at that, touching Isla's cheek tenderly. 'I don't think this is anything you can understand, Miss Scientist. I think this is something that's not meant to make sense.'

'But the stone, it goes back through time ... it doesn't do *this*.' Isla doesn't know why she's arguing the logic so much, perhaps because if it doesn't make sense then maybe it's not really happening.

'Says who?' Marina glances back towards the looming rock, standing in its usual spot with its usual air of ambivalence towards the world. 'Do you remember the story, Isla? About the stone? It was all so that the ocean could find the one she lost ...' She shakes her head, eyes coming back to rest on Isla. 'Whatever it is, I don't think we should waste any more time questioning it. And you should tell me what's brought you here.' Marina offers a hand to Isla and Isla decides after a moment that her mother is probably right.

Taking her mother's hand, Isla allows herself to be tugged gently forwards until they're walking alongside the lapping waves. 'I don't seem to ever have any control over where I end up with this thing, so I guess the answer to your question is that I don't know.'

'Well, what were you hoping for?'

Isla bites her lip, not wanting to admit to her mother that she may have driven her sister away. Twice. 'I was hoping to find Morgan. She's run away.'

'Hoping to find Morgan, or find a way to help Morgan?'

Marina pauses, looking intently at Isla. 'Morgan was always fairly crap at hide-and-seek. But she was very good at refusing to admit she'd been found. It's all very well you finding her, Isla, but how are you going to get her back?'

'I ... guess I hadn't thought of that.' Isla sighs, kicking at the sand with weary frustration.

'Why do you think she ran off?'

Isla purses her lips, resists the urge to just shrug away a question she doesn't quite know how to answer yet. But there is something else she needs to know first. 'Mum ... if this is the day after you died, how much do you know?'

Marina quirks an eyebrow. 'As in, do I know the future you've come from?' She shakes her head, squeezing Isla's hand. 'That's just for you, love.'

Isla nods, considering how this factors into what she wants to say next. 'The stone ... it took me to the past. And it kept showing me these moments of our lives. I thought it was showing me days that I could change, things that I'd missed with Morgan like – like not getting Dad to come to her sixteenth birthday, but I think the stone was trying to show me something else.'

'And your conclusion?' Marina asks with a good-natured grin. Isla sniffs, rubbing at her eyes because she forgot all the science-related jokes her mother would make to her and God, it hurts to know how much has left her mind over these years.

'You always told me to look after Morgan—'

'And you always did.' Marina is quick to interject, her expression full of an unwavering confidence. 'You bickered and rolled your eyes and all the rest but you always looked after her.'

'Right. And that's what I've tried to do ... but I did something wrong.'

Marina laughs at that, though it's laced with a deep sadness. 'You haven't changed a bit, eh? Still a perfectionist, even when ...'

She stops, looks back towards the sea with sorrow etched into the creases of her face.

'Even when I lost you,' Isla finishes, the words feeling like thorns in her mouth.

Marina can only nod it seems and for a moment there is only the sound of the waves and the wind, until she appears to gather herself together once more. 'What is it you think you did so wrong then, eh?'

'That's the thing, Mum ... I don't know. I've racked my brains over and over but it's a mess.'

'Have you asked Morgan?'

Isla snorts wearily at that. 'Repeatedly, but she won't tell me.'

Her mother raises an eyebrow, smiles wistfully as she nods. 'Yes, that's our Morgan. I imagine you're not asking right.'

'Not asking right ... Mum, surely there's only one bloody way to ask that question?' Isla rubs at her face wearily, feeling the drain of the day's constant revelations.

A hollow laugh comes from Marina and she shakes her head. 'Not with Morgan. Don't you remember how long it took us to get her to reveal what she wanted for Christmas every year?' She takes Isla's hand again, leading her a little further down the beach. 'You always thought you were so different from Morgan but you've got a lot more similarities than you realise ... if you really have done something wrong, as you so harshly put it, I imagine Morgan is trying to protect you from it. That's what you'd do after all, wouldn't you?'

'Of course ... but it's different; I'm her big sister. It's my job to protect her, not the other way round.'

Her mother shakes her head, a knowing spark lighting up her eyes. 'I'm not sure Morgan got the memo on that particular rule, my girl.'

Isla is silent at that, frowning at her own feet as she tries to comprehend what her mother means. It feels a little bit like trying to choose one single grain of sand from this beach. 'She's ... trying to protect me?'

Marina shoots Isla a grin, tapping her nose gently. 'Ladies and gentleman, we have a winner.' It's an altogether-too-reminiscent act and it sends painful nostalgia racing through Isla. She simultaneously wishes her mother hadn't done it and that she would do it over and over again, forever. Grief, a constant paradox.

'You're not the only sister in the family, Isla. Don't forget that.' Marina gives Isla's shoulder a reassuring squeeze before letting out a small, sad sigh. 'It would seem our time is up, love ...'

Isla's stomach lurches and she frowns. 'What ... what do you mean?' Her voice sounds tiny, almost childlike. It's the first day of preschool and her mother's breaking it to her that she can't stay with her, that she's got to go.

Her mother wears the same false smile of confidence that she did then. Except this time it's not fooling Isla one bit. And that's a whole lot worse.

Marina nods to something behind Isla, causing her to turn around. The impossible stone stands waiting, its cracked side spewing light out onto the sand. And, for once, Isla wants nothing to do with it.

'Screw that.' She sniffs, turning back to her mother. 'You don't have to go, I don't have to go.' Desperation is seeping into her voice, slowly like sludge. 'We can stay here, even if just for a bit longer ...'

'I wish it worked that way, Isla, but you've got a sister to find and I ...' She trails off, forces another smile as she shrugs slightly. 'I've got places to go too, I'm sure.'

Shaking her head rapidly, Isla grips onto her mother's hands with a sudden, fierce tightness. 'Please, Mum ... just another moment.' Her voice is calm but she can see the sand being sent into the air around the stone as the wind picks up and that sight is enough for panic to dig deep into her chest. She grips tighter, sure she's probably hurting her mother but unable to help herself. '*Please*, Mum,' she repeats, because now she's here with her again, Isla doesn't know how she ever managed without her.

Marina brings her close, wraps her arms around her. Isla can feel her fingers tangling into her curls, gently at first but then a little more frantic. She knows then, that her mother is feeling as panicked as she is. It doesn't help at all before she changed the past. She to know that, so when the wind inevitably reaches them seconds later Isla isn't ready at all.

Light floods Isla's world once more and she feels herself being tugged away. 'NO!' she bellows, letting go of every shred of composure she has left. 'I'M NOT GOING!' Isla digs her heels in with every bit of strength she can muster, screws her eyes shut as if ignoring the light somehow makes it no longer exist. 'PLEASE, LET ME STAY!' she screams, but nobody listens. She feels her mother's hands lifting away from her hair and knows then, knows it's futile.

And she doesn't want to waste any more seconds fighting it then, not when it's so obviously pointless. Fighting back her tears, Isla opens her eyes and looks at her mother. She doesn't know what to say; all these years she's wished she had one more chance to say something to her mother and now here she is with her mouth hanging uselessly open.

But what do you say? How do you say goodbye to a person you never expected to leave? Especially when you never thought you'd get the chance to.

All this turmoil must register on Isla's face because Marina touches her cheek with an understanding smile. 'Maybe we just don't say anything, eh?' The words are quiet and yet Isla hears them with crystal-clear clarity over the howl of the wind.

Isla scrabbles for the hand on her cheek and grips it tightly. It feels reassuringly solid at first but soon it begins to feel distant, faded. She knows the end of this impossible encounter has come.

'I wish you hadn't gone!' Isla cries out, needing for one second to be selfish and not worry about someone else being hurt.

Her mother's face is nearly hidden in the growing glow of the stone's power but Isla catches one last smile, though she almost wished she hadn't when it's full of so many big, scary emotions. 'I wish I hadn't too ...'

Then Isla feels her mother's hand fade away from her own, feels the beach disappear from beneath her feet. And she knows it's over.

She knows she's lost her mother all over again.

Eventually the light fades and the wind dies down. Too soon for Isla's liking; she'd rather spend an eternity lost in the chaos where she can grieve, uninterrupted. But the world comes back to her, piece by piece. She hears a jarringly comforting sound of rain pattering against a roof, sees a soft glow from a small night light and smells old, slightly damp wood.

It's all as familiar as a favourite pair of slippers. Isla feels herself draw a shuddering breath as memories wash over her, until she realises that she doesn't need the memory. It's happening right in front of her.

A triangular fort of blankets, propped up by an intricate arrangement of chairs and shelves, sways haphazardly in the corner of the room she's now standing in. Again it's all too familiar and Isla knows what she's going to find inside the fidgeting fort of blankets. For a moment she considers turning and running, because she's not sure she can face any more lost things today.

But when she comes round to the front of the fort, she's greeted by a surprise. There's no painful memory re-enacting before her. Instead, there's just Morgan and this time Isla is sure that it's her Morgan, the one she's desperately been searching for. She's staring out the window but the moment Isla comes into her view, she looks up. Isla's expecting tears or angry glares but there's none of that. Just relief.

'Isla,' she states softly. 'You came.'

And that's all Isla needs to finally let herself cry.

Thirty-Four

Crying is a funny thing, really. An instinct that everyone is born with to show their sadness or fear or even happiness by allowing their eyes to leak. Such an obvious display of vulnerability that makes no evolutionary sense, which is probably why it is really only humans who do it.

And perhaps it is why Isla has not let herself do it properly before now. She was surviving.

Because it's not as if she doesn't know *how* to cry. Isla can remember times when she cried entirely naturally. A childhood filled with falling over in rock pools, a schooling filled with the euphoric receiving of exam results and the painful lows of adolescent relationships. Plenty of opportunities for tears that Isla certainly didn't shy away from. Until her mother was gone and suddenly it didn't seem right to ever cry again. What was there left to be sad about? And besides, if she cried, then who was there to look after her?

Well, perhaps she's found the answer to that question now, in the dimly lit loft of her home. As she sits on the floor and feels herself cry as if it's the first time she's ever done it, Isla can feel a hand on her back. Morgan's hand, not doing anything other than reminding her that she's there. The sobs burn her lungs and sting her eyes, and make every muscle in her chest creak with complaint but at least, this time, she knows she's not alone.

Until suddenly, finally, it's over. Isla sucks in a breath that manages to stem the constant tide of sobbing and feels the flow of tears slow until they're just stuck, like treacle, to her cheeks. She's still trembling, but she can just about pull her head up to meet her sister's gaze.

Morgan, understandably, looks a little perplexed. But then she manages a sheepish smile. 'Jeez, Isla ... don't be so wet.'

The sarcasm is highly welcome and Isla hears herself laughing, albeit in a slightly distant way. She shifts a little, until she's no longer half-crumpled on the ground, and takes a good look at her sister. Morgan looks as tired as she feels and her eyes are a little red-rimmed but, other than that, she seems okay. And she's safe.

'Are you all right?' Isla asks softly.

Morgan sniffs, a little more shifty now. 'I could ask you the same thing ...'

'Oh, I'm fine.' Isla tries to brush it off, but then catches the almost disappointment in her sister's expression and remembers her mother's words. *You're not the only sister in the family.* Funny how something so obvious can feel so monumental. 'I mean, I'm not fine. I'm ...' She sighs, moves so she's sitting beside her sister in the muddle of blankets. 'Christ knows what I am.'

Morgan makes a small noise of amusement, though it's a little half-hearted. She pulls her legs up to her chest, rests her chin on her knees, then looks out of the small circular window they're sitting opposite. Isla follows her gaze, smiling faintly at the familiar sight of the ocean framed by storm clouds. Their own personal cinema; they used to come up here whenever there was a big storm and sit huddled in their blanket fort, watching the rain, wind and lightning pass by.

'Morgan, you scared the life out of me, disappearing on us like that. What happened?' Isla asks finally. Morgan doesn't say anything at first, which causes Isla to let out a heavy sigh. 'Do I not get to know, again?'

Morgan picks at the edge of the nearest blanket. 'Depends... are you going to tell me why you arrived sobbing?' she returns.

A rumble of thunder reverberates through the roof, making the wooden beams shiver. Isla decides to take that as a sign against her instincts to refuse her sister. 'I... It took me to see Mum.'

'What?'

'The stone, it took me to see Mum. To talk to her.'

Morgan is staring at her now, eyes wide and almost seeming to glow in the gloomy light. 'You saw Mum too?' she whispers.

'What do you mean – too?'

'I mean the general meaning of "too", as in "as well", as in "I also saw Mum".' Morgan sniffs, shaking her head. 'On the beach, the day after she died.'

'Yes, that's what I had!' Isla exclaims, an odd sense of relief inside her. Part of her was a little concerned that she had imagined the entire event.

Morgan smiles a little at that, then glances back out the window. 'I told her I was running away and do you know what she said? She said, "Make sure you hide where she'll find you." Like she knew that...' she trails off, her cheeks reddening a little as she realises she's talked herself into a corner.

'That you wanted to be found,' Isla finishes. Once she's received a nod of confirmation, she shifts a little closer. 'Which I guess leads us back to that question, Mogs... why did you run?'

Isla watches how her sister's head dips down and her lips purse tightly together. Deep in thought, just how she used to look when she was surveying a blank page in her sketchbook. Then she appears to make a decision, nodding to herself. With a deep breath, she twists round so that she can pull something from the back pocket of her jeans. The sight of the crumpled envelope in her hand sends a lightning bolt of fear through Isla's chest as she recognises it immediately. The lost letter, the one her sister never left behind before running away the first time.

'You ... you still have it?'

Morgan frowns at the envelope for a long moment, then slowly nods. 'I kept it in my suitcase. Not quite sure why. I guess I knew one day I would show it to you. And then when we had that fight a few weeks back I took it out and I've just been carrying it around since then, waiting for the right moment. I guess that's now ... I *think* that's now.' Isla hears the paper creak as Morgan's fingers tighten up against the envelope, as she battles against her own urge to hold on to it. It makes Isla feel even more wary of the letter within; can it still be so scary to hand it over, four years later?

'Well, you've got to show it to me now.'

With a weak smile, Morgan nods. 'I guess you're probably right. Promise me you won't be mad?'

'Depends what you've written ...'

'I guess that's fair.' With a sigh of inevitability, Morgan grips the envelope for one more moment before finally holding it out. 'It was a long time ago but, if I'm honest, I think it's still all probably true. Sorry.'

That stings; her sister very rarely says that word. And it's only when she's entirely certain that she needs to. Another rarity. It makes Isla deeply dread the contents of the envelope, but she knows she needs to do this. She takes the letter, feeling its weighty importance as if she's holding a boulder.

Morgan sits back a little, pleats her hands in her lap and gives Isla an encouraging nod. No getting away from this now.

She peels open the envelope, smiles faintly at how firmly it's been stuck down. After all these years, it's still a battle to separate glue from paper. Somebody really wasn't sure they wanted anyone to read this.

There's a strange feeling of nostalgia at seeing the notepad paper folded inside, the one with the seashell pattern in the corner. Isla remembers that notepad; she used it for writing shopping lists before she started using her phone instead.

The handwriting inside is scrawled and rushed, the handwriting of someone awake in the middle of the night and doing their best to remain undetected. But it's inescapably legible and Isla has no choice but to read.

Dear Isla,

So, I guess I've done it if you're reading this; I've left. I'm sorry and I hope you aren't too scared and angry. I mean of course I know you are both of those things but I promise you it's worth it. And I promise you this isn't some irritatingly dramatic adolescent act of rebellion. It's just necessity. I've tried to make sense of why I feel I need to leave, to help you make sense of it too. But it's hard, really hard. So I think it's best explained like this:

Do you remember when we found Mum's wellies? Back when she'd only just gone and everything was raw and angry. We were tidying up the study to try and help Dad from freaking out every time he walked past it and we found them under her desk, flopped over in the corner like she'd just kicked them off her feet before going to cook our dinner. We held one each and I remember that I cried hard enough to bring Dad running from

318

next door. But you didn't cry, not one tear. You just looked at them and held my hand.

I remember thinking about it later, wondering how you managed to keep so still and so composed when you were holding such a living part of her in your hands. I remember thinking that I wished I could be as strong as you.

Until it happened again, with something else. And again, and again, and again. You never once cried, even when Dad got so bad that he didn't come out of his room for a whole week. And then I started thinking about how many times we've sat and shared our sadness together in the past; like when you thought you'd done terribly in your biology A level and you sat in my bedroom all tearful until I made you feel better by doodling fish all up and down your arms.

And remember how we used to bicker constantly, like normal sisters do? How Mum would joke about handcuffing us to each other until we got along? And you would always have a comeback ready for me, no matter what. Then Mum went and you stopped. Like when I got suspended for getting into that stupid fight at school and I shouted such horrible things at you, and you just stood there and accepted it.

I didn't expect to lose Mum. But I certainly didn't expect to lose my sister too, especially when you're technically still here, living and breathing. Just not my Isla.

It scares me, I guess. It scares me that you've not yet let yourself feel any of what happened to us. Sure, you could argue that I feel it a bit too much but maybe I'm just trying to do it for both of us. And yes, I know you're hiding from it all because you want to be there for us. But that's not enough of a reason to tear yourself up from the inside, because I love you just as much as you love me (promise).

So I'm going to go. I think that might help. If you don't have

*to be strong for me any more, maybe you'll let it all out. I really
hope you do, Isla. Because I really miss my big sister.*

*Please don't try and find me. I can look after myself and I'm
not going to do anything stupid. I'm just going to give you some
space.*

Good luck.

All love,

Morgan x

A flash of lightning illuminates the room just as Isla finishes
the letter and she looks up, just in time to see her sister's worried
expression lit up in the harsh, unforgiving light.

She doesn't blame her for being worried. The letter is honest in
a way that Isla can't ever remember her sister being. Or perhaps
either of them being, which is probably part of the problem. The
words seem to have wrapped around Isla in a thick, smothering
cocoon that stops her speaking for a long moment, even when
she can feel her sister's desperation growing.

'I'm sorry,' Morgan blurts out once the moment has apparently stretched too long for her to bear.

Isla shakes her head. 'But I ... I did cry.' It's not exactly what
she expects to come out of her mouth. She was hoping for
something a little less defensive and little more well-formed.
'Didn't I?'

Morgan shrugs. 'I mean, maybe a little but ... it's not really
about the volume of tears you cried over the years, Isla, it's more
the fact that still, all these years later, when you appear in front
of me sobbing you refuse to admit there's something wrong.'
She glances around the dimly lit room, clearly trying to find
the answers amongst the ancient roof beams. 'We used to be so
close. We always had each other's backs and we had stupid little
traditions like – like coming up here to watch storms. And then

the first storm after Mum went you didn't want to come up here, which I could understand, but then the second storm you said you had to sort out the bills or something, and it kept on going.'

'I had to keep the house standing, Morgan. That was kind of important.'

Shaking her head, Morgan lets out a sigh of impatience. 'That's just it, Isla. Sure, it was important that we had enough money for food and that we had clean clothes ... but I don't think that was why you did it. I mean, who cares if the dishwasher made a funny sound for one evening, if it meant we got to be sisters again? No, I think you knew that if you sat up here with me and watched the lightning, you'd never be able to keep it all in.'

Isla hesitates, feeling a painful weight of emotion pressing against her chest. 'Morgan, I was just trying to keep you safe. I would do anything if I knew it would keep you safe and happy.'

Morgan glances up from her hands and meets Isla's gaze again. 'Like change the past?' There's a small, though terribly sad smile on her face that makes it all too clear to Isla what she's referring to.

'You ... you know?' Isla feels her voice crack into an almost croak of shock.

'That you made it so we were together when Mum died? Yeah, I know.' She shrugs, resting back against the sofa. 'I guess some memories are too big to be completely erased, just like my sixteenth birthday. So now it's like ... there's two different versions of that day and even I can't really tell which one is real any more. And if I'm honest, when I felt that change, that was when I decided I definitely had to leave again. Because nothing seemed to have changed – you were still trying to fix everything when I just wanted you to be, well, you ...'

'So that was all for nothing?'

Morgan shakes her head slowly, eyes a little out of focus as she stares at the window. 'No, I wouldn't say so. I mean, I think it does help to know that there's one version of that day where I'm not alone but...'

'But what?' Isla leans forward a little, sensing from her sister's deep frown that her next words are going to be important.

'But our mum died, Isla.'

The words are not a shock, of course they're not. But hearing them said so bluntly, so full of heavy truth makes Isla reel back as if she's been shoved. Morgan seems to notice this because she gives her an apologetic grimace.

'I know she died,' Isla whispers, trying her best not to sound defensive yet again.

'Sometimes I wonder if you do, though.' Morgan holds up a hand to stop Isla's instant reaction, shaking her head a little. 'I mean, of course you *know*. But... it's like you know that your sister lost her mother and your father lost his wife and that's awful but... you don't know that *you* lost your mother too. That you were just a kid yourself.'

'I was nineteen.'

Morgan sniffs, gives her a knowing look. 'Right, and when I was out in the world on my own at nineteen, that was all fine because I was a grown-up.'

'That's different, you were—'

'Grieving?'

Isla nods silently, feeling her throat drying up with every second that goes by, with every argument her sister makes that she can't quite find a way to argue against.

'Isla, *we* lost our mother. Both of us. And I think you've been so busy fixing everything you possibly can that you've forgotten. You lost her too. And more than that, you lost your whole life; your future, your freedom. And I guess your ability to just... sit with your sister and watch a storm.'

She wants so badly for those words to feel ridiculous and ludicrous, to be able to shrug them away as nothing. But she can't. Their truth is inescapable and she's cornered, trapped.

'Okay,' she whispers finally, feeling that horrible sensation of her throat closing up as tears once again rise into her eyes.

'Okay?' Morgan echoes, watching her as if she's a bomb about to explode.

'Okay, let's sit and watch a storm.'

They stay until the storm passes. They sit huddled in a fort that doesn't really fit them any more, until the clouds have lightened, the sea has calmed and the wind has quietened to its usual almost joyful bluster.

Isla almost wishes they could stay longer. There's a safety to be found here, in a strange little loft where there's no sense of time passing or expectations being held.

Maybe that's why she finally lets herself cry. A proper sort of crying, not just hysterical sobbing or a single tear rolling down her cheek. Just the silent kind, the kind that is only there to help rid you of some terrible sense of loss buried deep in your chest.

Silent or not, Morgan is quick to notice. She smiles weakly, almost apologetically, wraps her arm around Isla's shoulders and holds on tight. Isla gets the sense that she feels all too responsible for these tears and, to be honest, she would be right. But it's okay. The more she allows the tears to fall, the lighter she feels. And she realises just how much weight she has been carrying around.

But the storm passes and the still sky brings with it a sense of reality. They can't sit in this loft forever.

Something is bothering Isla, though. Aside from the unfamiliar feeling of damp tears on her cheek and the lingering weight of grief that one session of crying isn't going to lift.

'Morgan…'

Morgan looks over, tearing her eyes away from the window that she's been staring resolutely at for the past ten minutes or so. As if she's trying to give Isla privacy whilst being crammed beside her under a pile of blankets. 'Yeah?'

'Why Dylan?'

Her sister wrinkles her nose, obviously a little hesitant. 'Why did I ask him to help?' she asks and when Isla nods, she goes on with a sigh. 'He was the nicest guy I knew with a car, I guess. Remember how I did that summer job, at the café? Well, he would always park up outside and come in to grab a coffee. He was always so polite and patient, even when I kept screwing up his order. And he always asked after you … I figured, out of my available options, he'd understand the best.'

'He always asked after me?' Isla repeats, disbelieving.

'Ugh, you are so clueless.' Morgan rolls her eyes, absent-mindedly using her sleeve to wipe the lingering tears off Isla's face. It's entirely unexpected but entirely comforting. Then she narrows her eyes at Isla, suspicion rising. 'You weren't horrible to him, were you?'

Sniffing, Isla gives her sister a wry look. 'What do you think?' Then she slowly stands, careful not to knock over the fort in the process. 'Come on … who knows how long we've been gone in the real world.'

Morgan stands as well, surveying Isla with a concern that Isla is so used to wearing that it feels odd to see it directed back at her. 'You ready to go back? I mean, fifteen minutes of crying isn't really enough to fix nine years' worth of stuff…'

Resisting her usual instinct to lie, Isla shrugs. 'Probably not,

but it's a start. And we can't hide in this loft until it's all sorted ...
we might never leave.'

A thoughtful noise from her sister then Morgan nods her
acceptance. Her nod seems to carry some mystical power in
it because the moment she's done it, the loft is filled with the
all-too-familiar whirling wind and light of the stone moving
them on.

Isla expects a beach to reappear under their feet but it doesn't.
Instead, there's scruffy carpet, rain pattering against a window,
and the smell of damp, musty clothes lingering in the air. The
light of the stone clears away slowly but Isla has an idea already
of where and when they might be. Funny how certain smells
could stay in the memory for years, as though they've been
bottled and stored away, perfectly preserved.

Isla gets one whiff and remembers the taxi ride from the
train station, remembers how it was late and she stood, fidgeting
anxiously in the rain with no umbrella because who remembers
to bring an umbrella after receiving the worst phone call of
their lives?

The smell makes Isla's chest feel as if it's being squeezed in
a vice. 'I don't want to be here,' she murmurs, without really
thinking.

Morgan glances over, eyes darkening with concern. 'Why?
What's wrong? It's just your bedroom ...' She casts her gaze
around, clearly trying to spot some clue to explain Isla's sudden
terror.

'Yes, but ...' Isla tries to explain but the words are stuck in a
throat closed up with panic.

It turns out, though, that she doesn't need to explain. The
explanation arrives a moment later, as the door opens and a
younger Isla staggers into the room. The damp smell seems to

intensify as the rain-soaked young girl joins the rain-soaked pair of shoes she left on the radiator earlier.

'What is this?' Morgan croaks, taking a step towards Isla as the younger version stumbles across the threshold.

Isla takes a deep breath, dragging her eyes away from her younger self to look at her sister. 'This is it. This is why I don't cry any more.'

Thirty-Five

She tried so hard to be brave. Isla remembers how the effort made her muscles physically ache as if she'd just run a marathon. She came home to a house that felt gutted, hollowed out and ruined. She came home to a shadow of her father and a scared, confused little sister who looked at the world around her with complete betrayal.

So she forced every inch of herself to be brave, to not feel the way grief burnt against her skin. But of course that could only last for so long.

After she changed the day she came back home, Isla hoped distantly that perhaps this moment would no longer exist. But apparently not. She supposes that it makes sense; even if she came back on a different day, at some point she would have to face the emptiness of her bedroom and the dark, scary thoughts awaiting her there.

Morgan's hand slips into hers. She knows it's meant to be comforting but initially it makes Isla jerk with surprise, entirely on edge.

'What's going to happen here, Isla?' Morgan asks, apprehensive. She's probably never seen Isla look so stricken and, of course, that fills her with guilt. But she can't help it.

Shaking her head, Isla purses her lips together as she watches the younger Isla drag her suitcase to the corner by the window, then drop down onto the bed.

'Isla,' Morgan persists, 'tell me what's going to happen.'

'It's not…' Isla tries, voice raspy. She shakes her head, forces herself to focus. 'It's not like that, nothing's going to happen as such…' She trails off, eyes fixed on herself. The younger Isla is staring at her hands, flexing the fingers slowly. It felt as if she'd lost control of her body, Isla remembers. Shock had stolen the strength from her muscles, sapped it away.

'Then what is it?' Morgan asks, looking between the two Islas. 'What's so bad that it scares you so much?'

Isla doesn't need to answer, her younger self does it for her. Just as she's opening her mouth to respond, the younger Isla sucks in a deep breath and begins to cry. It starts silently and slowly, a small trickle of tears on her cheeks. But it doesn't take long for that trickle to become a torrent, for that silence to become a cracked cry. And soon the cry has grown into a beast that can no longer be controlled. Isla slides off the bed and lands heavily on the carpet, burying her face in her knees. The watching Isla knows she's trying desperately to smother the sound of her sobs but they still slip out and fill the bedroom, reaching the ears of two invisible sisters watching on.

It's a sound that Isla hasn't heard for a very long time but it doesn't stop it hitting her right in the chest like a bullet. She takes a step back, wincing as she hears her younger self's breath beginning to catch, hears it shortening until it's the rapid gasps of hyperventilating.

Oh, how she remembers that sensation. How she felt her chest tighten in a giant's fist-clench and was sure that this was going to be it; her turn to suffer a heart attack. How she felt tingles rushing down her arms and legs until she was sure she would never be able to move them again. She felt the urge to throw up rise in her chest, only for it to be replaced with the horrible swooping sensation of being about to faint. The room twisted and warped and even when Isla screwed her eyes shut, the darkness seemed to whirl about her like a hideous, shadowy hurricane.

Isla realises with a horrible jolt that she's no longer just remembering this feeling. As she's watching herself struggle to breathe, her own lungs seem to be constricting. As she's watching her younger hands grip her legs tightly, she feels her own hands begin to tremble.

A sob, deeply sown with fear, slips out of her mouth. 'I... I can't...' she croaks, turning and dashing from the room before she is forced to watch another second. There's a horrifying moment where the handle seems to resist her hold but then she's out in the corridor and there's blissful, silent air ready for her to breathe. Her legs collapse beneath her and she drops to the floor, just as Morgan returns to her side.

'Isla?' Morgan's voice sounds distant, as if she's still next door. But it's calm, steady, enough to bring Isla's eyes onto her. 'Isla, I think you're having a panic attack.'

Isla shakes her head, hands clenching together until she feels her fingernails digging painfully into her flesh. 'I... I can't be... not again...' She hears the words coming from her mouth, feels her lips moving, but again it's distant, as if somebody else has taken over. 'I wasn't going to have one again...'

Morgan snorts softly, dropping down to sit beside her. 'I don't think you get much choice when it comes to panic attacks,' she murmurs and there's a clear sense of experience in her words. That doesn't surprise Isla too much; after all Morgan has suffered her fair share of them over the years. Isla remembers the dark evenings spent in Morgan's bedroom during the first few months, where Morgan would shake and cry her way to calm and it would take every ounce of Isla's strength to stop herself from joining her.

The memory of that does nothing to help Isla and she lets out a groan as her chest tightens once more. 'I … can't …' she gasps out, shaking her head as tears slide down her cheeks.

Morgan's hands find hers, fingers tangling together. 'Isla, listen to me.' She shifts so that she's directly in front of her and Isla finds her gaze drawn to her sister's certain, unafraid eyes. 'You're safe. You're not dying. You just need to breathe. Do that for me, right now. Breathe.'

The idea of breathing seems entirely impossible to Isla right now and she lets out a rasping whimper to convey this. But Morgan isn't giving up that easily.

'Do it, Isla. With me.'

Amidst the fog of terror, Isla sees her sister's green eyes looking back at her. They're so full of certainty that she's going to be able to do this that Isla can't help but suck in a breath. It's short and frayed, barely worth doing as Isla's sure that it brings in no oxygen. But it gets things moving. Once that first breath is finished, Isla finds the strength to keep going. Morgan keeps her gaze fixed on her and begins counting, the numbers seeming to echo around Isla's head until they drown out the frantic screeches of panic.

She doesn't know how long it takes to drag herself back into calm. At some point, the world sharpens back into focus and her body stops feeling that it's being jabbed with thousands of tiny needles. Her chest loosens and her heart slows, until she's able to flop back against the wall with an exhausted sigh.

'I'm—' she begins but Morgan holds up a hand to stop her.

'If you start apologising I will slap you.'

Isla hears her own shaky laugh as Morgan comes to sit down

beside her. 'Fine ... no apology ...' she murmurs. 'Am I allowed to thank you?'

Morgan shrugs. 'You can but there's really no need ... I mean, you did the same for me more than once.'

Nudging her shoulder gently against Morgan's, Isla shoots her sister a smile. 'Well, thank you all the same.'

There's no reply from Morgan but there doesn't really need to be one. Silence settles over them, the calm after a storm. It's almost cosy, though somewhat marred by the distant, smothered sound of crying coming from Isla's bedroom. Isla thought she did a perfect job at making sure nobody could hear her but now she sees how futile an effort that was.

'Did you know I was crying in there?' Isla asks finally, after a few moments of trying and failing not to listen.

Her sister shakes her head slowly. 'No. Like I said in my letter, I never saw you cry ... I'm guessing from the rain outside that I'm just back from the park and skulking in the kitchen.' Morgan frowns at her own hands for a moment, clearly mulling things over. 'You said, before, that this was why you didn't cry any more. What did you mean by that?'

Isla looks towards her firmly closed bedroom door, tries not to picture the distraught young version of herself hiding on the other side. 'It was the first time I was on my own since I came back. I'd been so busy with everything; getting us back from the hospital, trying to make sure we ate, making sure Dad wasn't about to jump off a cliff ...' She snorts, trying to pass her words off as flippant. But she knows she's fooling nobody. So she carries on, forcing herself to explain herself when she really would rather not. 'I sat in the silence of the room and ... well, you saw. I let myself start crying and then it was like everything hit me at once. And it felt as if the oxygen was being sucked out of the house.' Isla pauses, feeling the sensations of panic beginning to creep up her back again. It's not until Morgan squeezes her hand that she feels able to continue, as though her sister is grounding her to the carpet and stopping her from being lost to the fog once more. Her own personal lighthouse.

'It took me ages to get calm again. I guess because I was doing it on my own. And then I sat there and thought – I can't do that, not ever again. There's no time and …' Isla feels the words trailing off as what she thought was a well-developed rationale unravels in the air. 'I guess it sounds pretty stupid now.'

'Yup.' Morgan shoots her sister a grin, shoulder bumping against hers. 'But it probably made sense at the time, right?'

Isla nods slowly. 'That panic attack felt like a luxury I wasn't able to have. And it started when I let myself cry so I figured I couldn't risk doing that again. After a few months it just became habit, I guess.'

Morgan is silent, which is enough for the sound of the younger Isla's crying to once again float into their ears, no matter how much Isla wishes it wouldn't. It seems so loud and desperate that she can't quite believe it's inaudible to those downstairs.

'I'm sure I calm down soon,' Isla sighs, shaking her head. 'Then we can stop listening to that racket.'

A snort from her sister is the only response she gets, then Morgan hops up with a sudden purpose. Isla watches her a little warily, not sure what this sudden purpose is going to lead her sister towards.

'You don't have to calm down soon,' she states with a piercing certainty. 'And you don't have to do it on your own, that's for sure.'

'What are you talking about?'

Morgan casts her eyes around the hallway. 'The stone must have brought us here for a reason other than just forcing you to see one of the worst moments of your life. It wants us to help. So we're going to help.'

With legs that still feel made of cotton wool, Isla slowly stands up as well. 'What do you have in mind?'

Morgan considers the question for a moment, brow deeply furrowed in thought. Then she steps towards the bedroom, places a hand on the handle and begins to turn it.

'Morgan, what are you doing?' Isla demands, foreboding fluttering in her chest.

'I'm opening the door.'

'Someone will hear!'

Morgan gives Isla an almost savage look of satisfaction. 'Exactly. Someone will hear and then you won't have to do this on your own any more.' Fierce determination radiates from her sister, daring her to argue back. 'And maybe it won't change anything, maybe it will. But I think it's worth a try.'

Isla flounders for a full five seconds in the hope of finding something that might convince Morgan otherwise, though she can't quite explain to herself why she feels the need to look in the first place. She supposes that the instinct to protect her sister against everything and anything is one that takes a bit of practice to suppress. It makes her feel a little sick to imagine her sister, nine years younger, potentially seeing Isla in such a state. But maybe it's worth it.

There's not much time to consider otherwise; the sound of the younger Isla's crying is well and truly free now, and it reverberates gleefully around the landing and down the stairs. Mere seconds pass before there's the thudding of footsteps on the stairs and the younger Morgan comes into view. There's a cautiousness in the way she approaches Isla's bedroom, but there's also a resolute lack of pause in her steps. She's not afraid, despite the grief that still hangs off her like a mist.

Part of Isla is scared to see this newly developing scene, but then she figures it's going to be in her memory anyway so she might as well. Besides, Morgan is already pulling her forward with a keen impatience, clearly desperate to see what her small change has achieved.

The younger Isla has sat up abruptly upon hearing her sister come into the bedroom, but there's no hiding the desolation painted across her face. Brushing away a few tears certainly isn't going to cut it. The younger Morgan sighs, moves over to sit beside her on the floor.

'You idiot, I knew you were pretending,' she mutters with only fondness in her tone.

Beside her, Isla fruitlessly tries for a few seconds to dismiss her sister's claims. 'I'm not, I really am fine,' she croaks, almost rasps. But her voice trembles with every syllable and so she gives up, shaking her head and allowing a few more tears to drip down her cheeks.

Morgan tuts, wrapping an arm around her shoulders. 'No, you're not. Nobody is anywhere close to fine.' It's a sentence spoken with the steadiness that her older sister has clearly been desperately searching for. And that is apparently enough to send Isla spiralling back into tears.

The sisters collapse into a hug filled with fierce protectiveness that Isla only ever believed she could possess. But now, seeing the tightly gripped fingers of her sister on her younger self's arms, she knows that's not true. That it's never been true.

'We can do this, Isla. We can.' It's a soft whisper from the younger Morgan but it's still audible and the older Morgan lets out a small sniff of agreement. Then she reaches across and takes her Isla's hand, squeezing so tightly that Isla wonders if they'll ever be able to let go again.

'We *can* do this, you know,' Morgan murmurs.

Isla meets her sister's gaze, wishing she could find the confidence she can see in her eyes. But the last few hours have been far too turbulent and confusing.

And maybe that's okay.

So Isla nods, smiles back at her sister. 'You could be right there.'

And maybe it's agreeing or maybe it's just relieved to finally see two sisters united, but that's the moment that the stone finally decides to take them home.

Thirty-Six

Dawn has fallen over their beach in a wave of soft, pink sunlight. Candyfloss clouds are swirled across the sky and the waves stroke the sand with almost tender gentleness, as if they're doing their best to leave no mark upon the shore.

It's utterly beautiful and, for one blissful moment, two sisters can stand and lose themselves in the artistic skills of Cornish nature.

Reality comes back all too quickly, though. The revelation that it is now dawn, when Morgan disappeared in the evening, crashes into their temporary peace and sends it scattering.

'Shit,' Isla whispers. 'Dad.'

'Dad,' Morgan agrees, glancing to Isla with a matching expression of concern. 'We should get home. Now.'

Part of Isla wishes she could ignore that fact and just stay on this beach a little longer. She wants to digest every little moment of the past few hours and what it means for her; she wants to let go of the stored-up tears she's becoming increasingly aware of having deep inside her. But she knows that can't happen just yet.

It will, though, and perhaps that's why Isla can find the strength to turn away from the sea and head back towards home.

When they enter the kitchen, there's a silence wrapped around the house like cotton wool. Soft and comforting and somehow, instinctively, Isla knows her father is okay.

They find him upstairs in his bedroom. Having crept up the stairs as though it's Christmas morning, they tap cautiously on the door before cracking it open an inch. Jasper is in his chair by the window, asleep until he hears the door creak and jolts himself into consciousness.

'Well, look what the tide washed in,' he grumbles, but there's a good-natured twinkle in the corner of his scowl as he observes the two sisters standing together at the doorway.

Morgan enters the room first, possessing a confidence that Isla is really missing right now. 'Well, to be fair, you did tell us not to bother coming home until we'd sorted out our differences.'

Jasper grunts as his far-too-big daughter squashes herself on the edge of his chair. 'And I suppose that had to take all night, did it?' he asks, eyes flicking between the two of them. Isla feels his gaze lingering on her still-rain-sodden clothes for a long second and, in an attempt to shake it away, she moves to sit on the edge of her father's bed.

But that turns out to be the wrong choice as Jasper appears to get a better look at her and frowns deeply. 'Isla... have you been crying? Are you okay?'

Morgan gives her sister a supremely smug look over the top of her father's head. 'See? I run off again but apparently you having a few tears on your face is more shocking.'

'Funny,' Isla shoots back, before returning her attention to Jasper. She can feel the instinctive 'I'm fine' rising up inside her but she pushes it back down again. 'It's okay, Dad,' she goes for instead, which somehow feels more honest. 'We've just... been working through things, that's all. There was a lot.'

Jasper quirks a single eyebrow with a precision that Isla always marvelled at. 'Is it to do with your little disappearing trips down to the beach?' he asks, then smirks at his daughters' dumbfounded silence.

Isla feels her cheeks warming, despite the morning chill wrapped around the house. 'You knew about those?'

A fond, slightly weary chuckle comes from her father. 'Isla, you are many things, but subtle is not one of them. You're normally on a routine as regular as clockwork but lately ... something's been drawing you away. And once Morgan was going along too, you were stuffed. This one's as subtle as red paint on snow.'

Morgan sniffs at that but doesn't bother to deny it. She does lean round a little to face her father better, before asking the obvious question. 'And you didn't ask where we were?'

Jasper shrugs, resting back a little in his chair with a comfortable sigh. 'You're grown women and you always came back, all limbs attached. Whatever you've both been doing, it was clearly something that was necessary.'

There's a slightly stunned silence as Morgan and Isla look at each other, conduct a wordless conversation to decide how much to tell. Then, in the end, Morgan gives a slightly shaky chuckle. 'Well, looks like someone isn't quite as clueless as he appears ...'

Another sigh comes from Jasper, as he gives Morgan a nudge off the seat in response to her teasing. 'Never forget how well I know you two.' He stands with a heavy grunt, moves over to Isla and places a gentle but much-needed kiss to the top of her head. 'You look a lot better without those tears stuck in your eyes, bud.'

Isla feels herself smile at that, and feels the smile reach right into the corner of her eyes, in a way she's sure she hasn't felt for a long time. 'I think so too, Dad,' she replies, though she knows they're not all quite free yet.

Jasper makes it halfway to the door before he pauses, turning back to survey the two. 'As much as I enjoy seeing you two working together … if it's all the same, I'd rather you didn't disappear on me again any time soon. Think we've had enough scares to last us a lifetime, eh?'

Isla is expecting a wave of guilt at those words; that's what would usually happen after all. But strangely enough there is nothing this time. Perhaps she knows that this was a scare that had to happen. Or perhaps, she reasons, as exhaustion drags at her eyelids, she is just too tired.

Jasper leaves the room a moment later, muttering something about needing tea and cereal. Though Isla slightly cynically suspects it's because he doesn't want to be involved in whatever emotional conversation may be coming.

But no such conversation arrives. Morgan clearly feels the same exhaustion as her sister, for she hauls herself over to sit beside Isla with all the effort of a fisherman bringing in their weighty nets.

With surprising synchronicity, both sisters flop back onto their father's bed. Isla allows herself a moment of distraction to wonder how long it's been since he's changed the sheets, before forcing herself to focus on the main matter at hand.

Her sister gets there first, though. 'You okay?' Morgan asks, and Isla hears the rustle of bed sheets as she turns her head towards her.

'I … I think so,' Isla finally manages to reply, each word having to be dragged kicking and screaming from the rather foggy depths of her head. 'I guess when I went racing into the stone to find you, I didn't quite expect – all of that.'

Morgan sniffs, smiling a little as she shuffles on the bed, until she can rest her legs across her sister's. It's entirely familiar but in a faraway manner, like when you visit your first childhood home. 'Hmm, I think I did …'

'Bollocks you did,' Isla scoffs, prodding her sister's nearest kneecap.

'It's true! Okay, maybe I didn't predict all of that but I definitely knew that, when you found me, I was going to give you the letter at long last.'

'When I found you?' Isla glances across at her sister. 'You weren't trying to disappear forever then?'

A small pause, then Morgan shakes her head. 'I never am, not really...'

'Morgan, I...' Isla stops, shakes her head. 'I was going to say I'm sorry for what I said in the cemetery, but I don't think that's quite right. I mean, of course I'm sorry for what I said, but it's more than that now. I guess I just mean... thank you. Because you're right; I'm not the only one who's been looking after this family, and though I'm still not sure you leaving was the best way to do it... I think what I'm trying to say is I understand a little better why you did it.'

Her sister shrugs good-naturedly but says no more, head coming to rest against Isla's shoulder with a weariness that is entirely understandable. Isla feels it too, a pressing sensation against her entire body that she's struggling to ignore for much longer.

Comfortable silence settles over the pair, a cosy blanket of peace. After a moment, Isla shifts to face Morgan a little more directly. 'So,' she begins, voice already feeling blurred around the edges as sleep begins to take hold. 'What now?'

'What now?' turns out to be a question that can't be answered immediately. It would seem that even the inscrutable power of an increasingly harmonious Morgan and Isla cannot solve that puzzle instantly. But it turns out not to matter all that much. For once, the future doesn't feel like a yawning expanse in front of Isla that shows no sign of changing. Instead, it's just a new inlet around the corner that she's yet to explore.

'What now?' just becomes a series of steps away from that long night and back towards normality. It becomes focusing on ensuring that nobody in the village finds out about Morgan's second attempt to disappear. It becomes a search for moments of peace where she can sit and think about the words written on that shell notepaper and resist the urge to try and somehow deny their truth.

There's a day when she becomes fixated on the idea of using the stone to go back and somehow make herself grieve properly, to somehow tell her younger self that all Morgan needed was her big sister. But when she suggests this to Morgan, her sister rolls her eyes and drags her as far away from the back door as she can manage.

'It's not about the past, Isla. There are no shortcuts here. You've just got to work out what it feels like for you. Now, not then.'

Isla can't find a way to argue against that. She's finding there's a lot she can't argue against with her sister these days.

A week goes by in these sticky patches of finding new 'what nows' and Isla is beginning to feel a sense of normality drifting back into their lives. The repetitive routine of work, evenings at home and errand-filled days off that once stifled her now feels a little more comforting.

But there are moments, when she's halfway through cooking dinner or when she's nailing together the dodgy dining chair for the umpteenth time, that she finds her eyes drifting to the noticeboard where her internship form is still pinned, fluttering in the draught of their old house. Then her routine stops feeling comforting again and she has to look away quickly, force herself to forget that this little potential for change exists.

It turns out, though, that change has its own, slightly more deviant way of finding her. Seven days after that long, scary night, it arrives in the form of a knock on the door to the octopus-feeding area.

Isla doesn't want to hear it because she has a feeling that she knows who it is. But the room she's working in is irritatingly silent so she really has no option but to turn around.

Of course, it's Dylan. Isla hasn't spoken to him properly since the day after Morgan ran away. She made sure to thank him for his help, the words stiff and wooden, but there wasn't anything else she felt she could say to him. In the end, it was just easier to avoid him.

Except now the amount of awkwardness hovering between them makes the air feel hot, stifling.

'Hi,' Dylan says after a long moment.

'Hi,' Isla replies, putting down her bucket of whelks.

'You're looking well. I mean, I guess that's not saying a lot seeing as last time I saw you, you were running on barely any sleep but...' He trails off as the thread of his compliment clearly falls away.

Despite her still-lingering anger, Isla finds herself smiling. 'Thank you,' she replies. 'Um... was there something you wanted?'

'Oh, right... yeah.' Dylan steps into the room a little more, rubbing at his arms as if the awkwardness between them is causing him physical discomfort. 'Listen, I could use your help. But, uh, it's a bit of an odd one...'

Thirty-Seven

Isla gets the sense that Dylan wishes he would rather not say exactly what it is he needs help with. Since he's said those words, he's been gradually shuffling back towards the door as if he might be able to rewind it all back.

Isla feels herself pitying him. Typical. She has tried so hard to be angry beyond all else and she is failing over one stumbled step backwards. And as Dylan narrowly avoids stepping in a bucket of leftover fish guts, Isla cannot take it any more.

'An odd one? More odd than me suddenly abandoning you on a cliff at dawn?' Isla quips.

Dylan stops, then grins in his usual wonky way, relief shining across his face. 'Um, actually it might be, though maybe I'm just used to you suddenly running off from me ...' he points out lightly, before hurrying on to presumably to stop Isla getting some sort of retort in. 'I just got a call from a mate who's a fisherman. Apparently there's a seal pup stuck in a net down on the beach by your house. My mate's on a boat and doesn't think he can get safely onto the beach with the tide as it is. I was going to see if I could get the poor thing, and you know that beach pretty well, right?'

Isla doesn't hesitate, which is strange for her. But then there is a marine animal in danger; she'd probably work with the devil himself to save one of those. 'Yeah, I know it well. You can't get a car down there, though. You'll have to carry the seal along the path to our house to get to the nearest road.'

'I'm sure we can manage, together.' His confidence does make Isla laugh a little; she's never tried to carry a seal pup, funnily enough, but she gets the sense that they're pretty heavy. But it seems his confidence is contagious because she finds herself nodding and beckoning him out of the room.

Isla drives them back towards Karrekoth. Dylan's Jeep is apparently full of seaweed sample boxes and if they do need to transport the seal anywhere, that's not really going to work. So Isla's battered and ancient Skoda is commandeered instead.

They both keep silent for the first few miles but, as Karrekoth comes into view, Dylan suddenly pipes up. 'I missed you this past week, you know. And I know I'm entirely to blame but, well, I just wanted you to know.'

'I missed you too,' Isla finds herself replying, before frowning at how those words have slipped out entirely of their own accord. She can feel Dylan's surprise radiating around the car and she sighs. 'Yes, I know – shocking. But even after everything … it's been strange not having you around.' She casts a glance at Dylan, who rapidly looks away to hide a smile. 'Don't get too excited, mind. I'm still furious with you.'

He's endearingly serious in his expression as he nods in response. 'Right,' he replies solemnly, before changing the subject. 'How's Morgan?'

'She's fine. Maybe even good. I don't think we're going to be doing any more night-time searches for her any time soon.'

Dylan nods as Isla takes the final bend into Karrekoth with a slight creak of complaint from her old tyres. 'Well, I'm relieved to hear that. Where did you find her in the end?'

Isla's ready for that one; she's been practising that answer in her sleep for the inevitable moment he or her father asked. 'Just in one of the caves on the beach. We used to play in there all the time.'

'Make sense,' Dylan replies and Isla feels herself relax a little, until his next question arrives. 'And how are you?'

Isla feels herself falter, and the car wobbles around the next bend as she temporarily forgets to concentrate on the road. How is she? She's not actually sure. Objectively, she thinks she's okay. Morgan's given her a lot to think about and sometimes Isla actually lets herself think about it. She's even let a few more tears escape, in the quiet of night when she's found her thoughts drifting back to the moment she was snatched away from her mother on the beach.

Meanwhile her family is safe and relatively content, which has always been the most important thing. But beyond that, well, nothing much has changed. She's still feeding fish in tanks and directing dippy tourists to the toilets.

'That's a long pause,' Dylan finally says, and Isla can feel his somewhat sympathetic expression burning against the side of her face.

'It's hard to say,' she replies, a little sharply until she forces herself to reel her defensive instincts back a little. 'Sorry. It's just ... everything's fine, but I'm not sure that's enough for me any more.'

A small snort from Dylan as they start up the drive towards her home. 'Thank goodness for that,' he comments.

'What do you mean?' Isla asks, glancing at him with a frown as she brings the car to a sputtering halt.

'I mean that you are so much more than this corner of the world. And I can't wait for you to realise that, once and for all.' He's out of the car then, before Isla can really respond or even fathom the meaning of his words. 'Come on! A seal needs us!' he calls from outside, as she finds herself stuck to her seat with slight bemusement.

'Seriously?' Isla splutters as she finally manages to stumble out of the car. 'You drop that bombshell on me and then just exit the scene?'

Dylan glances back to her with his trademark sheepish smile. 'Well, there wasn't time to do much else, and I didn't exactly plan on that coming out … like that. Now – seal?' he prompts, with a gesture towards the sea.

Isla isn't convinced at all by that answer but she's also not convinced that a seal can last much longer stuck in a net on a beach. So she's willing to leave it, for now. Sighing, she hurries past Dylan and beckons him round to the back of the house. He follows a little hesitantly, leaving a clear gap between them; a silent act of respect for the still raw wounds in their relationship.

It becomes obvious when they get down the beach why Dylan's fisherman friend couldn't get to the seal. Waves are furiously crashing against rocks, creating so much foam that the sea looks more white than blue. These fuming waves also explain why a seal pup has become trapped on the sand; being in that sea must be a bit like being in a washing machine.

Isla spots the poor creature first, lying prone in a tangled mess of green netting. As they approach it, it immediately begins a panicked thrashing that causes the net to cut deeper into its already bleeding fur.

'Shit.' Dylan comes to a halt a few feet away. 'It's bigger than I imagined.'

Isla rolls her eyes. 'You mean the super world-travelling marine biologist has never seen a lowly common seal before?' she asks, grinning. But then she's serious again, pulling out her phone. It takes her a minute to call her father and another precious minute explaining what she needs and why. But soon Jasper is hurrying down the path to join them, scissors in hand.

'You didn't mention him being here,' he comments gruffly with a nod to Dylan.

Isla has to marvel at her father's inability to recognise urgency, and ignores his words entirely, choosing to take the scissors from him instead. As she kneels down beside the seal, she hears Dylan quietly greeting Jasper and then her father's small grunt of a response.

A moment later, he's hunkered down beside his daughter. 'Interesting date; whose idea was that, eh?' he mutters, amusement lacing his voice.

'Injured seal, Dad,' Isla reminds him firmly, because she doesn't want to give his words a moment of her time when there's an injured animal (and when the words themselves make her head ache a little). As she starts to cut the net, Dylan also kneels down beside her and, together, the two men manage to keep the seal as still as possible. 'These cuts are horrible; we can't just let it back into the sea … especially not in these waves.'

'I'll call Marine Rescue,' Dylan says. 'Are … are you okay holding it on your own, Mr Pembroke?'

Jasper's response is a snort of amusement which Dylan wisely decides to take as answer enough. Once he's moved away, Jasper shakes his head. 'Am I okay holding it … where'd you find this dunce, again?'

Isla shushes her father impatiently, tugging the last bit of net away from the seal and wincing as it immediately starts wriggling again. 'Let go of it now, Dad. Just in case it tries to bite you. Then stand between it and the sea, we just need to make sure it doesn't try to go back in the ocean.'

Jasper shoots her a somewhat surprised look. 'Well, look at you. You know your stuff, eh?' he comments, standing up.

'It's almost as though I've read all about marine biology and worked at an aquarium for years.'

Her father smirks a little at the retort but says no more, as Dylan joins them again. 'They'll be about twenty minutes.'

'And until then … what, we play tag with a bloody seal?' Jasper grumbles.

'Ignore him,' Isla tells Dylan in an almost automatic way. Though, she reflects, at least her father is being embarrassing in an entirely different way. A normal way, probably.

When the marine rescue team arrive, everybody is thoroughly soaked. The seal has made many dashes towards the ocean and, despite having to half hobble on a cut-up flipper, it's still pretty speedy, so everybody has ended up having to wade into the water to keep the creature safe.

Still, even with sopping socks and a chill set right into her bones, Isla feels the happiest she's felt in weeks. A sense of purpose brings a warmth to her cheeks, despite the icy wind, and it's with a smile that she watches the seal being carried off the beach and away to safety.

It appears Dylan notices this smile too. Later, as she's giving him a lift back to the aquarium in dry clothes (courtesy of Jasper in Dylan's case), he makes a small noise of thought. 'So, you seemed to enjoy that.'

'Hmm? Oh … Yeah, I guess so.'

'You guess so?'

'Okay,' Isla sighs, 'Yes, I did … enjoy it. I enjoyed it a lot.'

Dylan nods slowly. 'Yeah, I thought so. That's why I asked the marine rescue people about vacancies …'

Isla almost sends the car off the road and the cliff at that. Once she's remembered how to hold a steering wheel, she spares him a brief glance. 'What?'

'They said to check the website.' Dylan shrugs. 'I know it's not exactly Hawaii but it's still a step away from this bloody place,' he says, gesturing to the aquarium they're now approaching.

'Do you think...'

'They'd take you? Isla, I'd argue that you know more about marine life than most of the South West combined. If somebody isn't willing to take you then they're a fool, and I'll happily tell them myself.'

The car comes to a shuddering stop in the car park but neither passenger nor driver make a move to leave just yet. Isla stares at the peeling building in front of her and tries to imagine not coming here every day. It's a little easier to do than before and she feels another smile inching its way onto her face. 'Maybe so.'

Dylan laughs, popping open the door. Isla can see Morgan stepping out of the aquarium and starting the walk towards them but she focuses back on Dylan for the moment as he speaks once more. 'I'm leaving for California in a month or so. It's a three-week exploration of jellyfish mating, or something... but how about this? By the time I go, you'll have left this place and found something else. Something better.'

Isla tries not to focus too much on the feeling of disappointment she has at knowing he's going to leave again. Even if just for three weeks. She keeps smiling, even if it is now a little forced. 'And if I do?' she asks. 'What's the prize?'

'Other than your own life fulfilment?'

Isla laughs. 'Can't put that on my shelf with my old swimming trophies.'

'Fine. You do that and I'll bring you back something from California for your damn shelf.'

Isla snorts. 'Wow, what an honour.' But then she grins, offering him her hand to shake. 'Fine, deal.' He shakes her hand, paired with one of his bemused chuckles.

'You're a find, Isla Pembroke.'

'Thanks, I think?'

'It's a compliment, honest.' He's moving to step out the car but Isla grabs onto his arm, halting him for a moment.

'Dylan, I...' He's turned back to her now, and Isla feels her mouth drying up a little. 'Look, what you did for Morgan... I can't say I agree with it or even fully understand your reasons for doing it but, well, if I had to choose anyone for my sister to ask for help running away, I'd probably choose you. And I know you kept her safe as best as you could.'

Dylan's cheeks flush red. 'That means a lot, Isla. Thanks.' And with that slightly flustered sentence, he clambers out the car and steps aside with an over-exaggerated flourish to allow Morgan access to his recently vacated seat. 'Your carriage, ma'am.'

'Thanks... Bye, Dylan...' Morgan responds in a slightly exasperated tone, watching him go with bemusement before hopping in and pulling the door shut. Then she reaches across and grabs Isla's hand to stop her from starting to drive just yet. 'What was that about, hmm? Have you been off for a secret make-up shag in a bush somewhere?'

'Of course, that's exactly what I'd do, Morgan.'

'Ugh, you're so dull. I need drama in my life, y'know.'

Isla starts to reverse out of the car park with an exasperated expression painted upon her face. She wonders how many times a day that ends up there. 'Well, we did rescue a seal together. Does that count as drama?'

'No way, shit!' Isla hears the creak of the passenger seat as Morgan shifts into a better position to gawp at her. 'That's awesome. What happened? Tell me everything, right now. Including the shagging part, obviously.'

Isla smiles at her sister's excitement, takes a moment to gather her thoughts and concentrate on turning into the main road before launching into the tale. As the words begin to tumble from her mouth, Isla can't help but glance towards the horizon. The clouds have lifted so she can see clearly for miles yet, somehow, the horizon seems a little closer. And Isla thinks she knows what that means.

Change is coming.

Thirty-Eight

Isla has seen change on the distant horizon for a very long time but, three days after she rescues the seal pup from her beach, that change seems to finally arrive. And it starts, as it often does, with Morgan. Her sister has been throwing almost wistful glances at her for the entirety of these three days and Isla is fairly sure she knows what Morgan is after, but she cannot accept it just yet. There's still a whirlwind of thoughts leftover in her head from the last visit she made into the stone and she's not sure she's ready for more.

But there's only so many times she can ignore a Morgan glance. Finally, as they're driving back from work, she gives up.

'Spit it out, Mogs.' She's trying to be more upfront with her sister, trying to fulfil Morgan's wishes from her four-year-old letter. It still doesn't feel entirely natural.

'So I've been thinking and … there's something we should do, back at the stone.'

She says it quietly, as if she knows it's controversial. But Isla still hears it over the creaks and splutters of her ancient car.

'The stone?' she echoes, briefly glancing at Morgan. Her sister is steadily picking at the edge of the window's shoddy sealant but Isla can still catch the look on her face. Deep thought. 'I thought you said we had to focus on the present, not the past? What do you want to do with the stone?'

'I've been thinking about all the moments you visited,' Morgan begins, looking up from her fiddling and over at her sister. 'They were all when we were alive, right?'

Isla nods. She's spent the last week gradually revealing all the visits she made, in the spirit of trying to be more open. Morgan listened carefully to each little tale and, though she didn't say much, Isla got the sense that her sister understood the reasoning behind each visit.

'Well, I think we should visit a time before we were born.'

'Why?' Isla asks, for it hasn't ever really occurred to her to do such a thing.

'Because.' Morgan stops abruptly and when Isla looks over at her, she is once again deep in thought. It takes her another minute to get the words together. 'We've spent so long trying to find these moments between us that might tell us something, or trying to change the days we didn't like. But I think we need to see where it all began, to see what brought our family together.' She pauses and even though Isla has her eyes on the road, she can sense her sister's apprehension. 'What ... what do you think?'

'What brought our family together ...' Isla echoes, half lost in her own thoughts for a moment as she considers her sister's proposition. Part of her is a little scared to go back to the stone, because the last time she used it her whole view of her life was tipped upside down. But she can't deny that Morgan's idea has worth. 'Did you have a particular moment in mind?'

Morgan shakes her head. 'Not really, but I think the stone will know. If we think hard enough about what we're after, it will do the rest. From what you've said, it always finds what you need. Even if it's a bit of a surprise.'

Isla has to agree with that. Even when she hasn't exactly

expected to end up where it's taken her, she can't deny that it has turned out to be precisely what she's needed.

'Okay, we can visit the stone.' Isla hears the unease in her own voice and it would seem that Morgan does too, because she reaches across and pats her arm.

'It will be a good thing, Isla. Trust me.'

Marina Pembroke loved to tell her girls how she met their father. She claimed it was a good lesson in the importance of apologies but Isla always suspected that their mother just enjoyed watching their father squirm from the other side of the room.

Either way, Isla heard the tale so many times that she could retell it back to front, upside down, in her sleep. Their father, a newly minted police officer transferred to the area (much to his chagrin), bustled into the post office one afternoon with a somewhat misguided sense of self-importance while following a lead on a string of pickpocketing incidents in the village. He asked their mother if she knew anything and then proceeded to comment on the somewhat haphazard organisation of the post office. The rest, as they say, is history.

History that would appear to be playing out in front of them right now. Morgan dragged Isla down to the beach straight from parking the car and, before she had a chance to really think about what was happening, they summoned the light of the stone and stepped inside.

And so here they are. Standing in the post office on the very day her parents met. Isla can tell that this is the right day from the fact that her mother has printer ink smeared across one cheek (a key detail from the story). Plus the calendar on the wall showing the date, below a rather twee painting of Karrekoth's church.

'God, those calendars were dreadful,' Morgan mutters from

beside Isla, though there's no need to keep their voices down; it's already entirely apparent that they're invisible. 'But you know what Mum used to say: keep the vicar sweet...'

Isla has to grin at that, flooded with the memory of Marina's falsely enthusiastic conversations with the vicar when he came round to sell the calendars every year. 'At least this one isn't covered in seagull puns...'

'Who knew there were twelve seagull puns in the world.'

They fall silent, no longer able to distract themselves in calendar talk. The sight of their mother, living her life with no sense of a time limit, lures them in like an anglerfish.

'This is the day they meet, right?' Morgan asks after a moment of watching their mother hunt around the counter for something. 'The day Dad comes in.'

Isla nods, eyes drifting over to the door. 'Yeah, it is ... any moment now, I guess. Lunchtime, Mum always said, right?'

Morgan nods, grinning a little. 'Dad always said he was too hungry to think properly; that's why it all went the way it did.'

'And Mum always said she'd had a disappointing sandwich so that's why she was in a mood.'

Giggling, Morgan loops arms with Isla. It's entirely natural and entirely comforting, and Isla feels as if she could spend forever like this; standing in the warmth and familiarity of this post office with her sister.

But time ticks on. They watch as Marina fishes out a squashed sandwich and eats it with a look of great derision, then throws the last bit in the bin with a sigh. They watch as she serves a few customers; they grin to each other as she feigns interest at Mrs Warren's moan about the terrible parking in the visitors' car park.

They watch the clock tick right on past midday and still there is no sign of their father.

'There!' Morgan says suddenly, just as Isla is beginning to

feel worry bubbling up in her stomach. Her sister is pointing towards the front of the shop and, through the slightly grubby windows, Isla can make out a uniformed police officer, stiffly walking across the harbour towards the post office.

Both Isla and Morgan hurry to the front, pressing up against the glass to watch his progress. It's so strange to see their father walking around Karrekoth with uncertainty, and with no awareness of the life-changing moment he's about to walk into.

Except he's not walking into it. Jasper walks straight past them without pausing, heading for the café.

'I ... I don't understand,' Morgan whispers. 'He's meant to come in here before going to the café. That's what he always said ...'

Isla feels her brow crinkle in confusion. 'Did he ever say why he knew to come into the post office?' she asks after a moment of just watching her father.

'Yeah, I think some woman told him ...' Morgan trails off and, when Isla looks over to her, her expression has changed. It's no longer confused but set in stone, a decision clearly made.

Isla feels a little nervousness fluttering in her chest like a trapped butterfly. 'Morgan?'

'Dad said the woman had red hair. He always used to joke that when he saw Mum he thought he'd wandered into a town full of gingers ...' Morgan snaps her head round to Isla, eyes a little wild now. 'It's you, Isla. You tell him to come in here. You get them to meet.'

'What?' Isla splutters. 'That's crazy!'

Morgan shakes her head, already opening the door and tugging them out into the warm sunshine. 'No more crazy than a time-travelling rock!'

356

'But we're not even visible!' Isla argues as she is rather forcibly pulled across the harbour.

'Oh, right. 'Cause the stone has never changed that when it needed to.' Morgan stops, rounding on her sister. 'You've got to do this, Isla. That's why the stone brought us here. It's you. You start everything. So go, now!' And with that she gives Isla a firm shove forward that almost sends her tripping into the nearby lamp post.

For a moment Isla stalls, anxiety pulling her back. But then her father makes to open the café door and she knows that Morgan is right. There's nobody else stopping him and directing him towards their mother.

It has to be her.

'Excuse me! Officer!' she shouts before she can think any further about it, chasing after Jasper. He comes to a halt, hand resting on the handle of the door as he turns towards her.

He seems so young that Isla would almost not recognise him, if it wasn't for the shrewd look of suspicion on his face. She's seen that look many times before, mainly when listening to a much-younger Morgan attempt to lie her way out of trouble.

'Yes?' he asks a little shortly, when Isla doesn't immediately launch into speech.

'You're looking for that pickpocket,' she finally blurts out, words slurring into each other so much that Jasper gives her a look of supreme impatience. Clearly he thinks she's an idiot, or drunk, or both.

'Yes … what of it?'

Isla hesitates, because she can feel the weight of her next words bearing down on her as though she's sinking underneath miles and miles of water. This is it; this is the moment that steers her father towards her mother, that will lead to her own existence as well her sister's.

And the moment that will eventually lead to her father's utter heartbreak.

That's what makes Isla pause, makes her mouth dry up. Should she lead him towards the love of his life, knowing that she will one day be ripped away from him? Are all the days before worth the days that come after?

Isla doesn't know the answer to that. She's not sure anyone does. But she does know that the stone has brought them here deliberately and, oddly enough, she trusts its judgement. Despite how ludicrous that sounds in her head.

So a moment later, hand slightly shaky, she points towards the post office. 'The woman in there, I think she saw something the other day when one of the incidents happened. She could be worth talking to.'

Jasper doesn't look entirely convinced, which is hardly a surprise. 'Right, well ... I'll be sure to pop in after my lunch ...'

'No!' Isla blurts out, before wincing at her own abruptness as it causes Jasper to look even more suspicious. 'Um, it's just she only works until one. So you'll miss her. So go now. Please.' She adds that final word as an afterthought, in the hope that it will smooth the deeply disapproving frown creasing her father's brow.

It doesn't really, but he does at least start towards the post office, albeit with a muttered curse that sounds a lot like 'shitting nutcase'. It's good to know her father's low tolerance for people hasn't changed over the years.

Isla watches him cross the road and stride rather confidently into the post office, feeling her heart thudding hard in her chest. Once she's sure he's inside, she returns to her sister.

She doesn't get much chance to catch her breath, as Morgan takes her arm immediately and pulls her back towards the post office. She appears to possess a disconcerting confidence that the stone will have switched them back to invisible, as she opens the door and breezes in, but sure enough neither Jasper nor Marina notice their entrance.

Then again, that might have nothing to do with their invisibility and everything to do with the intensity of their parents' conversation.

Marina is half frozen in the act of putting a stack of envelopes by the desk, the trademark startlingly green eyes narrowed in a way that Isla and Morgan both know to mean trouble.

'Sorry, what was that?' she's saying as her future daughters step inside, outrage lacing the edges of her syllables with vicious barbs.

'I said maybe you'd be able to remember if you saw a pickpocket if you weren't surrounded by chaos all day. I know this is a tiny village post office and all, but surely you still need some sense of organisation?'

Morgan lets out a low chuckle beside Isla, shaking her head. 'He really was an arse-brained idiot back then ...' she murmurs.

'Sorry, are you some sort of arse-brained idiot?' Marina snaps, just as Isla is wondering where on earth her sister learnt a phrase such as 'arse-brained idiot'. She drops the envelopes down on the desk, ignoring the way the pile totters then tumbles over.

'What?' Jasper splutters. 'I'm just trying to offer you some friendly advice, as your new neighbourhood officer.'

Marina laughs, the sound sharp and biting. 'Oh, is that what it is? I thought you were just being a nosy git.'

'Oi, there's no need for that! I'm a police officer, you know. There's rules about how you talk to one of us.'

Another laugh. Marina comes out from behind the desk, moving round Jasper with deliberate carelessness. 'Maybe in whichever big city you dropped in from there are. Here we treat respectful people with respect and idiots we show the door.' She's stopped by the door now, so close to Isla that she can see the precise group of freckles she has on her cheek. Her personal constellation, that's what Marina called them. And when Isla scowled at her own freckles, her mother would pretend to join them up with a pen and name them ridiculously complicated names until she couldn't keep scowling any more.

'So you're not going to tell me what you know? That's obstructing justice,' Jasper is saying, still under the impression that he can somehow win this argument.

'I don't know anything, now good day.' Marina pulls the door open, glaring at Jasper with such ferocity that it seems even he can't hold his ground any longer.

Isla knows what happens next, but it still makes her jump. There's an abrupt bang, a flash, and sudden darkness fills the shop. Beside her, Isla feels Morgan shift a little.

'The power cut...' she murmurs and when Isla looks at her sister, she looks utterly entranced in this moment.

There's silence from their parents for a minute, then Marina curses. 'Shitting hell, not again,' she groans, closing the shop door with a frustrated slam.

'You get many power cuts, then?' Jasper asks, as Marina stumbles back across to the till.

'I thought you were going?' Marina shoots back, before letting out a shriek as her foot connects with a nearby haphazardly stacked pile of magazines and she is sent tumbling to the floor.

Isla glances back to Morgan again, smiling. This is it; the moment where they stop arguing and start talking. The moment where Jasper realises how intensely captivating Marina's eyes are, and when Marina realises that there's a softness to this frowning police officer's face.

Jasper drops down beside Marina. 'You all right?' he asks gruffly.

'No! I've twisted my stupid ankle, haven't I?'

A hand slips into Isla's then. Morgan's. 'We should leave them to it,' she murmurs, when Isla crinkles her brow with confusion. 'I think if we stay any longer, it might be impossible for us to leave.'

Isla understands that fear entirely. She could quite easily stay here, watching her parents, forever. She wants to see Jasper help Marina into a chair and use the shop's ice-cream stock as a makeshift ice pack. She wants to watch as Marina directs Jasper to the fuse box and tells him the exact wiggle he needs to give the switch to get everything back on again. And she wants to be there for the moment Jasper leaves an hour or so later and Marina hobbles after him to give him a handful of sherbet lemons and her phone number.

But her sister is right. It's time to go.

'You okay?' Isla asks once they're outside, because Morgan may have been the one to lead them back onto the street but now she's looking rather wistfully at the darkened front windows.

'Yeah, fine. Just … missing her.'

It's a simple sentence and yet holds the weight of an ocean in each word, and Isla feels instinct take over. She smiles her agreement, then pulls her sister into a hug. Morgan melts into it immediately, nestling her head into the crook of Isla's neck. It does mean that Morgan's hair is tickling her nostrils, but Isla doesn't care.

She can't remember when she last hugged her sister like this without one of them being in tears.

Because, despite everything, there aren't any tears from either of them now. Just a quiet sense of reflection that lasts until there's the gentle sense of the floor being pulled from beneath them. The stone carefully deposits them back on the beach and Isla feels the wind wrap around them, almost as if it's adding its own arms to their embrace.

Morgan pulls away after another minute of silence that only feels comfortable. She smiles at Isla, eyes a little too bright but her expression steady. 'It was you all along.'

'I guess so ...' Isla replies. 'It hurt a little, doing that. Knowing that they were going to be heading towards heartbreak eventually but ... it was still good.'

Morgan nods her agreement. 'Yeah. A good hurt, like getting your vaccinations done. You know it's the right thing to do, even if it stings.'

Isla laughs, for only her sister would be able to conjure up such a simile for the occasion.

Suddenly, the wind picks up around them, howling in an almost alarmed way. Isla glances around the beach with a frown as a rumbling vibrates through the sand.

'Did you hear that?' she asks, glancing back to her sister.

'Considering that I have ears, yes ...'

Isla spares a moment to shoot a withering look at Morgan and her incessant sarcasm, before returning to trying to find the source of the sound.

It becomes clear a moment later, when the rumble turns into a cracking, creaking sound that comes from right beside them. From right inside the rock. Instinctively, Isla steps back, pulling Morgan with her. They stumble over the floor of the beach, until they can no longer feel the ground shaking quite so alarmingly beneath them, just in time to watch as the familiar small crack begins to stretch up to the top of the stone. It wriggles right up to the pointed summit, then splinters into dozens of smaller fissures that zip across the stone almost instantly.

There's stillness for a moment, and even the wind seems to stop in respect. But it's only for a moment, before there's one final almighty crack and the stone breaks apart. Shards of smaller rocks tumble down around their feet and the undulating waves of sand and pebbles that make up the beach's floor immediately pounce on the remaining stump of stone until it's completely consumed.

All that's left is a few larger broken pieces of rock, spread out across the sand around them like a destroyed jigsaw puzzle. Just like that, the famous stone of Karrekoth is gone.

And so, change begins.

Thirty-Nine

Isla Pembrooke sometimes wonders what it's like to not smell of fish. What it's like to not have constantly calloused hands from the onslaught of the elements. What it's like to not know the intricate details of a seal's dietary patterns.

But she only wonders this for a moment.

There is always an end to the cruel winters of Cornwall and, for Isla, she feels that end three months after the stone crumbles away in front of her and Morgan. It's a long winter; the destruction of said stone and the stitching together of a sisterhood does not make the dark months of wind and storms any easier to weather. Things are better but they're not perfect. There's still days of silence from Jasper, and still days of hollow sadness with Morgan, still days when Isla has to battle her own instincts and allow tears to fall. The stone was full of magic and surprises, but it could not fix everything. And perhaps it didn't need to. Perhaps being a little mended, but not perfect, is okay.

So the winter is survivable. They get through Christmas with a lot of food and Morgan's home-made and, quite frankly, lethal mulled wine. They count in the new year on the harbour wall, watching the distant lights of ships and listening to the echoing singing of 'Auld Lang Syne' from the pub, which casts a strange sense of enchantment over the moment. Isla and Morgan stay up until dawn, both finding it impossible to sleep for reasons that neither bother trying to understand.

And finally, the brilliant blue sky reclaims its territory over the clouds and brings back the tentative warmth of spring that Isla has missed so much, blessing their beach with calmer tides and gentler winds.

Isla finds her feet taking her there automatically once a day. Sometimes the sun has already started its journey down to the horizon, but Isla doesn't mind. She just tugs her coat a little tighter around herself and watches the world darken around her. Feels the comfort she's always felt in knowing that the tide will keep receding and returning, that the waves will keep crashing against the rocks. With change thick in the air, it's nice to be reminded of the constants.

March is firmly in place now, as Isla makes the same trip down the path and sits on the same flat stone she always does. It's all that's left of that mysterious, impossible rock now and, already, the locals are trying to weave new stories that might entice tourists to still visit despite their famous monolith being gone. Half-cooked tales of the old ocean spirit's grief finally crumbling down to something more manageable get passed around the village like a parcel. Whatever tale this stone now has behind it, Isla doesn't care; it gives her the perfect view of the sea, and reminds her that she doesn't need time-travelling magic any more. There's nothing to be found in the past for her now; she has to make the most of the present. A surprising lesson to learn from a time-travelling stone perhaps, but one that she appreciates nonetheless.

Today, with the wind calm and the sky clear, Isla doesn't stay alone for long. She hears the sure-footed steps coming down the path and doesn't need to turn round to know it's her sister. And if she wasn't totally sure, she certainly is when she hears

Morgan's quiet curse as she almost trips over a newly exposed root.

'Fucking tree,' Morgan grumbles as she plops herself down beside her sister.

'Hello to you too.' Isla looks over to her sister, automatically scanning to check how she is. Some habits never die, even after a few months of stability. Isla will always worry about Morgan, just as she's now sure that Morgan will always worry about her. A shared sisterly concern which feels entirely normal. 'How was the aquarium?'

Morgan wrinkles her nose. 'I swear, college cannot come fast enough. Somebody asked me what type of a fish was in this tank, right ... you know what tank it was? The sodding jellyfish tank. How the hell do you not know what a jellyfish is?'

'How old were they?'

Morgan laughs bitterly. 'Oh no, they weren't a child, Isla. They were full bloody grown, with wrinkles and everything.' She shakes her head, crossing her arms. 'How was superhero seal rescue?'

'Do you mean Marine Rescue? The actual name for where I work?' Isla feels her own pride still glowing strong in her words, even after almost two months of working there. She'd kept her word to Dylan, though admittedly it wasn't really about Dylan in the end. Once the stone was gone and there were just ordinary days left, Isla decided she really couldn't spend any more of them at the aquarium. She checked for vacancies, went for an interview and was peeling her photo off the aquarium's employee wall one week later. It's not exactly an internship in Hawaii, but it's a whole lot closer to it. At least everyone she works with recognises a jellyfish when they see one.

Morgan clearly notices Isla's still glowing pride because she rolls her eyes with a small noise of despair. 'God, you're so excited still; it's just weird. You probably have a crush on a seal or something, right?'

'You are disgusting. And for the record, I didn't even do any work with damn seals today. I was typing up a report about that minke whale we found last week. It's one of five spotted and rescued in the last month or so, which is apparently a lot higher than usual, so I was doing a bit of digging into why.'

Morgan wrinkles her nose and Isla braces herself for the onslaught of highly sarcastic teasing about to come her way. She's not entirely correct, though. Her sister's next words have an element of teasing in them but Isla is also aware of a large amount of fondness too. 'Who knew that your perfect, deadly boring job really did exist, eh?'

Isla shrugs, unable to deny it. Apparently frustrated that she can't get a rise from her sister, Morgan changes topic with the smoothness of a car trying to drive on sand. 'Dylan was asking after you, by the way. He was back in today to pick up some things for some talk he's doing in Liverpool.'

Isla feels a smile slip onto her face, almost secretively. 'Yeah, he texted me at lunch.'

'Cute. Did he court you successfully?' Morgan has found her older sister's cautious interactions with Dylan entirely baffling and has made it clear every step of the way. Isla deliberately stayed away from him in the weeks before he went off to California, a final signal that if he ever betrayed her trust again, it would all be over. Once he was back, though, they took slow, miniature steps towards … something. Isla still hasn't quite found the word to describe it yet, much to Morgan's intense confusion and frustration.

'We're going for dinner on Friday,' Isla replies, wriggling her feet down into the sand. She wishes it was warm enough to take her shoes and socks off but for now this slightly disconnected sensation will have to do. 'I'll be sure to give you the rundown on his courting, seeing as it's apparently the only thing you care about in life these days.'

There's no answer to that; just a shrug. Morgan lets out a slightly contented sigh a moment later, coming to rest her head against Isla's shoulder. It feels incredibly natural, but Isla still finds herself marvelling at that. Times have well and truly changed. She doesn't quite know how she's going to feel when Morgan goes off to start her art course in Plymouth, which is strange considering she's all too used to Morgan being gone. Surely it should be easier this time, when she'll actually say goodbye and when they'll actually know where she is? Apparently not.

'You will call me, won't you? When you're away?'

'You're asking me that now? I'm not going away for another four months, Isla. Plus I'm only a few hours away...'

'I know, but I just need to check these things.'

Morgan digs her chin a little into Isla's shoulder, causing her to squirm. 'Of course I will, idiot. I'm sending you smug photos of me painting while you're, I don't know, cleaning a seal's mouth out or something.'

Isla finds her sister's side and prods it until the chin is retracted from her shoulder. 'That's all I ask. I'll send you back a picture of the contents of said seal's mouth, shall I?'

Morgan grins, then lifts her head up as the sound of more footsteps reach her ears. They're slower, more careful. Isla suspects who they might belong to and is proved correct a moment later, when Jasper appears on the beach.

Isla has to remind herself that just seeing him on the beach is a big deal, even if he is still a little gaunter than she'd like him to be. There's a lot of memories for him to wade through down here, especially when there's not the distraction of an injured seal to chase them away. But Isla's been joined by him more and more over the last few weeks. Sometimes it's a silent visit, but it's a visit nonetheless and Isla finds endless relief in his presence.

'Should've known I'd find you down here.' He grunts as he picks his way over the stones and comes to squish up beside Morgan. 'It's damn cold down here; you're both barmy.'

Morgan makes a noise of agreement. 'Tell me about it. I only came down here to find her.'

'And I only came down here to have some peace so less of the complaining.' Isla shoots both family members a rueful look that succeeds in quieting them both. For a few precious moments anyway.

Soon enough, though, Jasper breaks the silence once more. 'I was going to make fish pie tonight. Bobby Mercer gave me some free haddock and plaice after I helped him fix a scratch on his boat. Lord, you would have thought the man had lost his firstborn child, the way he was blubbering on down the phone...'

Isla and Morgan exchange a look, both remembering the last time he tried to make fish pie and the resulting smoke-filled house. Isla bites on her lip, trying to decide how best to respond, before shaking her head and giving Morgan a little nudge, a silent relinquishing of control that happens more and more these days.

'Do you still remember how to make it, Dad?' Morgan asks with an impish sparkle to her eyes that only she can get away with. 'Without setting fire to the kitchen?'

Jasper shoots her a scowl that is intensely scrutinised by both daughters for signs of hollowness and defeat. 'It's not that hard, you just bung a load of fish with some sauce and cook it in the oven... pretty much.'

Morgan snorts. 'I'm sure that's how they do it in all the best fish restaurants.' But there's a grin on her face, clearly proud that her humoured teasing has answered the silent question hovering between the sisters. Isla can feel a smile resting against her own cheeks too; she knows that this is a long way away from staying in bed for weeks on end; she knows that this fish pie could give them food poisoning and she'd still treasure it.

'It sounds great, Dad. You'll need potatoes, though, and we've not got any.' Isla watches her father closely, not quite able to give up the instinct to carefully examine his reaction to any small setback.

'Bugger.' Jasper's response is entirely average. He chuckles, shakes his head. 'Sod it, I'll walk into town and get some.'

'You'll have to go to the supermarket at this hour, Dad. Shop shuts at six.'

Jasper scrunches his forehead in thought. 'Oh, well, in that case, screw the pie. I'm not giving that bloody place the satisfaction, just for some potatoes...'

Isla and Morgan share a grin. Their father's distaste for supermarkets and any large corporate shop in the area has only recently returned. Isla has found it highly ironic considering how much they've depended on such places over the past years. But it's a step towards the father she remembers from her childhood, the grouchy yet competent man who she relied upon so confidently. She's not going to complain for a second.

Jasper stands, stretches with a groan. 'I'd better get back on home then. Need to rethink the menu...' He glances at his watch. 'Don't be much longer, girls. Tide's coming in.'

'We won't.' Their answer comes in unison and Isla feels a rush of warmth from that. From the small smile on her father's face, she's fairly sure that he's feeling it too.

'See you in a bit.' He pats Morgan's shoulder, shoots a look to Isla that conveys a whole array of emotions.

Once he's gone, it's fairly easy to fall back into silence. For

Isla, it's a natural habitat and for once Morgan seems to be honouring that. They stay in this comfortable state for a few minutes and, although Isla could probably have done it for longer, she's not too bothered when Morgan pipes up.

'I was thinking today, how long it's been now without her here.'

Isla glances across at her sister, raising an eyebrow. 'That's cheery…'

Morgan shakes her head, frowning slightly. 'No, I mean… it always surprises me. That someone can be gone for so long and yet still have an impact every day.'

Isla finds herself intrigued by her sister's unusual display of philosophical thinking. 'Go on.'

'Well, think about it. Mum bought me that little easel when I was five and that's when I first really got into painting and drawing. And now I'm going to art school. And… she read you that same boring fish book every night when you were little and now you're rescuing seals.' Morgan sits back a little, resting against the slope of the rock. 'Even Dad cooking fish tonight is all because Mum pointed out, when he decided policing wasn't for him, that him being so handy with tools was a pretty good career move in a little seaside village where things get rusty and broken very quickly… if he hadn't started helping people out then he wouldn't have helped Bobby today and he wouldn't have the fish. See? She's still here, in all these little ways.'

Isla smiles at that, wrapping an arm around her sister's shoulders. 'I guess you're right. And we're sitting here together because she taught us that every good day ends with a trip to the beach.'

Isla feels Morgan nodding vigorously, her head bumping against her chin. 'Exactly. Exactly.' Her sister relaxes against her, almost as if she's relieved that Isla understands. And of course she does; Isla's felt that sensation more than once. Except now she feels the impact of her mother's life, not just her death. And that's a lot more hopeful.

Morgan stands up soon after that, dusting the sand off her trousers with a critical expression. 'I'm going to go check on Dad.'

'All right, I won't be long.'

Isla catches her sister's eye-roll but she can't help the attachment she has to this place. And while her fingers are beginning to go a little numb, she can't quite commit to leaving just yet.

Morgan heads off with a wave; Isla watches the confident way she picks her route back to their home path. She smiles to herself as she notices how high her sister holds her head, how her hair is pushed back from her face. How looking at her no longer brings a heavy sense of responsibility crushing down on her shoulders. Now her duty to look after her sister feels manageable, perhaps because it's no longer being held up by Isla alone. They're all sharing each other's loads.

That thought is comforting enough to warm her up for a few more minutes.

But soon Isla can feel the inevitable end to her beach visit drawing near. The tide is creeping ever closer, the sun is beginning to disappear completely behind the horizon, taking the last bit of warmth with it. Isla stands with a slightly regretful sigh, gives her legs a rub to get the circulation returning.

Then she turns to leave, ready to return to the real world now that it has more to offer. There's the prospect of fish and a dinner table filled with conversation; the prospect of a job that holds a purpose; a future dinner with a man who she knows has a good heart.

She steps over the stones, picks her way carefully back towards the path. As her feet leave the final rock and find the slightly sturdier ground of the path, Isla feels the wind begin to kick up behind her.

She turns, smiling at the familiarity of this breeze as it wraps around her and tosses her curls almost playfully. She tracks the wind's progress, as it dances across the sea, scattering it into new patterns, leaping through the waves and destroying their neat curls and ripples.

Isla watches the wind and the sea find a way of co-existing, sees the way the waves seem to accommodate the wind's movements. And in the distance, Isla can see the clouds beginning to darken. A rumble of something that sounds like thunder echoes almost ominously across the ocean. But neither the wind nor the sea pause in their incessant movements, utterly unconcerned by the prospect of a storm.

After all, what can a storm do to the will of the wind and the water?

Acknowledgements

I've yet to read a book that came into existence without an army of supportive people behind it and this story is no exception. As is often the case with my ideas, Isla's story started as a somewhat overcomplicated mess and so I have to start by thanking my incredible editing team at Orion for working your magic; Victoria Oundjian for your initial and exceedingly valuable discussions about what I actually wanted this book to do for the reader; Suzy Clarke for your incredible work untangling tenses which all the time travel does its best to muddle; and of course Harriet Bourton and Olivia Barber for your all round editorial wizardry. It has been such a privilege to work with you on this book; the passion you had for Isla's story has made writing it so much easier and your guidance and ideas have been so incredibly valuable. Thank you for your tireless work, your patience when I popped off and had a baby, and all your support throughout this process.

And of course I cannot mention any of those things without also mentioning my wonderful agent Jo Unwin. None of this book would exist if you hadn't seen some potential in me back at the start of my writing journey. Your support since then has continued to be invaluable; your confidence in me is sometimes all I need to keep on typing and that really makes all the difference. Thank you for guiding me through the world of writing, which continues to be very different to the world of teaching, and helping to make this book something I'm truly proud of (which takes a lot for this over-achieving author over here). Thank you also to whole team at JULA who have made running a literary agency in a pandemic seem almost easy.

A huge thank you to my squad of cheerleaders, without whom I'm sure I'd be on Chapter One still:

The incredible team at Cranbourne Primary School, for your infectious enthusiasm, support and praise that constantly remind me why I love being a writer. Thank you in particular to Lisa, for all your gorgeous WhatsApp messages; to Lara and Ruyan, for all your passionate questions and social media promoting; to Paula, for being the most supportive Head a juggling teacher/ writer could wish for; and to the wonderful Caroline and Natalie, for always keeping me sane(ish).

To my amazing friends, who have become even more valuable and treasured in the midst of a pandemic lockdown – Alice Keane, Megan Francis, Jessie Ravenscroft, Hannah Wise, Hannah Worth, Trina Moseley, Bella Roberts. Your messages of love and support for my first book have made writing a second one so much more meaningful, so thank you. Special mention to my group of incredible Mum friends – Emily Winter, Lucy Stephens, Stephanie Dallison – for always being there for me, whether it's a question about baby sleeping or a rant about book plotting. And of course, my guardian angel across the ocean – Vix Jensen-Collins. Thank you for battling my self-doubt for me, for making me laugh like a hyena, for gently pointing out the most obvious of typos, and for spending many a FaceTime discussing the ins and outs of various fantasy story elements.

Thank you to the Brown family, in particular Julia and Duncan, for being such incredibly kind and encouraging in-laws, I am truly honoured to be a part of your family. Thank you to my real-life fairy godmother Morwenna Banks for championing my writing from its very beginning, despite its cringe-worthiness, and for keeping Mum alive in my memories with your stories. Thank you to the Keily family, in particular my impossibly resilient grandmother Gillian Keily and the always 'plucky' KT's – Ruth, Mark, Eden and Ruby. Thank you to Patty Granny for the bucket loads of wisdom that I could pass on to my characters when they needed it most. And of course my gloriously mad family, the KBD's – thank you Jack for always being honest about my ideas; thank you Dad for showing me the true meaning of resilience, I've been so lucky to have had you by my side through our own grieving journey.

To my husband, Alex – you are my own personal magical rock, except you have yet to allow me to time travel (which I suppose I can forgive you for). Your calming presence, your love, your sense of humour is always exactly what I need. Thank you for wrangling our daughter so I could write this book and indeed this acknowledgement section. Speaking of which, a huge thank you to my newly arrived daughter Holly who has already managed to teach me so much about the unique wonder of motherhood. You are my glorious little ocean spirit and I love you so much. And thank you for those pregnancy/new-mum hormones that allowed some of the more emotional scenes of this book to come into existence.

But at the heart of this book is a mother and a sister, so I have to finish by thanking three very special people. My forever inspiring and forever missed mother, Deborah Keily, and my equally inspiring and loving 'step' mother, Mummy Lynne. You have both taught me so much about the unbelievably valuable relationship between a mother and a daughter which is so important to this story. And finally to my very own 'fierce whirling wind' of a sister, Alice. Morgan and Isla simply would not exist if I didn't have my own sisterhood to draw from. Thank you for all the laughs, hugs, cakes and madness over the years. There truly is no greater friend than a sister and I'm so blessed to have you in my life.

Credits

Tamsin Keily and Orion Fiction would like to thank everyone at Orion who worked on the publication of *The Surprising Days of Isla Pembroke* in the UK.

Editorial
Harriet Bourton
Olivia Barber

Copy editor
Suzy Clarke

Proof reader
Kati Nicholl

Audio
Paul Stark
Amber Bates

Contracts
Anne Goddard
Paul Bulos
Jake Alderson

Design
Rabab Adams
Joanna Ridley
Nick May

Editorial Management
Charlie Panayiotou
Jane Hughes
Alice Davis

Finance
Jasdip Nandra
Afeera Ahmed
Elizabeth Beaumont
Sue Baker

Production
Ruth Sharvell

Marketing
Brittany Sankey

Publicity
Ellen Turner

Sales
Jen Wilson
Esther Waters
Victoria Laws

Rachael Hum
Ellie Kyrke-Smith
Frances Doyle
Georgina Cutler

Operations
Jo Jacobs
Sharon Willis
Lisa Pryde
Lucy Brem